Driftless
DESPERATION

SUE BERG

LITTLE CREEK PRESS
AND BOOK DESIGN

MINERAL POINT, WISCONSIN

Little Creek Press®
A Division of Kristin Mitchell Design, Inc.
5341 Sunny Ridge Road
Mineral Point, Wisconsin 53565

Book Design and Project Coordination:
Little Creek Press and Book Design

June 2023

Follow Sue on Facebook @ Sue Berg/author
To contact author: bergsue@hotmail.com
To order books: www.littlecreekpress.com

Library of Congress Control Number: 2023909347

ISBN-13: 978-1-955656-57-3

Cover photo: Winds of Change, La Crosse, Wisconsin © **Phil S Addis**

ACKNOWLEDGMENTS

With each new book in the Driftless Mystery Series comes another opportunity for gratitude. So here goes ...

To Alan always, with love

To Little Creek Press for producing the best book possible.

To Driftless Mystery fans for reading and supporting my work and telling others about the series.

To my friend Beth Harris for being a sounding board and for traveling with me around the state, giving directions and loading and unloading books. Ughhh!

To Dick Wallin, retired DNR agent, for his expertise and knowledge of weaponry and law enforcement. Your suggestions improved the book tremendously.

Let us not become weary in doing good, for at the proper time we will reap a harvest if we do not give up.

—Galatians 6:9 NIV

DRIFTLESS DECEIT

"A smorgasbord of real-life issues including family loyalty, faith to forgiveness, and love both lost and found."
~Patricia Skalka, author of the Door County Mystery Series

"The ridges, valleys, and rivers of Southwest Wisconsin have provided the backdrop for many regional titles, and Sue Berg's *Driftless Deceit* doesn't disappoint in detailing the beauty of this rugged terrain. But Berg's gripping crime novel also paints an honest portrait of the crime and rural poverty that does exist beneath the bucolic veneer of this unique landscape."
~John Armbruster, author of Tailspin

OTHER BOOKS BY SUE BERG

Solid Roots and Strong wings—A Family Memoir

The Driftless Mystery Series:

Driftless Gold

Driftless Treasure

Driftless Deceit

FOREWORD
THE DRIFTLESS REGION

The name *Driftless* appears in all of the titles of my books because this region of the American Midwest where my novels take place is a unique geographical region, though relatively unknown. The Driftless Region—which escaped glacial activity during the last ice age—includes southeastern Minnesota, southwestern Wisconsin, northeastern Iowa, and the extreme northwestern corner of Illinois. The stories I write take place in and around La Crosse, Wisconsin, which is in the heart of this distinct geographical region.

The Driftless Region is characterized by steep forested ridges, deeply carved river valleys, and karst geology, resulting in spring-fed waterfalls and cold-water trout streams. The rugged terrain is due primarily to the lack of glacial deposits called drift. The absence of the flattening glacial effect of drifts resulted in land that has remained hilly and rugged—hence the term *driftless*. In addition, the Mississippi River and its many tributaries have carved rock outcroppings and towering bluffs from the area's bedrock. These rock formations along the Mississippi River climb to almost six hundred feet in some places. Grandad Bluff in La Crosse is one of these famous bluffs.

In particular, the Driftless portion of southwestern Wisconsin contains many distinct features: isolated hills, coulees, bluffs, mesas, buttes, goat prairies, and pinnacles formed from eroded Cambrian bedrock remnants of the plateau to the southwest. In addition, karst topography is found throughout the Driftless area. This landscape was created when water dissolved the dolomite and limestone rock resulting in features like caves and cave systems, hidden underground streams, blind valleys and sinkholes, and springs and cold streams.

About eighty-five percent of the Driftless Region lies within southwestern Wisconsin. The rugged terrain comprising this area is known locally as the Coulee Region. Steep ridges, numerous rock outcroppings like the Three Chimneys northwest of Viroqua, the classic rock formations of Wisconsin Dells, and deep narrow valleys contrast with the rest of the state, where glaciers have modified and leveled the land.

The area is prone to flooding, runoff, and erosion. Because of the steep river valleys, many small towns in the Driftless Region have major flooding problems every fifty to one hundred years. Farmers in the region practice contour plowing and strip farming to reduce soil erosion on the hilly terrain.

Superb cold-water streams have made the Driftless Region a premier trout fishing destination in the country. A variety of fish, including brook and rainbow trout, thrive in the tributaries of the Mississippi River system. The crystalline streams are protected by Trout Unlimited, an organization that works with area landowners to maintain and restore trout habitat. In addition, abundant wildlife such as deer and turkeys provide excellent hunting for the avid sportsman.

La Crosse is the principal urban center that is entirely in the Wisconsin Driftless Region, along with small cities, towns, and numerous Amish settlements. Cranberries are grown and harvested in bogs left over from Glacial Lake Wisconsin. At one time, cigar tobacco was grown and harvested throughout the Coulee Region, but foreign markets decreased the demand for Wisconsin-grown tobacco. However, tobacco barns or sheds are still found throughout the landscape and are an iconic symbol of a once-thriving industry. The region is also home to Organic Valley, the nation's largest organic producer of dairy products, organic vegetables, and fruits, particularly apples. Winemaking and vineyards have popped up in recent years, and apple production continues to be a staple in the Driftless economy.

After describing the area's geographical features, you can see why Wisconsin is the perfect setting for a mystery series! It's a wonderland of unparalleled geographical beauty, impressive wildlife, and friendly, memorable people. Enjoy!

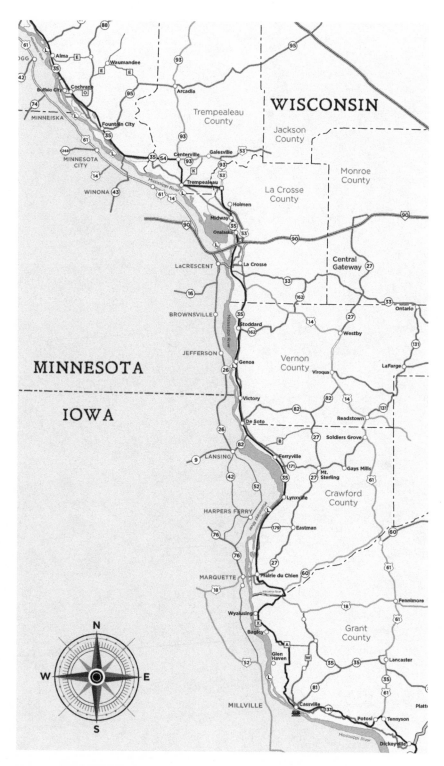

1

SATURDAY EVENING, SEPTEMBER 7

The sound of slapping waves on the sides of the *Geechee Girl* houseboat in Pettibone Harbor near La Crosse, Wisconsin, created a gentle, rhythmic cadence that was comforting. The houseboat swayed with an undulation that felt natural—a motion as old as the river itself. It reminded DeDe Deverioux of the river currents that rocked her grandfather's shrimping boat where they met the ocean tides in the early morning light. When she was a small child in the Gullah country of Beaufort County, South Carolina, that movement was a way of life flowing through her veins. Now as she sprawled in her chaise lounge chair under the flickering stars of a velvety black night on the Mississippi River near La Crosse, Wisconsin, she wondered what the next chapter in her life would bring.

Raised by her grandparents, Lorenzo and Hettie Deverioux, on the bayous and tidal creeks of South Carolina, the smell of river water and the life that teemed beneath filled DeDe with a deep longing for home in the low country near Morgan Island with its simple food, natural beauty, and unpretentious living.

She puffed lazily on her pipe—a habit she'd picked up from her grandma Hettie. Wisps of fragrant smoke rose into the air spiraling into ghostly gray shapes that swirled in the cool September night and then disappeared. In the distance, the bluffs along the Mississippi huddled like overgrown pouting children crouched along the shore. The light from a sliver of the gibbous moon shone on the dark surface of the water, leaving a rippling yellow crescent. Somewhere in the stillness of the night, a cackle of laughter and soft jazz music reminded DeDe of the sultry nights she'd spent patrolling the parishes of New Orleans as a city cop.

At age thirty-two, DeDe was still searching for a place to land. She tried teaching, but that lasted barely a year. Her inquisitive mind was restless, searching for some great mystery that needed a solution. She drifted from one low-paying job to another until a friend suggested police work. Though it seemed an odd career choice at first, the suggestion satisfied her insatiable curiosity about people and what made them tick. Her restless intellectual energy found its match in the challenges of detective work. Puzzling out the tangled tentacles of motive and opportunity focused her restless mind, gave her a purpose, and added meaning to her life. She had found her life's work, and there was no turning back.

Enrolling in the police academy was a cultural shock after her quiet and simple existence in the isolated surroundings of Wilkins on the riverbanks, where she lived with her grandparents on their small vegetable farm. River life was in her bones. She'd spent her Saturdays and summer months on her grandfather's small fishing boat trolling the tidal creeks, pulling in crabs and shrimp. DeDe could throw a cast net into a creek and retrieve a *ketch uh da day* as good or better than any man.

Despite the survival skills she'd learned from Grandpa Lorenzo, she soon discovered that her calm and deliberate manner in tense situations was critical to surviving the streets as a cop in New Orleans. Whether it was her simple, unsophisticated philosophy of life or her hardheaded, practical approach to problem-solving, DeDe thrived in difficult, challenging predicaments.

With three years of policing in New Orleans under her belt, she forged ahead with night classes until she became a detective. But wanderlust poked her in the ribs, and a few months ago, she'd decided to pull up stakes in her beloved south and move north. Grandpa Lorenzo and Grandma Hettie had passed on, so she used her small inheritance from her grandparents to buy a 1993 Harbor Master fifty-two-foot houseboat and began navigating north on the Mississippi River.

Maneuvering through locks and dams, she became an expert at traversing the currents and avoiding the dangers of the largest river in the United States. She'd been traveling now for almost three months—an extended and unintended vacation. Along the way, she fished and stopped periodically at farmers' markets along the river to stock up on fresh fruits and vegetables. With her fifty-pound bag of rice on hand, she could cook up a pot of gumbo or hoppin' john any night of the week.

Sitting in the blackness of the night on her houseboat in Pettibone Park, she wondered at the wisdom of moving this far north. September had already arrived, and the nights were cool and crisp. The brilliant colors of the hardwood trees and the sandstone bluffs that towered along the shores of the Mississippi complemented the cooler weather. However, living on a houseboat would not be feasible for much longer. She groaned with anxiety as she thought about what might face her in this northern climate. Wisconsin winters were notorious for heavy snow, bitter cold, and ice. *What do people do around here when it's that cold?* she thought. *Dat's enough to freeze da titties offa da witch.*

She'd applied for a detective position online at the La Crosse Sheriff's Department, resulting in a scheduled interview with Lieutenant Jim Higgins and Sheriff Davy Jones on Monday. The interview was only two days away. Now she wondered what she'd gotten herself into.

The river she understood; the people she wasn't so sure about, and the winter weather scared the bejesus out of her. She tapped the tobacco out of her pipe on the edge of the boat. The red coals hissed as they hit the water. She could still feel the heat in the pipe's bowl as she cradled it in her hand and stuck it in her sweatshirt pocket. It was her most treasured possession from her beloved grandmother.

Standing near the bow, she stretched her six-foot frame upward, her arms reaching for the stars. Silently she prayed a familiar Gullah prayer. *Twas mercy brought me from my Pagan land, taught my benighted soul to understand there's a God, and there's a Savior, too.* Then her voice broke through the dark night. "Well, Lord, you be watchin' over me," she finished solemnly, remembering the words spoken by her wrinkled grandma Hettie when she was just a child. DeDe knew who she was and who she wasn't, and she knew what she would bring to the job interview. She hoped it would be enough.

2

The evening sun was just beginning to sink behind Lieutenant Jim Higgins' house on Chipmunk Coulee Road south of La Crosse, Wisconsin. The woods that bordered the manicured lawn left odd, elongated shadows on the thick green grass. The wind blew gently through the trees, and shadows moved and swayed as if dancing to a rhythm all their own. Covered with cracks and crevices, the irregularly shaped sandstone formations at the back of Higgins' property provided excellent cover. A chipmunk scampered out from under a rock, trilled a warning at the man in camouflage, and scurried back into its underground burrow again.

Rolf "Maddog" Pierson leaned against the limestone rock outcropping, thankful for anything solid that would support his shaking legs. The irony of leaning on a slab of unforgiving rock for support instead of his own two feet was not lost on him. *The story of my life,* he thought. He'd promised himself he wouldn't drink while he was doing reconnaissance, but he gathered up what little courage he had, then pulled a half pint of vodka from his vest pocket and took a huge gulp. His eyes watered as alcohol slid down his throat spreading its warmth throughout his body. He needed something to steady his shaking hands and calm the wild beating of his heart.

He had thoroughly checked out Higgins' place when no one was around. The sophisticated camera mounted on a tree by the driveway aimed at the house's front entry was a problem he hadn't anticipated. It was some kind of expensive surveillance. The camera was too high to easily dismantle, and Chipmunk Coulee Road was too busy with traffic. The surveillance system meant he'd have to come up with another plan.

The reputation of Higgins as a determined investigator with the La Crosse Sheriff's Department was another roadblock in his plans. From everything Maddog had heard and read on the internet, Higgins was the synthesis of persistence and intelligence. He'd come after him with both guns blazing if Lillie went missing. Maddog harbored no illusions. Higgins would never give up his niece now that he'd bonded with her so completely.

Although Maddog was a burned-out druggie and alcoholic, he wasn't stupid, but a drug-addled brain could occasionally override an intelligent mind. Fully informed, coherent decisions often became a crapshoot. After all, the proof was in the pudding. Here he was, hiding behind some rocks doing surveillance on his own daughter. That fact alone made his situation hard to face in the light of day.

Regret, anger, and remorse went deep. At times, he felt like a lump of hot coal was burning a hole in his stomach. Walking out of the Wausau hospital higher than a kite almost six years ago, he left the baby girl behind without even signing the birth certificate. At the time, he was strung out on meth, desperate for his next fix. That monster—addiction—stalked his waking and sleeping. It strangled every good decision except the one to get high. Meth skewed his judgments until the only words to describe himself was harebrained loser. He was a hideous mess filled with deceit and shame. No one, except another addict, could ever understand.

Quietly he picked up his binoculars, turned toward the house, and knelt behind his rock perch. A hundred yards away, he watched the scene unfold. The squealing laughter of the little girl was infectious as she chased a squirrel up a nearby tree. The innocence of youth. He adjusted the lens to see her clearly—the blue eyes, the golden locks of curly hair, the obvious intelligence and curiosity that seeped from every pore. The little girl was so beautiful it hurt him to look at her. *That's my girl,* he thought wistfully.

Tears stung his eyes as he watched the impish child turn toward the dark-haired woman on the patio holding another little toddler, a curly-haired blond baby boy. They exchanged smiles and words, and Higgins lounged in relaxed contentment next to the woman. The little girl tilted her head back and laughed spontaneously with pure joy.

Lowering the binoculars, Maddog sat in his lair; hiding was a familiar methodology in his drug operation. His criminal forays required stealth and secrecy. After all, he ran one of the biggest meth labs in central Wisconsin on his old man's two-hundred-acre farm. The tentacles of his operation spread far beyond Marathon County, Wisconsin. Camouflage and subterfuge were his trademarks. He wasn't called Maddog for nothing. He'd earned his nickname eluding police and making drug drops in out-of-the-way places. And he'd killed a few men—one of the hazards of his profession.

He lifted the binoculars again to his red, bloodshot eyes. Another younger woman had joined the group. He scanned the house and lawn. The property was pristine and well-kept, with beautiful places for a child to run and explore. A creek, rocks to climb, trees in which to build a treehouse, a lush green lawn bordered by beautiful flowerbeds, and outside the perimeter of the lawn lay the mysteries and wonders of nature—a perfect environment for an inquisitive child.

Once again, regret stalked him, poked him, ridiculed him. What do you have to offer her? What could you possibly give her that she doesn't already have? Those were the questions that tormented him. He had nothing to give her except one thing—he was her real father. She was his blood. And by God, somehow, she would be his again.

He laid his binoculars down and hunched against the rugged rocks like an old man. Then glancing back over his shoulder for one last glimpse of the little girl, he slinked quietly into the woods, his plan gelling in his mind. He would return for the girl but not tonight. Later under cover of another night, the time would come.

3

SUNDAY, SEPTEMBER 8

"**B**apa! Bapa!" Lillie called, pointing upward to a tall maple in the backyard. "Look! There's something up there in that tree!"

Jim and Carol Higgins sat on the fieldstone patio at the back of the house on Chipmunk Coulee Road early Sunday afternoon. The trees were tinged with red, yellow, and orange, harbingers of things to come. The green oasis that surrounded their home had a tired look to it. Things were starting to decay and die in preparation for the dormancy of the winter season that would soon be upon them. Fall was unofficially here now that Labor Day had come and gone.

After church at Hamburg Lutheran up on the ridge this morning, Jim had grilled hamburgers and hot dogs. Now sixteen-month-old Henri cuddled on his lap, drinking his bottle, drowsy and contented. Stretched out in her chaise lounge chair, Carol watched Lillie running in circles around the base of a tall oak tree.

"It's a coon, Lillie," Jim said, startling Henri, who began to wail. "Oh, sorry, little guy."

"He's ready for a nap," Carol said, leaning over and taking Henri from Jim. Cradling the toddler in her arms, she stood up and said,

"I'll put him down, and then I'll be back out." She leaned down again and gave Jim a tender kiss.

"Mm, that was nice," Jim said, a dimpled smile creasing his face. He took a sip of his Spotted Cow beer.

"More where that came from," Carol said as she carried Henri inside. Jim didn't know if she meant kisses or beer. Either or both—it was all good.

Lillie ran across the lawn, her golden curls unfurling in the breeze. Coming up to Jim, she jumped into his lap, panting hard, her eyes full of childhood delight.

Jim pushed his nose into her hair, breathing her scent deep into his lungs, pulling her to his chest. Since coming to them more than a year ago under traumatic conditions, Lillie had made remarkable progress in adjusting to family life in the Higgins household. This week she'd begun first grade at St. Ignatius Catholic School in Genoa, wowing everyone with her uncanny ability to absorb information. Her mind was like a sponge. Jim and Carol still didn't understand where her prodigious curiosity came from, but questions bubbled out from a deep spring within her and left everyone wondering at her precocious intelligence. Jim leaned back, prepared for the onslaught of questions that Lillie would certainly ask.

"Will the raccoon come down all by himself?" she asked, turning her deep blue eyes to meet Jim's.

"He'll come down when he feels safe," Jim said. "He might have a home up in that tree. That's a common place for raccoons to live—in a hole in a tree or a burrow in the ground. She might have a family to take care of. Being twenty feet off the ground helps them feel safe from predators like nosy dogs." He shut his eyes and leaned back in the Adirondack chair, waiting for the next inevitable question. The late summer breeze was barely discernable, and it carried a slight chill, a reminder that the fall season had arrived. The air smelled of musky vegetation—sweet like honey. Warm and comfortable, Jim luxuriated in the bone-deep warmth of the sun's rays.

"What's a burrow, Bapa?" Lillie said, leaning back on Jim's chest, waiting for his answer.

"It's a place that a coon uses for its home. Sometimes they dig under a log, a bunch of rocks, or even an old barn or house." Jim's baritone voice rumbled quietly as Lillie took in this new information.

"What do they do in the winter when it gets cold?"

"Well, they sleep until it gets warm, and then they come out again. We read about that in one of your books, remember?"

Lillie continued asking questions until Jim noticed her body becoming limp and relaxed. Finally, it was quiet. Carol came down the stairs to the patio. Sneaking up to Jim, she stood before him, her eyes soft with affection.

"She's sleeping," Carol whispered. Jim opened his eyes. "Want to carry her in?"

Jim nodded. Shifting Lillie in his arms, he eased out of the chair and carried her into the bedroom, where he gently laid her on the bed. He closed the door quietly and wandered into the kitchen, looking for a piece of Carol's famous beet chocolate cake with fudge frosting. Balancing a plate of cake and a glass of milk, he made his way to the swoopy black chair in the living room. He was enjoying the cake immensely; Carol didn't usually make sweets. He took a big swig of ice cold milk and hunkered down to enjoy another forkful of cake.

"Jim?" Carol called from the bedroom.

"Yeah, whaddya need?" Jim asked, the cake perched temptingly on his fork.

"Could you come here a minute, honey?" Her voice sounded low and soft. Seductive.

Curious, Jim set his cake and milk on the end table and walked down the hall to the bedroom. Carol had recently painted and hung new drapes, so he supposed she needed help hanging pictures or something. He walked into the bedroom, stopped abruptly, and gaped.

Wearing only a diamond necklace, Carol was lying languidly on the turned-down bed linens, her brown eyes smoldering with desire. "I need you for just a little while," she said, crooking her finger at him. Jim's eyes drifted over her full breasts, dark nipples, and shapely legs.

He began undressing, first his T-shirt and then his Bermuda shorts. His eyes never left her face. "You never cease to amaze me, baby," Jim said, leaning over her. Carol took his hand and pulled him down to her, kissing him warmly.

"Surprises are the spice of life, Jim. You should know that by now," she said between kisses.

"Well, this beats chocolate cake any day," he whispered in her ear.

Later, Carol lay with Jim under the covers, spent and satisfied. "We should probably get dressed before Lillie wakes up," Carol said softly, "If she finds us like she did when we were in the tub together, I'm not sure I could answer her questions about why we're naked. Again."

"Don't worry. She'll have a healthy concept of marital love if she keeps catching us in these situations," Jim said, fingering the diamond necklace. They were face to face, cuddling together. Jim loved when passion opened the door to intimacy—soul to soul. "I love it when you wear this necklace," he said, looking intently into her brown eyes.

"Really? Why?" Carol's brown eyes moved across his face, trying to read the deeper emotion beneath the words.

"Because it reminds me how much you put up with last year when I was in the pits of my depression. I was pretty hard to live with for a while." He kissed her neck tenderly, then moved up to her lips.

"You were exasperating at times, Jim, but we're in this together no matter what," she said. Then her voice took on a softness. "I love you so much." He enfolded her in his arms. "I'm glad you've finally made peace with yourself ... and me. This necklace is a reminder of that."

Jim had endured a serious bout of situational depression when his sister, who was homeless, died in La Crosse's Riverside Park, with Lillie in tow. He put Carol through an emotional wringer as he struggled to understand the complicated family mess hidden from him since birth. He'd always remembered his childhood as idyllic, growing up on a dairy farm in a beautiful little coulee with his older brother, Dave. They got into their share of boyhood trouble and mischief, avoiding serious crimes and growing up to be good and decent men. Then last year, through a series of shocking events, he'd discovered he had a sister. It was a blow that sent him reeling with confusion and grief. When he'd finally climbed out of his blue funk, the gift of the necklace was a token of his love and commitment to Carol.

"It doesn't seem possible that it was more than a year ago when Lillie came to us, and I discovered I had a sister I never knew about. You were a week away from delivering Henri. The timing was not good. In fact, it was downright horrible." He shivered involuntarily. "Then we had that double murder to deal with. I don't want to relive that, either."

"I agree. But we weathered the storm. It tossed our boat around, but hopefully, we learned something in the process." Carol looked up at him. "I know I did."

"What'd you learn?" Jim asked.

"I remember something a seed corn salesman told my dad once. He had thirteen children, including a set of twins and a set of triplets. His famous saying was, "If you're going through a hard time, just be patient. This, too, shall pass," she said. "We went through a hard time, but I knew it wouldn't last forever. Everything resolves itself somehow."

"That's a lesson worth learning," Jim said, kissing her gently.

They were both drowsy, and a nap together would have been a perfect conclusion to the lovemaking, but the peace was short-lived. Crying wafted from the nursery.

"Oh, that's Henri. He's awake. I'll get dressed quick." Carol rolled out of bed, and Jim began to get up.

"No, no," she said. "You stay there. I'll go." She grabbed her clothes and dressed quickly.

Jim's phone buzzed. He got up, slipped on his boxers, and fumbled for his cell in the pocket of his shorts.

"Lt. Higgins."

"Chief, it's Paul. We need you over at 1156 George Street. Chief Pedretti's already here. Suspicious death."

"Right. I'm on my way." He grabbed a dress shirt and tie from the closet, slipped on a pair of khaki pants, and found his boat shoes. Walking into the nursery, he put his hands on Carol's shoulders and said, "Got a call over on George Street. Be back later."

Carol looked up at him. "Okay. Be safe." Henri's innocent brown eyes gazed at Jim, his blond hair mussed from sleep. Jim gently tousled his curls and kissed his little head.

"See you later," he said.

4

Jim cruised up U.S. Highway 35 along the Mississippi River in the late afternoon sunlight. Fishing boats bobbed on the current. A power boat pulled a skier who expertly carved twisting curves in the dark surface of the water. A group of bikers had stopped at a wayside to have drinks and snacks. Cruising through the tiny town of Stoddard, Jim stopped at Kwik Trip on the south side of La Crosse for a coffee and continued on his way.

Traffic was light. Zipping through town, he pulled up to the residence located two blocks north of the George Street viaduct. The home was a mid-century two-story dwelling with wooden siding, the paint faded to an anemic yellow. It was typical of the working-class dwellings in the area. Its fifty years of existence revealed significant wear and tear. One of the black shutters on a front window was sagging and hung at a tipsy angle. The front stoop had a slight list, and some of the shingles on the roof had loosened over the years and were rotted and curling. When Jim stepped on the porch, the weathered boards creaked ominously. Yellow caution tape encircled the residence, and the place was bristling with city cops, CSI techs, and other police personnel, plus the van from the county morgue. The front door was flung open. Jim flashed his ID for the officer stationed there, who nodded and grunted a greeting. A musty smell floated from the door—something old and dank, like moldy newspapers.

Seeing La Crosse Police Chief Tamara Pedretti standing off to one side of the living room, Jim walked up to her. She was dressed casually in a soft blue blouse and jeans but wore a cashmere navy jacket with her police chief badge conspicuously pinned on her lapel. Although she was heavy around the middle, her impeccable personal grooming was evident in her shining blonde hair styled in a French braid, painted pink fingernails, and tastefully applied makeup. She was still pretty, although the stress of balancing her job and family life took a toll on her emotions at times.

Tamara had worked her way up through the ranks. She was one of the few women police chiefs in Wisconsin, although women in administrative police positions were increasing around the nation. Her razor-sharp intellect, non-partisan demeanor, and sense of fair play made her popular among the city's residents. She could be seen often in and around local coffee shops and eateries, animated by the citizens' concerns. Holding listening sessions on the UW–La Crosse campus, students relied on her to maintain a rock-solid sense of security both on campus and on the famous Third Street procession of bars and taverns frequented by the college crowd. She butted heads, however, with anyone who challenged her authority. She was a stickler about form and protocol among her officers. She ran a tight ship. Jim liked her and admired her steely confidence.

"Tamara, haven't seen you for a while," Jim commented, standing next to her, watching the techs work the scene.

"Yeah. Funny how that works. We're in the same building, but we never run into each other. Heard about your baby. Congrats," she said, giving him a friendly smile.

Jim chuckled. "You're a year behind. And it wasn't one, but two." Jim sipped his coffee.

Tamara did a double take. He gave her a shortened version of the events surrounding Henri's and Lillie's arrivals. "It's been quite a year," he finished solemnly.

"Wow! And I thought I had it tough with three teenagers."

"Try becoming a father at fifty-two and inheriting a four-year-old who never quits asking questions." Then getting down to business, Jim asked, "So what have we got here?" He felt the weight of the crime seeping through the dim and gloomy atmosphere of the house.

Tamara glanced at her clipboard and gave Jim the bare facts. "Seventy-four-year-old male, Sylvester Kratt, widowed, retired from the La Crosse Rubber Mills where he worked for twenty-four years. Neighbors say he was quiet, kept to himself. Strangled. Violent struggle. The house wasn't broken into, so he might have known his assailant. Murdered. Now the question is why? That's where you come in, Jim," she finished, glancing at him, her face serious.

Jim and his young, dedicated team had a stellar reputation for solving difficult, enigmatic crimes. Jim thought their success was due to a lot of enthusiasm, an average amount of intelligence, the guidance of the Almighty, and sometimes a whole bunch of dumb luck.

He jotted down the facts she'd recited, then turned to her and asked, "Luke here yet?"

"Yeah, he's in the kitchen. That's where the victim's daughter found the body. She called it in."

"Right. Good seeing you."

"Wish the circumstances were different," Tamara said wistfully.

"Yeah, me too," he said, taking a few steps toward the kitchen. Then turning back to her, he said, "Hey, we'll have you guys out one night before the cold weather hits. Do one last grill out. We haven't seen your kids in a long time."

"Thanks. That'd be great. I'd like that." She smiled and turned to address another officer who was waiting to talk to her.

Jim walked through the cramped house filled with worn-out furniture, family pictures, and mementos. The carpets were faded, and cobwebs in the corners of the room swayed with the air currents.

The lingering smell of mold and old newspapers followed him. He jostled his way through the CSI people. Someone handed him a pair of blue paper booties which he slipped over his shoes before he peeked around the kitchen door. He snapped on a pair of blue latex gloves.

Luke Evers, chief medical examiner and coroner of the La Crosse County Morgue, was kneeling next to the victim lying on the kitchen floor, crumpled like a newspaper and obviously dead. Jim had worked with Luke for about seven years. He was efficient and resourceful, calm and unflappable. He was also Carol's boss.

Jim cringed at the sight of the purple bruising around the victim's neck and his vacant stare into oblivion. He looked away as his stomach turned over. "Luke, what's up?" he asked nonchalantly, keeping his voice neutral. "Anything interesting at this point?"

Luke acknowledged Jim with a nod, and they exchanged a serious glance. Despite Luke's composed demeanor, Jim knew that beneath the public exterior, he was a sensitive and caring man. He displayed a deep regard for the snuffed-out human being that lay on the faded, cracked linoleum floor in front of him. In their line of work, it was easy to become calloused. That was a slippery slope. Pretty soon, you were hard as nails and didn't recognize yourself in the mirror. He knew Luke was never callous about a death, maintaining a sense of propriety and respect for the deceased.

Standing and facing Jim, Luke said, "Well, he was strangled. Nothing's really out of place except the chair that was kicked over during the struggle. I'd say he died sometime late last night, possibly between ten and midnight. I'll know more after I perform the postmortem."

"Anything else?"

Luke nodded. "Yeah, there is," he said. He pulled Jim into a corner by the refrigerator. Speaking in hushed tones, he continued, "The techs found something, but they want to keep it under wraps until you see it. We're hoping you can figure it out."

A little chill ran up Jim's back. "Oh, yeah? What's that?" he asked, giving Luke a solemn stare.

"A women's locket was laying next to him on the floor and a note saying, 'I know what you did.'"

"Really?" Jim paused for a moment, his breath quickening. He cleared his throat. "The locket and note are bagged as evidence, right? When can I see it?"

"The CSI people bagged it earlier. It's back at your department locked in the evidence room, but I'll text you a photo of it." Luke frowned. "That's kinda strange, don't you think?"

"Yeah. Yeah, it is," Jim said, feeling the familiar knot of angst in his stomach. "Thanks, Luke. Send me that photo. I'm going to talk to the daughter today if I can." A couple of CSI techs hovered at the door, their faces impassive, waiting for access to the coroner. Jim nodded to them and then said to Luke, "You're busy. I'll talk to you tomorrow."

Glancing out the kitchen window to the small fenced-in backyard bordered by a narrow alleyway, Jim saw Paul Saner, a member of his team, talking to another detective, Sam Birkstein, in the shade of an enormous maple. He turned and brushed by the techs, went out the front door, and walked along a narrow strip of grass to the backyard. Clumps of neighbors and onlookers were standing along the back alley where several garages were located. Some were smoking, and some were sipping on a beer or soft drink. Jim could imagine the rumors being hatched and taking flight—all on social media, he supposed.

Coming up to the two detectives, he asked, "Been here long?"

"Nope. We just got the call about an hour ago," Paul Saner said. "Any more information? They didn't have much to tell us when we arrived."

Jim had worked with Paul for about four years. He was reliable, a bulldog at digging up financial connections in money laundering, racketeering, and drug traffic investigations. He always put his best foot forward in the community. His annual DARE presentations in the local public schools were a big hit with the kids. He often entertained the children with his exceptional piano playing and was frequently recruited to entertain the police and sheriff's personnel at various departmental functions.

Sam Birkstein stood next to him. His dark curly locks and luminous hazel eyes made him something of a heartthrob among the secretarial pool on the third floor of the law enforcement building on Vine Street. However, he had recently married Leslie Brown, another detective on Jim's team, much to the disappointment of his adoring fans. Jim was surprised the secretaries didn't wear black armbands to work every day when they found out he was permanently out of commission.

Sam stood in front of Jim wearing a pair of ragged cutoff jeans, flip-flops, and a blue and gold University of Michigan Wolverine sweatshirt. He frequently bought his clothes at Goodwill stores. He claimed the clothes were phenomenally low in price. Furthermore, he said his get-ups were part of his persona, aiding him in his surveillance of the drug underworld in La Crosse. Jim could see why, but he'd discovered through experience that locking horns with Sam about the professional dress code was a complete waste of his time. His warnings to him in the past about dress code compliance had been largely ignored, although Leslie had been a positive influence recently in his selection of attire. But clearly, he still had streaks of fashion faux pas.

"A woman's locket was found next to the body with a strange note. Sounds kinda weird," Jim said. The two men stared at him for a moment.

"How does this stuff always end up in our laps?" Sam asked disgustedly.

"We're detectives. Solving crimes is what we do. Well, at least that's what we try to do," Jim responded with a shrug. He gave Sam the once-over from head to toe. Sam returned his gaze with an air of detachment. "Who else's lap is it going to fall into? We're it, guys. You talk to any neighbors?"

"We canvassed the closest neighbors on either side of his house," Paul said, referring to his notes. "The city officers are continuing to talk to other people on the block. The Medfords and the Sloans were Sylvester's closest neighbors. Nice people. Didn't have much to say about Sylvester. Said he was quiet and kept to himself. Not a lot to go on."

"Did they notice anything odd last night?" Jim asked.

Sam piped up. "The Medfords went to bed at about nine-thirty, and the Sloans were out bowling at the Stardust Lanes over on the south side with friends. They had a few beers and got home about twelve-thirty this morning. They didn't notice anything out of the ordinary. No lights were on when they came home as far as they can remember."

"What about the daughter who found him?" Jim asked. "Did you talk to her?"

"She was already gone when we got here. We'll have to talk to her tomorrow," Paul said.

"That's okay. I'll go over and talk to her now. We won't get much more information about the scene and victim today, so unless you run across some other connections, we'll meet tomorrow morning." Jim said, turning to leave.

"Right, Chief. Tomorrow," Sam said.

5

By six o'clock on Sunday evening, Jim was making his way along Eighth Street to Heather Lovstad's residence. The temperature was warm, and he drew in a long breath of fresh air through the open window, trying to erase the smell of the dilapidated house from his memory. The aroma of fresh bread from Festival Foods bakery made his stomach cramp with hunger. An image of a gooey cinnamon roll covered with sweet icing popped into his brain. However, Carol had recently been on a kick to limit their sweet intake since they'd both gained a little weight. *I could cheat,* he thought. But when he pictured Carol giving him a brown-eyed stare with her raised eyebrows, he stepped on the gas and zipped past the grocery store.

He was familiar with the Cass and King Street neighborhoods which were peppered with historic mansions. Many featured turrets, wrap-around porches, ornate doors, and stately gardens surrounding the imposing homes. He'd only lived three blocks east of here before he'd bought his current home in the country on Chipmunk Coulee Road south of La Crosse some twenty years ago. Nothing had changed too much.

Jim drove up to a small, neat compact house on Cass Street situated in the middle of a generous lot. The residence was sided in light yellow vinyl with dark blue shutters. Tall, mature shade trees stood along the street, and a curving sidewalk led to the front entrance embellished with low evergreen shrubbery. A separate garage was set back behind the house. It was cheerful and welcoming. A purple clematis to the left of the door climbed on a framework, its tendrils creeping across the frame. Its sweet scent reminded Jim of Carol's skin after a bubble bath. He rang the doorbell. Then he heard footsteps and a yapping dog before the door rattled and opened.

"Lt. Higgins?"

"Yes." Jim flashed his ID. "You must be Heather. May I come in?"

"Sure." She held the door open while a little white dog barked and woofed at Jim's shoes. After showing Jim to the small living room, Heather scooped up the little pet and took him to another part of the house.

"Sorry about that. He's not used to company," she said apologetically.

"No problem."

Heather sat on the couch opposite Jim. She was a large woman in her mid-forties, somewhat overweight, although she was tastefully dressed in blue jeans, a coral sweater, and casual loafers. Her thick brown hair had a blonde streak that swooped across her front bangs. Her small, furtive eyes looked Jim over as she plopped on the leather couch, slumping into the cushions, tucking one leg up under the other. Without makeup, the shock of her father's death was evident in the dark circles under her eyes and her pale complexion. She waited patiently for Jim to begin. He reached into his suit jacket and retrieved his small memo pad and pen.

"First, let me extend my condolences on the death of your father," Jim said seriously. Heather nodded, not making any comment. Jim continued. "So, I'll get right to it, Heather. Where were you last night between nine and midnight?"

"I was at La Crosse Distilling with friends from eight until about eleven. When I got home

I went straight to bed."

"Your friends can verify that?" Jim asked.

"Oh, sure." She gave him the names of the three friends and their cell numbers. "Have you ever been there? Their Fieldnotes gin and vodka are great."

"No, I'm not much of a drinker. It's down near Riverside, isn't it?" he asked, feigning an interest.

"Yeah, Vine Street. It's a fun place to go for a cocktail."

"I'll remember that." Jim moved the conversation back to the inquiry. "What kind of work do you do?"

"I'm a secretary at Lowe, Pritchert, and Hanson Law Office downtown on Pearl Street. I've worked there for almost twenty years now. Started right out of high school." She smiled wanly.

Jim noticed her large muscular hands absent of rings. "Are you married?"

"Divorced, no children." She paused, her face reflecting frustration. "Don't you want to know something about my dad?" she asked impatiently.

"Yes, I'm getting to that. So, your dad must be a widower or divorced. Is that right?"

"A widower. My mom died suddenly in 2011 after a massive stroke."

"I understand your father worked at the La Crosse Rubber Mills. When did he start there?"

"He worked there twenty-four years." She did a quick mental math calculation for a moment. "He started in 1986 and retired in 2010 when the company moved to Portland, Oregon."

"So, he must have worked another job other than that one. If my math is right, he started at the rubber mills when he was thirty-eight."

"Yes. Before that, my parents owned a farm near Readstown, south of Viroqua, off Highway 14 on County Trunk T. My dad milked cows and tended bar in Readstown. Kind of an odd combination, but during the eighties, many farmers had a hard time staying afloat. There were suicides and lots of auctions, sort of like it is today. My mom never liked the farm, so they sold out and moved up here when he was hired at the mill."

Jim sat back in the La-Z-Boy chair and made a few notations on his memo pad.

"Tell me about this morning when you found your father," he said, laying his pen and pad aside to listen.

"Okay. I got up about nine and had some coffee and a little breakfast." She stopped briefly and cleared her throat. "About one o'clock, I decided to go get groceries. I usually stop at my dad's once a week to check on him, and after I bought my groceries, I stopped at the house. That's when I found him on the floor and called 911."

Jim watched her as she gave her account. She seemed relaxed and comfortable telling what had happened.

"Heather, when your dad was found in the kitchen, a couple of items were found next to the body that were puzzling. Did you notice them when you found him?"

Her brow creased, and her face paled significantly. "No, I never went into the house. I drove up in the back alley like I always do, walked across the lawn, and went to the back door, which leads into the kitchen. The door was locked, and when I saw him collapsed on the floor, I immediately called 911. I'm like ... very squeamish, and I didn't want to be in the same room as a dead person."

Jim sat silent for a moment. "Don't you have a key to your dad's house?"

"No. If he was gone when I stopped, I'd just come back later. He was almost always home on Sunday morning."

"And you never saw the items lying on the floor next to him?" Jim asked, keeping his voice neutral.

"No."

He decided to move on. "What kind of a relationship did you have with your dad?"

"Whaddya mean? He was my dad," she said defensively. Jim noted the slang and her bristling attitude. It seemed an uncharacteristic response from a professional person, but he knew that emotional baggage could suddenly rear its ugly head without warning.

"Yes, I know that, but can you describe your relationship? Were you close to him?" he asked calmly. He shifted in his chair and crossed his legs. He gazed at her, waiting for her answer.

Heather began picking at a loose string on her sweater. Nervously, she brushed her hair away from her face. Jim noticed a change in her demeanor. Heather had tensed up, and she uncrooked her leg from beneath her. He tried to reassure her.

"Take your time. Whatever you tell me will remain confidential."

"My dad had some problems," she said, her eyes flitting around the room. "My mother was a fine woman, and I really think she loved my dad, but she was never enough, you know?" Jim could see tears welling up in her eyes. He nodded, not from understanding, but to give assurance.

"What kind of problems did he have?" he asked, fixing her with a cool stare.

"He was addicted to pornography," she said softly. "There were other women." Several moments of silence passed. Jim knew from past experience in his career as a cop that pornography addiction led down a very rough road—broken marriages, infidelity, incest, and a host of other heartbreaking sexual and relational problems. Heather wiped away a tear and went on.

"I didn't know any of this about my dad until later when I was older. In my early twenties, my mother told me about it. I was shocked. I mean, I'd seen *Playboys* and stuff like that, but I couldn't imagine my dad looking at such disgusting images." She spat out the words, her nose turned up in disgust. "The humble dairy farmer, the family man. What a joke!" After a few moments, she went on.

"Then there were the other women. After I found out about all of that, I became very uncomfortable around him, thinking he was going to try something on me. Our relationship changed from a normal father-daughter relationship to ... I don't know. I felt like I never really knew who he was. It's very complicated and hard to explain. I just didn't feel safe with him anymore, so I avoided him. When Mom died, I checked on him occasionally only because I promised my mom I would, but my feelings for my dad are very conflicting. Sorry," she said softly. By now, the tears were wet on her face.

"Did he ever sexually abuse you?" Jim asked gently. Heather's eyes hardened, and her head jerked up.

"I never gave him a chance. Didn't let him get that close," she said defiantly, wiping away her tears.

"I'm sorry about that, but I had to ask. Are you an only child?"

"No, I have a brother who lives in Rockford, Illinois. He's a waterworks engineer and is employed by the city to keep an eye on municipal water sources. Purity and pollutants. That kind of stuff."

"I have a picture of a locket I want you to look at." Jim scrolled through the photos on his phone and handed it to Heather. She looked at the jewelry, then carefully shook her head.

"Sorry, I don't recognize it. Should I?" she asked, looking up at Jim. "Is it important?" A tear glistened on her cheek, and she wiped it away on the sleeve of her sweater.

"Yes, it's important, although we're not sure why yet. You're sure it doesn't look familiar?"

She nodded vigorously, looking at the image again. "Never saw it before. What was the other thing you found?"

Jim leaned forward, placing his elbows on his knees, his hands clasped. "There was a note that said, 'I know what you did.' Can you shed any light on that?"

Heather sat stock still—whether from shock or something else, Jim wasn't sure. She looked up at him, her pupils small and dilated. "I have no idea what that means or who would have written it. But I will tell you that with all my dad's sexual promiscuity, someone could have decided to deliver a dose of revenge. Maybe an enraged husband." She shrugged her shoulders. "If I think of anything, I'll call you."

Jim stood. "Thanks, Heather. Call me on my cell if you think of anything that might be important. Sometimes the smallest detail can make a difference," he finished as he handed his card to her. "Do you have any questions for me?"

She shook her head and walked Jim to the door.

Back in his Suburban, Jim couldn't help but wonder at the revelations Heather shared. In his years as an investigator, he knew better than to try and predict what people might tell him. He'd been surprised, shocked, and horrified at the confessions he'd heard. *Desperate Housewives* had nothing on the common ordinary citizens walking around the streets of this town.

Still, the most telling information he'd heard had nothing to do with what they'd discussed during Heather's interview. *Why didn't she ask him what they knew about the killer?* Jim thought. And something more disturbing: *How did she know when she looked through the kitchen window that her dad was already dead?*

6

Leslie Birkstein unlocked the back door of the duplex on Cliffwood Lane beneath Grandad Bluff, a huge six-hundred-foot limestone bluff that overlooked the city of La Crosse and provided a panoramic view of the Mississippi River Valley. She stepped inside with Paco, her black lab. He'd been her constant companion, first in the U.S. Army, where they worked together as a team locating hidden IEDs in Iraq, and then later, as her constant and loyal companion in civilian life.

Paco made a beeline to his water dish, lapping noisily, slobbering water onto the hardwood floor. Then he turned his attention to his kibble, crunching with gusto as bits of chewed-up dog food escaped from his mouth and littered the area around his dish. Leslie headed for the shower after sweating through a three-mile run on the trails in Hixon Forest near the apartment. Sam was still out on the murder call that had been reported about two that afternoon.

As she was about to step into the shower, she heard someone come through the front door.

Her instinctive fears stemming from her experiences of sexual and physical abuse sent chills down her back. Her anxiety spiked at unexpected sounds—even in her own home. "Sam? That you?"

she yelled, sticking her head around the bathroom door, her heart thumping nervously.

"Yeah, Lez, it's me. I'll start the grill. We've got some pork chops, right?" Sam asked, opening the refrigerator and sorting through the contents.

"Bottom shelf in the meat drawer. I'm taking a shower. Be out in ten minutes. Make some camp potatoes, okay?"

"Yep. Sounds good. Will do." He heard the bathroom door close and the shower start.

Sam fired up the grill on the rear cement patio, returned to the kitchen, and seasoned the pork chops. As he cut up potatoes, onions, and carrots onto a large piece of aluminum foil and slathered butter and olive oil over the top, he thought back to their wedding just two months ago.

They'd foregone a big expensive affair and opted for a quiet ceremony at the Friendship Gardens along the confluence of the Black and Mississippi Rivers in La Crosse. Sam's father, a Lutheran pastor, had performed the ceremony, and Paul Saner, his detective colleague, had provided some beautiful music. The afternoon was a godsend, with typical early July weather, sunny and hot but not stifling. They'd invited only immediate family and members of the detective team. Lillie Higgins had been the miniature bride. She proudly carried a basket of roses, hyacinths, and daisies and was accompanied by Paco, who carried the wedding rings in a little box tied around his neck.

Sam still couldn't believe he was a married man. It felt so right. Although their relationship had been rocky at first, Leslie was the girl of his dreams. A painful separation and months of reflection had helped them realize they were truly in love. Now when he woke up next to her every morning, he thanked God for her. And he regularly prayed that the issues of PTSD from her military service and the traumatic abuse she'd endured from her former boyfriend would fade and become just a bad memory. She frequently endured recurring nightmares that left her in a cold sweat. *Don't get complacent. She'll still need counseling,* he thought.

He walked out to the patio and laid the tin foil packet of potatoes over the red coals. Then he smelled something lovely—a jasmine scent. Turning around, he watched Leslie plop down in a plastic lawn chair on the patio with Paco, who remained vigilant by her side. She ruffled his ears, and he licked her hand affectionately.

"Smelled you before I saw you," Sam said, winking, grasping the tongs, and leaning down for a kiss. "In my experience, that isn't always a good thing, except if it's you. You always smell good. What's that stuff you're wearing anyway?"

"Something I got from your mom—Pink Peony—so I'm sure it's perfect, right?" She smiled wickedly. Leslie was still trying to adjust to Mrs. Birkstein's bent for perfection. She still felt as though she hadn't been accepted yet. Somehow she hadn't risen to Mrs. Birkstein's exceptionally high standards. She knew her mother-in-law's expectations in dress, decorum, and housekeeping were ridiculously high. At this point in their relationship, Leslie wasn't sure if trying to please her was worth the effort. *I mean, who dusts their pillows?* Leslie thought.

"Be careful now! She's still my first love," he teased.

"Don't remind me. Your mom's your first love, and Paco's mine, so we're even."

Sam grimaced. "Oooo. That was a low blow."

"Sorry. Just joking. So, what's with the murder?" Leslie said. "Anything interesting?"

"Strangulation over on the north side. Don't know a whole lot yet." He went back into the kitchen and returned with the pork chops, which he placed on the grill grate. The fire flared, and the smell of cooking fat and meat filled the air. "We'll know more tomorrow." He sat down opposite her in another chair, the tongs in his hand. He noticed her tanned legs beneath the white terrycloth beach cover-up. She was gazing at him with tender affection.

"Higgins show up?" she asked, flipping her wet hair over her shoulder.

"Oh, yeah. He said a locket was found next to the victim with some kind of puzzling note," Sam told her.

"Oh, boy, that sounds spooky," Leslie said, rolling her eyes.

"Don't worry. Tomorrow at this time, we'll know a whole lot more," Sam said, strolling to the grill to check the pork chops.

"Maybe. But I'm guessing we'll probably be more confused than we are right now."

She's usually right, Sam thought. "That does seem to be the way it works," he said.

7

At eleven o'clock Sunday night, Ezekiel "Zeke" LaSalle parked his Chevy pickup along the curb, flicked off the headlights, got out of the cab, and walked to the truck box. He put on an orange safety vest and grabbed a pair of well-worn leather gloves and two orange safety cones he'd bought at a garage sale for five bucks. Walking under the streetlight on the 800 block of Ferry Street, he set up the cones and aimed his flashlight at the ragged pothole that yawned up at him. Like a dentist inspecting a bad tooth, he took a screwdriver from his back pocket. Kneeling by the hole, he pried the loose gravel and blacktop to the center, where it formed a small pile of rubble. *Maybe I should have been a dentist,* he thought, chuckling to himself.

Returning to his truck, he retrieved a whisk broom and small dustpan and strolled back to the cavity in the pavement. Sitting on his haunches, he heard a car slowly approaching. He pivoted and swore quietly. *A cop.* Just what he didn't want to have to deal with tonight.

The squad car rolled to a quiet stop. A door slammed. Footsteps approached in the beam of the headlights.

"Are you that pothole artist guy?" the cop asked.

"Yup. Just preparing this hole for a mosaic masterpiece," Zeke said, looking up at the cop.

"Does the mayor know you're doing this?" the officer asked, walking closer. Standing up, Zeke shrugged his shoulders. They squared off in an easy manner.

"I don't know," he said, the pothole gaping upward between the two men like a big black eye. "Would he mind? It doesn't seem like the city street crews are getting the holes filled. I'm beautifying the environment. At least that's how some people see it," Zeke explained, friendly-like.

The cop nodded, a wry expression on his shadowed face. "That's one viewpoint. Doesn't bother me any." He came to some kind of conclusion about the situation and said, "Well, at least I know where one of your so-called masterpieces is. I'll stop and take a look tomorrow. Until then, you have a good night. Don't get hit or run over. And you didn't talk to me, right?" the officer said, turning back to the squad car.

"Right," Zeke replied. A few minutes later, the cruiser rolled quietly down the street, its taillights glowing like two orange embers.

He turned back to his work, evaluating his next step. He went to the truck box again, took down his water and quick set mortar, and began mixing. Lifting a completed mosaic of an American eagle out of the truck, he lugged it to the pothole, then returned for the mortar. Fifteen minutes later, the pothole had been filled and embellished with a stylized American eagle mosaic which, along with the mortar, plugged the unsightly cavity. The eagle stared up at Zeke with a haughty eye as if to say, *You really expect me to live in this hole?*

"New home, Mr. Eagle. Good luck," Zeke said, saluting ceremoniously.

As he drove back to his place on Ninth Street, Zeke chuckled to himself. During the day, he was a registered CPA, performing private tax preparation and advising his clients about savvy investment strategies in the office at the back of his house. By night he worked on his mosaics in the dim and dusty basement of his home. Shelves stacked with baby food jars of colored glass, pebbles, rocks, and other assorted paraphernalia lined up like a parade along the wall.

"A bunch of junk," his wife told him when she ventured down the stairs. She regularly had fits about the dust that floated up from the basement and coated the kitchen countertops with a fine white powder. "Couldn't you have found another way to express your artistic urges?" she'd asked.

He remembered exactly where he had been when he decided to pursue this art form—eighth-grade world history class with Mr. Ives. Zeke had been fascinated by the Greco-Roman world of the fourth century and the creative genius of mosaic artists who immortalized history with pieces of tesserae and grout. He could still feel the gritty surface of his first mosaic, a world history project that depicted colorful fish swimming in a deep blue sea. Assembling the picture with small pieces of colored glass and stone and cementing it into a permanent piece of artwork left him with a feeling of accomplishment and pride, even though it weighed a ton. It was the beginning of a fascination that has lasted until now.

He was constantly amazed at every pothole masterpiece. They were always inspirational. Emblematic symbols, numbers, mascots, sports team logos, historical figures, and other sundry objects were all fair game, as well as special numbers and birth dates. That people ignorantly drove over the top of them didn't bother him in the least. He was making an eyesore into something beautiful.

Recently, his notoriety spread when an article about him appeared in a local magazine touting the La Crosse area. Phone calls were coming in. People wanted to dedicate a pothole to a person or a cause. Zeke donated half the money to the cause and kept the other half for his efforts. Three hundred dollars could buy you some street creds in an ancient art form. Cool.

He was still puzzled about the order he'd received the other day, though. An anonymous donor honoring something—just a date, 10/8/77. Yellowed paper in a common white envelope. Odd. And the donor wanted the mosaic to be placed in a pothole on Sunset Street on the south side. That was even weirder. But whatever. The donor had left him five hundred bucks in cash, no questions asked. He wasn't complaining. *Just do it*, he thought.

8

MONDAY, SEPTEMBER 9

On Monday morning, Jim Higgins and Leslie Birkstein examined the evidence left at the crime scene Saturday—a small golden locket about the size of a quarter on a fine gold chain. Then there was the cryptic note written in block print—I know what you did. Jim felt his heart flutter as he looked at the mysterious message. Somehow the simple penciled note on the notebook paper left him feeling queasy and out of sorts. It reminded him of a past note he'd received at his home almost two years ago from a very disturbed bomber. *I hope history isn't repeating itself,* he thought.

"Well, Chief, I think this locket and note are the keys to solving this case," Leslie announced. He glanced at her and noticed the serious attention she gave to the evidence. Dressed in her classic chic style—a light green sweater, gray dress slacks, and an unusual artsy gold pendant—she looked pulled together, confident, and professional. *Sam is one blessed fellow,* Jim thought. *Now if he'd take a few cues from his wife about his clothes, I could quit fighting with Sheriff Jones about the dress code.* Sometimes his confrontations with Sam reminded him of past arguments with his son, John, when he was in junior high.

They locked the evidence room door and turned the corner continuing their discussion as they walked down the hall.

Jim said, "Yeah, I agree with you. Those two items are key pieces of evidence, but right now, I've got an interview at ten I have to prepare for." He stopped and turned, facing Leslie, when they reached her office door. "This is the last candidate we're interviewing for the systems information manager for our investigative department," he told her.

Leslie looked confused. "The what? I thought you were hiring another detective."

Jim sighed and rolled his eyes. "According to the county board, we're hiring a person to help us do online searches, document acquisitions, and evidence processing—whatever that bureaucratic bullshit means." Jim turned up his nose at the confusing title. "I'm sure all the applicants will be totally confused about what they'll be doing in this position by the time we're done. Typical government claptrap." Then lowering his voice, he added, "But I have the authority to decide the person's assignments, so really, the position's name and description are just a formality. There are ways around this BS." He waggled his eyebrows at her.

Leslie shook her head and gaped. "I'm confused. Are we hiring a detective? Yes or no?"

"In my book, we're hiring a detective, but you didn't hear that from me," Jim finished, pivoting and walking down the hall to his office. "I'll let you know how it turns out," he said, giving her a frustrated wave.

Half an hour later, Jim was on the first-floor administrative wing of the La Crosse Law Enforcement Center. He walked down the empty hallway to Room 167, where he found Sheriff Davy Jones seated at a long conference table reviewing his notes and applications. Jim nodded and sat down, scrolling through his texts and emails.

Looking up as Jim settled himself at the table, Jones asked grumpily, "Getting anywhere with Birkstein's get-ups?"

"Leslie seems to be having a positive effect. We can always hope," Jim said, smiling.

Within five minutes, two La Crosse County board members, Tom York and Stephanie Stoneman, joined them. Davy Jones texted his secretary to bring down the final candidate so the interview could begin.

DeDe Deverioux had taken special care with her appearance. Her hair was smartly styled and glossy, her tasteful makeup complimented her dark ebony skin, and her fingernails were lightly coated in clear nail polish. Behind her large glasses, her brown eyes were warm and gracious. A gold silky long-sleeved blouse and black pencil skirt were draped elegantly over her big-boned six-foot figure. She gave off a vibe of casual competence and relaxed friendliness. To Jim, she seemed like a down-home country girl nervous about making the right impression. It wasn't until she began telling her story that he realized how wrong first impressions could be.

After introducing her to the committee, Sheriff Jones looked up from his application form and said, "Tell us about your background, Ms. Deverioux."

DeDe began. "I grew up in the Gullah culture in the little town of Wilkins near Morgan Island, South Carolina. My ancestors were Black slaves brought here from Sierra Leone, Africa, in the mid-1700s. I was raised by my grandparents, Lorenzo and Hettie Deverioux, from the time I was a small child. I don't remember my parents. My grandparents told me my father was killed in a gang shootout near New Orleans, and my mother died a few years later from alcoholism. Someone in Social Services had sense enough to ship me up to my grandparents, or my story might be very different." She paused, making eye contact with everyone at the table. Then she continued in a soft, musical voice that Jim found hypnotizing.

"I graduated from Wilkins High School in 2005. I was unsettled for a time, but I went on with college and earned a bachelor's degree in sociology from the University of South Carolina in Beaufort. I taught a year in a rural country school." She paused. "That wasn't for me," she said, smiling softly. "I love children, but teaching them is a whole other ball game." The group chuckled quietly.

DeDe went on. "After skipping around at low-paying jobs, a friend suggested police work. It sounded crazy to me, but when my grandparents died within the same year, I didn't think I had anything to lose. After graduating from the police academy, I served on the New Orleans city police force for five years and went to night school to become a detective. That's really what I want to do."

"How did you get to Wisconsin? Seems like a long way from home," Jim commented. He leaned back and listened, impressed again with her calm manner.

"Well, it's a lot farther than I planned to go," she said seriously. "But I like what I see. River life is all I've really known. Right now, I live on a houseboat in Pettibone Harbor." DeDe noticed their surprised looks, but Jim understood the emotion behind the decision. His love of the river had been nourished in his young life, and that love had never left him either. He considered his houseboat, *The Little Eddy*, sacred ground.

"Well, living on a houseboat won't work during the winter in Wisconsin," Sheriff Jones said brusquely, giving her a hard stare. His abrupt remarks were typically Midwestern—straightforward and to the point—something she had observed in several exchanges with the locals over the last few weeks.

"Oh, I know that. I'm prepared to make other arrangements. The cold weather will be new to me. You know, I've never seen snow, although I've heard a lot about it," she said naively.

"You've never seen snow?" Ms. Stoneman asked, her eyes wide with disbelief.

DeDe smiled ruefully. "No, ma'am. And that's the truth." Then her eyes brightened. "But have you ever seen a shrimper in his boat on an early mornin' rockin' in a tidal creek throwing out a cast net and haulin' in a mess a shrimp?" she said, her native drawl slipping into her speech.

Jim covered a grin with his hand. *Comin' back at you, Ms. Stoneman. You go, DeDe,* he thought, smiling at her. Right then and there, he decided he liked Ms. Deverioux just fine.

9

By early afternoon, the third-floor classroom at the law enforcement center on Vine Street was packed with county and city cops, detectives, crime scene techs, and the county coroner and medical examiner. Everyone was waiting to hear the specifics about the strangulation that had occurred on Saturday night on George Street.

The classroom was drab, painted a typical bureaucratic beige with a heavily trafficked dirty, gray carpet which added to the dismal effect. A photo of the victim had been hastily taped to a large whiteboard. The name of the victim was scrawled across the top of the photo. It was a typical first step in investigating a suspicious death. The staff felt the whiteness of the board glaring at them with defiance, empty of motives or theories.

Luke Evers had completed the autopsy on Sylvester Kratt, and he was leaning against the wall waiting for Jim Higgins to give him the go-ahead to start. He stared pensively out the row of windows that faced Vine Street, a patch of blue sky peeking through some fluffy white clouds. His demeanor was serious and somber.

Jim had been circulating around the room with DeDe, introducing her to the investigative team. In a surprising move, Sheriff Davy Jones had convinced the committee to hire DeDe Deverioux on the spot. Leslie, Sam, and Paul welcomed her warmly.

Jim walked briskly to the front of the classroom and stood behind a white plastic folding table. He rapped his knuckles loudly on the table. People who had been having animated conversations stopped talking. One by one, they began focusing their attention on Jim, who stood at the front of the room.

"Alright, people. Let's get started," Jim said in a businesslike tone. "As most of you know, Sylvester Kratt of 1156 George Street was found strangled in his home early Sunday morning, September 7. The death is being treated as a homicide at this point. Luke has the results of the autopsy." Jim stepped back along the nearest wall, waiting for the gruesome details he always dreaded. Another life snuffed out, another killer on the loose. He thought about the challenges of hunting down a murderer. Butterflies flitted in his stomach, leaving him feeling irritated and nervous.

Luke Evers stepped to the front of the table, where he laid down a few notes. He got started.

"The victim, Sylvester Kratt, age seventy-four, was strangled in his home at about 11:30 p.m. on Saturday, September 7. During the strangulation, the hyoid and thyroid cartilage were damaged and displaced due to the pressure of the ligature on the neck. Compression on the carotid arteries by the ligature caused cerebral ischemia to take place rapidly within ten to fifteen seconds. Due to air hunger, violent struggling continued until the victim was unconscious. This may account for the scuff marks on the linoleum floor and the overturned chair in the kitchen. There was significant bruising around the outside of the neck, and the ligature did penetrate through the skin layer about a quarter of an inch. The techs did not locate a ligature or rope. Questions?"

"Was there any evidence of drugs, prescription or otherwise, in the blood?" DeDe asked. The crowd looked over at her, and a slight whisper rippled across the room. Chief of Police Tamara Pedretti and Jim exchanged a glance.

"The blood toxicology tests are in the lab right now. Why do you ask?"

"No reason, but in my experience, strangulation takes muscle. It's not easy to do, even on someone elderly like Mr. Kratt. Victims fight, kick, knock stuff over," DeDe explained. "You said there was minimal disturbance at the scene, so I wondered if the victim was incapacitated by drugs first. I've run across it, although it's unusual," she finished. She met Jim's eyes. He gave her an approving nod.

"Don't know yet, but I'll see what the report says," Luke commented. "I didn't find any injection sites, but they're hard to spot. I'll check again."

"Just an idea," DeDe said thoughtfully.

"And a good one," Luke remarked.

Moving on, Jim directed a flurry of reports that reviewed the facts at the crime scene. The CSI techs were still processing everything, but they had found a set of tire tracks in the side yard near the border of Kratt's property. DNA hits looked sketchy. Fingerprints were nil so far, but it was early. However, DNA was being extracted from the locket, but without a source, it was basically useless. It

would be filed for the time being with all the other evidence. Whoever committed the crime had been cautious, careful, and quiet.

After filling in the whiteboard and following up with other questions and discussion, the meeting broke up. Jim called for a powwow in his office. With the growing size of his team, the office felt cramped and crowded when everyone trailed in.

"So tell me what you make of the necklace and the note," he said, grabbing a piece of paper from his printer on the credenza, looking up at them. He walked to the window and cranked it open to let in some fresh air. He made eye contact with each detective.

Paul rubbed his chin and started. "The necklace is a major clue. It seems like a hint at a previous incident, maybe an unsolved death. The words of the note suggest that someone knows about something Sylvester did—a crime of some kind." He finished and looked at

Sam. "Maybe someone witnessed it goin' down, and they decided to deliver retribution as their own form of justice?" He shrugged his shoulders as he finished talking.

"That's what I think, too. Maybe an unsolved murder from the past, but the crime was never solved and . . ." Sam's voice drifted off.

"And now a relative or friend or lover is getting even," Leslie said, finishing Sam's sentence.

"So you're proposing that the victim, this Kratt guy, was involved in an old unsolved crime?" Jim asked, sitting behind his desk, doodling on the paper. It was quiet for a moment, everyone deep in thought. When no one answered, he went on. "Leaving clues with the body makes me think something's unresolved and Kratt has gotten his due justice. All speculation at this point, but we've gotta start somewhere."

"Maybe a partner who participated in the crime is getting rid of Kratt, who wanted to cleanse his conscience and confess?" They all turned and looked at DeDe when she spoke.

"Interesting take. Hadn't thought of that," Paul replied, lifting his eyebrows. "The note suggests that Kratt did something bad. Someone somewhere knows about something he did. Must've been really bad for him to be strangled." More silence.

Jim started again. "Of course, the killer could be a total fruitcake, and he put the necklace and note there to distract us from the real reason for the murder. But it seems we're all in agreement about an old unsolved crime. It might be murder, or it could be something else. Abduction? Rape? Abuse? Is that what you're thinking?" Jim asked. Jim thought about Sylvester's pornographic addiction problem.

When no one responded, Jim continued. "One thing you should all know is when I talked to the daughter, she shared that her dad had an addiction to pornography and had been unfaithful to his wife over the years."

"That's interesting but hardly uncommon nowadays," DeDe said.

"It's a place to start," Jim said. "DeDe and Leslie, why don't you start combing the police archives down on the second floor? See what you can dig up about unsolved murders or other unsolved crimes in the area," Jim ordered. "Paul and Sam, I want you to try and find some work acquaintances of this Kratt guy. Let's get a better handle on the man. See if they have any ideas about his death. Family problems, financial, whatever. Keep the sexual stuff in mind." Jim sat back. "I'm going to review my notes on the interview with Heather, Kratt's daughter. I might talk to her again if something pops out at me. The family history sounds somewhat chaotic. Let's meet back here tomorrow morning about ten."

"We're on it, Chief," Paul said, pivoting and walking out of the office.

When everyone had filed out, Jim walked out to the lobby. Emily Warehauser was seated on her throne as secretary extraordinaire, perched over her computer, her fingers flying over the keys, which was unnerving to Jim, especially when he recalled his two-fingered hunt-and-peck style.

"Emily—" Jim said, leaning over the counter. That's all he managed to get out before she quit typing and looked up at him anticipating his question.

"Yes, an office for DeDe?" she said, amazing Jim with her intuitive secretarial sense. "What about that little corner room across from Leslie? It's small, but a desk and a filing cabinet will fit. We can probably squeeze in a wastebasket, too. That's how tiny it is, but at least it's private. I'll get a name sign in the hallway, too."

"Sounds good. You'll take care of it?"

"Already called the custodian. He's on his way up with the stuff, sir," she said briskly.

"Good. Thanks," Jim said sincerely. He pivoted and returned to his office. He opened the folder that contained the notes from Heather's interview. Once more, he was confronted with the hidden motives of the human heart. One thing was sure—the darkness of the sin-sick soul had splattered its violent inclinations onto another human being. Like so many times before, his team would try and uncover the identity of a killer still unknown and loose on the landscape.

10

TUESDAY, SEPTEMBER 10 – EUGENE, OREGON

Professor Margretta Yelski Martin walked briskly into her office at Friendly Hall, the main administration building on the University of Oregon campus in Eugene. The misting rain that had been a hazy permeable sheet was now a full-fledged downpour. The fall colors outside her office window blurred into a Monet-like collage of smudged bronze, brick red, and dark sage. In the distance, she could barely make out the blue shadow of Spencer Butte, rising lazily above the farmland of the Willamette Valley. The scene left her feeling homesick. La Crosse, Wisconsin, was a long way from Eugene, but the scenery here reminded her of home. She hadn't been back to Wisconsin for a visit since her mother's death in early 2002.

In a moment of time, she found herself traveling back in her mind to the idyllic autumn days of 1977 in La Crosse. The river city in the heart of the Midwest held many fond childhood memories—their old Victorian mansion on Cass Street, Sunday afternoon hikes along the trails in Hixon Forest, walks along the Black and La Crosse Rivers, and hours spent in her father's office at the university. Her journey to becoming the biology department chair at the university in Eugene had been an outgrowth of her father's influence.

Stanley Yelski had been well-versed in the area of molecular biology, which he'd taught in the science department at the University of Wisconsin–La Crosse from 1968 to 1996. She could still remember the enthusiasm in his voice when he talked about the microscopic world of cells, DNA, nucleic acids, and the biosynthesis of proteins within each cell compartment. His ability to describe the microscopic world built a bridge for her insatiable curiosity and inspired her at an early age to walk in her father's footsteps.

Margretta recalled the musty smell of her father's small, cramped office. The narrow window gave an uninspiring view of the parking lot at Stevens Hall, but inside the office, the walls were covered with huge colorful posters of cells and nuclei and mitochondria. A model of spiraling strings of DNA sat on his desk, and the floor-to-ceiling bookshelves were bowed with thick, mysterious volumes like Lehninger's *Principles of Biochemistry,* James D. Watson's classic volume *Double Helix*, and Lewin's *Genes XI.* The volumes on microbiology in his office alone would have kept a budding genetics scholar in reading material for years. After her father's death in 2001, Margretta had them shipped to Oregon, where they now graced the library in her stately home in Eugene.

As a budding intellectual, Margretta had spent hours sitting on the floor of the office, legs crossed, with a volume from her dad's collection open on her lap. Her young developing brain sucked up information about the enigmatic nature of microorganisms, organisms with their own rules and principles. At first, everything about this microscopic world was a mysterious puzzle, a universe of wonder and mystique. But gradually, over time, an amazing world opened to her as she soaked in the principles of microcosms.

Her intellectual strength and insatiable curiosity about the natural world began in that simple, unpretentious cubicle of her father's university office. There she'd been inspired to reach further and higher than she could have imagined. Those memories always left her with a feeling of nostalgia and a deep gratitude to her father for the beginnings of her illustrious career.

Now Margretta Martin presided over the development of biology course offerings at Eugene. Under her leadership, the university's reputation as a research facility in cellular biology was well known throughout the U.S. In addition, degree programs in evolution and marine conservation were just a few of the hundreds of other biological fields of study the college promoted.

In addition, Margretta had been a vocal proponent for the study of genetics, and she'd led the university to develop a state-of-the-art research lab in genomics. Her generosity in donating millions of dollars from her deceased husband's estate to the facility gave her the privilege of naming it—Chrisley Genomics Lab, a combination of her sister's and father's names, Christina and Stanley—a fitting tribute to the two people who framed her work ethic and inspired her drive to succeed.

Turning away from the office window, Margretta noticed the stack of correspondence and graduate study proposals stacked on her desk. *The buck stops here,* she thought. Looking at the pile, she knew the truth of that statement every day. Someone was always attempting to rally her support and enthusiasm for some groundbreaking and exciting aspect of research in the graduate studies program: genome editing and mapping, DNA biorepository sampling, and "snips" (single nucleotide polymorphisms) which were used to predict people's risk of contracting particular diseases.

Still, despite all her success in the biological world, the autumnal season led her down the slippery slope of hopelessness, despair, and depression. The anniversary of her younger sister's unsolved abduction and disappearance was a wound that broke open and bled fiercely over all her triumphs and achievements, leaving her discouraged with disappointment and sadness.

Standing next to the desk in her office, she replayed the familiar scenario in her mind again, contemplating its ramifications on her life. She allowed herself to slip into the black hole of that awful October night in 1977. She could still taste the salty popcorn on her tongue when the doorbell rang at her parents' residence early that evening. She had just finished studying for a chemistry test and was enjoying a brief hour of watching television.

The police officer had stood inside the small vestibule that led to the living room, nervous and fidgety in his pressed blues, as he informed her parents about the strange phone call to the police station. Something was wrong at the Blackmans; someone had heard repeated screams coming from inside the home. Eventually, a neighbor had walked to the home of Professor Blackman, where fifteen-year-old Christina Yelski was babysitting their little two-year-old toddler, Dorian. When Christina didn't answer the locked door, the police were called.

Entering the house, they found the two-year-old child sleeping soundly in his crib. However, a bloody trail led to a basement window that had been pried open. In searching the yard, a shoe and a hair barrette were found belonging to the young babysitter. Over the next several days and weeks, the police found a trail of clothing scattered at different locations until the evidence disappeared southeast of La Crosse near the little town of Westby. Christina's body was never found.

As time passed and the clues faded, the Yelski family experienced a roller coaster of emotions. Their hope was renewed when detectives and investigators called them periodically, assuring them they would never give up the investigation. That was followed by the anxiety of imagining Christina's last moments and what she'd suffered. They plummeted into despair when the weeks turned into years, and no progress was made in the case. Margretta was convinced her parents had died of broken hearts.

After their passing, Margretta kept her sister peacefully enshrined in her memory. She'd purged her home of all the physical reminders of Christina's life; photos, birthday cards, and letters were tucked in a box and placed on the top shelf of her bedroom closet collecting dust. It was just too painful to be reminded of the tragedy every day.

But the human heart must make sense of loss somehow. Each year on the anniversary of the horrid crime, Margretta waded through the shrine she'd constructed in her heart, feeling the empty loneliness of her only sister. She remembered the times when they laughed until their bellies ached at some silly girlish joke, the whispered secrets they'd shared about boyfriend crushes, and the moments they'd revealed their dreams and future plans.

Recognizing the familiar blackness descending upon her soul, Margretta opened her phone, punched in a number, and waited for an answer on the other end.

"Thorsen Counseling Services. May we help you?"

"Yes, I'd like to make an appointment with Dr. Goosen," Margretta said softly. "Anytime next week will work."

11

On Monday night, Leslie Birkstein was having a nightmare. The bare branches of the trees scraped against each other in the wind and shifted like spindly claws grasping at a rising moon. Wispy fog rolled off the sullen river in waves snaking through the skeletal trees, hissing like a restless serpent. It was cold. Leslie shivered as she fought to contain the terror that filled her chest.

As Leslie walked softly on a thick bed of fallen leaves, the moon gave just enough ambient light so she could find a way through the tangled undergrowth. Her fear threatened to suffocate her. A branch crackled behind her, snapping under the weight of something. Her imagination filled in the void. She stopped walking, her heart pounding. Looking backward, she sucked in her breath when she saw the silhouette of a large, muscular man in the distance. She was sure now—Wade had come for her.

She turned and began running, but the footsteps slapping the hard earth behind her were confident and unrelenting. She was certain he would crush her if she resisted him. Suddenly, she tripped on a branch, fell to the ground, and screamed. Startled, she jerked and woke up in bed next to Sam. She was sweaty and distraught. Her heart threatened to jump into the next county.

Sam snored softly beside her. In the moonlight, his unshaven face was slack with sleep, his wavy hair dark on the white pillowcase. Leslie slipped quietly out of bed and tiptoed to the kitchen. She turned on the lights and flicked the switch on the electric tea kettle. She took a mug from the cupboard and set it on the kitchen counter. Hearing the commotion, Paco padded into the room from his bed in the hallway, whining and licking her hand. Leslie leaned over and kissed his great black head.

Would these dreams always plague her? When would they finally be over? Tears filled her eyes when she thought of the recurring nightmares that continued to stalk her. Watching comrades being blown to bits by IEDs in Iraq and a harrowing near-death experience of physical abuse from a man she thought she'd once loved had left her psyche fragile. She'd worked hard to make peace with her turbulent history, but it seemed no matter what she did, the terror haunted her, thundering roughshod over all the progress she'd made.

When the water boiled, Leslie poured the steaming liquid into a mug and added a peppermint tea bag and a generous portion of honey. She carried it into the living room and snuggled on the couch with a throw over her legs. Paco sat protectively at her feet.

The past came in, plopped down next to her, and refused to leave. Sitting in the dark, she brooded, images of Wade at the edges of her memory. The violence that had intruded into her life seemed to penetrate her brain like water soaking into a sponge. Memories of friends from Iraq appeared and floated in the night air like ghosts— Sully, Raiford, Jenny, Mitchell. All dead from the same explosive IED that blew them into the next kingdom. She stroked Paco's regal head, and he groaned with pleasure when she scratched behind his floppy ears.

Sipping her tea, she looked up when she heard a rustle in the hallway. Sam walked into the living room in his boxers and T-shirt, hair tousled from sleep.

"Lez? What's going on?" he asked, squinting at the kitchen light.

"Just a bad dream," she said softly.

He stumbled to the couch, sat down next to her, and gently pulled her into his arms. "I'm sorry. How can I help?" he asked sleepily, kissing her cheek.

"You've already helped just by being here." She nuzzled her head under his chin. Taking his hand, she clasped it tightly, the fear oozing out of her. "I'm sorry I woke you. I tried to be quiet."

"Wade or Iraq? Which one this time?" Sam asked, staring into the dark, wondering when the demons were going to leave his wife alone. He said a silent prayer that God might grant her some peace.

"I refuse to verbalize it and give them a life."

"Atta girl," he said. They sat quietly for a while until Leslie finished her tea. "Come on. Let's go back to bed," Sam suggested, standing and pulling her up.

They walked to the bedroom and crawled under the covers. The quilt felt good against the cool night air that wafted through the window, gently moving the sheer curtains. Sam spooned up next to Leslie's back, cupping her breast in his hand. Soon she could hear his breathing, deep and regular. She was comforted by his solid presence next to her, yet she envied his easy, unperturbed sleep.

But Sam had changed, too, since he'd been shot in the chest a year ago during a confrontation in the parking lot at the law enforcement center. His carefully constructed worldview had been damaged by the shooting, and his naive attitude that nothing bad would ever happen to him had to be revisited. Holding onto that philosophy was a dangerous gamble for a cop. It left you unprepared for the realities of chasing down unpredictable, desperate criminals.

Lying next to him now, feeling the warmth and solid comfort of his body, she prayed he would always be here for her. *I will never leave you nor forsake you.* That was one of Sam's favorite Bible verses and the one he had chosen as part of their marriage vows. But Leslie knew promises in life were fleeting—after all, they lived in a fallen, depraved world. People promised and people failed. All she could do was take each day as a gift. That was the closest thing to assurance she had. It would have to do.

12

The Higgins' home on Chipmunk Coulee Road off U.S. Hwy. 35 sat on a wooded ten-acre lot. A small creek meandered through the northern edge of the property. Along that same edge, an outcropping of limestone lay in oblong humps; one looked like the figure of a sleeping camel, and the others etched the skyline in castellated and craggy formations that resembled the ancient ruins of a forgotten castle. The morning sunlight was just sifting through the massive maples, elms, and pines, leaving smears of yellow patches on the lush lawn. A clump of huge white pines in the northeast corner whispered quietly in the morning breeze. The summer songbirds had fled. Although the woods were surprisingly quiet, mourning doves cooed softly on the roof of the small pole shed where Jim kept his gator and riding lawn mower plus an assortment of other power and garden tools.

When Jim had purchased the home with Margie, his first wife, almost fifteen years ago, it was a small bungalow in desperate need of updating. They'd remodeled and added on over a period of ten years, making it a comfortable abode. New windows, tan siding, flagstone sidewalks, and a concrete driveway brought it into the modern world. A three seasons porch and a flagstone patio out back had been added on the southeast corner of the house, which overlooked massive flowerbeds and stone-lined walkways, which had been Margie's pride and joy.

The twins, Sara and John, had already graduated from high school when the property was purchased, but they came home from college on the weekends, and it gradually became their home, too. Nowadays, John and his wife Jenny lived in Holmen, and Sara lived in the newly constructed apartment downstairs.

The basement apartment had initially been a source of conflict between Carol and Jim. Would they use it enough to justify the cost? Was it for guests, or would they rent it out? They discussed their options for months until finally deciding to go ahead with the project.

With Carol's talent for decorating and eye for detail, Jim's woodworking talents, and a hefty portion of their savings, they'd transformed the dingy basement into a chic, modern one-bedroom oasis complete with an ensuite bathroom and full kitchen. Sara's teaching salary at the local Catholic school in Genoa would never have been enough to afford anything so grand. But so far, it had worked out well; Sara exchanged some rent for babysitting services.

It was seven-thirty on Tuesday morning. Waiting in the dining room, her briefcase next to her, Sara leaned against the wall, trying to be patient while Lillie chomped on a piece of toast, strawberry jelly smeared across her face. Henri chased Cheerios around the tray on his highchair, cooing happily in the morning hustle and bustle, getting a few in his mouth but throwing the majority of the little o's on the floor. Carefully wiping the jelly off Lillie's face with a wet wipe, Carol grabbed her backpack from the hook in the entry.

"Lillie, time to go, honey," Sara encouraged gently.

Popping the last bite in her mouth, she lifted her backpack and took Sara's hand. Carol leaned in for a kiss.

"Where's Bapa?" Lillie asked, fixing Carol with a blue-eyed scowl after the peck on her cheek.

"Probably getting dressed for work," Carol answered. Before she could grab her, Lillie had escaped Sara's grasp and hurtled down the hallway to the bedroom. Sara let out a frustrated sigh.

"Don't fight it," Carol advised, giving Sara a seasoned look. "She's impossible without her fist bump and kiss from Bapa."

With Lillie on the road to school with Sara and Henri content after a bellyful of oatmeal, Jim and Carol settled down to a quiet breakfast. It had taken a while to develop a routine when Carol had returned to work part-time in August and Lillie had started first grade. Over the last few weeks, their mornings were finally beginning to jell. Peace reigned—at least for today.

The sunshine left puddles of brilliant, pooled light on the driveway, fallen leaves littering its surface like pieces of iridescent, broken glass. A blue jay landed on an arborvitae bush near the front entrance, and he cawed raucously at the occupants inside. Soaking in the peace and quiet, Carol nibbled a cup of yogurt with granola and sipped her coffee while Henri played on the floor with his toys. Her view of the backside of the *Wisconsin State Journal*, where Jim had retreated for his morning snippet of news, irritated her.

"Jim, will you listen a minute?" she asked impatiently.

The paper rustled, and Jim moved it to one side, looking over at her. His blue eyes were pools of cool intelligence. Framed by a light blue oxford shirt and a red Ferragamo tie in a palm tree print, his tanned face seemed exceptionally focused on her. His odd blond-gray hair was tousled and casual.

"Do you think we can take another overnight camping trip on the river with the kids before it gets too cold? Maybe this weekend?" she asked, sipping her coffee, looking at him over her mug. "The weather's supposed to be beautiful."

"Hmm. Maybe. But this murder on George Street is going to take front and center. If we do anything, it'll be spur of the moment. You should be okay with that after our little impromptu love fest Sunday afternoon, right?" A grin crept across his face.

"Opportunities like that don't come along every day," she said, smiling mysteriously. "But keep the camping in mind, okay?"

"Sure. Lillie and Henri would love it," Jim said reasonably, returning to his paper.

Now as Carol sped up Chipmunk Coulee Road after dropping Henri at the sitter's house, she wondered about the text left on her phone by her former husband, Matt Donovan: "Could we do lunch today? Need your help with something. MD"

Hiding things from Jim was not her style, and although the text made her uneasy, she knew her feelings for Matt were high on a shelf somewhere—out of sight, out of mind. After twenty years with very little contact, they had both moved beyond their marriage disaster. *Water over the dam,* she thought. Still, she couldn't allow any hint of impropriety with Matt taint her relationship with her husband. Jim wasn't possessive or jealous, but his moral compass would go into a wild spin if a past lover re-entered her life for any reason. After rocky circumstances had strained their relationship last year, she was in no hurry for a repeat performance.

She pulled her Toyota SUV into the Vine Street parking lot and sat in her car contemplating her next move. Grabbing her phone from her purse, she texted a brief message: "Lindy's on Main @noon. Sharp. CH"

Carol tucked her phone in her purse and made her way toward the law enforcement center. Swiping her badge across the back door entry, she walked down the hall to the coroner's office with an unsettled weight hanging over her. Why would Matt contact her now, twenty years after their divorce? She shook her head as if trying to dislodge a nest of bees that had invaded her thought processes. She'd just have to wait and see what he wanted.

13

That same morning, DeDe Deverioux and Leslie Birkstein sat at a large worktable on the second floor of the law enforcement center in a cramped room with one small window facing the east. The overhead fluorescent lights hummed with an irritating buzz, making their work seem even more tedious. Leslie imagined the table had been worn smooth by the shuffling of paperwork performed by poorly paid secretaries, but in reality, it was just an old table that had probably been dug out of some custodian's collection of hodge-podge discarded furniture in a dark, dusty closet of the law enforcement building.

Since yesterday afternoon, the two of them had been searching online for past unsolved crimes in Wisconsin, including murders that had taken place over the last thirty years. The archival evidence from cold cases in the La Crosse County area was stored on the second floor in a secure, locked room lined with beige filing cabinets stuffed with thick manila file folders. They hadn't even cracked open the thick manila file folders yet, unsure where or even how to begin.

"Any luck on your end?" Leslie asked, giving DeDe a frustrated glance.

"There are more unsolved cases here than any cop would want

to admit, that's for sure," DeDe replied. She stretched her arms to the ceiling in a languid motion.

"How's life on the houseboat?" Leslie asked, switching the topic.

"Quiet, which I like, but it's lonely. I miss my grandparents. It's gettin' colder, too. Just exactly when does this snow y'all talk about arrive?" Behind her glasses, DeDe's brown eyes reflected a glimmer of anxiety.

"Snow? Well, that depends on a lot of factors." Leslie started explaining. "Sometimes, it comes as early as October and hangs around until April. But there are always exceptions to the rule. Some years we don't get snow until after Thanksgiving. But I've also read somewhere that snow has fallen in Wisconsin every month of the year."

DeDe did a doubletake. "I sure hope that's not the case this year."

"That's the problem. You never know for sure. Have you found another place to live yet?"

"Nope. I figure I can stay on the houseboat until mid-October. Does that sound reasonable?"

"Workable but maybe not as reasonable as you think. Let me know if you need some help finding a place." Imitating DeDe, Leslie leaned backward in an arching motion, stretching to relieve the kinks in her back and neck. Hunching over her laptop screen for hours at a time left her with knots in all the wrong places. "I found out there are at least ten cold case murders in central Wisconsin alone over the last twenty years. Who knew?"

"Only ten? That's manageable. The last count in New Orleans for unsolved murders was upwards of seventy-five, and the numbers just keep rising."

"Is that why you left?" Leslie asked, her curiosity aroused. She leaned back and stretched out her legs, preparing to listen.

DeDe shrugged, then hesitated. She thought, *A bad marriage is something I'm not comfortable telling you about yet.* Instead, she said, "I had a case of wanderlust, I guess. After my grandparents' deaths,

I couldn't see returning to Beaufort County to raise vegetables and catch fish in tidal creeks, although honestly, I do miss that simple lifestyle. And truth be told, the daily violence that confronted the NOPD was starting to get to me. It seemed like we never got ahead of the criminals—we just barely contained their activity. I'm too young to be burned out, but I was disillusioned. *And then, of course, there's JuJu,* she thought. "So I hopped on a boat, and here I am, the proverbial fish out of water."

Suddenly Jim's familiar face appeared in the door frame.

"Hey, making any progress?" he asked as he approached the table. He looked refreshed and confident. Then he noticed the girls' somber expressions. "What's wrong?" he asked, his brows knit together in a scowl.

Leslie glanced at DeDe, then back to Jim. "I don't know, sir. This seems like an impossible task. If we just had more to go on, we might be able to zero in on one of these crimes."

DeDe turned toward him. "It's not slim pickin's, sir. There are plenty of crimes to choose from, but we need a reference point," DeDe finished lamely. "Something to focus on."

"Okay. Let's approach it differently, then. Narrow your search to include the unsolved crimes in the immediate vicinity. Think about Sylvester's age; at seventy-four, that means any crimes he committed could be within a forty- to fifty-year range. And remember, he's lived around here his entire life. The note suggests that someone knows something he did. So whatever that was probably happened in this area."

Jim paused a moment, then went on hurriedly when the women didn't respond. "That's totally arbitrary, but you have to start somewhere. Make a list of victims, motives, and evidence. We'll start with that and see where it takes us. Sam and Paul are out trying to kick up anything that moves. They might uncover something from the crime scene that will help us or something from their interviews might provide a lead. We've got the necklace, and hopefully, we'll get some latent prints or DNA from the house. Once you get some stuff together, bring it to me, and I'll start looking, too."

Leslie frowned, then shrugged her shoulders. "How far out from La Crosse do you want us to go?"

"Start with a fifty-mile radius and see what you can find. That help?"

"Yeah. It does. It's a starting point. Thanks," DeDe said, smiling.

"You're going to want to look at forensic evidence, crime scene materials, investigators' notes, that sort of thing," Jim said.

"That's still a huge task," Leslie said. "What's our time frame?"

"Don't have one until something else turns us in another direction," Jim answered. "We've succeeded against terrible odds before, Leslie." Jim turned to leave the room. "Do me proud, ladies," he said over his shoulder.

14

Paul and Sam were on the north side of the city at a place called Little Jo's on Rublee Street, wolfing down scrambled eggs, sausage links, hash browns, and toast. Cassie, their waitress, had been regularly refilling their coffee cups, giving Sam a few lingering glances.

Working with Sam made Paul feel *very* middle-aged. Sam wasn't much younger than him, but his curly locks, innocent expression, and wide-eyed wonder about the world made Paul feel like a hardened veteran cop. The young girl's second glances at Sam made him remember days of cruising for girls, going on dates, planning beer keg parties—all the stuff associated with youth. Now he was a seasoned married man with a little girl and a second baby on the way.

Brushing some crumbs from the front of his dress shirt, he took another drink of coffee. His dark hair was styled and gelled, his hazel eyes bright from a good night's rest.

"Do girls always do that when you're around?" Paul asked, chewing on a slice of toast.

"Do what?"

"Come on. They're coming on to you. Shit, you don't have to do anything except just sit there, and they're falling all over you."

Sam screwed up his face in disgust. "That's ridiculous. I have no idea what you're talking about," Sam said. "Besides, I'm married. I have my own set of problems."

"Thunderclouds on the marital horizon? Not finding your bliss?" Paul asked. Noticing Sam's worried look, he dropped the teasing banter. "Talk to me. What's going on?"

Sam let out an ominous sigh. "It's just that Lez still has a lot of problems with bad nightmares. I wish that crap would quit, but it just keeps haunting her. She had another bad one last night. I've tried to be there for her, and she says it helps, but I don't know . . ." His hazel eyes clouded, and his voice drifted off as he watched the traffic outside the window.

"Patience, man. You're at the same place Ruby was a while ago. It's a long process. My flashbacks are less frequent now, and they aren't as devastating when they come. Recovery takes time." Paul took a sip of coffee and continued. "Leslie suffered a lot, and it takes a toll on your mind and soul. Usually, the partner, if they stick around, needs to adjust, too. You have to come to a place of acceptance. Her trauma will resolve itself eventually, but you also need to understand her trauma is a part of who she is now. You can't erase it, but you can make peace with it ... sort of."

Sam leaned back in the booth listening carefully to Paul. He would know about trauma. He'd been seriously injured during a shoot-out in an ambush of a fugitive that went wrong down in Vernon County.

"Yeah, I guess you'd know."

"So do you. You've been wounded. Are you done with your sessions yet with Doc Riley?"

"Yeah, I guess it helped, but my faith helped me more."

"Well, there's that, too," Paul said quietly. "Don't give up, Sam. It'll get better. Patience is the key, and being there for her is exactly what you should be doing."

They silently finished their breakfast, refused more coffee from Cassie, paid the check, and headed out into the cool September morning. Traffic was picking up on George Street as commuters wove in and out of congestion, making their way to the industrial park where Kwik Trip headquarters, several start-up companies, and other businesses were located. As Paul pulled away from the restaurant, a biker whipped around him, pedaling easily and fearlessly in the bustling traffic.

Fifteen minutes later, Paul and Sam breezed into Jim's office. Jim was on the phone. He held up a finger, talked awhile longer, then stood up.

"What'd you find out yesterday about Kratt?" he asked impatiently.

"Not much we didn't already know," Sam started. "Loner, good worker, quiet, kept to himself." Sam shrugged and looked over at Paul.

Paul continued. "After talking to the neighbors and others who knew him at his job, we're stymied. What about his past before he came to La Crosse?"

"He was a dairy farmer down by Readstown, tended bar to make ends meet. But he had that serious addiction to porn, and there was infidelity in the marriage. I didn't detect any sexual abuse in the daughter, but things on the home front were strained," Jim told them. "Her relationship with her dad was superficial at best, but I feel there's something ugly below the surface that she's not telling me."

Paul's eyebrows flicked up in surprise. "Interesting," he mumbled.

"I found out where his farm is. I'm heading down there to talk to some people," Jim said.

"We're going to check in with the crime scene techs back at the house," Sam said.

"You do that," Jim said as he grabbed his suit jacket and headed for the door. Switching off the lights, he said over his shoulder, "Let's meet later this afternoon and compare notes."

15

Lindy's Sub Shop on Main Street in downtown La Crosse was hopping with the lunch crowd on

Tuesday at noon. The locals liked the place. The food was tasty and cheap, and you could get in and out within half an hour. Carol dodged traffic as she hurried across the street and made her way inside. Walking into the sub joint, she realized she was nervous in a scatterbrained, teenage kind of way. *This is a big mistake,* she thought. *Matt's the last person I want to see.*

The tempting smells of fresh bread did nothing except make her stomach churn, but not from hunger. She hadn't seen Matt in several years, although occasionally, she'd read an article in the entertainment section of the *La Crosse Sentinel* about his band and the local music scene. Matt traveled with his country-rock band Mississippi Mud on the weekends, and his job during the week sorting mail at the post office kept him hidden, out of circulation. It wasn't surprising that they never ran into each other anymore, which was fine with Carol.

Standing in line waiting to order her sandwich, she felt someone touch her arm. She turned and came face to face with Matt Donavan. He smiled, his eyes searching her face looking for something.

Approval? Affection? Acceptance? *Nothing's really changed,* Carol thought. *He still needs the adoring crowds. He always had to be the center of attention.* He gave her a neutral peck on the cheek.

"I'm over in the corner by the window," he said, a hint of a smile curling his lips.

"Okay. I'll just get a sandwich and join you," Carol said weakly, her eyes distrustful.

By the time Carol found her way through the lunch crowd with the sandwich in her hand, ten minutes had passed. Matt had finished his salad, and he watched her intently as she started devouring her roast beef on rye.

Sitting across from him, Carol evaluated her former husband with an up-close-and-personal gaze—the large expressive eyes, the carefully styled wavy hair, somewhat long, gray showing through here and there, a pair of sunglasses perched on the top of his head. *The cool music star,* she thought. He was wearing a white T-shirt that said "Harvest—Neil Young," overlaid with a black leather jacket. Obviously, he was still trying to project the mature yet hip image. But all that didn't fool Carol. The pronounced crow's feet at the corners of his eyes, the wrinkles of skin that sagged just a bit in the neck area, and the flat depressive demeanor he couldn't hide weren't lost on her. Aging really was the great equalizer.

"Are you going to stare at me the whole time I eat this?" Carol asked, her brown eyes flashing.

"You've still got a lot to stare at, baby," he said seductively, his white teeth gleaming.

"Stop it," she said crossly. "So, tell me. What is this help you said you needed?"

Ignoring her question, he asked, "How's the marriage going? Saw your announcement in the paper. I've heard about Jim around town. He's got quite a reputation as a cop. A lieutenant. Impressive." His eyes had turned serious, the friendliness gone. His voice had an edge to it. Carol met his cool gaze with one of her own.

"Our marriage is great. Jim is very attentive—he loves me fiercely. And, of course, he's a great dad to our two little ones. You know, I never thought I'd be a mom. That has been an experience I wouldn't trade for anything. We're very happy, thank you," Carol said, but her voice had picked up a defensive tone.

"Wow! Sounds like a rockin' good time. A cop who actually has a life. Now that's something to crow about."

Carol glanced at her cell, which was lying on the table. "Listen, Matt. You're on the clock. You have exactly fifteen minutes to lay out this big problem you've got that you need my help with." Her irritation was growing by leaps and bounds.

Matt hesitated, then made a gesture with his hands. "Well, I may have misspoken." He waited a moment, then laid a hand on his chest and said, "Personally, *I* don't have a problem." Then he pointed at her. "But you're going to have one real soon." He dipped his chin and opened his eyes a little wider.

"You and your little family."

Carol frowned, feeling a tightness in her chest, an anxiety that sat there like a rock. She stopped eating her sandwich. A hunk of roast beef fell on the table, but she didn't bother to pick it up. "That sounds like a threat. What's this about?" Her voice was louder than she'd intended, and the couple in the next booth looked over at them, their eyes widening in alarm.

"Settle down, darlin'," Matt said softly, leaning toward her, smiling reassuringly at the couple across the aisle. He waited a few moments, then continued in a hushed tone. "A guy I know from the music scene in Wausau looked me up last weekend. We were talking about bands and guitar players, stuff like that, and how bad the music scene has gotten. The bars where we play are dens of drugs and other iniquities which I won't mention. Probably human trafficking, for all I know. Nothing like the good old days when it was couples out on the town, having a few beers and dancing to some good, loud rock 'n' roll. Which is why I don't take my band on the road much anymore." He took a big breath.

"Anyway ... we got on the topic of fights we'd seen, then to cops, and one thing led to another."

He paused. Carol jumped in.

"Where is this going?" she asked rudely. "Get to the point, Matt." She pushed a strand of hair behind her ear. Her sandwich lay unfinished on the parchment paper. She gave him a hard stare, frustrated with his subterfuge.

"When we were loading up our gear in the back alley after our gig, my friend had a conversation with a guy from Wausau who's searching for his little girl. Says the grandmother took her and left town, and he hasn't been able to track her down. Says the girl is his daughter, and he wants her back. Her name is Miss Lillie—"

Carol felt like the floor had disappeared, and she was falling somewhere deep and dark and cold. Her pupils dilated, and there was a ringing in her ears that wouldn't stop. To say she was dumbstruck would have been an understatement. She lost track of time. The noisy lunch crowd receded into the background. Clutching the edge of the table, she heard Matt mumbling on and on, but it was wasted on her. Finally, she recovered. Matt's words drifted back into her brain over the hubbub of the sandwich shop.

"Carol? Honey? Are you listening? Talk to me," Matt said, leaning over and grabbing her hand. "Are you having a heart attack?"

Carol looked over at Matt and slowly withdrew her hand. In a voice she didn't recognize, she said, "Is this your idea of a sick joke? That you would perpetuate a vicious rumor like this about my family when I am finally so happy is unbelievable! I don't believe a word of it!" The volume of her voice ramped up. People began staring, their sandwiches held in mid-air.

"It's vile and cruel! That you would use my children to drum up some kind of relational rescue between us is beyond belief. You can take your stupid rumors and stick them where the sun doesn't shine!" By this time, she was yelling. She threw her napkin down on top of her uneaten sandwich. Her face was flaming, her eyes snapping with anger. She jumped out of the seat and grabbed her phone and purse. Matt clutched her arm, but she jerked it off. "Don't touch me! And don't you ever call me again."

The lunch crowd went silent, zeroing in on the commotion. Matt, always the entertainer, turned to the crowd, shrugged his shoulders nonchalantly, and said, "Once a drama queen, always a drama queen. What can I say?" He hurried after her, scurrying through the mute crowd.

Carol ran out into the street, where a pickup truck squealed to a stop when she blindly stepped off the curb directly in front of it. She held out her hand, mouthing the word, "Sorry." The driver flipped her off and tore away in a huff. With shaking hands, she unlocked her Toyota and started the car just as Matt ran out of the shop and hollered at her from the curb. She ignored him and rammed down Third Street, doubling back until she came to Vine Street. By now, she was crying. She wiped the tears away, angry that she had ever agreed to meet Matt. What kind of a stunt was this?

Pulling into the law enforcement center parking lot, she sat in her car, leaning her head on the steering wheel. Finally, she wiped her face with a baby wipe and pulled lipstick from her purse. She stared at herself in the rearview mirror as she smeared some pink gloss over her pale lips. *You look like hell. Pull yourself together,* she thought. *No one else knows about this.*

Her phone buzzed, and she looked at it briefly. A text from Matt: You didn't let me explain. There's more that you don't know. M" Carol ignored the text and pushed the phone deep into her purse.

Then an image of Lillie came into her mind. She could see her azure eyes, petite button nose, and sunlit golden curls. She heard her squeaky little voice and her never-ending questions. Carol started shaking again. Fear rolled over her in waves. *How in the world am I ever going to tell Jim?*

16

By the time Jim got out of the office, put gas on his Suburban, and picked up a sandwich at Kwik Trip, it was past noon. He took his time driving southeast out of La Crosse on U.S. Hwy. 14. The bucolic countryside flew by. The autumn colors along the steep hills and sandstone bluffs hinted at things to come. Jim loved the fall season with its brilliant palette and cooler temperatures. He thought of those lyrics by James Taylor: "frost on the pumpkins and the geese have gone to fly." Country homes and farms whizzed by his window bringing back memories of childhood days on the farm in Blair with his parents and his older brother, Dave. Then he thought about Juliette, the sister he'd never had the chance to know and love. *You've made your peace with that,* he thought. *Don't go there.*

Huge self-propelled choppers were busy grinding up golden stalks of corn into silage. Wagons hauled it out of the field, filling elongated white silo bags resembling swollen white plastic worms. The air had a musky smell to it. Jim rolled down his window, enjoying the warmth of the early afternoon sun on his arm. He found some easy jazz on the radio and tapped his thumb on the steering wheel to the rhythm of the music.

When he passed the wayside above Ten Mile Hill, his memory

flashed back to the truck bomber who had led his team on a twisted manhunt that ended on Halloween night on Grandad Bluff high above La Crosse.

Working his way southeast, he drove through the little hamlet of Coon Valley, known for its pure, clear creeks and streams where some of the best trout fishing in the upper Midwest could be found. As he drove over the bridge into town, the Coon Creek sparkled in the brilliant sunshine, the currents creating little white ruffles as it flowed around hidden rocks below the surface. The main street was a collection of early 1900 mortar and wooden buildings: a phone company, an antique shop, a funeral home, and a couple of bars and restaurants. The calm and placid atmosphere was typical of so many small towns across the state. He braked and lifted a hand in a friendly wave when a couple of pedestrians crossed the street slowly and leisurely headed for The Stockyard, a local saloon and eatery.

After passing through Viroqua with its bustling main street businesses, he continued south on U.S. Hwy. 14. Before coming to Readstown, he turned left and headed north on County Road T, which ran parallel to the main highway. Winding his way along the county road, he followed Heather Lovstad's directions until he came to Getter Road. According to Heather, the former Kratt farm was the second place on the left. Jim turned into a driveway filled with potholes and bordered on both sides by fenced cow pasture. He slowly made his way toward the cluster of buildings. The Suburban rocked from side to side when he came to a low dip in the middle of the driveway.

Huge maples spread their branches over the large four-square farmhouse, and a clump of birch stood in the middle of the circle drive. The house needed a good coat of paint. The graying, weathered siding gave the place a forlorn disposition, like a pouting child sent to the corner. Once red but now faded to a dusty rose, a derelict barn stood to the left of the house where a half dozen Hereford beef cattle ate silage from a bunk.

In his investigative career, Jim had learned to take a few minutes to get the lay of the land, especially when he was on someone else's property. Sitting in the Suburban an extra minute, he watched for movement, for signs of life, for normal daily activities—somebody feeding cattle, the chuffing sound of a milker pump coming from the barn, a tractor running, or the ripe, pungent odor of manure as someone cleaned the barn. Usually, a mixed-breed mutt was there to greet him. Maybe a few stray cats or some chickens were pecking here and there. It seemed unnaturally quiet. The house was shuttered and dark as if no one lived there. His cell chirped in his suit jacket and made him jump.

"Higgins."

"Jim?"

"Yeah, honey. What's up?" Silence followed, then what sounded like crying. "Carol, what's wrong?" Carol rarely called him at work, so this mid-day interruption was unsettling.

"I took the afternoon off. There's something I need to talk to you about."

Jim was confused. He frowned because it reminded him of another morning almost two years ago when she'd finally come out and told him she was pregnant at forty-two. He knew that couldn't be the case today since he'd taken care of those possibilities with a vasectomy last winter. Instead, he said, "Can't it wait til I get home tonight?"

"Well, I guess so. I just needed to hear your voice. I love you, honey."

"I know that. So, what's going on?"

"I called Sara, and she'll take care of the kids tonight. I'm packing a light supper, and I'll meet you at Pettibone at five. Will that work for you?"

"You want to take *The Little Eddy* out on the river tonight?" he asked, the pitch of his voice rising with consternation. *This is getting weirder by the minute,* he thought.

"Uh-huh. Is that okay?" She sounded needy and scared, which was very uncharacteristic of her.

"Sure, I guess," he said grumpily. "I'll meet you there, but bring me a pair of jeans, my boat shoes, and a sweatshirt, okay?"

"Yes, I'll do that. Gotta go. Bye, love." And the line went dead.

As he put the phone back in his jacket, he was startled when a man walked up from behind the Suburban and stuck his head in the open truck window.

"Help ya? Are you lost?" he said in a loud voice.

Jim jerked and leaned away from the man dressed in an oil-spattered sweatshirt, well-worn Redwing work boots, and patched blue jeans. A DeKalb seed corn hat was plopped on his head at a funny angle. He was clean-shaven, but swatches of graying brown hair stuck out from under the hat, reminding Jim of the scarecrow in the *Wizard of Oz*. The man's hazel eyes were intense but friendly.

Jim stuck out his hand. The two men shook, and Jim climbed out of the Suburban and casually leaned against the door. His heart was still pounding from Carol's odd phone call and the farmer's abrupt greeting. He flashed his ID, then introduced himself. "Jim Higgins. I'm an investigator with the La Crosse Sheriff's Department."

"Clyde Reinhart. You're kinda far from your stomping grounds, aren't you?"

"You might say that, but I get down here every once in a while," Jim said. He paused briefly. "I understand this used to be Sylvester Kratt's farm. Did you buy it from him?"

"No, I'm the second owner. Jerome Kirking bought it from Sylvester, and I bought it from Jerome. He lost it in foreclosure back in 08, and I bid on it at the sheriff's auction. That was ten years ago."

"So, you've never met Sylvester?"

"He drove down here once a while back. We visited in the yard. He looked around from behind his steering wheel and left. Haven't seen him since."

"So where does this Jerome Kirking live?" Jim asked.

"You sure you want to go there?" Clyde asked suspiciously. "The guy has a few screws loose if you ask me."

"I'm trying to find some people who knew Sylvester personally. Did you hear about his death?"

"Read it online in the *La Crosse Sentinel*. And that's exactly why you should be careful if you're going to talk to Ophy—that's short for ophidian."

Jim looked confused. "What's that mean?"

"It's the scientific name for snake." Clyde paled noticeably, and he looked nervous. "He earned his nickname honestly by cheating everybody in the county. And some say he's into witchcraft. I know his wife is, but he never actually said he believed in that horseshit. He's been in jail for a couple of DUIs and D&Ds. Somebody told me the other day he's been cookin' meth somewhere on his eighty acres, but I don't know if that's true." He shrugged noncommittally. "Just saying you better be prepared. When you're dealin' with Ophy, you're dealin' with a whole lot of bad."

Jim considered his points. "Thanks for the warning. Can you tell me where he lives?"

Clyde crooked his finger at Jim and directed him to the hood of the Suburban. He leaned over the hood, took a seed corn tablet and pencil out of his shirt pocket, and drew a small map for him. "Easy to get lost back in these hills, and he doesn't like anybody comin' unannounced. The only way into his property is by a field road. It's landlocked." He seemed uneasy. "Don't tell him you talked to me."

"No problem. I'll be careful," Jim finished as he took the crude map and climbed back in his vehicle. "Thanks. I appreciate it."

He followed the rutted circle drive out onto the gravel road. Glancing occasionally at the map, Jim stopped and pulled over when he located the dirt lane that functioned as Jerome Kirking's driveway. Reaching under the front passenger seat, he found his Kevlar vest. Undressing from the waist up, he slipped the vest over his T-shirt and rebuttoned his dress shirt, leaving his tie and jacket on the front seat. He'd nagged his team to wear their vests when in doubt. Sam wouldn't be here if he hadn't worn his a year ago.

"No sense in being stupid about this," he said quietly to himself. He unlocked his glove box, withdrew his holster and pistol, and laid them on the seat. Carol's words came back to him: "Remember, you have more people to think about now. It's not just me anymore." He sat in the truck for a moment thinking about his two families: the twins, John and Sara, now independent and living their own lives, and Lillie and Henri, who depended on them totally each day for every need.

Jim started driving up the field road overgrown along the edges with sumac, prickly ash, and locust interspersed with larger white pines and hardwoods. The single-lane dirt track wound its way through some undulating hills. Jim's Suburban sloshed across a small creek and climbed along the road through the brush and tree cover. The overgrown foliage created a dense atmosphere that barely let in the bright sunlight of the afternoon. Knee-high timothy and grama grass brushed against Jim's vehicle like waves washing against the side of a boat. After several hundred yards, he drove into a sunny clearing.

A small cabin-like structure sat in the middle of the cleared field. Its brown color had faded over time, and it looked tired, gray, and small. A porch built of questionable materials and poor workmanship tilted precariously away from the front of the house, its railing tweaked and partially collapsed. Sprawled on a red plastic lawn chair, a calico cat snoozed in the afternoon sun. A larger pole shed stood behind the cabin about fifty feet, the sliding door yawning open in the sunshine. Jim could see a broken-down Farmall H sitting in the darkened recesses just inside the door.

Around the entire property, garbage and junk of every imaginable kind lay in drifts: a decrepit wheelbarrow without a wheel, piles of garbage bags that had burst open, their contents puking out on the ground, bikes without tires, a rusted 57 Chevy, and a graveyard of farm machinery in every shape and color lay in various states of disrepair and neglect. Among the detritus, a couple of sows were wandering, snorting and rooting in the dirt, and a half dozen chickens were pecking around in the grass. A skinny Holstein heifer was tied to the fender of a rusted John Deere B tractor, where she grazed contentedly on timothy grass.

Jim placed his revolver in the holster under his arm, put on his suit coat, and carefully stepped out of his Suburban.

A whiskered, unkempt man suddenly appeared from inside the cabin. His wife-beater T-shirt was more gray than white, and his Oshkosh bib overalls were ripped and covered with ground-in dirt and oil. On his feet were a pair of men's slippers encrusted with pig shit. He placed his hands defiantly on his hips.

"What the hell do you want? How'd you find me?" he yelled, his voice gravelly and threatening. "You sellin' somethin'? Cause if ya are, I ain't in'erested." Even from a distance, Jim could see his alcohol-glazed eyes inspecting him, sizing him up. *Could be some meth, too,* he thought. *Take it easy.*

Jim slowed his speech and actions, making sure his response could not be interpreted as confrontational, but even that was no guarantee the guy wouldn't explode if he perceived some kind of threat.

"I'm looking for Ophy," Jim said quietly. He crossed his arms over his chest and waited.

"Well, you found him. Whaddya want?" the man barked cantankerously. He looked Jim over with one eye cocked shut, his hands on his hips in a rebellious stance. His unwashed shoulder-length hair was encrusted with dirt and oil, and it stood out from his head like the fur of a scared cat.

"Did you hear about Sylvester Kratt?" Jim took a few more steps toward the man.

"Yeah. I heard he bit the big one." The man's gravelly voice had grown suspicious, the irritation at Jim's surprise visit now blanketed with fear. Ophy stepped down from the crooked porch and slowly made his way toward Jim. He stopped ten feet in front of him. "You got some ID?"

"Absolutely." Jim moved his hands carefully, then reached into his jacket and opened his ID badge. The smell coming off Ophy was nauseating—a mixture of human sweat and filth and pig shit. Glancing down at his grungy slippers, Jim leaned away from him, trying not to be too obvious.

"Whaddya want to know?" Ophy asked, spitting a stream of tobacco juice on the ground near Jim's foot. *Don't spit on my shoes, bud,* Jim thought, gritting his teeth.

"You knew Sylvester. Tell me about him."

"We were classmates in school down at Kickapoo. After high school, we both started farmin'. We helped each other with crops and other stuff. Got to be pretty good friends. Haven't seen him much since he sold the farm. Why do ya wanna know this stuff?" His eyes seemed to finally focus on Jim.

"He was murdered, and we're trying to get a better picture of him as a person. Know anybody who'd want to kill him?" Jim held Ophy's alcohol-induced gaze, his blue eyes drilling into him.

Ophy didn't answer right away. Jim thought maybe the question had blown right over him.

"Do you know any—" he started to repeat.

"Yeah, I heard ya the first time. And no, I don't know anybody who'd want to kill him."

"Can you think of any reason someone would murder him?"

"Hell if I know. He was quiet, but he did like that awful raw porn. And he fooled with quite a few women over the years. I don't have no idea why anyone would want to kill him. Maybe some husband found out that his wife couldn't resist Sylvester's charms." He laughed raucously, then shrugged his shoulders. "Me—I got my own sets of problems," Ophy said, rocking back on his heels. "Ain't got time to be worrying over others."

"Do you know any of these women who had affairs with Sylvester?"

"All just rumors. It's not like I went spying on the guy. That's his own private business."

"You have a cell phone?"

Ophy whipped one out of his back pocket. "You bet. I'm a technological wizard with this thing," he said, smiling for the first time.

"You live with anyone here?" Jim's eyes wandered back to the primitive cabin.

"Nope. My wife left about six months ago. Haven't seen her since she drove off with my vehicle. It was the only decent thing I owned, too." Jim noticed he didn't seem too upset about his wife being gone.

"Okay. Will you take a card and call me if you think of anything about Sylvester that might be helpful?" Jim asked politely.

"Sure," Ophy said, stepping closer and taking the card. "Ya know, for a cop, you ain't too bad a guy."

"Thanks. I appreciate it." Jim pivoted and walked back to his Suburban, keeping his pace slow and deliberate. Climbing in, he started the vehicle and backed up, hoping he wouldn't puncture a tire on a sharp piece of junk. The temperature had skyrocketed, so before Jim got to the gravel road, he stopped, stripped off his shirt and suit jacket, and unbuckled the vest. Then putting his shirt back on, he laid the tie and suit jacket on the passenger seat and pulled out on the gravel road.

Jim had seen a lot of poverty and destitution as a cop. When children were involved, it was heartbreaking. Ophy Kirking had fried his brain with a little too much of everything, but at least his wife had enough sense to leave him, and hopefully, she had enough sense to never come back.

17

By four o'clock Tuesday afternoon, Jim was back at the law enforcement center riding the elevator to his office on the third floor, still trying to get the smell of the pig manure out of his nostrils. Walking past Emily's desk, she waved him to a stop.

"Jim, just a fair warning. Your office has become a dumping ground of cardboard boxes," she said seriously. "Actually, right now, it looks more like a garage sale."

"What? I'm not following you." He fixed her with a stare and a frown to match. Emily's nose crinkled at the odor that had followed him from the elevator.

"Just prepare yourself. And don't yell at me when you see it." Her eyes were wary.

"Fine. Don't worry about it. I'll handle it."

Jim pivoted and continued down the hall, turned the knob on his office door, and walked in. Piled against one wall were cardboard boxes stuffed with file folders overflowing with paper. The mountain appeared to be tilting, threatening to tip and swamp Jim's office in a sea of documents.

"What the—" Jim sputtered, still standing by the door.

"Hey, Chief. I see you found our discoveries. There they are—all the files of all the cold cases from the last forty years that occurred within a fifty-mile radius of La Crosse," Leslie said, coming up behind him, looking at the mess. He turned and gave her a wide-eyed stare. "Actually, there are still a few more on their way from surrounding counties, and some of the case files have been transferred to digital storage. Those are on our laptops, so we can pull them up."

"Yeah, but—"

Leslie held up her hand to stop him. "I distinctly remember you saying we should bring the stuff up here and you'd help us get started." Leslie tilted her head and lifted her eyebrows.

DeDe's voice erupted from the hallway where she stood in the doorway to the office. "You know what my Grandma Hettie used to say?"

"I have no idea, but I'm sure you're going to tell me," Jim said, looking over his shoulder at DeDe. He waved her in, his shoulders slumping.

"Dog got four feet but can't walk but one road." DeDe lifted her chin as she gazed back at Jim.

"And that means?" Jim asked, confused. Leslie grinned wickedly.

"No matter how many things you'd like to do, you can only do one thing at a time. We did one thing at a time—found the cold case files—and here they are." DeDe swung her arm toward the documents like she was blessing them.

"Right." Jim walked deeper into his office still staring at the mountain of boxes. He stood with his hands on his hips contemplating how to get started. "Don't let the public see this. They'll think we've never solved any crimes in this county for the last fifty years." Leslie and DeDe stifled a grin. Jim continued, "So I guess we should make a plan?"

"We have a plan," Leslie said with confidence. Jim continued gawking. *When did I lose control?* he thought.

DeDe disappeared and returned to the office with a large map of Wisconsin affixed to a corkboard.

"We found the board in the basement. The map came from Walmart. Here's what we think we should do," DeDe said, her voice calm and deliberate. For the next ten minutes, the women rolled out their plan of attack. Jim occasionally nodded, all the while feeling that the investigation had been highjacked or micromanaged; he wasn't sure which but wisely kept his mouth shut.

When the women finished their pitch, Jim said, "All I want right now is to get this in another room. This," he pointed to the boxes, "is not going to work in here. Once we move the boxes, we can organize it."

"Well, what about that meeting room down the hall?" Leslie suggested.

"Doesn't have a lock," Jim said.

"Is that a problem?" Leslie asked. "We can have one installed if we need it, right? Does the budget allow for a new lock on a door?" Her sarcastic tone was not lost on Jim.

"Consider it done. Tell Emily to order it," Jim said, walking over and picking up a box. They'd no sooner moved all the boxes out of Jim's office than Paul and Sam strolled in.

"Jeez, what's that smell? Pig shit?" Sam asked, his nostrils flaring. Jim ignored him.

"Find out anything, guys?" Jim asked, looking back and forth at them.

"Nope. We've been hitting dead ends all day." Sam loosened his tie and pulled up a chair from the corner. Stretching his legs out, he crossed his feet and let out a sigh. "We spent some time at the house going through stuff. We'll go back tomorrow. How about you?" he asked.

"Well, I got into a situation that was pretty sketchy. I even wore my vest," Jim said. Paul's eyebrows raised a notch. Jim went on to explain his visit to Ophy Kirking. "The only thing that came out of it was that Sylvester was a womanizer and porn freak. That could describe an awful lot of men in this day and age. And it doesn't help explain why he was murdered."

Paul was still standing in the middle of the room, a frown creasing his face. "Chief, that necklace. Does it have any marks on it? You know, like a maker's mark or a date? That kind of thing?"

"What made you think of that?" Sam asked.

"*Antiques Roadshow.* Watch it every Monday night," Paul answered. *Another sign of middle age,* he thought. "Maker's marks can be really tiny and sometimes go unnoticed, but a mark might give us something to work with."

Jim shrugged. "I don't know. I didn't think of that." He glanced at his watch—quarter to five. "Look, guys, I need to meet Carol at Pettibone at five. The necklace is in the evidence room. Leslie knows where it is if you want to look at it. Go for it," Jim said, grabbing his suit jacket. "I'll see you tomorrow morning about eight."

As he turned to leave, Sam said, "You better get the shit off your shoes before you see Carol."

18

The swirling water of the Mississippi River spread like a curving chain that sparkled in the evening sun. The blue bowl of the overhead sky provided the perfect backdrop for Canadian geese that formed a V against the drifting red and pink clouds. Their *honk-a-lonk* calls urged the flock to their marshy destination somewhere along the Upper Mississippi Flyway. A candy apple sun burned toward the horizon, its rays spreading out, coloring the waves of the river current until it looked like spilled blood laced with streaks of gold.

Jim fired up the engine of *The Little Eddy* and navigated the boat into the main channel of the Mississippi River from the dock at Pettibone Park. The soaring bluffs had an easy familiarity, like the presence of an old friend. Jim breathed deeply, his senses heightened by the beauty of the September evening. The air was saturated with humidity; a storm was brewing in the west. In the distance, cars and trucks rumbled noisily across the big blue bridge that spanned the bustling river, its long steel arms stretching into Minnesota and back to Wisconsin—an exchange of traffic that continued 365 days a year. Steering into the current, Jim nudged the engine up a notch and eased his way south along the shoreline.

The lofty bluffs above the river were craggy sandstone terraces interrupted sporadically along the shoreline by grassland and stands of hardwoods. Here and there, Jim caught a flash of metal and glass from the traffic along U.S. 35, the Great River Road. Stoddard came into view and then the old river town of Genoa. Walleye fishing was best along this stretch, and Jim had spent many hours casting and reeling in beautiful fish. Eagles soared above on heated thermals, their wings outstretched, their eyes searching for prey despite the lateness of the day.

Carefully piloting the houseboat through U.S. Lock and Dam #8 near Genoa, Jim navigated the backwaters below the dam with a casual expertise that came from years of experience on the river. Carol had scarcely said a word since Jim met her at the dock in the Pettibone Park marina where they'd loaded the boat with a cooler of food and drinks.

As he trolled slowly through the tangle of islands that made up this section of the Mississippi River, Carol caught his eye, her expression serious. Her brown eyes held his gaze, and his stomach flip-flopped. Feeling uncomfortable, he thought back to the phone conversation earlier in the day. Jim wondered if he'd done something stupid or offensive; he was far from perfect. But he knew that after almost three years of marriage, Carol was not a nitpicker. Something had rocked her world, and he was afraid to find out what it might be.

They cruised downstream a mile or so to a pristine sandbar dotted with reed canary grass, tufts of riverbank sedge, and immature stands of cottonwood and willow. Jim ran the prow up on the shore of the sandbar and athletically jumped onto the tiny beach. Tying the craft to a clump of white birch near the shoreline, he helped Carol unload the dinner while she spread a blanket on the sand. He returned to the boat, changed into his comfortable clothes, and rejoined her.

Nearby, a belted kingfisher rattled loudly at them from the branch of a pin oak that hung precariously over the water. Except for the bird's squawking, the quiet was exquisite. Suddenly in a flurry of wings, the feisty bird retreated to a tree farther inland, focusing his distrustful eyes on them, scolding them for invading his space.

Carol's aloof disposition disturbed Jim, but he stayed silent and began unpacking the food she'd prepared. He got the feeling this wasn't one of her surprise romantic interludes. Although the weather was glorious, and they'd enjoyed other idyllic trips on the river, there was nothing amorous about this situation.

He handed her a plate on which he'd spooned some potato salad, placed a piece of fried chicken, and dished up some cubed watermelon. Giving it to her, she smiled weakly and mumbled a thanks. He fixed another plate and sat down. By now, the silence was no longer a welcome reprieve. After a few bites of chicken and salad and a swig of Spotted Cow beer, he made an attempt at conversation.

"Your call this afternoon surprised me," he said, keeping his voice calm.

"I'm sure it did," she said softly, her eyes focused on the slow current of the river. *Just wait til you hear what this is about,* she thought.

A half a mile away, a huge river barge punched through the current, weighted down with a load of harvested corn, squatting low in the water. In its wake, the water heaved and raced to shore. A little chipmunk *chirred* from a fallen log and then darted back into his underground hole.

Jim looked over at Carol. She was picking at her food, and her body was tense and rigid.

"Carol, what's going on?" he finally said. "Tell me. You're like a coiled spring ready to explode outta the shoot."

She looked at him and drew in a long, deep breath. "Okay, I guess there's no good time. I have to confess something, and it's not going to be easy."

Jim stopped eating, laid his plate on the blanket, and turned to face her. *She spent a shitload of money, and she's feeling guilty,* he thought. Then—*An affair? Never.* Then—*What is going on?*

"I'm listening." His heart thumped unsteadily. His investigative senses kicked in. He swallowed anxiously. *Don't jump to conclusions. Just listen.*

"I met Matt for lunch today."

After an awkward pause, Jim said in a reasonable tone, "Alright. I don't think that's the end of the world, but I'm not really happy about it, so why don't you explain why you did that." *Especially without telling me,* he thought. He realized he sounded condescending, like her father, instead of her husband, but it was too late now.

Carol didn't seem to notice. "He texted me with the ruse of needing help with a problem, and I fell for it. I met him at Lindy's, but it went badly. Very badly. But not for the reasons you're probably thinking." A grasshopper landed on the blanket, and Jim flicked it off impatiently, feeling his irritation building.

"Carol, I don't know what to think," he said sharply. He ran his fingers across his chin, then laid back on the blanket, ignoring his food. He propped himself up on his elbows. He tried to lighten the tone of his voice. "Maybe if you keep explaining, I can understand this whole thing a little better."

The sky had turned into a twisting kaleidoscope of swirling orange and pink hues. On the opposite side of the river, just above the Minnesota bluffs, a gray bank of clouds was beginning to form, hinting at a change of weather. Carol continued staring at the evening sky ahead of her and started her explanation again.

"There's this guy Matt knows from the music scene in Wausau who told him Lillie's dad has been looking for her. He's been searching the area, but he's come up short—so far. He wants her back, Jim. He's been trying to find Lillie since she disappeared with Juliette two years ago." It was quiet for a long moment. She continued to sit like a statue on the blanket, her face devoid of emotion.

"What are we going to do, Jim?" she asked softly. Her hands lay in her lap like two limp dishrags. She looked exhausted and afraid. Jim sat there while trying to wrap his head around what she'd told him. He noticed she'd started shaking, and she was trying not to cry.

Turning to him, she said with emotion, "We can't lose her, Jim. She's our baby girl. We promised Juliette that we would love her and take care of her. We're her family now."

He sat up, grabbed her hand, and pulled her over to him, wrapping his arms around her. Despite the alarm and panic snaking into his gut, he was convinced this was somebody's ill-informed concept of how they'd come to have Lillie in the first place—some crazy rumor had taken over.

"Okay, let's think this through." Jim stroked Carol's arm, trying to reassure her. He started using his hand to emphasize his points. "It's not like we stole her off the street or something. This must be some botched misunderstanding. We went through all the proper channels when we adopted Lillie. I'm in law enforcement, for Pete's sake. Do you think I'd do something like this illegally?" By now, his voice has ramped up in volume. Exasperated, he sat up straight.

Carol interrupted. "Don't yell at me, Jim."

He swallowed hard. "Sorry. I didn't mean to yell." He started again, toning his voice down. "It's just that the State of Wisconsin awarded Juliette full custody of Lillie. Her mother signed off on her parental rights and then died of a meth overdose. The dad—whoever he is—never signed the birth certificate. We have no idea who this Joe Schmo is. Juliette's will is a certified, registered document that specified I was to be Lillie's legal guardian. We went through all the proper channels in court. Let's remember the facts, honey."

Carol turned her head and looked him in the eye. Her nostrils flared, and when she started speaking, her voice was firm, and her eyes flashed. Jim was familiar with that look. *Oh boy, here we go,* he thought.

Carol began. "First of all, don't condescend to me, Jim. I know the facts as well as you do. But Lillie's mother was a meth head. Those kinds of people don't live by the rules. She died of an overdose and probably didn't even remember the sex once it was over—or who the guy was, for that matter. It was likely another addict like herself, and she did it for her next fix. Of course, I could be wrong, but whatever." Now her voice ramped up. "For some reason, this guy who claims he's the father has realized he has a little girl somewhere. What if he finds Lillie? What then, huh? Is he going to stalk us? Kidnap Lillie? What?"

Jim attempted to answer, but she harshly cut him off. "And don't say I'm exaggerating. Stuff like this happens all the time. But you, being in law enforcement, would already know that, right?" Carol's voice had taken on a desperate edge, and she blinked rapidly.

Who's yelling now? Jim thought. Her challenge sat between them like a poke in the eye. Tears shimmered in her eyes. The silence dragged on.

Jim kissed her cheek. "Well said. Good points. Did you warn Sara to be extra careful about the kids tonight? Tell her to lock the doors?" Jim's voice was calm, but his suggestions unhinged Carol.

She stiffened, then said, "No, I told her that we'd try to be home by eight. She was fine with that. I didn't tell her anything else. I wanted to talk to you first."

"And you chose to do this when we're miles downriver from La Crosse on our houseboat? Honey, what were you thinking?" he asked, irritated, his blue eyes intense.

"I don't know—I panicked, I guess. I'm sorry, but I didn't know how you'd react to the news, and I didn't want Lillie getting wind that there might be a problem. She's very smart, you know," Carol said defensively. "And she just started accepting the fact that we are really her parents. I don't want anything to mess with that security."

"Well, you're right. She is very smart," he said. He pulled his phone from his jeans. He had two bars. Dialing Sam, he explained the situation. "Yeah, I'll call Sara and explain things. Would you mind parking in the driveway til we get home? We should be there in an hour or so." He listened. "I owe you, buddy. Thanks."

"What'd he say?"

"He's on duty in the driveway until we get there." Jim punched in their home phone number and talked to Sara, careful not to alarm her. When he hung up, he said, "I don't know about you, but I'm hungry." He picked up his plate and resumed eating.

"I'm sorry, Jim, but I did what I thought was best."

"I know, baby. You better eat something," he said gruffly.

His anger was building, especially when he considered the veiled threat that came along with the information about Lillie's father. *I'm her father now, buddy, whoever you are,* Jim thought angrily. *There is no way on God's green earth I will ever give up that child. She's my baby girl despite the DNA.*

"I know where I'm going when I get home," he said, tearing a chunk of meat from a drumstick with his teeth, his jaw working furiously.

"Matt's?"

"You got that right."

19

By eight-thirty that evening, Jim was driving north through La Crosse up Losey Boulevard to Campbell Road. Traffic was light, and the sky reflected a pink afterglow just above the western horizon as dusk settled over the city. Extracting information from Matt Donovan about Lillie's long-lost father would be like pulling a rotten tooth without Novocain. It was probably a dumb rumor started at a biker bar by a bunch of boozers. But, despite Jim's belief that the rumor was more bluff than truth, he couldn't let it go when it came to Lillie and Henri's safety and security. It'd be a dereliction of his duties as a father.

He pulled up to the duplex at Campbell Road. Stepping out of his vehicle, he walked to the front entrance of the duplex on the right and rang the doorbell. The streetlights were just beginning to hum to life as twilight descended. Leaning on the porch railing, Jim watched the lights winking along the street. The sky had become dark, and a low rumble of thunder hinted at a storm brewing in the west. In the stillness that had settled over the city, kids were outside riding their bikes, and a couple of boys were playing catch with a football beneath the street lights. The air was sultry with the smell of ozone and the coming rain.

Jim recalled the look of anxiety and fear on Carol's face when she'd told him the outrageous story. He was confused by Carol's gullibility in trusting her former husband's character and motives. They'd never really discussed Carol's marriage to Matt, but Jim knew that their relationship had more than the normal issues all couples faced—Matt's problems of alcohol dependence and multiple infidelities continued for over five years until divorce seemed to be the only solution. Jim couldn't believe Carol had the desire to see him again. Why would she want to revisit that relationship?

He was confident the life he'd built with Carol was rock solid. He was as deeply in love with Carol as she was with him. Still, it irritated Jim that she had so quickly run to Matt's aid—she should have known better—but he excused it. Carol's commitment to him and their family was enduring and unshakable. He loved her for that; the other stuff was extraneous bullshit or a lapse in judgment that happened to everyone once in a while.

The door swung open. Matt Donavon stood in front of Jim barefooted in a white T-shirt and black jogging pants, eating a bowl of Wheaties. His eyes widened with surprise at the sight of Jim standing on his stoop. A couple of drops of milk slipped off his lip into the bowl. After a few seconds, he shut his mouth and resumed chewing. Regaining his self-assured confidence, he waved Jim into the apartment with his spoon.

"I thought you might show up," he said, walking into the living room furnished with IKEA bookcases, end tables, and a huge leather couch. A wool rug with a swirling pattern of deep red, gray, and teal muffled the sound of their feet. Five guitars of various makes and colors were hanging on the wall as well as an iconic poster of the Eiffel Tower in a slick silver frame. A big-screen television was tuned to *Great Performances* on PBS; the volume seemed deafening to Jim. Eric Clapton was jamming, his extraordinary guitar virtuosity filling the room with its magic. It was easy to see Matt was enthralled with the man and his music.

"God, Clapton is an absolute genius," Matt said, his eyes glued to the set, ignoring Jim. Shoveling another spoonful of Wheaties into his mouth, he slobbered milk down the front of his shirt. Jim blinked at the uncouth mannerisms. When he realized Matt had no intention of engaging in conversation with him, he picked up the remote and flipped off the TV.

"Hey! I was watchin' that," Matt complained, his juvenile temper flaring, his dark eyes flashing.

"You upset my wife. I want you to tell me about this guy who thinks he's going to reclaim my daughter," Jim said carefully, his blue eyes fixed intently on Matt.

"Well, you must know by now, after a couple of years of marriage to Carol that she can be something of a drama queen when she gets pissed." His eyes were hard and uncompromising. "Don't forget—been there, done that." He punched the air with his spoon. "She made a huge scene at Lindy's today. She embarrassed the hell out of me, and I was just trying to help her out."

Jim stood in front of him for a moment and analyzed this character out of Carol's past. He could understand the initial appeal—the rocker type, dark, good-looking, loaded with talent. But things fell off the cliff when you scratched beneath the surface. Anybody needing his former wife's approval this badly had some serious problems.

"This isn't about Carol," Jim said, giving Matt a cool stare. He leaned toward him and put some bite in his words. "This is about some scuzzball who thinks he can waltz into our lives after six years of absenteeism and threaten us with some crap about being Lillie's father. That's not happening," Jim lectured, his index finger pumping up and down. Underneath, he was fuming.

"I was just tryin' to do you all a favor," Matt said, holding his spoon out in a helpless gesture while he balanced his cereal bowl in the other. The bogus innocence infuriated Jim. He stared at Matt until he squirmed.

"Who's this guy who didn't have the balls to sign his name on the birth certificate but seems to think he can reclaim his lost child now after six years on the run? He's gotta be some kind of meathead loser. I need a name!" Jim demanded loudly.

"Whoa! The cop has arrived!" Matt tipped his chin up, giving Jim a defiant stare.

"Deal with it. His name," Jim said, his eyes lit up with righteous anger. Moving a few steps closer to Matt, Jim repeated, "I need a name." Matt held up his hand in a stop gesture, backed up a few steps, and gave him a petulant glare.

"Okay, okay," he whined. "My band played at a bar in Wausau—The Black Bear Inn—over on Jackson Street, and Steve Kolstad, a music friend of mine, introduced me to this guy who claims to be your daughter's real dad. He knew her nickname. Miss Lillie, right?" The corners of Matt's mouth curved up in a slight grin. Jim wanted to punch his lights out.

"His name," Jim barked.

"Maddog Pierson, the biggest meth dealer in central Wisconsin."

Jim felt his stomach contract. His eyes widened in shock. "What?" he whispered. "Maddog? You met him? What was he doing in public?"

"Did you want me to get his autograph?" Matt said with snappy sarcasm. "Or maybe I should have stuffed and cuffed him? Yeah, I met him, and I told you—he's lookin' for his daughter." He drank the milk from the cereal bowl in one guzzle, watching Jim over the rim of the bowl.

Maddog Pierson was well known for his meth production and sales. Law enforcement all over the state had been on the lookout for him for months. The police were sure he had several safe houses throughout the state where he kept himself tucked away out of the public eye. Jim was surprised he'd risked a public appearance. If he was willing to be seen in the open, maybe his threats about reclaiming Lillie should be taken seriously. Suddenly Jim's sense of uneasiness increased.

"Cops in every county have a warrant out for his arrest. You're sure it was Maddog?" Jim asked.

Matt glared, setting the bowl on the coffee table. "I looked him up online. Believe me; it was him. I was standing in the back of the bar at one in the morning, loading up our band equipment after our gig, and I overheard Steve and him talking. It wasn't like he was out in the open having a beer with the boys. We were in an alley behind the bar. There weren't many people around."

"Where's Maddog now? Have you seen him? Is he in La Crosse?"

Matt turned his mouth down, lifting his shoulders in a shrug, displaying an innocence he didn't possess. The bluster continued. "I have no idea. Only met him that one time." He crossed his arms over his chest in a defiant gesture.

"How'd you connect him to Lillie?"

"He mentioned the name Higgins. I put two and two together since I keep tabs on Carol's fabulous life now that she's married to a detective. A lieutenant, no less." His voice dripped with sarcasm.

"You had your chance with Carol. Did anybody ever tell you that you're a complete pain in the ass?"

"All the time, *Lieutenant*," he said, saluting cockily, his eyes gritty and hard.

Jim bit down on his jaw, cutting off a response, trying to stay respectable. "Thanks for the tip," he said as he pivoted to leave. "If you get any more information from your friend, I'd appreciate a call."

"Sure, no problem. And, hey, I gotta say. Carol's still pretty fierce, you know," Matt said. Jim slowed down but kept his back to Matt and continued toward the door. "She always was a looker."

"You got that right," Jim said over his shoulder. "You should see her with nothing on but a diamond necklace." He let himself out and strolled to the Suburban with a grin.

"Deal with it, bud," he said softly, feeling a surprising sense of satisfaction.

20

WEDNESDAY, SEPTEMBER 11

Stepping on a wooden building block as he stumbled around the kitchen in the dim morning light, Paul Saner dramatically hopped around on one foot in the kitchen, mumbling to himself, "The hazards of being a parent. Damn, that hurt." He leaned against the counter, inspecting his foot, wiggling his toes for good measure. Then he leaned down and picked up the random block.

The morning was damp; a front had moved in overnight, and a soft rain was steadily falling, blurring the lines of the neighboring houses in the shrouding mist. Although Paul loved their new home in the Market Street neighborhood of La Crosse, he missed the dramatic views of the Mississippi River from their old Grand River apartment near Riverside Park. The big blue bridge that spanned the river to Minnesota was an iconic symbol of the city, but the home they'd bought here over a year ago gave them more room for their growing family.

"What was that yell all about?" Ruby asked, strolling into the kitchen. Her belly protruded noticeably under the sheer white cotton pajamas she wore. She was entering her sixth month of their second pregnancy. Paul was hoping for a boy this time. Her auburn hair cascaded down her back, a tangle of curls that ended just above her tailbone. Paul noticed her full breasts beneath the sheer fabric, and he let his mind wander among some lovely seductive thoughts. *She's so beautiful when she's pregnant,* he thought.

Ruby started the morning coffee routine, scooping Starbucks breakfast blend into the basket and filling the coffeemaker with water. She mindlessly punched the brewing button and sat down at the table.

"Play me something this morning. Maybe a little Mozart or Schumann?" Ruby suggested, rubbing her expanding tummy. "Something to go with my morning coffee and toast and stretch marks."

"Mmm. okay. I know just the piece. See if you can guess what the music is suggesting."

Paul walked to the corner of the living room where the baby grand piano sat waiting. He positioned himself on the bench, pulled out a piece of music from a stack he kept on the floor, and began playing. His long, slender fingers caressed the keys as the notes floated in the air, tumbling over themselves with elegant beauty and grace.

In the middle of his performance, Melody stumbled into the living room clutching her favorite Winnie-the-Pooh fleece blanket. She stood quietly beside the piano because this was their morning routine—music before breakfast. Her shining eyes watched her father's hands move gracefully over the keys. She tugged on Paul's arm.

"Me, Daddy! Let me play," she demanded, her fingers tapping Paul's arm.

Continuing with the piece, Paul leaned over, "Wait. A little bit longer," he said softly. After several moments, he ended the music with a flourish, the last chord echoing in the room. Melody clapped enthusiastically.

She clamored into Paul's lap, her strawberry blonde hair disheveled from sleep. Paul took her right-hand pointer finger and guided her through a rendition of "Twinkle, Twinkle, Little Star" while he played the accompaniment with his left hand. He heard a rustling behind him. Ruby wrapped her arms around his shoulders and planted a kiss on his unshaven cheek.

"Time to get dressed, Melody," she said. The little girl slid from her father's grasp and toddled into her room, her diaper sagging, dragging her blanket behind her. "Pick out your outfit. I'll be there in a minute, baby."

Paul swung his legs to one side of the piano bench and stood up.

"What was that piece?" Ruby asked. "It was very beautifully performed."

"That was 'Kinderszenen,'" he said, arching one eyebrow. "You understand German?"

"No, I don't, but it sounded playful, so maybe something to do with children?" she guessed, tipping her head. Her green eyes were like the depths of an ocean tidal pool.

"Hmm, you're not only beautiful but brainy, too. 'Scenes from Childhood' by Robert Schumann," Paul teased. "An appropriate piece for our stage of life, don't you think?"

"The 'kinder' gave it away," Ruby said. Paul looked at her, nonplussed. "You know. Kindergarten?"

"Oh, sure. Hey, I'd love to continue this discussion, but I've got to get ready for work. Although, you're looking so fetching in those pajamas, my thoughts are straying to other things," he said, grabbing her and kissing her neck. She giggled infectiously.

"Must be that 'just crawled out of bed in my pajamas look' everyone's going for these days," she said into his shoulder. "Later, buddy." Ruby untangled herself and headed for the bedroom.

In the next half an hour, Paul shaved, showered, and dressed. Ruby left for daycare with Melody. He locked up the house and headed to Vine Street, parking his Ford F-150 pickup in the law enforcement center parking lot. Riding the elevator to the third floor, he walked into Jim's office. Immediately he noticed Jim's steady, intense gaze focused on his computer screen.

"Morning. What's going on?" Paul said, standing next to Jim's desk, casually sipping his coffee.

Jim locked eyes with Paul. Clicking out of whatever he was researching on the computer, he stood up and parked his hands on his hips. He wore a white oxford dress shirt with a tiny blue pinstripe, a Brooks Brothers red and blue paisley tie overlaid with a soft wool navy suit coat and gray flannel dress slacks. His clothes looked sharp, but the dark circles under his eyes conveyed worry and the disquiet of a sleepless night.

"What do you know about Maddog Pierson?" Jim asked bluntly.

"Probably the same things you know. Notorious for escaping the cops. Big-time drug dealer. Your all-around sleazy criminal. He's at the top of the state's most-wanted list. Escaped numerous high-speed chases with the Marathon County cops, one of which left three innocent people dead when he tore through an intersection at 29 and 97. Has a network of dealers throughout the state. Supposedly worth millions. All in all, an extremely nefarious character. Everybody's looking for him. Why?"

"He thinks he's the father of Lillie," Jim said, his intonation flat, his eyes dark.

Choking on his coffee, Paul sputtered, "Say what?" His eyes grew large with the shock of the idea, and he wiped coffee from his chin. "Are you serious?"

Sauntering into Jim's office, Sam looked at both men and asked, "What are you talking about?" He was dressed in a pale pink button-down shirt, dark blue tie, and navy dress slacks. Standing in front of Jim's desk next to Paul, he looked confident and professional. He noticed Jim's dark mood and said, "Everything okay this morning, Chief?"

Paul looked totally confused. "Why wouldn't everything be okay? What happened? What'd I miss out on?"

"Sam watched over the house while Carol told me about this mess with Maddog. Why she chose to tell me when we were on *The Little Eddy* halfway to Lansing is beyond me, but whatever." Jim continued the story about the convoluted circumstances surrounding Lillie's gene pool. He ended by saying, "Believe me, Maddog's DNA is the last thing I want swimming around in Lillie's bloodstream." His blue eyes gazed intensely at the two detectives, his anger simmering beneath the surface.

"So, what's your plan? You can't exactly hide out until he decides to make a move." Sam shrugged, sipping on his coffee. "Life goes on, but you're sort of damned if you make a move and damned if you don't."

"Yeah, tell me about it. Carol and I still need to talk about that," Jim said. His voice hardened. "But mark my words, that loser will be having no contact with Lillie. None. Not now. Not ever." Jim's jaw was set in a rigid line. Even as he spouted his angry defense, he knew he had no control over what Maddog might be planning. Jim's eyes misted with tears when he thought about Lillie. She was a beautiful, exceptional child, and he was bound to her with cords of love. Protecting her from the likes of Maddog Pierson was what he was prepared to do with his life, if need be.

"Got it, Chief. Let us know if we can help. I'll put some feelers out with my drug contacts around town. See if they've heard anything." Moving the conversation along, Sam said, "So what's on the docket today with the George Street murder?"

Paul offered a plan. "I'm going to take a closer look at that locket—"

Sam interrupted. "I'm still going through some paper from the house. Personal stuff, newspaper clippings, junk like that."

"Sounds good," Jim said. "I'll help the girls with the cold case files, although that may be a complete dead end. Haven't got much else. Who knows? Maybe something will pop out at us." But he knew the longer they went without solid circumstantial evidence, the more difficult it would be to apprehend Sylvester Kratt's murderer. Their files would be slapped into a manila folder marked Cold Case like so many of the others they'd uncovered. To top it off, the distraction of Maddog's pernicious parental claims would be grating at the edges of his mind all day.

By ten o'clock, the work on the Kratt case was moving forward, but the going was tough, like slogging through a dump filled with insignificant rubbish. Nothing was standing out. Still, DeDe and Leslie were making incremental progress in sorting and identifying unique evidence in each cold case which was better than nothing. The chart they'd devised was filling up, and the pinpoints they'd added to the Wisconsin map made it look like a colorful pincushion.

At twelve-thirty, Carol knocked on the door where Jim, DeDe, and Leslie were elbow deep in dusty files.

"Hey. Wondering if you want to go to lunch?" she asked sweetly, addressing Jim.

"Yeah. Let me get my jacket," he said, standing up and leaning backward to get the kinks out of his back and neck. While he walked to his office, Carol visited with the girls.

"Tough going, huh?" she commented, her brown eyes sympathetic.

"You could say that, but we've already eliminated some cases, so by tomorrow, we may be able to zero in on more of the local ones," DeDe said. "We might actually uncover an unsolved case that could tie in with the Kratt murder. CSI is still sorting through what they found in the house." Her voice rolled in smooth, easy tones, the vowels delicate and gentle; her Carolina upbringing oozed out in her diction. "Before you go, ma'am, I wanted to ask if you and Jim would come to my houseboat Friday night for a mess of dirty rice and chicken. The team's coming over, and I'd love for you to bring your little ones. I've heard so much about them that I just have to meet them in person."

"That would be lovely. If it rains, you can come over to our house and use my stove. How's that sound?" Carol asked, smiling broadly.

"That sounds jes' fine, ma'am," DeDe said, flashing a huge smile.

"By the way, please call me Carol. We don't stand on tradition around here." Jim appeared at Carol's elbow. "Ready?" he asked.

"Let's go," Carol said, smiling. She twiddled her fingers at the girls.

Jim drove to Harley's restaurant at the foot of Hedgehog Bluff through the dismal misting rain, and they asked for a table on the back patio, which was under a protective awning. Because of the drizzle, most people sat inside, so the patio was pleasantly quiet. Jim wove the conversation around to Maddog, thinking the quiet secluded setting was a good place to discuss their options without anyone overhearing their conversation.

"Do we have to ruin our time together talking about the likes of that man?" Carol asked, exasperated, snapping her napkin open on her lap with a flourish. She'd spent some time on the internet researching him, and everything she read about him made her shudder.

"Well, it's a despicable topic, but we have to figure out a few things pretty soon. We all need to know where Lillie is and whose care she's in all the time," Jim shot back. He made an effort to keep his voice calm and evenly modulated. "I don't like this any more than you do, but facts are facts. This Maddog sounds like he's determined to reconnect with Lillie, but that will happen only over my dead body," Jim sputtered, his face suddenly dark with anger.

"Honey, you need to calm down, and don't talk about being dead," Carol started, but Jim interrupted.

"Calm down? Sweetheart, who was the one in tears last night?" Jim stared at her, his blue eyes direct and piercing. "After my conversation with Matt, I will do everything I can to protect Lillie, but the facts are not comforting. Maddog is loose on the landscape. No one seems to know where he is. People keep saying they've seen him, but so far, guess what? He's nowhere to be found. He's one of the biggest drug dealers in the state. He's on the hunt for Lillie, and it isn't going to take him long to find us. Those facts alone keep me tossing and turning at night when I think about what he might be planning."

The waitress set their plates of food in front of them. Jim asked for a refill of his iced tea, poured ketchup on his hamburger, and took a bite. Carol's fork hovered over her taco salad.

"What?" Jim asked, wiping ketchup from his mouth with his napkin, regretting his tirade when he looked at the sad expression on Carol's face.

"What about God?" she said. "You're always telling me that God has his protective hand over our family." Her brown eyes were soft with emotion. "What about that? Are we just going to throw Him out the window now?" Jim could see the blur of tears forming in her eyes.

He reached across the table and laid his hand over hers, then grasped her fingers firmly. Looking into her eyes, he said softly, "You're right, honey. God is watching over our family. Thanks. I needed that reminder."

They ate silently for a few moments, each lost in thought and speculation.

"There is one person we could totally trust with Lillie's safety. No one would think to look for her there. If we need to whisk her to safety, it'd be perfect," Jim stated, holding a fry mid-air, deep in thought.

"Sara?" Carol asked.

"Nope. Someone who has always had our best interest at heart, love."

"I don't know. Is God being eliminated from the list?"

"Well, no. Obviously, God takes care of us. But He also uses people we know to help us. What about Gladys Hanson? Her place would be a perfect haven for Lillie. Gladys is loving but tough, and Lillie loves her to pieces. Her place is out of the way but in plain sight. She's practical, and she loves Lillie and Henri as if they were her own grandchildren. And believe it or not, she's dealt with some very tough situations over the years as a social worker. She's familiar with the emotions that go along with tense conflicts, especially when you're talking about the placement of children in adoptive homes and the land mine of emotions that goes with parental rights."

Carol stayed silent for a few moments. Jim bit his tongue, not wanting to tread on her thoughts. Then she said, "You know, Jim, that's a plan that might work. Have you talked to her?"

"Not yet. But I'll call her tonight and have a chat." Jim noticed Carol visibly relax as she leaned back in her chair.

"Anything as precious as our children is worth fighting for," she began. "Lillie is our daughter, not only on paper but in our hearts. I will never give her up to anyone else. And that's a promise." Jim noticed the burning emotion behind her eyes.

"Well, we may be in for it. It could be a rough road. You ready for that?" he asked, taking a drink of tea.

"Absolutely. God gave us Lillie, and I believe that was His plan all along. He rescued her from the street and put her in our arms. And that's where she's staying." Jim loved her words of confidence.

"Couldn't have said it better myself," he said. He just wished he felt the same bravado, but underneath, he was skeptical. There were so many factors to control to keep Lillie out of harm's way. He wasn't sure he could juggle all of them, leaving him feeling overwhelmed. Then a thought came to him—one he desperately needed. *Do not fear, for I am with you. I will strengthen you and help you; I will uphold you with my righteous hand.*

Jim closed his eyes briefly and felt a comforting reassurance wash over him. *Whatever happens, God already knows—and He's with us.* That's the only promise Jim had right now. It was enough.

21

Paul Saner sat at his desk, staring at the delicate gold locket from the murder scene on George Street. The necklace lay in front of him on a piece of white paper. He'd borrowed a high-intensity lamp from Leslie's stash of tools, and its beam illuminated the details of the jewelry. Through the magnifying glass suspended from a stand above it, he could see the delicate filigree etched along the edge of the lovely heart locket. The gold necklace radiated a warm glow under the high-beam light as he gazed down at it. He hoped it might be engraved with initials, but there weren't any.

Pulling on a pair of latex gloves, he found the maker's mark on the back of the locket—a faint VCA and the letters 750 were barely visible, but they were there. Van Cleef & Arpels. Paul felt a twinge of satisfaction as he continued to take notes on his yellow legal pad. Hovering over the necklace, he turned the locket over again and studied the front. He could envision the locket on a young girl. Perhaps it was a gift from her father or her boyfriend. Maybe she'd worn it to prom or her graduation. It was a beautiful piece made with only the finest materials and with great care, as one would expect from such a distinguished company as VCA. He could imagine giving it to his daughter, Melody, on her sixteenth birthday.

As he continued to examine the locket under the magnifying glass, he noticed a faint black line along the edge of the heart encircling its circumference. He squinted at it as he peered through the glass again. He dug in his pocket and found his jackknife, which he carefully inserted into the dark line. When Paul twisted the knife slightly, the locket suddenly popped open. Inside was a photo of two teenagers, their goofy smiles tugging at Paul's emotions. His heart thumped hard. *Who were they?* He pushed his chair back and walked down the hall to Jim's office, where he was working.

"Chief, I need you in my office for a minute," Paul said seriously, his head peeking around the frame of the door.

Jim looked up casually. He noticed Paul's somber expression. "You find something?" he asked, getting out of his chair.

"Yeah, but I need another set of eyes," Paul said.

Jim followed Paul down the hall into Paul's office. Both men walked to the desk and hovered over the locket under the high-intensity lamp. Paul pointed at his discovery.

"It's a photo of a couple of kids. It was inside the locket," he said, straightening up and moving aside so Jim could take a closer look. Jim hunched over the photo, adjusting the magnifying glass.

"It's small, cut from a bigger photo. Look at the clothes—looks like mid to late seventies, maybe," he said in a hushed tone. Jim lifted his head and briefly stared into space, remembering an event from his past when he was just eleven. *Couldn't be,* he thought. His eyes drifted back to the photo, but he couldn't shake the feeling he'd seen this girl somewhere before.

"There's a house in the background, but it's barely visible. Too much of the photo was cut away when they tried to piece it into the locket. Still, we might be able to identify it somehow. Let's get this photo out to the public. In the meantime, take it down to Heldrich Photography on Winnebago Street. Lois specializes in helping people identify family members in photos. Carol had her do some work for her. Ask her to enlarge it—maybe try to get a little more detail.

Maybe she can identify the type of paper used and possibly the kind of camera. That will help pinpoint the date of the photo within a couple of years. What else did you find out?" Jim asked, standing and facing Paul.

Paul grabbed his yellow legal pad from his desk and started reading his notes. "It's a Van Cleef & Arpels locket. They're a highly reputable company that produces expensive jewelry, and usually, their pieces are considered heirlooms that are passed down from generation to generation. The 750 indicates it's eighteen karat—all of their jewelry is seventy-five percent gold. And there's a partial serial number. Right there," he said, pointing to the edge of the locket with the tip of a pen. Jim looked again. CL 8497, but the last number was smudged; the bottom curve was there, but the rest was missing.

"Yeah, the last number could be a three, a five, or an eight. Should be easy enough to determine with a call to the company. Explain that it's part of a murder investigation. See what you get," Jim suggested. "It's a start, anyway. This is good, Paul. Really good work."

"So, did you and Carol come up with a plan for keeping Maddog away from Lillie?"

"We're relying on our Higher Power for protection." Paul's eyebrows shot up, but he stayed silent. "We talked about some options at lunch, but we're not sure if they're viable yet." Jim's face hardened, and he looked out at the traffic furiously speeding along Vine Street. The weather outside was unpredictable—raining one minute or sunshine trying to shine through the thunderclouds the next.

"Let me know if there's anything I can do to help," Paul offered.

"Will do," Jim said simply.

Meanwhile, Sam was in his office plowing through boxes of personal effects from the Kratt home on George Street. The CSI team had boxed up drawers of personal papers—birthday and Christmas cards, certificates of various kinds, funeral folders, church bulletins, boxes of photos, newspaper clippings—all of it collected over a lifetime. *The accumulation of stuff,* he thought.

Now he slogged through it like a peon with his nose to the grindstone. He hoped he wouldn't leave behind this much ephemeral litter when he was dead and gone. But he knew already from his brief two months of marriage how easily possessions could pile up. Just last week, Mrs. Brown had arrived with five boxes of high school and college odds and ends she'd gathered from Leslie's bedroom in Decorah. All of it was still in their spare bedroom, where Sam was sure it would remain for some time, probably until they decided to turn the room into something other than a catchall for junk. Then they would have to give it a home somewhere else, hopefully in the trash.

Sam continued rummaging through the boxes of paper. He bounced between losing his concentration, daydreaming, and focusing on the task. Sifting through the archives, the musty smell of the yellowed papers hung in his nostrils. Sam was surprised to see that his fingertips had turned black from handling the old newsprint. Looking toward the window, he noticed the dust motes in the shaft of sunlight that filtered into the window. Hearing a quiet knock on the door, he looked up as Leslie came into his office, distracting him further.

Sam focused on her blue eyes first, then the long, straight blonde hair and beautiful, flawless skin. Even though it was near the end of the day, her clothes seemed unwrinkled; her sweater and slacks hugged her lanky figure. Sam's eyes traveled to her breasts, then back to her face.

"Bored?" Leslie asked. "I saw that look." He gave her a sulky glance and smiled wickedly. "I guess I can allow that from my husband, but only when no one else is around, big guy."

"I have been hellishly bored all day," Sam replied. "But you're just the person I wanted to see, and my fantasies are running wild right now. We could shut the door and—"

"Sam," Leslie interrupted. "We said we'd never do it at work, remember?"

"Worth a try," he said, smiling. He patted a chair beside him. Leslie sat down, and something light and floral, like lilacs, drifted from her into the air. Ripping open a bag of Cheetos, she leaned over and offered him some.

"How do you not gain weight when you eat this junk?" he asked, eagerly diving in and popping the crunchy treats in his mouth. He licked the salt from his lips.

"The key is to exercise regularly, and then you can allow yourself forbidden fruit."

"Mmm, forbidden fruit … now that's a subject we could discuss at length."

Leslie shook her head gently. "Sam, you've got a one-track mind."

"That's true. You'll find out about that tonight. Are you and DeDe getting anywhere on your cold case files?"

"Not so much. Sorting and organizing, but that's about it for the moment."

"How's DeDe doing, do you think?" He looked over at her as he continued perusing the files. He reached in the nearest cardboard box and grabbed another handful of paper, plopping it on the desk with a thud. Dust blew out of the pile, and Leslie waved her hands back and forth, attempting to direct the dust elsewhere. "How's she adjusting to Wisconsin?" Sam repeated, sneezing loudly.

"Oh, I think she's fine. I called Bandbox Realty today and hooked her up with an agent. She needs to find an apartment soon before it gets too cold. She just left to look at some places, and I didn't feel like working alone. Anything I can help you with?"

Leslie noticed Sam suddenly very focused on a newspaper article from the pile. Picking it out of a bunch of yellowed documents, he laid it down and started reading. A quietness settled over the small office. He was wearing his hair a little shorter these days, but it still curled gently around his ears.

"Hey, did you find something?" Leslie asked, leaning over to see what was so intensely interesting.

"I don't know. Maybe ..." His voice drifted off as he continued to focus.

Leslie glanced at the title, "Missing Babysitter's Disappearance Remains Unsolved." The date of the *La Crosse Sentinel* Sunday edition was October 23, 1977. The headlines were like a brisk slap across the face. A black-and-white image of a pretty girl sat under the bold print.

Sam's finger moved carefully down the page, stopping now and then to read the details. "Whaddya think, Lez?" he said vaguely. "Why's this Kratt guy got this article? Seems like a strange thing to save for forty years, don't you think?"

Leslie recognized that tone of voice. Cautiously she said, "Sam, let's not give too much importance to this right now. It's early in the investigation. Besides, people save things that are memorable, and a disappearance like this in a small college town would be something you wouldn't easily forget. He could have clipped it out of the paper and probably never looked at it again."

Sam glanced over at Leslie, noticing that special look she always gave him when he was about to jump into the deep end of theory building.

In almost everything, she was his tempering agent. Despite his training, Sam tended to get wild notions about cases they worked on, going off half-cocked when there was little factual evidence for his theories. This often led the team into strange territory. The problem was that his zany ideas were often accurate, which didn't always translate into an advantage for Leslie. She was the one who had to play devil's advocate and talk him down from the ledge he'd crawled out on, frequently without solid circumstantial proof. Sometimes she thought she missed her calling—maybe she should have been a lawyer or a psychologist.

Right now, he was staring at her, his hazel eyes intense. He ran his fingers through his dark wavy hair and took a deep breath.

"I know, Lez," he started saying. "I know. I need to check my wild assumptions at the door and let the evidence guide me to what really happened." She held her hand up, and he gave her a high five, leaning back in his chair. His tie hung loosely around his neck like a deflated windsock. He looked tired, and his clothes were wrinkled and dusty. "The evidence should inform my theories instead of the other way round," he repeated. "I get it."

Sam sat forward again, the intensity returning. "It's just that I think this might be significant in this case somehow. I don't know if it ties in, but it might be relevant." He carefully laid the article aside. "Maybe it will correlate with something you find in those cold cases."

"Well, you're making progress. At least you didn't use the f-word," she said.

"Hey! I don't ever use the f-word!" he said, looking peeved.

"Not that f-word; the f-word that stands for feelings as in 'It *feels* like this might be relevant.' I'm proud of you, honey. You're getting there." She grinned.

He made a rude sound, gave her a disgusted look, and continued paging through the mountain of documents. "That's what I get after sitting here all day looking through this dusty crap—ridicule and sarcasm. By the way, it's your turn to cook tonight. Did you remember?" he said, looking over at her.

"Yes, and I'm glad to do it. Any requests?"

"Yeah. How about some f-ing fish?"

Leslie giggled. "Grilled salmon it is."

22

The sun was beginning to sink in the west. Its rays filtered through the border of huge maples in Jim's backyard as he drove into the garage. The drive down Chipmunk Coulee Road was quiet. Jim met a farmer pulling a gravity box full of harvested corn, and a garbage truck was heading toward U.S. Hwy. 35. The wooded valley sparkled with red and orange tongues of sunlight that glowed as they touched the grass, making everything seem magically alive. Walking into the entryway from the garage, Jim heard Lillie giggling and squealing while Henri stumbled after her, babbling empty threats.

Coming around the corner into the living room, he threw his suit coat on the swoopy black chair. He stood there watching Lillie and Henri play. *They're so innocent, but the evil in the world is bound to bump up against them and hurt them,* he thought. His stomach rolled over. He wasn't sure if it was from hunger or anxiety. He felt Carol's arm around his waist. Looking down at her, he could see the happiness and contentment in her eyes. He kissed her lightly on the lips.

"Look at them. They're really starting to bond, Jim," she said wistfully, her brown eyes shining.

Why couldn't life always remain this simple? he thought.

"Bapa!" Lillie shouted, running into his arms. Jim knelt on his haunches and tenderly kissed her cheek. "Watch, Bapa! Henri's getting really good at chasing me! Pretty soon he'll catch me!"

Henri had been slow to get the hang of forward mobility, but Lillie had made him the focus of her attention. Now she walked up to Henri and helped him stand. She stood a few steps away and urged him forward, clapping her little hands energetically. "Come on, Henri. You can do it," she said gently. Henri's big brown eyes zeroed in on Lillie, and he took several confident steps until he fell into Jim's arms. Jim buried his nose in Henri's soft blond locks and took in his scent. Lifting him, he turned to Carol.

"What's for supper? I'm famished," he said, taking off his tie and flipping it on the back of the chair.

"Lasagna, French bread, green beans, cabbage salad, and ice cream with strawberries," Carol said, taking Henri, who'd reached out to her with chubby arms. "Come on, you little bruiser." Turning to Lillie, she said, "Go wash your hands, Lillie, and come to the table, please."

Placing Henri in the highchair, Carol scurried around getting dinner on the table while the toddler banged noisily on his tray with a spoon. Jim sat down and breathed deeply. Domestic life always had a calming effect on him. Now he took in the atmosphere of their home. It felt secure and stable, and happiness permeated its walls. He couldn't ask for more, but he knew it could all change in a moment. He thought again of Carol's words at lunch. God was watching over them, and that thought alone helped lessen the tightness in his chest.

"Beer or wine?" Carol asked.

"A Leinie's would be great."

Carol brought him an opened bottle, and Jim drank a long swig of cold beer. Lillie slid into her place at the table, and Carol prepared to say grace. Jim was a stickler about family meals, although he knew that many families never sat down together and broke bread. The tradition came from how they'd both been raised—parents who had insisted on fellowship at the table around good home-cooked food. They were determined to raise their little family the same way, the world be damned.

Jim credited his conversational skills, impeccable manners, and tolerance for subjects and people he didn't always agree with to family mealtime. His parents had welcomed many to their simple home. Some guests were gracious; others were not. But all were treated with respect and tolerance, which Jim thought was lacking in today's culture.

The odd thing, Jim thought, *is that people were more alienated than ever despite being plugged into technology twenty-four hours a day.* To Jim, eating together seemed like a logical place to begin a renewal of relationships, to catch up after a long day of ceaseless activity in the rat race. A prayer, a meal, and good conversation created an opportunity to throw technology to the wind. In his experience, nothing took the place of face-to-face discussions over a plate of tasty cuisine.

"Bapa?"

"Yes, Lillie. Tell us about your day, sweetheart. Did you learn anything new today?" Jim said, leaning over and cutting some lasagna into small pieces for Henri. He put a few green beans on his tray.

"First, I wanna know somethin'," she said, raising her index finger. "Why do we pray when we eat?"

"We need to thank God for his blessings, and that includes food," Jim explained. "You must pray at school, don't you?"

"Oh, yes. We pray in the morning. And then we pray before lunch, and then we pray before we go home," Lillie informed them, tearing off a bite of French bread. "That's a lot of praying, Bapa." Jim smiled and nodded. Lillie turned to Carol and said, "Mama, this food is so good."

Carol smiled tenderly, and she caught Jim's eye. There were times she still couldn't believe the change that had taken place in her life since she'd met and married Jim. Now she was a mother—an event she never believed would happen, especially at her age. Jim returned her gaze with a steadfast glimmer in his eye and a hearty grin.

"This lasagna *is* delicious, love. Thank you," Jim added, enjoying another forkful.

"So what about your day, Lillie?" Carol asked. "Anything exciting happen at school today?"

Lillie tipped her head, and a quizzical expression crossed her face. "Well, today I saw a man watching the playground. It seemed like he wanted to talk to me. He kept staring at me, but Mrs. Schneider said I should ignore him." She stabbed a green bean with her fork. "I think he was taking some pictures." As Lillie continued to rattle on, Carol felt a wave of alarm. "But the rule is we have to stay on the playground and not wander in the street. We're learning about stranger danger. What's wrong with strangers anyway?"

Carol and Jim exchanged an alarmed look and stopped eating. Jim gently lowered his fork to his plate, cleared his throat, and focused on Lillie. Suddenly the room seemed close and stuffy. *Stay calm; don't panic,* Carol thought as she glanced up at Jim.

"Bapa?" Lillie's blue eyes searched his face. Then she turned her gaze on Carol. "Mama? What's wrong?"

Jim nodded. "Mrs. Schneider is exactly right. When you're at school, you should always stay where your teachers can see you. You do that, don't you, Lillie?" Jim asked, his blue eyes serious.

Lillie shook her head up and down and pushed her curls away from her face. "Yeah, but sometimes Rory Fischer wants to hide behind the lilac bushes so he can kiss me. But that's yucky. I'm not doin' that."

"That sounds like a good plan," Carol answered, her face somber.

"I agree," Jim said softly.

After the meal, Carol took the kids and headed for the bathtub. Jim could hear giggles and splashes echoing down the hall. He rinsed the dishes, loaded them into the dishwasher, and wiped the counters and table. Then he walked down the hall to his den and closed the door. Punching a number in his cell phone from a list of emergency numbers taped to the top of his antique oak desk, he waited for an answer.

"This is Schneiders. May I help you?"

"Yes, this is Lt. Jim Higgins calling. Is your mom home?"

"Just a minute, please," the voice responded. Jim heard some rustling and talking on the other end.

"This is Louisa Schneider."

"Hi, Mrs. Schneider. This is Jim Higgins, Lillie's dad. She mentioned an incident at school today I wanted to follow up on. Something about a man watching her while she was playing outside, possibly taking photos. Could you tell me about that?"

"Oh, that was during morning recess. Lillie came to me and said someone was watching her from the street, but when I went to the fence, the car was gone. I never did see the man she was talking about. I just chalked it up to her vivid imagination. This sounds important. Is it?" Her voice had taken on an apprehensive tone.

"Yes, it's very important. Listen, I need to apologize. We probably should have called earlier. I'm sure you know that Lillie is adopted. We've recently received a report that Lillie's biological father is trying to find her. We're not sure of his intentions since he hasn't contacted us, so we're sort of in the dark. We heard through an acquaintance of Carol's that he's been trying to locate Lillie." Jim twirled a pen through his fingers as he relayed the facts.

"Your daughter, Sara, filled us in on some of the details about Lillie. Does her father have court-appointed visits?"

"No, no. In fact, he never signed the birth certificate, so this whole report is upsetting. We didn't lend much credence to it because we thought he was out of the picture. But when we were told about his search for Lillie, and when I found out who he was, I did some research. Just so you're aware, he's a dangerous individual if all the reports about him are true—and I know they are." The line was so quiet Jim wondered if they'd been disconnected.

"Mrs. Schneider? Are you still there?" Jim asked.

"You don't think he's a school shooter, do you?" Mrs. Schneider asked. Jim could imagine her alarmed expression.

"I believe his main interest is in Lillie, but nothing is beyond the scope of possibility at this point."

"I think the best thing to do would be to call Father Knight. Do you know him?" she asked.

"Oh, yes. I know him well. I'll give him a call. And please, just be observant and follow your instincts if you feel something is strange. Okay?"

"Yes, Lt. Higgins. I can do that. Thanks for calling."

Jim hung up. He sat in the deepening twilight inside his cozy office. The night outside had morphed into a dusky gray, and the shadows of the trees reflected on the windows in dark, shifting shapes. Jim rubbed his eyes, got up, walked to the window, and stared into the darkness. Had Maddog already been here? How did he know Lillie went to school at St. Ignatius in Genoa? If he knew about Lillie, then he probably knew about Sara and Henri, too. Jim felt a dark web of distrust and fear fall over him. He shivered involuntarily as if standing in the shadow of a frozen mountain. He jerked nervously when Carol walked into the darkened room and touched his arm.

"The kids are ready for bed. Do you want to say good night?"

"Sure."

"Jim, you're pretty tense. You just about jumped out of your skin just now. Are you okay?" He turned to Carol and wrapped his arms around her. He held her for a few moments, feeling some of the tension melt away.

She pulled back and gave him a questioning look. "I talked to Mrs. Schneider—" he started.

"Bapa, are you coming?" Lillie yelled.

Rolling his eyes, he kissed her lightly and whispered, "Later."

After reading a few stories, Jim tucked Lillie in while Carol gave Henri a drink of milk, then slipped him into his crib for the night.

Watching Lillie sleep, Jim sat in the rocking chair and let his eyes wander around the small bedroom that was her exclusive domain. Elsa, her *Frozen* doll, was her constant companion, especially at bedtime. She lay right beside Lillie, her eyes staring at the ceiling in the dark; the doll's blonde hair was almost the same color as his daughter's.

Jim's eyes strayed to the framed white feather pressed under glass that hung just above Lillie's bed. It was a constant reminder to them what Lillie already knew—God's angels were always with us, guiding and protecting us. The feather had floated from the sky and landed on Juliette's tombstone on the day of her memorial service at Hamburg Lutheran Cemetery. No one knew how it had gotten there, but Lillie insisted she'd seen an angel hovering over her grandma's grave, and the white feather was proof of the angel's existence. No one had a better explanation. Jim believed her, and gradually over the last few years, Carol started to believe, too. Tonight, spiritual beings were the topic of conversation again.

When she was tucked in her bed, Lillie's blue eyes studied Jim's face. Not much escaped her notice, even though she was only six years old. With a luminous, serious expression, she said, "The man I saw today didn't have a nice shadow, Bapa."

"Shadow? What do you mean?" he asked, frowning. Jim never knew what might come out of Lillie's mouth. He would've loved to spend a day inside her pretty little head. He was sure her thoughts would bowl him over.

"He was dark like night. Will he hurt me?" Her eyes were wide with concern, and Jim saw the beginning of some tears.

Jim knelt next to her bed, leaning over her. Stroking her little cheek with his thumb, he held her gaze, feeling the importance of her question weighing on him like a heavy stone. *Don't blow her off.*

"I'm checking into that. You're safe here, Lillie. We're going to do our very best so that no one can hurt you, baby." He kissed her nose, and she grabbed him tightly around his neck. She smelled of baby lotion and toothpaste, and her firm squeeze left Jim feeling an intense fatherly urge to protect her.

"I believe you. I love you. Night, Bapa," she whispered, rolling on her side.

"Night, Lillie. Love you, too," Jim said, pulling the quilt over her shoulders. He leaned down and kissed her cheek tenderly.

Getting out of the rocking chair, he quietly snuck out of the room and softly closed the door behind him. Then he tiptoed down the hall and peeked in for a quick look at Henri. The soft glow from the night light illuminated his golden curls and long eyelashes lying against his chubby cheek. The sight of his baby son tugged at Jim's heartstrings. *So precious. They grow up way too fast.* He laid his hand briefly on his little chest. Then he turned and went into the living room, where Carol reclined on the sofa.

"Well, everything seems copacetic. All is well at the hour of eight," Jim said in his deep baritone voice. Noticing Carol's serious expression, he walked over and plopped on the couch, grabbed her feet, and gave them a good rub. "You look like you need a massage."

"A massage isn't going to help what's been dished on my plate," she said curtly. "So what's the deal?" she asked, pulling her feet away and sitting up.

Jim filled her in on the call he'd made to Mrs. Schneider. Then he told her about Lillie's shadow man. "She senses some kind of danger."

Carol looked at him with an inscrutable expression. "She has a gift, Jim. She sees spiritual dimensions ... realities ... shadows that others can't see."

"Or won't see," Jim said.

"That, too. Tell me, what's your plan? It looks like Maddog is serious about this," Carol said. She leaned forward into a sitting position and reached for his hand. Jim could feel her shaking.

"Take it easy, honey. I'm going to call Father Knight and Gladys and get a plan in place. I'll alert the local law enforcement up and down the river and in surrounding counties. Everyone wants to catch Maddog just as badly as Marathon County does. Hopefully, we won't have to use our plan, but this guy is elusive and slippery. And Sara needs to be fully clued in. Why don't you go down and talk to her while I make a few calls?"

"Right. It'll feel good to actually do something proactive." Carol swung her legs from the couch and headed for the downstairs apartment.

By ten-thirty, they'd talked everything over, Jim had made the necessary contacts, and the plan for their family's safety was in place. Everyone who was important had been notified and was on board.

"You call day or night," Gladys Hanson commanded. "I'll do all I can to help. Tomorrow I'll prepare the bedrooms so everything's ready."

"Thanks, Gladys. You're a trooper." Jim could imagine her white hair encircling her head like a cloud and her no-nonsense gritty demeanor creasing her wrinkle-lined face. Despite her gruffness, she loved Jim's family as if they were her own. Gladys had shared some difficult emotional journeys with Jim. First, when his beloved Margie had died of breast cancer, and then when he had uncovered the truth about his unknown sister, Juliette. Jim loved Gladys as if she were his own mother. She was his confidante, counselor, prayer warrior, and friend.

"I've seen a lot of this kind of thing in my day. It's never pleasant, but prayer helps. I'll do that, too," she promised firmly. "Just remember Joshua 1:9: Do not be terrified; do not be discouraged, for the Lord your God will be with you wherever you go."

After they had tea, Jim and Carol went to bed. Carol snuggled on Jim's shoulder as he gently held her. The stress of the last few days seeped away, and after a few moments, he heard her deep, regular breathing. But Jim lay in the darkness staring at the ceiling, praying they'd done enough. Praying their plan would work.

23

THURSDAY, SEPTEMBER 12

By nine o'clock the next morning, Jim was sitting in the small room on the third floor of the law enforcement center surrounded by mountains of cold case documents trailing back at least twenty years and, in some instances, forty years, which seemed ridiculous. His thoughts tumbled over one another. Didn't they have any more evidence about this Kratt murder than to be grasping at straws from the past? The locket and the mysterious note suggested a person had been wronged. But how? Weren't there facts that could help them from the crime scene or something that had been found at the Kratt home that would give them a direction? Except for the necklace and the note, they'd come up empty. There didn't seem to be any witnesses to the murder. Neighbors were helpful, but they hadn't noticed anything of importance that could lead to a solid suspect. At the same time, Jim's concerns about his family's safety haunted his waking hours and robbed him of his sleep at night. He was beginning to feel frayed around the edges.

Frustrated, he got up suddenly, grabbed his coffee cup, and left DeDe and Leslie staring after him. He went down the hall to his office and slammed the door behind him. He stood by the narrow window and looked down into the parking lot of the law enforcement complex. Information about Maddog swirled in his head, but trying to predict the criminal's next move was an exercise in futility. Jim felt so impotent in the face of this shadowy threat.

Most people would dismiss Lillie's dark perception of the man she saw at St. Ignatius school as the product of an overactive imaginative mind that was untrained and raw. Jim knew differently.

From the first moment he'd met Lillie a little over a year ago, it was apparent that she had a keen, deep-seated intelligence few other children possessed. John and Sara, fraternal twins from his first marriage, were blessed with good minds and strong personalities for which he was thankful.

But Lillie's gifts were unique and remarkable. He supposed nowadays she'd be called gifted. Intellectually he knew this was true—her reading and math skills were well beyond her biological age—but she'd also been given a spiritual insight that was deep and authentic. She saw things that were invisible to others. Sometimes it scared him; other times, he was strangely comforted by her simple childlike faith in God and the angels, those invisible spiritual entities that ministered to believers throughout the world.

Today his mood matched the dark, threatening weather outside. He knew the signs of depression—he'd had serious bouts of it at various times in his life. He wasn't depressed now, but his anxiety levels spiked when he thought about the dangerous criminal who was focused on his family. Jim imagined Maddog's attention honing in on Lillie, and he realized he was gritting his teeth. *Lighten up. Concentrate on the tasks at hand.* It seemed disaster was stalking him like the roaring lion Scripture talked about.

He sat down at his desk and turned his office chair toward the long, narrow window. The sky had turned a deep indigo, and thick purple clouds in the northwest boiled with energy. In the distance toward Grandad Bluff, a flash of lightning streaked across the sky like a broken arrow, and the thunder that followed boomed across the valley. Soon large raindrops began pelting the window sounding like angry slapshots on ice.

His phone buzzed. He picked it up.

"Hey, Lt. Higgins. This is Stephanie Holt downstairs in the lab. Just wanted to let you know we did get some prints from the back door of the Kratt house. Not sure whose they are, though. They're not in the system. They're not Kratt's either, but they might prove helpful down the road. Also, the note seems to have been written on old paper, like maybe thirty years old. We thought that might be significant somehow. The ink used to write the note was a standard fine-tip black marker, the kind you can buy at any discount store. But the paper left us wondering."

"Really? That is interesting. Anything else?"

"Well, Sam is looking through all the paper stuff. I don't know what he found."

"Yeah, I'm going to get together with him this morning. Thanks, and let me know if anything else comes up."

"Will do." She clicked off.

His phone buzzed again.

"Jim, Luke here. Just wanted you to know we did find a significant amount of Versed in Kratt's blood. I doubt he'd have taken that much, even if it was prescribed. My thoughts are someone slipped it into something he drank before he was strangled."

"Hmm. Interesting. Thanks, Luke," Jim said.

Jim sat still, his mind swirling with the Kratt case. After a few moments, he got up and went to find Sam.

Sam was at his desk, focused on the task of sorting through the paper ephemera from the Kratt house. Jim walked in, found a chair, and sat down. The room smelled musty and seemed heavy with humidity from the rain outside. Papers were heaped across his desk, and smaller boxes leaned against the wall. Jim crossed his arms over his chest and propped an ankle on one knee.

"Have you found anything worthwhile in all this stuff?" he asked Sam, his eyes scanning the piles. Jim noticed Sam's hair was stylishly cut, his clothes surprisingly professional. *Leslie's having a positive influence,* he thought. *Maybe Jones will get off my case. The sooner, the better.*

Sam looked up and pursed his lips. "Maybe. Is there some reason this Kratt guy would have hung onto a *La Crosse Sentinel* newspaper clipping about the Christina Yelski disappearance that happened over forty years ago?" His hazel eyes studied Jim, waiting for his reaction.

Jim stared at him blankly. "I don't know. People hang onto stuff all the time for a lot of different reasons or for no reason at all. From the looks of it, he seemed to be something of a hoarder. What are you thinking?" Jim asked. He leaned back in his chair, waiting for Sam's explanation. *Here we go. Another one of his crazy theories.*

"What if the clippings numbered in the twenties? What would you say then?" Sam sat back and clasped his hands behind his head.

"Do they?"

"Yeah, twenty-two so far and counting," Sam told Jim.

"What? That is unusual." Jim got out of his chair and came around the desk. Sam had organized the clippings in chronological order from 1977 to 2016. They marched across the top of his desk like soldiers on parade. The sources varied from newspaper clippings to articles from the internet and local interest magazines. All had been printed from a computer printer. Suddenly Jim felt a glimmer of hope. *It might be a dead end, but it's something.*

"Was there a computer in the house? Maybe a laptop?" Jim asked.

"Nope. But any of this stuff you could find using a computer at the public library." Sam swept his hand above the papers in a broad gesture. "They have Wi-Fi and printers, too," he said. "I called the La Crosse Public Library. Kratt came in occasionally, did some research, and had things copied. The articles were inserted through these other documents, so I think Kratt kept searching for leads in the case, wondering if the police were figuring out Christina's disappearance. Then when he found an article, he would slip it in among his other paper collections. Helluva a lot of junk. No wonder people get buried under their stuff. I don't know, but that's the scenario that makes the most sense to me."

Jim chewed on his lip. He studied the collection intently. "The guy had some kind of obsession about the disappearance of this girl," Jim said as he sorted through the articles, stopping and reading briefly about things that interested him. Suddenly, it all flooded back into his memory.

Jim stopped reading, looked off into the distance, and thought back to October 1977. It was a long time ago, but he remembered exactly where he'd been when he heard about Christina Yelski, similar to the way older people remembered where they were and what they were doing when John Kennedy was assassinated or the way younger people today recalled where they were when the Trade Center bombings happened on September 11.

In 1977, Jim was eleven and in the sixth grade at Blair Middle School. He was sitting in the second row by the window in Mr. Harris' math class, where they were studying algebraic expressions and variables. Somebody had brought up the Yelski girl's disappearance in class. Mr. Harris allowed the class to discuss it for a few minutes, but he was too seasoned a veteran to let them get totally distracted from the math work in front of them.

Then Jim recalled seeing her photo in the *Sentinel* as he sprawled on the couch in the living room that same night. It had affected him profoundly because she was only a few years older than him. That event had rocked the secure world he'd inhabited with his parents and brother. He thought of the photo Paul had found in the locket. He stared at the girl's pretty likeness in the newspaper. *Was it the same person?* Several seconds passed.

"What's your take on this?" Jim asked, his eyes shifting back to

Sam. He ran his hand through his hair in a nervous gesture. Sam noticed his exhausted look.

"I could be mistaken, but who do you know that keeps a running file of an investigation into a cold case unless you knew the girl and wanted justice or were somehow involved in committing the crime? What other options are there?"

"Maybe he was going to write a best-selling true crime novel?" Jim said skeptically. He lifted his eyebrows and shrugged. Their eyes met.

"Not," they both said at the same time, shaking their heads.

"There's no indication he was a writer of any kind?" Jim asked. Sam shook his head in the negative. "Maybe the case just interested him in some way that we'll never know about," Jim suggested.

"Highly unlikely, Chief," Sam said, unconvinced. "The dates of these clippings stretch over forty-some years. That's more than simple curiosity."

"The newspaper clippings are significant in some way," Jim said. "Did Kratt know Christina? Did he witness the crime? Or was he involved in the disappearance, and somebody who knew about it gave Kratt the justice they thought he deserved?"

"That's what we don't know," Sam replied. "But it's also a possibility that these clippings are unrelated to Kratt's murder, and it was just some kind of crazy hobby." Sam thought a minute and shook his head again. "But I think this is more than a coincidence, and you know what you always say."

Jim looked at him curiously. "Careful with your use of "always" and "never." Most events don't conform to rules that are that simplistic." Jim waited, intensifying his stare at Sam, and then asked, "What do I always say?"

"There's no such thing as coincidences when it comes to murder," Sam finished, crossing his arms over his chest and leaning back in his office chair. He looked pleased at his conclusions.

Jim silently nodded his head in agreement. "We need to meet and get everybody on the same page." He leaned over the random papers that threatened to overtake Sam's desk. "Let's get this stuff on the board, Paul can tell us about the locket and the photo inside, and maybe we can start making some connections. We need to figure out some people to talk to." He looked at the clock. "Let's meet at one o'clock down the hall in the big classroom."

24

Paul had spent a good part of the morning researching the photography businesses listed in the yellow pages. In the La Crosse vicinity, thirteen landscape photographers and twenty-seven were identified as portrait photographers. Of those forty studios, twenty-two did not exist in the late 1970s. That left eighteen possibilities that might give them information about the locket photo. As he called each business on the list, he questioned them about the email he had sent yesterday with the partial photo found in the locket, but one after another purported no knowledge of the individuals in the photo. Not one identified the photo in the locket as even vaguely familiar. He was treated with a polite detachment by some and outright disdain by others until he finally slammed his fist on his desk in disgust.

Deciding to act on Higgins' suggestion to talk to Lois Heldrich, he drove out of the Vine Street parking lot at about eleven o'clock, passing the La Crosse Post Office on the way to the Heldrich studio. He swung onto Fifth Street, traveling south through traffic until he came to Winnebago, where the hubbub thinned. Along the street, spacious lawns of brilliant green were lined with massive hardwood trees that shaded the sidewalks. The thunderstorm was easing up, but a light rain was still falling. Heading east to the 1600 block, he came to the Heldrich Photography Studio.

The business was tucked behind a home that had dark natural cedar siding and cedar shake shingles. A small handcrafted wooden sign stood near the driveway, indicating the office hours of the photography studio. Bordered along the lot by a row of evergreens, both structures resembled English cottages, diminutive and charming. Paul hopped from his truck with the photo from the locket tucked in his jacket pocket. He trotted quickly down the cement driveway through the misting rain and entered the front door of the studio. Shaking the droplets of water from his jacket, he rang a little bell on the counter to announce his arrival. While he waited for someone to appear, he strolled around the studio studying the photographs that were tastefully displayed on the sand-colored walls; modern family portraits in sleek frames hung next to restored generational vignettes of immigrant families.

Promptly an older lady with silver-gray hair cut in a simple bob approached him with a friendly smile. She had a narrow face, and her bright green eyes were framed with a pair of artsy glasses that swooped up in a dramatic curve at the corners. Paul guessed her age to be mid-sixties.

"Can I help you?" she asked. She folded her hands on the counter and patiently waited. Paul flashed his ID. "Hi, you must be Lois."

She nodded. "Yes, I am. Is there something you needed?" she asked.

"I'm Detective Paul Saner with the La Crosse Sheriff's Department. Lt. Jim Higgins suggested your services. I have a few questions for you about a case we're working on."

"Oh, yes. I know Jim. I did some work for his wife, Carol. He used to live in the neighborhood with his first wife, Margie, over on Cass Street. I'm so glad to see he remarried. He's such a great guy. I restored some vintage photos for Carol, which is my specialty, and sometimes I help people identify relatives in the photos. It's kind of a passion of mine."

Paul reached into his suit jacket and withdrew the photograph he'd discovered in the gold locket. He laid it down, and Lois reached underneath the counter for a magnifying glass. She examined it carefully.

Paul began to explain. "We're curious about several things. First, who are these people? Identifying them would give us a huge break," Paul said. "Second, where was the photo taken? And third, when was the photo taken? Any of that information would give us a direction in the investigation."

Lois looked up. "Well, I'm still in the process of transferring my photography to digital storage. It's a huge job. I started in the business part-time about forty years ago back in the mid-seventies. I've been working backward in the process, and I'm now starting on photos from the late eighties." She took another look at the photograph. "If this was taken in the La Crosse area, then negatives should exist somewhere. I will certainly look through mine. But I would recommend you send out the photo to every photographer in the area that was in business in the seventies and ask them to check their negatives to see if they took this photo."

"I've spent the entire morning doing that. I emailed all the photography studios around here that existed in the seventies yesterday and then followed up with a phone call this morning. No one recalls these two people."

She smiled when she saw Paul's discouraged look. "Well, that was a shot in the dark. Are you telling me I'm your last great hope of identifying these people?"

"Yeah. I guess you're it. Any idea when it might have been taken?" Paul asked.

"Well, if you look at the necklines and style of the clothes, it suggests the seventies.

"Okay. Any other ideas?" Paul asked.

Lois shook her head. "I'll work on it on my end, but I think you should go public—Facebook, Snapchat, Instagram. Someone in this area might recognize these people. Let me make a copy." When she'd returned from the back room, she gently slid the photo across the counter toward Paul.

"Thanks for your help. If you discover anything, just call me," Paul said as he laid his card on the counter.

"I certainly will," Lois said smiling, adding, "Go public; it's your best bet."

25

By one o'clock in the afternoon, Jim and the team were gathered around a whiteboard in a classroom on the third floor of the law enforcement center. They discussed their discoveries and updated the board with photos, facts, and theories about the Kratt murder. The multiple newspaper clippings were taped on the board in chronological order. Motive and opportunity were still vague. Jim felt the passage of time ticking by without any substantial leads.

Mostly his thoughts were of Lillie and the scenarios that could happen. Even as he imagined them, he knew the frustration of trying to predict the random actions of a burned-out drug dealer, but he couldn't seem to control the scenes that kept appearing in his mind, flashing a warning like heat lightning before the arrival of a violent storm.

"When I talked to Lois Heldrich this morning, she recommended we go on social media with the photo. She thought somebody might recognize the couple," Paul started. "I checked with the photographers who were working in the area in the seventies and early eighties. No one remembered the kids."

"Let's put it out there on the web," Jim said. "Paul, you take care of that and get it to the TV stations and to the *Sentinel*."

"What if someone else involved in the original crime has been targeted by the killer? Releasing the photo to the public could motivate them to kill again," DeDe commented. Everyone listened intently. Sam stared uneasily at the floor, deep in thought. Jim shuffled nervously on his feet. *Dealing with criminals was a total crap shoot*, he thought—*still was and always would be.*

He turned to Leslie and DeDe. "That might be a risk we have to take. How are the cold cases looking? Are there any that are standing out?"

"We started looking at cases that were within a hundred-mile radius of La Crosse that might be worth considering. We specifically looked at cases where the victim was female and found wearing jewelry. We thought the necklace suggested that," Leslie explained. "Do you want me to give you the details now? There are about ten cases that seem to fit the parameters of our evidence."

"Just tell us about the Yelski girl's disappearance for now since Sam found those clippings and articles at the Kratt house," Jim said, frowning. "We don't believe those news articles he saved were a coincidence."

Leslie paged through her notebook, stopping at the notes she'd taken about the disappearance of the La Crosse teenager.

"Okay, here it is," she said, moving her finger down the page. "Christina Yelski was babysitting at Professor Morris Blackman's home the evening of October 8, 1977." Leslie continued scrolling down the page of notes. "Neighbors heard a couple of screams and went to investigate. The doors were locked, but Christina didn't answer, so they put in a call to the La Crosse Police Department. When police arrived, they forced entry and found the two-year-old Blackman child sleeping soundly in his crib. Christina was gone. A bloody trail upstairs led to the basement, where someone had broken the window to get into the house. Police concluded that Christina had been taken out of the basement window. One of her shoes was found near the curb on Sunset Street—that's on the south side—and a hair barrette was found in the Blackmans' yard. There were no witnesses, although many people in the area were interviewed."

Leslie looked up, noticing the deadly quiet in the room, everyone imagining the girl's horrific experience. Paul stared into space; he'd gone somewhere else thinking about Melody wearing a gold locket for her sixteenth birthday, going missing, and never seeing her again. A sense of horror and then anger filled his chest.

"Did you want me to continue?" Leslie asked softly.

Jim blinked hard, swallowed, and nodded. "Yeah, let's hear the rest of it," he said softly. He leaned his haunches on the table and crossed his arms, giving Leslie his attention.

"Over the next several months, two more pieces of Christina's clothing were found; a wide headband that matched the long-sleeved shirt she wore that night was found on County Road Y in Vernon County near Avalanche, and her blood-stained underwear was discovered by a county worker when he was patrolling along Seas Branch Road. Since then, no traces of the girl have ever been found."

DeDe Deverioux had been silent during the litany of the girl's ordeal. Now she stood up, stuck up her index finger, and said, "I'll be right back." She walked briskly from the room down the hallway and returned a few minutes later with a piece of paper in her hand.

"This piece of information is from an interview conducted by Vernon County Sheriff Tim Landry in 2005," DeDe said, glancing at the date at the top of the transcription. "A man in a bar in Readstown was overheard by the bartender referring to a recent suicide in Readstown as the guy who was, and I quote, 'involved in the Yelski thing,' unquote. That's what the bartender said he heard. The bartender was a man named Rollie Gander. He relayed this information to the Vernon County sheriff. Seems that someone else knows something about the Yelski girl's disappearance, sir," DeDe finished.

"I want you girls to follow up with this Gander guy and see where that goes."

DeDe nodded as she looked across the table at Leslie. "Sure. We can probably do that this afternoon."

Paul's cell vibrated in his pocket. He stepped away from the group and answered. Everyone talked quietly, and finally, Jim ended the discussion and looked at everyone expectantly.

"All right. Let's make a plan. There are people out there," Jim pointed to the window noticing the brilliant sunshine, "who know something about this crime and the Yelski incident. The two may be connected. We need to work it from the beginning—witnesses, evidence, law enforcement who dealt with the crime, relatives, anyone who might still be alive who remembers details of the event."

Paul interrupted as he slipped his phone into his pocket. "Chief, one more thing about the photo. I thought from the beginning that the girl in the locket and the photos in the newspaper articles of Christina looked like the same person to me. That was Lois on the phone." Jim locked eyes with him. "She said the photo was taken with a 1977 Pentax K1000—a rather expensive camera that took very good pictures. The paper used was something called Panalure paper—a bromide paper, very sensitive."

"How does she know that?" Jim asked, sitting up a little straighter.

"She took the picture. She has the negative and the camera. The girl in the photo is Christina Yelski." Paul let that sit for a moment. Everyone stood stock still. Silence reigned for several seconds.

"I don't need to tell you what a break this is. This is huge," Jim finished, shifting his eyes from Paul.

Paul nodded in agreement. "Lois has prepared a full-size photo from the negative. I'm going back over there to pick it up."

"Damn. This is big," Sam whispered. "A forty-year-old crime that suddenly reared its ugly head again. Unbelievable."

Leslie remembered Sam's theories. *Where does he get those ideas?* she thought.

"Well, people, we have a working theory," Jim said. "The evidence we have seems to suggest that Sylvester Kratt was murdered because he knew something about the Yelski girl's disappearance, or he was involved in her murder somehow. That's what the facts seem to suggest, but keep an open mind about other possibilities when you talk to people. We've got a direction. Let's not waste it."

26

When the meeting broke up, Sam and Paul decided to go to the Yelski home on Sunset Street to try and recreate the scene of the Yelski girl's disappearance. They'd reviewed the investigators' notes and decided to look at the neighborhood's layout and surroundings. Even though forty years had passed, the neighborhood footprint was very similar to when the crime had been committed.

"The disappearance of the Yelski girl resulted in the largest manhunt in the history of La Crosse. Sounds like they pulled out all the stops in order to try and find her," Sam said. He loosened his tie, pulled it up over his head, and threw it on the seat of the Jeep. "Boy, I could go for a cold beer right about now."

"If someone did that to Melody, I'd kill the bastard," Paul said vehemently. His face was dark with anger. He glanced at Sam and noticed his shocked look. "What?"

Sam's eyebrows lifted. "You'd have to find him first. The parents of this girl must have gone through hell and back. And that's an ordeal I wouldn't wish on any parent," he said reasonably, although he appreciated Paul's sentiment.

"Well, wait til you're a parent. Then you'll understand."

"I'm waiting. A little too soon, yet."

Sam thought about having children with Leslie, but he was still wrapping his head around being married. Sometimes his chest tingled when he thought about how much he loved Lez. It wasn't just her physical beauty, although that was certainly a blessing. He loved her for her tenacity—that stubborn refusal she seemed to possess in the face of overwhelming odds. She'd survived a horrific attack by her former Army boyfriend when he had imprisoned her in a wooden box for over eighteen hours. Sam realized he was flexing his jaw just thinking about Wade Bennett. He relaxed and took in a deep breath. He attributed Leslie's survival to prayers and God's protective hand, although he still couldn't understand why God had let her suffer so long. The whole experience had left her with deep-seated emotional wounds. Now, as her husband, he frequently had to mop up the results of that. But he was glad to do it.

The furious rain that had blanketed the region during the morning hours had let up, and the clouds showed patches of blue poking through. The wind was blowing in gusts, and huge droplets of rain from the trees splattered onto Sam's windshield. The streets were wet and slick. Sam swerved here and there to avoid several rain-filled potholes.

"Doesn't the city ever fix those holes?" Paul complained.

"Call the mayor and complain. I hear he's pretty progressive. Maybe he'll listen to you. You're a taxpayer, but I doubt you'll get very far."

Losey Boulevard was busy with traffic. As he approached the intersection of Losey and State Highway 33, he noticed a familiar figure drifting through the abandoned Kmart parking lot. He seemed to be on the verge of falling down, but his wobbling gait continued in a generally forward direction.

"What are you doing?" Paul asked as Sam turned onto 33 and then cruised into the Kmart parking lot and killed the engine on the Jeep.

"Gotta talk to one of my informants. Just wait here a minute," Sam said, opening the door. He walked toward a man hunched over

SUE BERG

as if hunting for something he'd lost, shuffling lazily toward the street.

As Sam approached the man, he lifted his hand in greeting. "Hey, Marcellus. What's the haps?"

"Nothin' happenin'. Just making for my woman's house over on Barlow. Whadda you want?" he sneered. His eyes wandered subversively past Sam to the traffic on the street. His dark hair was dirty, squashed down on his head with a Menard's brimmed hat. Sam noticed his unlaced shoes, bare ankles, and ripped jeans.

"Are you hungry?" Sam asked, offering him a Snickers candy bar from his pocket.

"What? You my keeper now? Why'd I be hungry? My woman's a good cook." His eyes finally met Sam's in a nervous flitting glare and then slid away. The man's brain cells had been cooked with a host of illegal substances. Conversations with him were brief and tended to stay on the surface of things. It was like inching a jig next to a bass and waiting to see if anything would strike.

"Heard anything about Maddog Pierson being in town?" Sam asked, slipping the candy bar back into his pocket. The man swayed ominously as if he was going to topple on the pavement, then he exerted some self-control and straightened up. Sam fixed a perceptive stare on him. *Trying to maintain eye contact with Marcellus was impossible*, Sam thought. His eyes bolted away and careened everywhere else, looking for a place to land, everywhere except Sam's face.

"Who's Maddog?" Marcellus asked, ramming his fists in his pockets.

Sam lifted his hands in front of him in disbelief and shook his head. "Don't give me that crap. Everybody doing any dealing knows Maddog Pierson. In Wisconsin, he's to the drug world as beer is to the bar scene. Have you seen him around?"

Marcellus began shuffling away, but Sam stepped in front of him, leaning down to look into his eyes. "Look me in the eye and tell me you haven't seen him or heard he was in town."

"Why you think I should help you? I don't got to do nothin' for you, honky man."

"Come on, Marcellus. It's a simple question," Sam said, trying to hide his impatience.

Marcellus looked away, watched the traffic for a few seconds, then said, "The word on the street is he's looking for some kid, but I don't go stickin' my nose in other people's business," he snarled, his tone surly.

"Where'd you see him last?" Sam asked, putting a little grit in it.

"I don' remember. I already tol' you that," he said, trying to hold Sam's stare. He sighed when he realized Sam wasn't going to give up. "Last time I seen him was on the south side in an alley back by that rehab center behind the hospital," A bead of spittle landed on his unshaven beard and sat there.

Sam knew he was lying. In fact, he doubted Marcellus would recognize the truth if it materialized into human flesh and came up and shook his hand. "Where'd you see him last?" he repeated.

"Don' need to talk to you, man." Marcellus made a stumbling move to get around him.

Sam held up his hands and began backing away. "You're right. You don't need to talk to me, and the next time you get hauled in, I don't need to come to your rescue, bud," Sam said, turning and walking back to the truck. A few seconds passed. Sam was almost to the Jeep when Marcellus shouted after him.

"Might be at the La Crosse city harbor behind Lutheran. Heard he's got a boat there."

"Got it," Sam said, waving briefly over his head, walking toward the Jeep.

Climbing in the truck, Sam fired up the engine, thought again, and grabbed his phone in the console. He punched his speed dial and waited.

"Higgins."

"Chief. The news on the street is that Maddog has a boat docked at the La Crosse Municipal Harbor behind Gundersen."

"Okay. I'll check it out."

"Be careful. You might want to wear a vest. Maybe take some backup with you. Maddog'll blast you if he feels threatened at all," Sam warned.

"Got it. Thanks." Higgins hung up.

Sam drove out of the lot and turned left on 32nd, then right until he pulled up to the former Blackman residence on Sunset Street. It was a typical residential area, filled with homes built in the sixties. Sam was sure it had been lively with young families at one time. Now it seemed deserted, but it was early afternoon, and most people were still at work.

Sam and Paul got out of the truck and approached the house. The residence was well-kept, a ranch-style home with a field stone fireplace located conspicuously in the front of the house, flanked on each side by a large window. The street and nearby houses were quiet. The house seemed deserted; the windows were dark with pulled shades. No one appeared to be home. Sam rang the front doorbell and waited. Nothing.

"Well, this was a waste of time," Paul said, rolling up the sleeves on his dress shirt.

"We can try later," Sam said, stepping away from the entrance.

They climbed back in the Jeep and began to drive away. Suddenly Sam caught a glimpse of something literally buried in the street. He braked, pulled over to the curb, and shut off the Jeep.

"What now?" Paul asked, leaning out of the window. "Another rabbit trail?"

"Rabbit trails sometimes lead to other things, buddy," Sam said circumspectly. He walked into the street and knelt down to inspect the filled pothole. Paul came up behind him, leaning down, peering over his shoulder.

"What is it?" he asked as a group of teenagers flew by in an SUV, the radio blaring hip-hop into the air.

"Don't know but look at the date—10/8/77. That's the date of Christina's disappearance." Sam stared off into the distance. "Somebody filled a pothole on the street where Yelski was last seen as a tribute to her."

"You don't know that. That's a pretty big assumption, a gigantic leap. Not too logical. But, it is strange. Who does this kinda stuff?"

"Don't know, but we better find out. Somebody's on a mission. Whether it's pointing us toward the killer or reminding everyone the crime's not solved, or for some other weird reason, this is probably important."

Sam took out his cell phone and took a few pictures of the mosaic. Then he walked to the curb and stood on the sidewalk while he dialed La Crosse City Police. He finally got through to Chief Tamara Pedretti and explained what they'd found.

"It's a pothole filled with the date of Christina Yelski's disappearance?" Tamara asked, incredulous. "How do you find this stuff, Sam?"

Sam rubbed the side of his face. "Well, I guess it mostly finds me. The pothole is filled with a mosaic. Actually quite well done. Do you know who does stuff like that, or is this just a one-off?"

"I'll check around with my officers. Maybe somebody knows something. I'll call you back. Hopefully, within a few minutes."

"Right." Sam hung up. A few minutes later, his phone rang.

"Birkstein."

"Sam. The artist is a guy over on Ninth Street South. He's a CPA and has a business in his home. Some guy named LaSalle. My secretary says he does mosaics around the city. He recently did some murals at the Onalaska Clinic and in the Logistics Health lobby. His latest romp in the art world is potholes. Go figure. Good luck," Chief Pedretti told him.

"Hey, thanks." Turning to Paul as he put his phone in his pocket, he said, "Let's go see the pothole artist."

"The what?"

"Never mind. Just get in the Jeep," he said.

They drove through traffic across town while Sam told Paul about the pothole artist. He turned on Jackson, then turned on Ninth Street.

"There it is," Paul said, pointing to a sign on the lawn that said LaSalle Tax Preparation and Financial Planning.

Sam pulled up to the curb and parked in the shade of an ash tree. They stepped out and made their way around the side entrance of a two-story home and walked into the office. A balding middle-aged man stood by an open filing cabinet dressed in a yellow dress shirt, blue print tie, and navy trousers. He looked up at them and flashed a friendly smile.

"Hi. Can I help you?" he asked, closing the file cabinet.

Paul and Sam flashed their IDs and introduced themselves.

"We have some questions about a pothole mosaic on Sunset Street over on the south side," Sam began. "The dates displayed in the pothole may be important to an investigation we're conducting. Could you tell us about it, Mr. LaSalle?" Sam watched the man carefully.

"Hmm, the pothole police, eh?" he asked jokingly. Then in a friendly way, he continued. "Call me Zeke." He stretched out his hand and shook with Paul and Sam. He had an open, honest face and a good-natured demeanor. "Tell you what. Why don't we go downstairs to my basement studio, so I can look up the records on that one. I've done quite a few now throughout the city, and I can't remember the details of each one," he said as he maneuvered his way around the two men and led them through the kitchen to the basement stairs.

"Watch your head," he warned as he descended a narrow flight of stairs, turned on a landing, and entered a large basement room that had been converted into an art studio. One wall was filled with open shelves crammed with small baby food jars and pint canning jars full of stone and glass. Narrow windows near the top of the wall provided some illumination though it was still dark. Zeke flipped on a light. A long old wooden table was covered with newspaper and grouting tools. Other utensils lay haphazardly on the tabletop, along with a roll of cheesecloth next to the tools.

"It's dusty down here. Drives my wife nuts," he said casually, grinning to himself. "She's at work. She's a nurse at St. Francis."

A drawing for the next street art mosaic design lay on the table. Throughout his studio, sketches of previous pothole mosaics hung helter-skelter from the wall where they had been attached with duct tape. The wet smell of dirt lingered in the air. Plastic plates filled with colored marble and glass sat on another table near the work surface. Next to the table, a large, debarked tree stump was strewn with a steel-headed mallet and several broken and chipped pieces of marble. Seeing Sam looking the stump over, Zeke explained.

"That's where I chip my pieces of glass and stone to fit the images I make," he explained. "I started my career in advertising, but I couldn't stand the pace of it," he continued as he opened a beat-up filing cabinet and took out a folder. "So I got my license in accounting and started my own business so I could do art when I wanted to. And lately, this pothole thing has really taken off. I'm even getting calls from larger cities like Milwaukee, Green Bay, and the Twin Cities."

Sam liked the feel of the studio. It had a relaxed vibe. He could see Leslie doing something artsy like this. "So, how much time do you spend on your art?"

"Oh, it depends. Some weeks, maybe five to ten hours. Other times as much as twenty or thirty, but that depends on my tax work and accounting load. It's not tax season now, so I've had more time to do mosaics."

Zeke shuffled through the paperwork in the manila folder and pulled out a yellowed piece of paper. "Oh, yeah. I remember this one now," he said softly as he stepped over to a map of the city of La Crosse. He pointed to Sunset Street, where an X16 marked the spot.

"That one was odd."

"Oh yeah? How's that?" Paul asked, giving Sam a perplexing look.

"The donor wanted that specific date—10/8/77—and it had to be installed in a pothole on Sunset Street as close to the 697 residence as possible. Very strange. Plus, the donor didn't leave his name, but he left me five hundred bucks cash in a plain envelope. I only charge three hundred, but it must have been important. He wanted to be sure I did it, I guess. He specified the date. That's it," he said, looking over at Paul and Sam. He handed the yellowed scrap of paper to Paul, who'd put on a blue latex glove.

"You keep saying 'he.' Was the customer a man or woman?" Sam asked.

Zeke turned his mouth down at the corners. "Don't know. Couldn't tell from the note."

"Do you have a security camera on your property?" Paul asked as he inspected the paper.

"No, this neighborhood's been pretty safe so far," Zeke answered. "I haven't felt the need to have one."

"Looks like the same kind of paper we found at the murder scene," Paul said.

"Murder?" Zeke said, his eyes widening.

"We're investigating the murder of Sylvester Kratt over on George Street last Saturday evening. You might have heard about it on the news. We found something at the murder scene that used this kind of paper. We're going to have to bag this as evidence," Sam said, pointing to Paul, who was holding the paper between his thumb and index finger.

"Just wait. I'll get you a bag upstairs," Zeke said as he took the steps by two and returned with a baggie. Paul slipped the paper into it.

"Can you tell us anything else about this mosaic?" Sam asked.

Zeke studied the floor intently. "Well, I have a drop box out by the entrance of my tax office for pothole orders. You probably noticed it when you came in."

Paul and Sam nodded.

"People leave me their information, and then I contact them about the project they want to do, and we go from there. This one just listed a date with the money. No contact information. So, I did it and installed it."

"When did you get this request?" Paul asked.

Zeke picked up the folder from the table. He scrolled down the page using his finger to find the request. "I got it on August 28, and I completed the project and installed it just a couple of days ago on September 11. It was pretty simple—just numbers."

Sam jotted the information down in his memo notebook.

"Okay, that helps. Let us know if you hear anything back from this person," he said as he handed him his card.

They thanked Zeke, trooped back up the stairs, and left by the side entrance.

"Whaddya think of that?" Paul asked Sam when they were driving back to Vine Street.

"Somebody's leaving some pretty obvious clues," Sam said, resting his arm on the open driver's window. "First the note at the murder scene and now a message in a pothole. If we can figure out who's leaving them, we'll have accomplished something."

"Good luck with that," Paul said sourly, slouching in the seat.

27

By four o'clock, the team had gleaned little in the way of hard, circumstantial evidence. They possessed a young girl's necklace, a note written on yellowed paper, the instructions for the pothole written on paper similar to the note found at the murder scene, fingerprints of an unknown person at the Kratt house, and the records of the interviews conducted after the Yelski girl's disappearance. Neighbors of Kratt had not noticed anything out of the ordinary at the home the night of the strangulation. For all practical purposes, there had been no witnesses to the murder.

Despite the break by Lois Heldrich, who'd identified the girl in the photo as Christina Yelski, there was little to go on. They didn't know who the young man was in the photo with her. Sam and Paul had discovered the puzzling mosaic in the pavement near the Blackman home on Sunset Street. Interesting, but it didn't bolster anyone's confidence that the disappearance of Yelski or the murder of Kratt were linked. After Sam and Paul's interview with Zeke LaSalle, the mosaic note was taken to CSI techs to be analyzed to see if the paper matched the note found at the murder scene. There might be a connection between the two notes, although no one was sure about that yet. Right now, everything was conjecture and pie-in-the-sky theory.

"So now we're getting messages in potholes?" Jim asked, cutting a piece of apple with his jackknife and popping it in his mouth. His eyes blinked in confused doubt. "Don't let this get out to the public. I can see the headlines already, and it gives me nightmares." He held up his hands and did quotes in the air. "'Detectives Get Secret Messages Buried in Blacktop.' That'll earn us a lot of points with the public. It definitely doesn't sound professional," he mumbled grumpily as he chewed on the apple.

"Gotta go with your gut, Chief. To me, the pothole seems totally random and goofy, but it is a message of some kind. Whether it's a tribute or another tidbit left for us to chew on, I don't know, but it's pretty weird," Paul remarked, standing with his hands in his pockets.

"We've got to consider that it might be the killer's way of distracting us from clues we already have," Sam commented. "Confusing us. Leading us away from what really matters."

Jim shook his head. "Don't worry. I'm already confused enough for everybody." He was standing behind his desk, feeling like his mind had turned to mush. "I don't know what to think of it. Did you pick up that photo from Lois?" he asked.

"Yeah, it's in my office. But I already know where the house is," Sam answered cockily.

"How do you know that?" Paul asked.

Jim looked over at Sam. "Yeah, how do you know that?" he asked.

"The Yelskis lived near the university over on State Street. That picture of Christina is taken in front of Yelskis' house. I've driven by the house lots of times on my way to work, but we need to identify the guy in the photo. Maybe a boyfriend. There's only one other sister, right?" Sam asked.

"Yep. I'm going to give her a call," Jim suggested, throwing his apple core into the wastebasket. "Let's go look at this photograph," he said, turning and marching down the hall. Sam and Paul followed him. Entering the office, Sam picked up a large white envelope, opened the clasp, and pulled out the eight-by-ten photo.

The details of the tall three-story Victorian house were evident—gingerbread fretwork around the porch and the eaves, a stunning turret, and an expansive wraparound porch on the north and west sides of the home. Lilacs and hydrangeas bloomed in profusion beneath the porch railings, and the small postage stamp yard was groomed with the precise hand of someone who understood how to enhance a property's value using shrubbery and flowering bushes. In front of the house, Christina and her mystery beau stood on the yard arm in arm, their smiling faces reflecting an affection that seemed to go beyond friendship.

"You know, I think I recognize that place, too," Jim said, letting his eyes wander over the details of the home. "We lived in the Cass Street neighborhood for about ten years, and we used to pass this place on our walks with the twins." Turning to Sam and Paul, he continued, "I want you to get the physical evidence from the Yelski crime from Lez and DeDe. Let's get some DNA tests started on the clothing and see what's there. Maybe we can pull something out of it that will help give us a direction. I'm going to call the Yelski sister."

"We'll get on it, Chief. Good luck with the sister," Paul said as he put the photo back in the envelope.

"We haven't had much of that yet," Jim said gloomily as he disappeared down the hall. Entering his office, he walked to his desk, sat down, and perused the file folder with the Yelski case until he found the name of the sister. He found it interesting that she had continued to keep in contact with the police. Then he called information.

"I need the number of a Professor Margretta Martin in Eugene, Oregon," he said.

He heard the standard "Just one moment, please" response, waited, and then wrote the number on his desk pad. Then he punched the number into his cell. Leaning back in his chair, he swiveled toward the narrow window, noticing the crisp fall day. Overhead the brilliant blue sky was filled with puffy white cotton-like clouds that were forming ice cream cone scoops in the sky. In the distance, the trees in the city and along the towering bluffs had taken on a slight wash of fall pigments. In a couple of weeks, everything would be exploding in a riot of fall color—fields of golden corn swaying in the warm wind, glowing orange pumpkins lying fat and lazy at farm stands, and bittersweet vines clinging tenaciously in ditches and along fence rows.

"Professor Martin," a pleasant voice said.

When Jim heard the voice, he sat up attentively and turned back to his desk, resting his elbows on the desktop.

"Hello. This is Lt. Jim Higgins from the La Crosse Sheriff's Department. I was hoping you could give me a few moments of your time to talk about your sister Christina's disappearance. Recently, some new events here have brought the crime back into the spotlight, so to speak." Jim waited, wondering what it would feel like to have a wound break open again, to have another reason to hope, to have another grasp at a conclusion and a possibility of justice. Silence followed. Finally, Margretta spoke.

"Oh, my. I didn't expect this. I'm sorry—you've caught me off guard, I'm afraid." Her voice was unassuming and delicate.

"I apologize. There's no easy way to approach this subject, which I'm sure is very painful for you. I'm sorry, ma'am. I didn't mean to upset you," Jim repeated sincerely.

"Could you fill me in on what's been going on?" Margretta asked softly.

"Sure, I'd be glad to," Jim said. He told her about the circumstances of the Kratt strangulation, the gold locket with the picture, and the odd note left next to the body. When he was finished, the line was quiet.

"This is unbelievable," Margretta said softly. Jim could imagine trying to take in all the events that had happened this last week from the perspective of the lost girl's sister.

"I realize this is probably a terrible shock. You must have some awful memories of your sister's abduction," he said sympathetically.

"Unless you lived through something like that, it's hard to relate. My memories of my sister are still precious to me. She was a lovely, intelligent, caring person," Margretta started. But she couldn't hold it together and began to weep softly over the phone. How could she tell him of the years of psychiatric care she'd received to help her cope with her loss, the years of tormented guilt, wondering if there was something she could have done to prevent the awful event? How could she tell him of the beauty of her younger sister, how she looked up to her and tried to model her life after her? All to have it come crashing down in a moment in time on a beautiful Wisconsin October evening when her whole life loomed in front of her, laden with promise and plans?

After a moment, Margretta regained her composure and started again. Her voice was subdued but stronger now, and although she couldn't see the caller, she knew her words were creating a bridge from her dead sister to an investigator 1,500 miles away.

"She had dreams of becoming a nuclear physicist. She wanted to work in the NASA space program, and she had the smarts to do it. The mystery of her death and disappearance has haunted me ever since the day it happened. Anything I can do to help bring her killer to justice—just ask." As she'd talked over the phone, a determination and a gritty resolve came through in her voice.

"We really appreciate that," Jim said. "If you don't mind, I'm going to ask some questions that might help us sort out some things on our end. Do you have time for that?" Jim asked.

"Actually, I would love to fly out to La Crosse and talk to you in person," Margretta offered.

"Can you arrange your work schedule to do that on such short notice?" Jim asked skeptically.

"I'm the head of my department. It's not a problem. I haven't taken a vacation in over ten years. I have over one hundred personal leave days built up. Believe me, it's not a problem," she repeated in a voice used to giving orders.

Jim smiled. She sounded authoritarian, but there was a hint of Midwestern practicality beneath the words. "If that works for you, we'd be grateful for the help, although I have to tell you that you would be on a consultant basis only."

"In other words, you're calling the shots," she said bluntly.

"Absolutely. It won't work any other way."

"No apologies necessary. I totally understand, and I can live with that. It will take me a day or so to get my calendar cleared and schedule a flight to La Crosse. But I should arrive no later than Sunday. How does that sound?"

"Great. We'll look forward to it." They exchanged contact information, and when Jim hung up, he felt a pressure release in his chest. Maybe Margretta could shed some information on the original crime that would lead them down a different path.

28

Carol had finished her office work at the morgue by four-thirty, and she picked up Henri at the daycare center shortly before five. As she drove through Chipmunk Coulee in the fall afternoon, the beautiful day was lazy with bright sunshine, a blue sky, and the smell of corn drying in the air. But it was lost on her. She barely noticed the crisp air that wafted through her partially opened window. Carol braked hard when a pheasant flew up along the roadside, its burnished gold and red feathers flashing in the brown roadside grass. She accelerated again as patches of shadow and sun flitted across her windshield. Although little Henri babbled happily in his car seat, Carol's thoughts were far away, a scenario playing in her mind—one that she couldn't control.

In the past few days, she found it almost impossible to stay calm and focused on the tasks at hand when she thought about Maddog shadowing them. Some notorious criminal was making plans to steal Lillie away from them, and the very thought toppled her reasoning power like a wrecking ball and left her breathless and scared. She guessed most parents would feel the same way and took comfort in that. Since they'd developed their plan, Carol felt more composed, but her determination to protect Lillie shifted with her moods, especially when she let her thoughts run ahead of her. Confronting a hardened criminal was not in her skill set, but she counted on her tiger mom to roar to life if Maddog appeared anywhere near their home.

She slowed and pulled up to the mailbox on the opposite side of the road, unclasped the latch, took out the mail, and threw it on the front seat. Turning into the driveway, she punched the garage door opener and drove into the yawning darkened space. Lifting Henri from his car seat, she grabbed the diaper bag and the mail from the front seat, anxious to get inside and begin preparations for supper. Her hands were full, so she probably wouldn't have noticed the binoculars lying outside on the threshold to the hallway entry from the garage, but the note attached to them caught her eye. She set Henri down and grabbed the binoculars and note.

Hello. I found these binoculars back by the rocks when I was cleaning up some stray brush. Sincerely, Tom

At the top of the note was the lawn care agency's logo—Midwest Landscape Services of La Crosse.

Carol clasped the note in her hands. The binoculars burned like a torch held against her skin. She pushed down the urge to panic and call Jim. *No, he'll be home soon anyway,* she thought. Taking Henri inside, she laid the mail on the buffet in the dining room along with the binoculars and the note and walked into the kitchen. *Carry on,* she thought. *Jim'll know what to do.*

Meanwhile, Jim had stopped at Blooms Galore on Third Street, his favorite floral shop. Walking into the little boutique, he blinked rapidly, his eyes adjusting from the brilliant sunshine outside to the fluorescent lighting inside.

"Oh, Lt. Higgins! So nice to see you again," a friendly young woman said, looking up from her work. "May I help you?"

Cut flowers, the trimmings of leaves and stems, a spool of florist wire, and a pair of sharp shears were scattered on a worktable behind the counter with a pitcher of water nearby. Jim liked coming here because it reminded him of the little shops they'd visited along the

Champs Elysee in Paris on their honeymoon. Displayed on shelves above the worktable were rows of vases—some in pastels and cut glass, others in bold colors and interesting shapes.

Jim eyed the vases and pointed to a dazzling crystal vase. "Nice to see you, too, Ingrid. I'd like a dozen yellow roses in that vase, please, and maybe add some of those purple irises."

"Mmm, you have good taste," Ingrid commented as she headed for the cooler. She reached for the roses, the irises, a bunch of greenery, and the baby's breath. As she arranged the flowers, she said, "There are cards for a message. Is this for delivery, or will you take it with you now?"

"I'll take it with me, thanks," Jim said. "And I'll deliver the message in person. No need for a card." He smiled broadly. He laid a hundred-dollar bill on the counter and grabbed the vase. The young girl yelled thank you as Jim went back out onto the bustling street.

Walking to his Suburban, he felt hopeful. He supposed it was naive to believe that yellow roses could actually make the world seem brighter and more optimistic, but at this moment, it's what he wanted to believe. As a cop, he knew the Kratt murder was far from being solved, and the Yelski girl's disappearance seemed to be muddying the waters. Maddog had failed in his efforts so far, and he thanked God for his protective care. Going home on a beautiful fall day to a family who loved him and cherished him made the surreptitious nature of his work recede into the background, even if only for a couple of hours.

Walking through the door from the garage a little after five, he could smell something delicious, filling the house with a wonderful aroma.

He yelled, "Hi, babe. I'm home!" He walked into the kitchen and came up behind Carol, kissing her on the neck. She pivoted and leaned against the counter, her warm brown eyes turning up to him. Her face was flushed from the heat of the stove, and her eyes had a luminous, shining quality that made Jim glad she was in his life.

Eyeing the flowers in his hand, she kissed him affectionately.

"Oh, they're gorgeous, Jim. What's the occasion? It's not our anniversary yet," she said as Jim set the bouquet on the counter.

"Isn't love enough of a reason?" he asked, leaning against her body, and planting a kiss on her mouth.

"Mmm, that was nice," she said, enjoying the saltiness of his lips. She pushed against him from the counter, picked up the flowers, and set them on the buffet in the dining room. Then she came back to the stove.

"Love's the best reason there is for giving flowers," she said. She stopped, then with a little smile playing on her lips, she said, "To see a world in a grain of sand and heaven in a wildflower, hold infinity in the palm of your hand and eternity in an hour."

Jim returned her smile. "William Blake. Very good, honey. Not only are you a fabulous cook, but you quote poetry, too. Can't lose on that deal."

"Learned that in fifth grade. It's kinda corny, but somehow it just stuck. So, how're things going with the investigation?"

Jim leaned against the counter as he began talking. "Slow, but we had an odd thing happen today." He told her about the pothole mosaic.

Stirring the gravy, she leaned over and adjusted the heat on the burner as she listened. "I think I've heard about that guy or read about him in the paper. Here's a heads up—that pothole stuff might just be some ruse to get you distracted and off track."

"That's exactly what Sam said."

She rapped the wooden spoon against the kettle. "You'll be careful, won't you, honey?" she asked, a frown wrinkling her forehead.

"As careful as you can be when dealing with miscreants," he said, spearing a pickle from the jar on the counter and crunching on it. "You can't fix stupid, and most criminals I've met aren't exceedingly smart, although I'm sure there are some who are." He walked to the fridge, opened the door, and pulled out a Leinie's.

"Can you set the table? This is just about ready. And then get the kids from the backyard. Ask Sara to join us, too," Carol said.

After the evening meal and bedtime rituals were over and the kids were in bed, Carol and Jim sat on the patio around a cozy fire he had built in their outdoor fireplace. Sara had retreated to her basement apartment and had pulled the blinds on the patio door. The evening was hushed; the birds had quieted. A few fireflies darted in the tall grass next to the woods, their phosphorescent lights blinking on and off with some invisible code. The warmth of the fire glowing in the velvety night penetrated their frayed nerves, and the hectic pace of the day began melting away. Jim clasped Carol's hand.

"Jim, I have to tell you something," Carol started, her voice edgy.

He groaned. "Just when I was thinking we could have a quiet, peaceful night." *Maybe make love later,* he thought. He sighed. "What now?" he asked, cranky that the tender mood was receding fast.

"Honey, you have no idea what I'm going to tell you. It might be something good," she said accusingly, her brown eyes flashing.

"Is it?"

"No."

He pulled his hand away and sat forward in his Adirondack, leaning his elbows on his knees, staring into the fire. He turned his head and looked at her. "Okay, let's have it, but I could have used some good news," he said huffily.

"I'm sorry, but when I came into the house this afternoon, there was a set of binoculars and a note by the garage door entry. They're in on the buffet. Tom, the guy from Midwest Landscaping, said he found them back by the rocks when he was mowing and clearing dead brush. It looks like Maddog has already been doing some spying. God, I hate that man, and I've never met him!" she spat with vehemence. She sat hunched in her chair, feeling as if the woods had eyes, that some invisible menace was focused on them right that instant.

Jim leaned back in his chair and stared at the sky's constellations.

Although he was furious that Maddog had been on his property, he stuffed his disgust, trying to remain calm.

"That doesn't surprise me. After all, he knows where Lillie goes to school. He's got connections all over the state, I'm sure. But we're not going to do anything until I check out some other information I found out about him today."

"Oh yeah? What's that?"

"You have to trust me on this," he said, his face hardening in the reflection of the fire.

Carol sat up straighter. "Jim, I thought we had an agreement— no secrets, remember?"

He closed his eyes briefly, not wanting to argue and spoil the mood of the evening, although it seemed to be going down the tubes quickly. They'd already had arguments about involving Carol in his cases. They'd come to an uneasy truce. "I know. We did agree to that." Jim hesitated, debated with himself, then decided he didn't want to start lying now. "Okay, so here's the deal. Sam found out from one of his drug informants that Maddog may have a boat at the municipal harbor in La Crosse. I haven't had time to check it out. Been too busy chasing down these leads in the Kratt murder. But I'm going to check into it; I promise you that."

"Then what?"

"I don't know. First off, I don't know if the rumor is true, but moving drugs via the river would be a smart way to deliver his cargo with minimal interference from cops. Maybe he's looking to expand his drug trade into this area, although we already have plenty of drugs. If he's transporting drugs, we'll take him down and throw him in jail. But we need hard proof that there are drugs on the boat or that drugs are being transported by boat. Either way, he's a fugitive from the law, and he needs to be arrested. I talked to the harbor master this afternoon. We'll probably have to do some surveillance. We don't want him skipping on a false arrest. That's where it gets sketchy. So . . ." Jim's voice trailed off into the night air.

Carol interrupted. "If he has a boat, can't you get a search warrant? I mean, the guy has terrorized half the state of Wisconsin. He's sold drugs all over the place. Wouldn't that hold up under the court's scrutiny if you applied for a warrant?" Carol reasoned.

"Yes, most likely. Anyway, like I said, I still have to do some checking on all this before we storm him. He's made enough money selling drugs to buy every boat at Skipper Bud's tomorrow in cash if he wanted to." He sighed heavily. "I sure would sleep better at night if he was locked up."

"Well, that's what we both need—some sleep—preferably without Maddog prowling at the edge of our dreams," Carol said. "Jim, we're giving him way too much power. I'm sick of all this, and we haven't even met the guy yet. Not that I want to. It's like chasing a ghost."

"Well, it's not likely that we'll meet him anytime soon," Jim said angrily. "He's not going to knock on our door and ask Lillie to come out and play."

She stared into the fire like someone who'd lost track of time. After a few quiet moments, she grabbed Jim's hand and pulled him up. "Come on. No more Maddog talk or speculations. I've got something better in mind." Jim tweaked his eyebrows upward. "How about a session in the soaking tub?" she asked with a beguiling smile. "We haven't done that for a while." She leaned against his chest and kissed him sweetly.

"Mmm … a soak in the tub and a session in bed? I hope I can hold up," Jim said, putting his hands behind her neck and kissing her intensely. He gazed at her face, his blue eyes deep and clear, his hands running down her back to her rump.

"You always have so far, baby," Carol whispered seductively, returning his kiss.

By midnight, Carol had been sleeping soundly for an hour. She'd rolled away from Jim, and he tenderly draped the bed covers over her exposed shoulders, her hips rounded under the sheet. She groaned a little but didn't move or awaken. Silently, Jim slid his feet to the carpeted floor, stood up, and in the dark, pulled on a pair of boxers and a T-shirt that he'd purposely left next to the bed. He grabbed his cell phone off the nightstand. Sneaking out into the hallway, he closed the bedroom door silently.

The house was dark and quiet. A gibbous waxing moon was just setting, but it provided enough ambient light that Jim could make out the familiar layout of the house once his eyes adjusted. Without turning any lights on, he entered the back hallway leading to the garage. There he slipped on a pair of well-worn jeans he'd hung on a coat hook earlier, grabbed a black hoodie off another hook, and pulled it over his head. Slipping his feet into a pair of athletic shoes in the hallway, he tiptoed over the carpet to the front door. Once outside, he breathed deeply of the still night air. The scent of evergreen enlivened his sense of smell, and he noticed inky shadows shifting across the driveway.

He walked to his Suburban, still parked in the driveway in front of the garage, quietly opened the front passenger door, used his key to unlock the glove compartment, and reached in for his Smith and Wesson M&P 9, which he'd had customized with a laser light and a loaded chamber indicator. He fished out his shoulder harness and finagled it under his sweatshirt, then holstered his gun.

Quietly closing the door on the Suburban, he began walking in the dark down Chipmunk Coulee Road toward U.S. Hwy. 35. He dug his phone out of his jean pocket and flipped it open. The blue light illuminated his worried expression. With his thumb, he punched in Paul's number.

"Hey, Chief," he heard Paul say softly. "I'm on my way."

"I'm walking down Chipmunk Coulee toward 35, coming up to the curve where the bait shop used to be."

"Be there in a minute."

Jim closed his phone and tucked it back into his jeans. He was always amazed when he worked nights during a stakeout or other surveillance at the noises that punctuated the darkness. The atmosphere was filled with the rustlings and skitterings of nocturnal creatures. Jim's ears tuned to the sounds as his footsteps joined the nocturnal symphony. Somewhere in the woods, an owl hooted. The air was still, and the trees stood like silent sentries along the road, their leaves occasionally whispering in a sudden breeze. Jim heard Paul's pickup before he saw it. He stepped off the road and waited on the shoulder.

When the dark blue Ford F-150 truck got closer, he stepped out into the beams of the headlights. Paul slowed and crunched to a stop in the gravel alongside Jim. He opened the door and climbed in.

"How ya doin', Chief?"

"I've been better," he grumped. "I hope we can find out what this guy is planning. Then maybe I can do something about it. That's a big maybe." In the lights from the dash, his face was a mask of anxiety.

Paul drove silently through the south side of La Crosse, making his way through a complex of businesses near the river behind Gundersen Lutheran Hospital until he came to Houska Drive. As he drove, he thought about his career at the sheriff's department—drug busts, traffic fatalities, murders, recovering stolen property. He had survived some gripping experiences together with Jim. Now he supposed he could add breaking and entering to them. He squirmed uncomfortably. He sure hoped Higgins knew what the hell he was doing.

Weaving in and out of the darkened businesses in the industrial park, Paul came to the harbor parking lot adjacent to the municipal marina. A few vehicles were parked in the lot. At the far end, the marina office was locked up tight. Paul parked the truck at the far end of the parking area and killed the engine. The boats in the marina bobbed in their moorings.

"Saddle up, partner," Jim said. "You carrying?"

"Yep. Wearin' your vest?" Paul asked.

"Nope. This is just a look-see. I talked to the marina manager before I got home today. When I described Maddog, he said he'd cruised in late Tuesday afternoon. He didn't know if he was staying on the boat. He didn't think so. Supposedly he's in slip 45 on the end of the middle pier. Let's just take a walk and see what's up."

"Sounds good," Paul said, but once again, he silently questioned the wisdom of Jim's decision. This could turn out bad—really bad.

"You okay with this?" Jim asked, glancing at the side of Paul's face.

"Let's get in and out as quickly as we can," Paul said, his voice husky.

The two men disembarked, strolled through the parking lot, and began walking out over the water along the second pier. It was very quiet, and despite the darkness, a luminous pathway of moonlight reflected on the water. Occasionally, dark clouds floated by, briefly obscuring its light. Boats swayed gently, water lapping quietly against the hulls, which were tied securely in their slips. Covered with canvas, they were shielded from the wind and rain, battened down against the elements. Everything was hushed and tranquil, but somewhere a cat meowed. The trees rustled gently in a sudden breeze, and then it was quiet again. Their footsteps reverberated on the pier as they walked toward Maddog's slip.

Stopping at slip number 45, Jim and Paul stared at the boat. It was a late nineties model cabin cruiser. The forward cabin was offset with a double berth. The raised helm seated at least six, and wide side decks made movement on the boat easy. Jim was sure the price tag would have been well over fifty thousand. No one seemed to be on board.

They stepped onto the deck, and the cruiser responded with a slight rocking motion. Jim reached into his pocket and removed his set of lockpicks. He worked the locked door until it finally clicked open with a *snap. This could get us shot,* he thought, *and in serious trouble if we get caught.* Then the anger rose in his belly like a burning fire. *Screw it,* he thought. *I'm doing what I have to do to protect my family.*

Silently opening the door, Jim began his descent into the boat, his heart stuck in his throat. He withdrew the Smith & Wesson pistol, prepared to confront Maddog if needed, hoping it could just be an information-gathering foray. Jim cleared the boat and breathed a sigh of relief. Paul stayed on the stairs, his head and chest exposed, scouting the marina for any unexpected visitors.

Walking through the kitchen and dinette area, Jim stepped down into the master bedroom. The smell of sweat, cigarettes, and pot saturated the sheets and blankets, which were tangled in a lump on the mattress. Jim began looking at the contents in the drawers of the sleeping berth. Using the flashlight on his cell, he rifled hurriedly through the items: condoms, an unopened pack of cigarettes, T-shirts, underwear, a couple of pot pipes, and a bag of marijuana. He was about to move on when underneath the other stuff, his eyes caught the corner of a Walgreens photo envelope. He laid his gun on the bed, pulled the photos out of the envelope, and used his cell to illuminate them.

The detail of the pictures stunned Jim and took his breath away. Lillie's features were clearly visible—her tendrils of golden hair reflecting the sunlight, her intelligent eyes, her heartbreaking smile— and his house in the background. All taken in his own backyard. *Damn you,* Jim swore silently, choking back his anger. He holstered his gun and slipped the photos in a baggie.

Suddenly, Paul leaned into the cabin. "Chief, somebody's comin'!" he whispered hoarsely.

Three figures stood in the parking lot, arguing loudly. As they argued, their voices carried over the water. Jim scrambled up the stairs, flipped the lock, clicked the door shut, and crept along the port side to the stern. Kneeling next to Paul, he pointed to the water. Using a ladder, he eased himself into the river. Paul followed. By this time, the arguing group was walking across the pier to the boat.

The water was cold, and instantly their soaked clothes felt heavy and clumsy, threatening to pull them under. They silently dog-paddled among the moored boats, stopping briefly, clinging to the sides of the boats, and ducking under the piers while they gradually swam toward shore. Weaving in and out of the shadows, they managed to avoid detection. When they reached the edge of the shore, they hovered like a couple of turtles, their heads above water, their bodies submerged in the dark river. A hedge of lilacs and hawthorns hung over the bank and provided some shadowy cover.

They stayed submerged in the river until Maddog entered the boat with a man and a woman. Lights flickered on inside the cabin, and the muted sounds of conversation drifted over the dark water. The argument continued.

Jim and Paul heaved themselves out of the river onto the bank and silently squished their way back to Paul's truck parked in the deep shade at the end of the parking lot. Opening the doors and climbing in, Paul waited a few minutes before starting the engine. Other than the muffled purring of the motor beneath the hood, the dripping water from their clothes was the only sound in the truck. Paul flicked the heater on high and waited until the windshield fog had cleared. Then he drove out of the parking lot back to South Avenue, where both men banged their doors securely shut.

The tension in Paul's chest felt like a balloon about to pop. He let out a whoosh of air. "Find anything?" Paul asked, breathless.

Jim pulled at the waistband of his jeans. He held up a small baggie with several photos. "He's been photographing her in my own backyard, the damn pervert," Jim snarled.

"God, it's worse than I thought. How could he possibly think he's going to get away with this? What're you going to do?" Paul asked, absorbing Jim's anxiety and anger.

"Move to plan B," Jim remarked solemnly.

"What's that?"

"You don't honestly think I'm going to tell you that, do you? Taking care of Lillie and Henri is my job, and nobody else's. No one's going to know about my plan until it's necessary."

Paul gave him a shocked glance. "Chief, you can't do this alone. You've tried that before. Remember your plan to meet that deranged bomber on Grandad Bluff? We've been there and done that. I'm not up for a catastrophe, especially one that involves a six-year-old girl and a toddler," Paul reminded him roughly. Jim silently shook his head.

"There's no other way. When I initiate my plan, Lillie and Henri's location cannot be compromised for any reason."

"Well, damn!" Paul yelled. He hit his fist on the steering wheel, knowing he couldn't convince Jim to give up his stubbornly held strategy. Paul looked over at him, his eyes blinking rapidly. "If you need help, you call. I mean it," he said resolutely, his eyes like dark stone chips.

"You got it, buddy," Jim said, clasping his arm. "Thanks."

The trip down Chipmunk Coulee Road felt like they were driving in a tunnel under the sea. The green of the trees at the edge of the headlights and the blackness of the night numbed their emotions. Jim was shaking—whether from cold or fear, he wasn't sure. About five hundred feet from Jim's house, Paul pulled off the highway onto the shoulder and stopped the truck. Jim climbed out.

"Thanks, buddy," he said softly to Paul. He jumped down from the truck and waved Paul away. He started walking up the road. The quiet was exquisite, and he thought it would help calm him down, but as his feet echoed on the pavement, he realized he was trembling with rage and anger.

He hated the uncertainty that had crept into the peaceful oasis of his home. He'd always been able to shelter his family from the unsavory nature of his work in the past. Now it felt like everything he'd done previously to protect his family had evaporated into thin air. With a pair of binoculars and a camera, this lowlife drug dealer had disrupted everything they'd worked so hard to give Lillie and Henri. Fear and distrust had invaded, and it seemed so damned unfair.

He worked his tongue against his cheek as he thought about the explanation he would have to give Carol in the morning. Moving Lillie and Henri to Gladys' place would set off alarm bells of insecurity and distrust, something Lillie had already experienced when she was homeless. He could imagine her upturned blue eyes searching his face for answers. And her questions. God, her questions would torment him. But his greatest fear was that she would not be able to trust him anymore, and that was something he couldn't abide. Fortunately, little Henri was too young to understand the menacing situation, but kids could easily pick up on fear.

Jim's legs felt like waterlogged timbers as he trudged up the driveway. He left a trail of wet footprints behind him that would evaporate by morning, but the problems still facing him wouldn't disappear. They were as real as the cool hard steel of the revolver in his armpit. There were no easy answers, but he intended to protect his family, come hell or high water.

29

FRIDAY, SEPTEMBER 13

Carol and Jim woke early in the dim light of dawn as they'd been doing lately since things had gone awry. Jim felt like the captain of a space shuttle that had suddenly lost its tether to earth's gravity, severed by some great cataclysmic event. He imagined them floating randomly without direction in the darkness of space, without a clue of what to do.

Without backpedaling, Jim calmly told Carol what he'd done during the night.

"You did what?" Carol exclaimed. She sat up suddenly in bed, her eyes wide with alarm. Jim cringed at her reaction. He found her hand, but she pushed it away.

"I had to find out if his intentions were serious, honey. Paul was with me. Maddog's been here on our property, and he took pictures of Lillie. I wish it were different, but that's the deal," Jim said, sitting up next to her. His eyes were puffy from lack of sleep, and he shivered when he thought about his clandestine swim in the harbor.

Carol flopped backward in bed, collapsing on the pillow, staring at the ceiling. "When did you get in the habit of performing illegal searches and breaking and entering?"

"You wouldn't believe how many times cops conduct clandestine searches without a warrant. And no, I'm not in the habit of doing them. In fact, I don't do them. But this is different. This is a personal threat to our family. I had to investigate. I had no choice. And I found out that Maddog is serious."

"Couldn't we have assumed that without you putting your entire career in jeopardy? Jim, what were you thinking?" The silence filled Jim with guilt and second-guessing. Carol continued to stare at the ceiling stubbornly. "What's the plan now?"

Jim turned toward Carol, taking her hand. This time she gripped it back, turned toward him, and brushed her fingers through his hair. "Well, I think we should continue to stay here as long as we can. At the first hint of trouble, we move the kids to Gladys'. You'll go, too. In fact, tonight, I want you to pack some of the kids' extra clothes and a few toys—whatever you think you'll need—so that we're prepared at a moment's notice. If you go with the kids, that'll make the transition a little easier. Hopefully, we won't have to do it for a while, but . . ." He stopped, not wanting to think through the ramifications.

"Maybe we should just ignore the degenerate and live our lives as best we can," Carol huffed, turning on her back. "I'm not crazy about leaving our home because of some shadowy threat looming on the horizon. It just goes against every principle of our right to feel secure in the privacy of our own home. Dammit!" She slammed her fist down on the mattress with a force that surprised Jim. More silence. Finally, she said, "Did you remember we're going to DeDe's houseboat tonight?"

Jim rolled out of bed. Standing, he looked down at her and said, "No, I forgot that. We'll go, but let's take the kids on the river this weekend. I need to relax and get out of here. I feel like a prisoner in my own home, for Pete's sake," he finished. "And yes, this whole thing ticks me off, too." He turned abruptly and went into the adjoining bathroom.

"Okay. Let's take the kids on the boat," she said. But her stomach clenched in anxiety even though escaping to the wilds of the river had an allure she found very appealing. Then her doubts rushed in again like floodwaters breaching a dam. "I guess I haven't convinced myself we're going to be okay yet," she mumbled to herself.

"What'd you say?" Jim asked, leaning his head around the door frame, meeting her gaze.

"Nothing."

30

Friday morning dawned beautiful with a clear blue sky and the husky glow of pink on the horizon above the bluffs, although a chill permeated the atmosphere. Fall color was beginning to blush on the trees along the river, and the temperatures hovered in the upper fifties. DeDe woke in the bedroom of the houseboat as it rocked gently in the current in Pettibone Harbor. Her hunt for an apartment yesterday afternoon yielded two possibilities—neither ideal, but both better than a boat.

She'd finally decided on a small two-bedroom house that had been recently refurbished and updated. It wasn't fancy inside, but it was clean and well-kept, and the rent was within her budget. A tiny fenced-in lawn out back bordered South Avenue, the same busy street where Gundersen Lutheran Hospital took up three city blocks of space. She imagined hearing every ambulance and rescue squad siren, but that was no different from her environment in New Orleans. She'd signed the contract, then headed to Slumberland to order a couch, a recliner, a queen bed, and a kitchen dinette set to be delivered on October 1 to the residence. She'd decided to use other basic household items from the houseboat until she got on solid financial footing.

She eased out of bed, wincing when her feet hit the cold floor. She tiptoed into the bathroom and started the shower, stepping out of her nightie into the warm water. In a couple of minutes, she'd finished. Dressing quickly in the tiny bedroom, she pulled on a geometric print shell and black slacks and wrapped herself in the warmth of a gray mohair sweater. Silver jewelry completed the look. Her lifestyle demanded a simple approach to her wardrobe. In one tiny closet, she could grab any article of clothing blindfolded, knowing the pieces would complement each other.

Glancing around, she decided her boat was ready for company. There was plenty of seating on the forward deck. She'd swept the boat last night and wiped down the surfaces. Her bar, although not fancy, was stocked with a good assortment of hard liquor and beer. The vegetables for the dirty rice were prepared, and the chicken was seasoned and waiting in the refrigerator. *Dinner would come together easily*, she thought. She was looking forward to a different setting other than work where she could get to know her colleagues a little better. She fixed her hair, did a quick application of light makeup, drank a strong cup of coffee, and ate a couple of scrambled eggs and toast. Then she called a cab and headed for work.

Walking off the elevator on the third floor of the law enforcement facility, Emily greeted DeDe with a casual smile.

"Find a place to live?" she asked, looking up at DeDe from her desk chair.

"Yes, a house over on South Street near Gundersen," DeDe said. "It's small, but it'll feel like a mansion after living on a houseboat. Now I just have to get my boat winterized, and I can move the end of September. On warm days, I can probably walk to work."

"Any problems, just let me know. I know a lot of realty people around town," Emily said.

"Thanks. I appreciate all your help," DeDe replied as she walked down the hall to her office. She sat down at her desk and glanced at the picture of her grandparents in the small frame. She missed them deeply. Their lined, weathered faces spoke of resilience and wisdom, and she'd always be thankful for their guidance and love in her formative years. Without them, she wasn't sure where she would have ended up. Her cell buzzed.

"DeDe Deverioux. La Crosse Sheriff's Department. How can I help you?" There was a slight pause.

A husky voice swam over the line, "Hi, baby. Know where I can find a good detective?"

DeDe's brain froze, and her heart skipped a few beats. She felt faint. She was glad she was sitting down, or she'd have fallen on the floor.

"JuJu, where are you?" she managed to whisper, her breath catching in her throat. She squeezed her eyes shut for a second, then stared at the photo of her grandparents. *Grandma, where are you when I really need you?* she thought.

"Where am I?" the voice said with exaggerated impatience. "Well, I've spent the last three weeks driving north, trying to find you. When I realized you weren't coming home, I hopped in my car and headed up here. Pretty good detective work, huh?" The line was silent. Not getting a response, Jude went on. "I'm exploring this fine city of La Crosse. They might be in need of a good Southern chef somewhere around here, don't ya think? You going to help me find a place to serve my grub?"

"Oh, JuJu. You show up at the most inopportune times," DeDe groaned.

"Well, excuse me!" he said sarcastically, anger spilling over into his voice. "But the last time I checked, I thought married people worked out their problems—together." Then his voice softened. "Sorry. I didn't want to start like this. I've missed you, baby. Really, I have."

"Well, I'm working until four. My houseboat's at Pettibone Marina. I'm sure you can find it. But I'm having my friends over tonight for dirty rice and chicken."

"Well, that'll be just fine. Don't you think they should meet your husband?"

After a long silence, she finally said, "I guess they will now that you've arrived on my doorstep."

"Well, thanks for the vote of confidence," Jude said, sounding hurt. "Hey, I'll pick up some stuff at a farmers' market and cook with you. How's that sound?"

"That's fine. My slip number is 67. There's a key under the flowerpot by the door. I'll see you around four." DeDe closed her phone.

As DeDe sat in her darkened office, her thoughts clumped together like tumbleweeds blowing across a prairie. JuJu. Here. In La Crosse. She could imagine him sitting on the deck of the houseboat, his black skin glistening in the afternoon sun, sipping a beer with a smile on his face and a load of secrets locked behind his dark eyes.

Jude Delaney's veiled past had been the main problem in their marriage. His refusal to share anything about his family history had been like a spike being driven through their relationship. Despite DeDe's attempts to wring it out of him, he remained firmly entrenched in silence.

"There's nothin' in my past that has anything to do with this moment right now," he'd said softly but firmly when they'd last made love. She'd tried everything—probing questions, empathy and understanding, and finally, when he'd refused to reveal his secrets, she'd run away. Now she could add panicked flight to her list of attempts—and failures. She shivered with dread when she thought about the conversations they still had to have if they wanted to save their marriage—*wanted* being the key word.

She heard muffled conversation coming down the hall.

"I'll see you later. Love you," Sam said.

"Okay, later," Leslie said.

DeDe twisted her chair to face the door, heaved herself up, and crossed the hall to Leslie's office. Poking her head around the door frame, she asked, "Got a few minutes so I can cry on your shoulder?"

Leslie noticed the apprehensive tone in her melodious voice and the downcast expression on DeDe's face. "Absolutely. Come on in and sit down," Leslie said, waving her to a chair.

DeDe walked in with sagging shoulders, plopped unceremoniously in a chair, then rubbed her face with her hands. Leslie removed her lightweight jacket, hung it on a hook next to the door, and sat down at her desk. She wore a pale pink cashmere sweater, pencil skirt, and practical brown skimmer flats. "So, what's up?" she said expectantly, turning to face her.

DeDe leaned forward, her elbows resting on her knees. "My husband's in La Crosse as we speak," she said, her words clipped and factual, their eyes meeting across Leslie's desk.

"Oh. I see," Leslie said hesitantly, although she really didn't understand. Confusion creased her face. "I didn't know you were married. Is there a problem? He's not going to hurt you, is he?" Leslie asked, her eyes widening with alarm.

"No, no," DeDe said emphatically, waving her hands in front of her. "Jude's a wonderful man, but we've had some problems in the past, and I ... well, I ran away. Obviously, *that* didn't work," she said, chiding herself. "Maybe he should be the detective, and I should be the chef. After all, he successfully followed me up here from New Orleans."

Leslie stayed quiet, anticipating an explanation of some kind. DeDe leaned back and kicked her feet out in front of her. Pinching the bridge of her nose, she rambled on.

"He's a very well-known chef in New Orleans. We met at the five-star restaurant he owns— Louisiana Bistro. I started frequenting the place in the evenings at closing time after my NOPD street beat, and over time I found myself falling for him. He was charming and funny and very kind. When he asked me to marry him after our whirlwind romance of three months, I said yes." She clasped her hands in front of her, then dropped them back into her lap.

"We were so happy, so in love, but when I started asking about his past, he clammed up, got angry, and was adamant that his past had nothing to do with our future. Of course, I gave the classic response that married people shouldn't have secrets. Blah, blah, blah. I couldn't leave it alone, and he wouldn't tell me, so I took off."

"Runnin', huh?" Leslie asked. DeDe nodded. "Am I just here to listen, or do you want some advice?"

DeDe sat back in her chair as if bracing herself for bad news, her face stoic and serious. "Go ahead. I can take it," she said.

Leslie wasn't so sure. "Well, believe it or not, I did the same thing with Sam."

"You did?" DeDe grabbed the corner of her glasses and pushed them down on her nose. She peered at Leslie, her brown eyes wide with surprise. "Seriously? You hit the road, too?" she asked dubiously. "Boy, you and me got a lot more in common than we thought, huh?"

"Yeah, we do. Seriously. I was so scared of the feelings I had for Sam. At the time, I believed I would bring him nothing but bad luck. My bucket of problems looked huge, overflowing like a sewer, so I ran to Chicago."

"Didn't work?"

"Obviously not. We were married and very happy, but for our relationship to work, we both had to lose our egos. Listen, let me tell you something. First," Leslie held up her index finger, "your husband followed you all the way to Wisconsin. That says something. He must love you very much." DeDe's demeanor softened with emotion, her shoulders sagged, and tears filled her eyes.

"Second," Leslie held up another finger, "people's past can either challenge them to rise above it, or it can keep them imprisoned in its chains. That might be simplistic, but let's briefly go with that assumption. If he's a successful chef, then his past, whether good or bad, must have motivated him to do something with his life. That's a positive thing, don't you think?"

"Yeah, I guess. I hadn't thought of it like that," DeDe replied. "But what if it's something really bad?"

"Like what?" Leslie challenged her, turning her hands palm-side up. "When you don't know what it is, it's all conjecture. You're worrying about something that might not even exist."

DeDe shrugged and looked away from Leslie's intense gaze. "New Orleans is a tough place to grow up," she said, picking at a loose piece of yarn on her sweater. "Lots of bad stuff happens there. I've seen stuff that would turn anybody's dreams sour. I just don't understand why he can't tell me how he grew up. Why can't he trust me? It makes me wonder if he's done something criminal."

"Well, you're a detective, and apparently, you've become a little cynical. That happens in our line of work. Why haven't you investigated on your own? If he has a record, you can easily find that out."

"I'm afraid of what I might find," DeDe answered dejectedly.

"That's what I'm telling you. You might be afraid of something that doesn't even exist." Leslie's eyes were filled with sympathy. "Listen, if we're really being honest here, every relationship is a risk. Exposing your heart and your innermost feelings to someone can make you feel very vulnerable. But there's also great reward in that. Sam took a chance on me. He doesn't know half of the trauma I endured in Iraq, and I'm not going to tell him. I don't want his pity, but I need his love and stability in my life. When things get tough, Sam's there. Maybe that's the way it is with your husband. He doesn't want to be an object of pity in your eyes. I don't know too many men who would want that," Leslie concluded.

"You mean he'd rather be my hero than risk rejection for a past he couldn't control?"

"Yeah, maybe. That's something you'll have to consider. Just be ready to be very patient. Don't demand. It's kind of like the sand in the hand thing," she finished, leaning back in her chair. When she thought about all she'd said, she wondered when she'd become a counselor. Usually, she was the one seeking advice. Now she was giving it. She smiled at the incongruous nature of their conversation.

DeDe's looked perplexed. Her eyes were question marks. "The what?"

"Okay, this is my psychobabble for the week. Some famous guy—I don't remember who—said that love is like sand held in your hand. If you hold it loosely, with an open hand, the sand will stay where it is. The minute you close your hand and squeeze or you try to hold it too tightly, the sand trickles through your fingers. If you give the person freedom and respect, your love will likely remain intact. Hold too tightly, and love slips away and is lost. That's my version anyway."

"Wow! That's kinda like something my grandma Hettie used to say—*Mus tek cyear a de root fa da heal de tree*," DeDe said.

Leslie's eyebrows scrunched together. "What's that mean?" she asked, enjoying the sound of the rounded vowels rolling off DeDe's tongue.

"You must take care of the root in order to heal the tree."

Leslie smiled. "That might be another way of looking at the problem. Sounds like wisdom to me."

The office was quiet for a moment. DeDe stood up and said, "Whatever happens, you're in for a culinary treat tonight. Jude is an excellent chef, and he's promised to help me in the kitchen."

Leslie's phone beeped. She listened and responded with a few monosyllabic answers.

"Higgins wants us in his office. Right now."

31

While DeDe and Leslie were analyzing their marriages, Jim was in Sheriff Davy Jones' office on the first floor of the law enforcement center. He sat in the chair across from Jones' desk, one leg propped on his knee, calmly trying to hold it together while the sheriff chewed him out. Davy's face was crimson, and he pushed back the few strands of hair remaining on his bald head that had flopped over his forehead. The tan uniform shirt he was wearing strained at the buttons. Davy stood defiantly behind the desk, his fists parked on his hips, his potbelly sagging over his belt, and his eyes looking like pieces of flat steel. Jim hoped he wasn't gearing up for a heart attack.

"What in the hell made you think you could bag Maddog's boat on your own without a warrant —and with Saner in tow?" Sheriff Davy Jones asked angrily. He bit his words off as if he were tearing up a piece of steak.

When Jim refused to answer and remained silent, Jones erupted again.

"Well? Say something, Jim! Explain this to me!" he repeated loudly, waving his arms wildly. "I don't ever remember you doing anything this asinine in your entire career!" After a few moments, during which he could hear Jones' heavy breathing, Jim finally spoke.

"I had a lapse in judgment, sir," he said calmly, lifting his icy blue eyes to meet the sheriff's belligerent stare. He uncrossed his legs and continued sitting, his arms crossed over his chest.

"You're kidding!" Jones said, his eyes growing larger. "A lapse in judgment? That's your excuse? Jim, in our profession, we rely on *not* having lapses in judgment. There's got to be something else that's going on. You're one of my most experienced, trustworthy officers. Hell, you could do my job if you had to." Jones tensed, looking like he was going to vault over his desk and tackle Jim to the floor. "Well? Aren't you going to defend yourself?"

Jim held his hands up in front of him. "All right, I'll try to explain. First of all, I was well aware that what I was doing was illegal." Jones' face fell in disappointment. Jim shifted uneasily in his chair. He didn't like to disappoint anyone, especially a lifelong friend and colleague.

"Well, I'm glad you know that breaking and entering is illegal. We're making progress. Keep going," Jones said sarcastically, a little calmer, making a circular motion with his hand.

"Second, I was not aware that city police had a surveillance team already watching Maddog's boat."

"Communication, Jim," Jones said brusquely. "Our department relies on it."

Jim launched himself out of the chair. "What? And I'm supposed to read minds? There were no meetings, emails, or other communication that would have let us know Maddog was even in town. My wife discovered his presence through her ex-husband. How's that for detective work? So you're right, Davy—communication is key, and it goes both ways," Jim said tightly, his dimple denting his cheek as he gritted his teeth. "But you know as well as I do that every officer has his sources ... and no, I'm not divulging mine to you," Jim reminded him firmly when Davy looked like he was about to interrupt him. Jim knew he was teetering on the edge of insubordination, but he continued anyway, feeling his control dissolving. His voice was ominous, his intentions prickly as he continued.

"Third—and this is the most important part—Maddog believes he is the biological father of my adopted daughter, Lillie, and he's been making threats that he wants to regain custody of her. He has no legal rights as a parent since he never signed the birth certificate and hasn't been around for six years, but that doesn't seem to matter to him. Apparently, he's suddenly feeling parental. He's been seen watching Lillie at St. Ignatius school in Genoa, and he was on the back of my property and did surveillance with binoculars and took photos with a camera."

"How—"

"Don't ask me how I know that. Various sources." Jim's voice was tight and hard. "I don't know yet what I'm going to do about this threat, but Carol is scared to death, and frankly, if I catch up with this loser, I'm going to break his meat-lovin' skull!" Jim shouted. Jim's flushed face and blazing eyes made the silence that had descended seem deafening.

"Jim, why didn't you come to me?" Davy asked quietly. Jim took a deep breath, grasping at some vestige of control. He aimed for an objective tone in his voice, but it came out apologetic. Although he was furious, he was also thoroughly embarrassed. He plopped back in the chair.

"Because I wasn't sure if any of the rumors were true. I heard from a source that he was in town looking for Lillie, and another source told me about the boat down behind the hospital. I didn't anticipate being surveilled in the process." He groaned, then said, "Shit happens, I guess." Jim closed his eyes, leaned forward, and bowed his head, resting his elbows on his knees. After a moment, he looked up and said, "I apologize if I put you in an awkward position."

Jones took a deep breath and finally sat down at his desk. He waved his hand raggedly in Jim's direction, the wind taken out of his sail. "No problem. Apology accepted. I guess Chief Pedretti will have to get over the fact that we stepped on her toes and interfered with her investigation. Narcotics have their shorts in a bind, but they'll have to get over it."

"I can talk to Pedretti—" Jim started, but Jones nodded in the negative.

"No, after what you've told me, I can understand that your emotions got ahead of rational thinking. If anybody pulled that shit on my kids, I'd probably go ballistic, too. We've got enough pressure to endure without our families being threatened besides." Jones paused, and something like sympathy crossed his face. "Listen, like I said, you're one of my most reliable, stable officers, so I'm just writing you up with a reprimand that will go in your permanent employment file. I'm not asking for your badge or putting you on administrative leave. You've been an excellent police officer—stellar—and everyone is allowed to screw up once, especially when you're trying to protect your own family. Now, tell me, what's your plan?"

"I'm moving the kids and Carol to a safe place until we can get a hold of this guy," Jim said succinctly.

Suddenly, the energy seemed to have been sucked out of the room. Silence hung over the two men like a wet towel thrown over a campfire. The vehemence and accusatory tone that had characterized their conversation disappeared like a wisp of fog.

Standing up, Jim said, "I appreciate it, Davy." He left the first-floor office and took the elevator to the third floor. Emily glanced up as he got off the elevator.

"Morning, Chief." Then she did a double take. "Jim, are you all right? You look strange."

"Believe me when I say I have good reason to look strange. No interruptions for about an hour, Emily," he said seriously, turning and walking to his office where he closed the door carefully behind him.

32

By ten-thirty on Friday morning, DeDe and Leslie were climbing into Leslie's Prius in the parking lot of the law enforcement center. Leslie drove the little car in and out of the snarled traffic downtown, braking suddenly when a motorcyclist veered around a truck ahead of her. The coffee they'd picked up at Kwik Trip sloshed in the cupholder, threatening to spill onto the carpet.

They crossed the big blue bridge over the Mississippi River and headed to the Root River Senior Care Center in Houston, Minnesota, to interview the neighbor of Professor Blackman. Mrs. Jewel Loiselle was one of the few remaining witnesses who'd watched the horrible events unfold at the professor's home the night of Christina's abduction in October 1977. Higgins had insisted on re-interviewing anyone who still had memories of the event. Someone might recall critical details about the incident that had been overlooked, he'd said.

"Do you think Higgins is right to put so much weight on this Yelski cold case?" DeDe asked, her voice shadowed with doubt. She watched the scenery slip by—the luscious green of the alfalfa fields, the soaring sandstone bluffs along the river, and the sunshine that still felt warm like summertime despite the march toward fall.

Leslie watched the road over the steering wheel. "What else do we have to investigate? No witnesses to Kratt's killing. Kratt was a loner with few associates, a history of pornographic addictions, maritally unfaithful, a necklace, and a strange note left at the scene." Leslie's face darkened with the implications. "I wonder if the note and locket left at the scene were meant to mislead the investigation from the beginning, possibly to draw us away from someone who wanted to get away with murder and cleverly invented a way to focus our attention on another unsolved crime, but Higgins sense of things is unusual in this case, and other options aren't presenting themselves." She looked over at DeDe, her eyes troubled. "I don't know what direction to take, either, although Sam also seems convinced the two crimes are related. Those newspaper articles in Kratt's personal effects are hard to dispel as a mere coincidence."

"It's a weird set of circumstances, for sure." DeDe slipped the large duplicate of the locket photo from the envelope and stared at the two teenagers. "What about the guy in the picture with Christina? Must be a boyfriend. They seem very friendly. They're holding hands, and they look happy."

"The tip line's been getting some calls since the photo was published in this morning's paper and was on the TV news last night. But nothing solid has come from that yet," Leslie told DeDe. "It's likely a boyfriend. The challenge is to find him."

After crossing the big blue bridge into Minnesota, Leslie headed west on Highway 16. The primary geographical feature in this extreme southeastern corner of Minnesota was the Root River which flowed gently through the valley of the same name. The idyllic waterway traveled east for more than eighty miles, eventually emptying into Navigation Pool #7 south of La Crosse.

As Leslie drove, the bluff country rolled out before them. Sections of the river revealed exposed limestone, and large flat rocks hovered over the riverbank in places. Occasionally, DeDe would spot some people gently paddling canoes or kayaks in the warm, golden sunshine squeezing a few more glorious moments from the summer-like day. Wisps of red and orange on the trees created a palette reminiscent of the French Impressionists. Focusing on an object in the landscape from high in a dead elm near the highway, a red-tailed hawk appeared regal and attentive from his lonely perch. Leslie pointed at him over the dash as she slowed the car and pulled to the side of the road.

"*Buteo jamaicensis* … commonly known as the red-tailed hawk. Watch him. He's got his eye on something," she said, pointing at the bird. The hawk peered intently at movement in the field, then lifted off with his powerful mottled wings, his red tail acting like a rudder. A harsh *keeer* came through the open window as the raptor bore down on a field mouse, grabbing it expertly in its sharp talons. Flying to a nearby tree, he began ripping open the mouse, feasting on its innards.

"Glad I'm not a mouse," DeDe said, frowning.

They drove for a while in the bright sunshine. The blue sky was intense and cloudless, like an upside-down metallic bowl curved gracefully over the lush green land. As they entered the outskirts of Houston, Highway 16 morphed into West Cedar Street. Leslie turned left on Henderson, drove a couple of blocks, and arrived at the nursing home, a bureaucratic brick structure shaded by mature maple and oak trees. Someone on a riding mower was expertly cutting the huge lawn, and the adjacent parking lot was full of cars. The air smelled of cut grass and musky leaves. Parking the Prius, the two detectives walked into the entrance of the sprawling care center.

A young receptionist at the front desk looked up when they walked in. She wore mint green scrubs, and a stethoscope hung limply around her neck. Her blonde hair was neatly clipped with a wide barrette on the top of her head, and a pair of hot pink glasses framed her green eyes.

"Can I help you?" she asked, snapping her chewing gum.

DeDe glanced at the name tag on the girl's smock. "We hope so, Samantha," she said pleasantly. Both women flashed their IDs.

"We're wondering if we could talk to Mrs. Jewel Loiselle."

"Are you guys cops?" Samantha asked breathlessly, her eyes riveted on their IDs.

"Yes, we're detectives," Leslie responded. "Could you tell us where we could find Jewel?"

"Let me see what wing she's in," Samantha answered. "I'm new here and don't know all the residents yet," she explained. Samantha turned to her computer and began pecking the keys, snapping on her gum as she gathered information.

While DeDe and Leslie waited, a commotion in the lobby attracted their attention. An elderly gentleman was heading toward the entrance doors. His mission—to escape the immediate environment. He muttered beneath his breath, his walker squeaking ominously as he propelled himself forward in a tottering shuffle. Coming from behind him, a nursing assistant trotted hurriedly to his side.

"Mr. Everson, where do you think you're going? Were you going to leave me behind?" she said good-naturedly as she gently clasped his arm. She smiled warmly at him. "You can't go without me."

"Gettin' outta here," Mr. Everson gasped in a panic. "They're after me again."

The scene was interrupted by the young receptionist's voice, and DeDe and Leslie's attention turned back to the young woman in front of them.

"Jewel Loiselle is in the Evergreen wing, right here to your left," she pointed, "Room 148 at the end of the hall." Samantha handed them a card with the information. "She should be in her room, although she might be napping right now." The young girl shrugged her shoulders. "You'll have to take your chances."

"Thank you," DeDe said. "We'll find it."

"Yeah, you should be able to. You're detectives, right?" the young girl joked, elbowing the girl standing next to her at the receptionist's desk.

"We can handle it," Leslie said dryly.

They proceeded down the wide hallway where wheelchairs and walkers were parked, along with metal carts stacked with towels and sheets and another cart filled with medications. A few nurses padded silently in and out of rooms, carrying paper cups containing medication, which they administered to the residents. Leslie tapped politely on the door of room 148.

DeDe noticed the smell of Listerine and the lingering aroma of toast and coffee as they entered the room. A single bed was situated along one wall, and the tightly packed space was filled with knick-knacks and healthy, vibrant houseplants. Near the bed sat a maple dresser where family pictures occupied a prominent place. Next to the window, an elderly woman hunched in a wheelchair and looked longingly at the beautiful oasis outside.

"Mrs. Loseille?" Leslie asked quietly. The older lady turned to her, and a friendly smile creased her wrinkled face. She was tiny and appeared to shrink farther into the bright red, white, and blue afghan that covered her lap and legs. Her white hair was thin and fluffy, and little bare patches of her pink scalp showed through here and there. But a pair of bright, attentive blue eyes looked back and forth at the two women standing in front of her.

She held out her hand, and Leslie grasped it firmly. It felt like a little bird's wing.

"Hello. Do I know you, dear?" she asked sweetly. Her airy voice floated within the cramped environment of the room. As her smile faded, it was replaced with a frown that creased her forehead.

"No, you don't know me," Leslie said. She introduced DeDe, each of them flipping their ID badges open. Then she told her, "We're investigating a recent murder that we think might be tied to an old cold case. We're wondering if you could tell us about the night Christina Yelski was abducted in October of 1977. We understand you were a neighbor of the Blackmans at the time."

Jewel seemed to retreat for a moment, and Leslie feared her understanding and memory might be compromised by dementia.

She sat quietly, and finally, after a few moments, Jewel's eyes focused, her thin lips twitched, and she began to speak.

"My memories of that evening are just as clear as if they'd happened yesterday," she began, her eyes brightening. Her voice became insistent, and her eyes seemed to focus on a point directly in front of her. "My husband and I were watching television in the evening as we usually did. Our kids were in their bedrooms doing homework. The neighborhood at that time was full of families with children. There were almost forty children in a two-block area. It was a great atmosphere to raise a family. Our kids never lacked playmates or friends." She paused a moment in her trip down memory lane, her eyes drifting back to the two detectives. Then she started again.

"The night was cool. As I said, we were watching TV, and our living room windows were open slightly. My husband, Pete, thought he heard a scream outside somewhere shortly after eight o'clock, but I hadn't heard anything, and we both dismissed it. We thought we were being silly. Some kids were still outside playing tag or something and assumed they'd been playacting. Then about five minutes later, Pete heard what he thought was another scream. That time, I heard it, too. So, he got up and went to the window. Didn't see anything, but he was uneasy about it."

"Did he notice anything out of the ordinary when he looked out the window?" DeDe asked.

Jewel smiled mysteriously. "Well, he didn't, but I did earlier. I never told the police this when they interviewed us. Actually, I forgot about it and remembered it later, but I never bothered to call it in. I didn't think it was important, I guess. Now, after all these years, I suppose it doesn't really matter anymore," she finished wistfully.

Leslie felt a chill run up her spine. "What did you forget to report, Jewel?"

"The Blackmans never knew it, but I saw Eric Osgood sneak in the back kitchen door about six-thirty." She sat up straighter as if she was a key witness in a trial and on the stand.

"Who's Eric Osgood?" DeDe asked.

"Eric was real sweet on Christina. Both the kids were juniors, and they'd gone to homecoming together the week before. The glow was still there. Know what I mean?" she asked, her tiny white eyebrows lifting delicately. She seemed pleased to tell this unknown tidbit of information.

"They were in love?" Leslie suggested.

Jewel giggled and waved her tiny hand in the air. "Puppy love, maybe," she suggested. "But your first love is always special."

DeDe fumbled with the envelope and pulled out the photo. Handing it to Jewel, she asked, "Do you recognize these people in this photo?"

Jewel smiled knowingly. "Oh, yes, that's Christina," she said, her finger shaking slightly as she pointed to the teenager. "She babysat our children on occasion, too. And that might be Eric." She pulled the photo closer and scrutinized it with an intense gaze. "Yes ... I think that's him." Jewel handed the photo back to DeDe.

"Did you see Eric leave again that evening?" Leslie asked.

Jewel nodded vigorously. "Oh, yes. He left around seven-thirty. I was just finishing the dinner dishes, and we were going to watch *Masterpiece Theatre* on television. I looked out my window over the kitchen sink and saw Eric wave to Christina and walk down the street."

"He was there a little over an hour?" DeDe asked.

"Yes, I'd say so," Jewel said.

"Anything else you can remember?" Leslie asked.

"Well, you probably know this, but my husband is the one who finally went over and knocked on the Blackmans' door when we heard the second scream. When he couldn't get Christina to answer, he called the police. They came and discovered she was missing."

"Did you observe any vehicles in the area that weren't familiar?" DeDe asked.

"Well, like I said, the neighborhood was always busy. Lots of families. I never noticed anything unusual that week—nothing except Eric visiting Christina while she was babysitting at Blackmans." Jewel sat back in her wheelchair, looking exhausted from the short exchange.

"One more thing. Did you see Eric Osgood return again after seven-thirty?

"No. He never returned that I knew of," Jewel said.

"And you definitely saw Christina alive when Eric left at seven-thirty?" DeDe asked.

"Yes, they kissed at the door," she said matter-of-factly.

"Is there anything else you can remember, Jewel?" Leslie asked.

"No. I've told you what I know. I always felt so bad about what happened to her. She was a sweet girl—smart, too." They waited a few more minutes, but soon Jewel's head bobbed and lolled to her chest. She'd fallen asleep.

DeDe and Leslie turned and quietly exited the room. Walking down the hallway, Leslie approached a nurse who was talking to an aide.

"Excuse me," Leslie said politely. "Could I ask you something about Jewel?"

"I can't give out information about patients," the nurse said, frowning. "HIPPA laws." She was a heavyset woman with short, frosted brown hair, a pudgy face, and dimpled hands. The frown on her forehead, her arms crossed over her chest, and her formidable wide stance seemed to challenge the detectives' authority to ask about personal patient information.

"Yes, I understand," Leslie said. "But we're from the La Crosse Sheriff's Department, and we just interviewed Ms. Loiselle about a current investigation we're conducting. We just wondered how reliable her memory is."

The nurse's stance relaxed a little. "Well, her memory isn't exactly a health condition, so I guess I can tell you what I know about that."

"Great. We'd appreciate it," DeDe said.

The nurse eyed her cautiously, then continued. "Jewel can't remember what happened yesterday." Leslie's heart sank at this piece of information. "But her long-term memory is excellent, and according to her family, what she remembers is exactly the way they remember it. But if I ask her tomorrow who her visitors were today— she'll have no memory that she even talked to you."

"So, in other words, her memory of an incident forty years ago would be more accurate than her memory about anything that happened yesterday?" Leslie asked.

"That's exactly right," the nurse said, finally smiling. "Her long-term memory is usually crystal clear."

"Thanks. That's good to know," DeDe said.

Back on the road to La Crosse, the two women discussed the ramifications of the new information.

"Why would someone withhold such an important piece of information in an abduction case?" DeDe asked, sounding frustrated.

"Assumptions," Leslie answered brusquely.

DeDe frowned. "What do you mean?"

"People assume that what they know isn't important, or that it won't have any bearing on the case, or they're trying to hide something."

"But it's like a puzzle," DeDe said, moving her hands in front of her as if she were putting things in order. "All the pieces need to be put into a coherent whole before the picture becomes clear. And the fact that Eric Osgood visited the home the night of the abduction is very important. In fact, it makes him a person of interest. No one knew about him until today. I don't remember reading his name in any of the interview notes."

"You're right. I don't remember seeing his name, either. He also might have seen something that could lead to other suspects."

"He could have swung back to the house and witnessed the abduction. At any rate, it's a new twist."

Leslie made a wry face and became philosophical for a moment. "You and I both know that investigations are a fluid process. If you follow a rigid protocol, you can miss the human factors in a case— the emotions, motivations, and fears that drive everything. The facts and the human passions need to be woven together to understand the whole. That's what makes this work so interesting—and frustrating."

"Well, ain't dat da truth," DeDe said, slipping in some Carolinian lingo.

Leslie smiled. *But the truth can be mighty slippery sometimes,* she thought.

33

The atmosphere in the old shed was dim and dark, although the sunshine outside was brilliant. The smell of mud and the aroma of cured tobacco had permeated the wood over the years and still lingered in the shed, along with piles of obsolete machinery. Sunlight streamed through a couple of holes in the patched, rotted roof, leaving buttery yellow puddles on the dirt floor. Dust motes drifted lazily in beams of sunlight. Inside the dark interior, planks of vertical pine were punctuated with a pattern of sunlit stripes; the rusting hulks sat as silent witnesses to the brutality taking place inside. Chirping noisily in the rafters, sparrows hopped from pole to pole, oblivious to the drama unfolding below them.

Maddog Pierson had enough illumination to accomplish the task at hand. He had no patience for traitors and demanded complete allegiance in the ranks of his drug operation. People who betrayed him—lowlifes like Marcellus Tate Brown—found out quickly what Maddog would do to someone who sold him out. Marcellus was having a very bad day, and it was about to get worse.

"How ya doin' now, Marcellus?" Maddog asked through clenched teeth as he hoisted him upward by his left ear. "Are you ready to reconsider your options?" He hovered over the snitch like a medieval inquisitor, his long hair brushing the sides of his unshaven face. His eyes were pinpoints of flat black anger, and he focused them on the whistleblower duct taped to an old wooden chair. Maddog released his captive's ear and noticed the tears running down Brown's cheeks.

In the background, just a few feet on either side of the drug lord, two enforcers stood in the shadows, their huge arms crossed over their chests, awaiting orders. Both men were gargantuan, their necks as thick as a man's thighs, their dull eyes devoid of emotion, their bodies hard as iron. They were trained to maim and kill.

Maddog reached out and grabbed a loose corner of duct tape and ripped it off Marcellus' mouth.

He screamed, his skin instantly puckered, turning bright pink. He spat on the dirt floor of the old shed. In the throes of severe drug withdrawal, Marcellus leaned forward and vomited on his clothes, gagging repeatedly. His body screamed with pain, and chills came over him in waves causing his teeth to chatter in his head.

"Not feelin' so good today, huh?" Maddog asked, feigning sympathy, stepping around the puddles of vomit.

Marcellus shook his head weakly. He was seized again with abdominal cramps, and he leaned forward and groaned in pain. His clothes were soaked in sweat and smelled sour, and his hair hung limply against his face. Pale and clammy, he grimaced when he tried to move his swollen hands and feet, which were taped to the old wooden chair. He had wet and soiled his pants. Marcellus was sure he was going to die.

"Let's talk about what you told that stupid cop the other day," Maddog began calmly. "Take your time, buddy. We've got all day and night if we need it." He grinned wickedly, leaning down and making eye contact with him.

Marcellus whimpered like a child, and his voice came in hoarse rasps. "I just told the cop that I thought you had a boat down behind the Lutheran hospital," he groaned weakly. "That's all I said."

The flat, broad hand struck him across the face, his neck

whipping sideways from the blow. Blood ran in a stream out of his nose and dripped off his upper lip onto his T-shirt. His eyes glazed over with shock and pain.

"That's it? You expect me to believe that?" Maddog shouted, angrier now.

"It's true. That's all I said." Marcellus' eyes rolled upward in his head as he shut his eyes.

"Who's this cop?" Maddog demanded loudly.

"His name's Sam something. I don't remember."

Another vicious slap sent his head jerking in the other direction. He felt like his teeth would fall out of his head. "You need to think a little harder, my friend," Maddog reminded him, his voice ominously quiet.

It was silent for a moment. Then Marcellus whispered, "Birksomething. Sam Birk ... stein."

"That's better. We're making progress," Maddog said soothingly, patting the prisoner's head like an obedient dog. "Now, tell me some more about this deadbeat Birkstein,," he began. He gave his cohorts a dark glance and nodded imperceptibly. Each man nodded in sync, their faces etched with grim determination. Maddog continued to question Marcellus about any plans the detective might have revealed, but Marcellus adamantly insisted he knew nothing. Maddog finally left the shed and walked out into the woods. He didn't like screaming and knew plenty would come from the shed in the next few hours.

Instead, he walked a half mile to the edge of a bluff overlooking a beautiful valley where a creek wandered through a stand of hardwoods. Holstein cows grazed in a lush green pasture along the hillside. Sitting on the limestone rock ledge, he dangled his feet over the rim. His thoughts drifted again to his innocent lovely daughter, Lillie. Plans were being made, plans for an exchange. But he wasn't ready yet. He was still getting a handle on this Higgins guy. The guy had some bravado coming on his boat and stealing the pictures of Lillie.

To be honest, he barely remembered the sex he'd had with the woman six years ago. He guessed that nowadays, people would say they had a relationship. What a joke. They were both higher than kites at the time. She claimed he was the father, but she was so delusional at that point in her addiction that he could have said the father was Santa Claus, and she would have believed it; he probably would have believed it, too.

He still didn't understand why he felt such a compulsion to get the girl back. Oh, she was a beautiful little thing—almost like a make-believe fairy nymph. In his most honest moments, which were few and far between, he was tiring of the brutal business of the drug world. No one appeared to be who they said they were. It was all smoke and mirrors. Maybe that was the appeal of being a father. He could finally come clean and be an honest, decent person.

Maddog envied Higgins' family life. They seemed so happy. He was seized with envy when he'd observed them behind the rocks on the detective's property. Higgins had a beautiful wife, a lovely home in an idyllic setting, and two gorgeous little children who looked to him for security and love. It was easy to see that Lillie had an incredibly strong connection with Higgins—one that could not easily be erased or substituted with someone else, least of all him.

Shaking his head sadly, he thought about love. That was something that had eluded him since his childhood. But he desperately wanted someone to love him as Lillie loved Higgins. Someone whose eyes shone with trust and innocence when they looked at him. He'd never experienced that. He'd walked away from that possibility when he left the hospital in Wausau the day Lillie was born—a mistake that would be hard to rectify now.

But now's my chance to change everything. I finally have a worthy opponent, he thought, *and a prize that will be worth the effort.* He tilted his head back in the warm sunshine and let his mind wander. *So much to do, so little time.*

34

Jim, Paul, and Sam huddled around a map of Wisconsin in the classroom on the third floor of the law enforcement center. The colored ends of stickpins stuck in random locations on the map reminded Sam of the failures of law enforcement to solve every single case. The frustration of the Kratt and Yelski cases filled him with deep-seated frustration. *Why couldn't anything ever be easy?* he thought.

Off to the side of the Wisconsin map, Jim had enlarged a La Crosse and Vernon County map which he had juxtaposed and stapled to the corkboard. He moved his finger from the scene of the Yelski abduction along a line paralleling U.S. Highway 14 southeast toward Vernon County.

"Alright, guys. Yelski was abducted here," he said, pointing to the Sunset Street crime scene, "and we don't know where she ended up, but the discarded clothing indicates a path that vaguely follows Highway 14 southeast of La Crosse along here." His finger moved slowly, stopping at the pinpoints that indicated the location of the articles of clothing that had been found.

"Forget about trying to find a body," Paul said. "After forty years, that will suck up any momentum we've got going. She could be buried anywhere."

"Margretta Yelski wouldn't feel the same as you about that," Jim reminded the two detectives.

Sam shrugged his shoulders casually, his eyes glued to the map. "Stick to finding Kratt's killer, and it may lead us to some new information about Yelski," Sam added. Paul nodded silently.

Jim dropped his hand to his side. "I agree, but if the two crimes are linked, then knowing as much about Yelski's abduction as possible might give us some other persons of interest that could lead us to new suspects and motives," Jim said.

"True," Paul added.

"Pie-in-the-sky bullshit," Sam said sourly. Jim gave him a withering glance. Paul frowned ominously.

"Well, thanks for your vote of confidence," Jim said, the sarcasm in his voice pronounced, "but the identification of the girl in the locket photo is a major piece of evidence that we can't ignore. And finding it at the Kratt crime scene suggests some kind of link."

"Seems logical. Maybe the girls will uncover something this morning," Paul said. "You got any better ideas?" he growled, staring at Sam. Sam scowled back like a pouting teenager.

Jim thoughtfully studied the map, then turned when DeDe and Leslie walked through the door, chattering back and forth.

"Speak of the devil. What's up? Find anything?" Jim asked, glancing hopefully from one woman to the other.

"Our interview with Jewel Loiselle was interesting," DeDe replied. "She claims she saw a teenage boy named Eric Osgood visit the Blackman home between six-thirty and seven-thirty the night of the abduction. She identified Eric from the photo with Christina. Said they were sweethearts, had gone to Homecoming together, and seemed to have a puppy-love relationship, whatever that means," she finished, rolling her eyes.

"She knew Eric how?" Jim asked.

"Well, she knew Christina because she'd babysat for her kids, and Eric lived nearby and had attended her church," Leslie said.

"Okay. That's good," Jim said, feeling hopeful for the first time in days. "You keep at it and find out where this Eric is now. We're going to want to interview him as soon as possible." Turning to Paul and Sam, he asked, "Anyone else in the investigator's notes that we should interview again? What about the Blackmans?"

"Mr. Blackman passed away in 2011, but Mrs. Blackman is still alive and lives in Winona." Sam looked at the clock. "We're heading over there for a scheduled interview at one o'clock."

"One other thing," Paul inserted, "Van Cleef and Arpels jewelry, according to their website, is very high-end. Most pieces range in the thousands of dollars. I looked online at a ruby and diamond ring priced at a quarter of a million. I think this necklace cost a significant chunk of change. It doesn't seem likely that a university professor like Yelski could afford it on his salary. And I checked into the serial numbers. They are used to identify their different jewelry lines, like the Alahambra line. They won't tell us anything more specific than that. Just so you know," he finished.

"That might be significant somewhere down the road," Jim added. Then, turning down the hall, he said, "Paul, walk with me a minute." When they were out of earshot, Jim stopped and faced him. The overhead fluorescent light in the inner hallway shone down on the two men and hummed with an irritating low-grade buzz.

"Just a heads up. Jones knows about our trip to Maddog's boat last night. I got dressed down this morning. I'm pretty sure you'll be hearing from him. I think he's cooled off since he talked to me," Jim told him. "Maybe my meeting took the piss and vinegar out of him, but I doubt it."

"How'd he find out?" Paul asked quietly, his eyes uneasy.

"City police were conducting surveillance on the boat." Paul covered his eyes with his hand, then let it slide down his face, letting out a sigh at the same time. Jim continued, "And you know, there are quite a few guys over at city who would just as soon cut my throat as work with me. Still, you gotta remember that what we did was illegal. Pedretti is ticked off. There'll be consequences."

"What's going to happen now?"

"I got a letter of reprimand in my file, and I'm hoping you'll receive the same treatment. If Jones calls you in, be ready. He's furious."

Paul's cell buzzed in his pocket. He glanced at the caller, then looked at Jim. "Jones," he said.

"When you don't play by the rules, shit happens," Jim said, clasping Paul's shoulder. "Sorry." His blue eyes were like brittle pieces of broken glass. "Don't deny it. Fess up. You'll do better that way."

Paul spoke into his cell. "Yes, Sheriff. I'll be right down," he said as he walked away, rolling his shoulders.

Jude Delaney wandered through the Cameron Street farmers' market, awed by the multicolored rainbow of garden vegetables, fruits, and flowers spread out before him in the tiny mobile booths. He'd been to farmers' markets all around New Orleans. Apparently, Wisconsin was just as adept at farming if the produce was any indication. He was excited by the variety of peppers, tomatoes, carrots, cauliflower, and cabbage available to customers. Jude quickly filled his rolling hand cart with the items needed to contribute to DeDe's dinner plans. Then seeing a beautiful bouquet of fresh flowers, he purchased them and bought some tempting homemade raspberry muffins for breakfast. Finishing his shopping, he walked briskly to his Lexus and headed to the houseboat in Pettibone Harbor.

Jude liked the simple, down-home vibe he was feeling the last few days in this river city. He'd grown up next to water his whole life and couldn't imagine living anywhere that didn't have a lake, river, or ocean close at hand. Wisconsinites were friendly and unassuming, straightforward and honest in their exchanges with him, and he found himself warming to them.

Driving to the harbor, the sight of the big blue bridge that stretched across the Mississippi, the iconic symbol of this river town, filled him with nostalgia. How many trips had he taken over the CCC, the Crescent City Connection, the twin cantilevered bridges over U.S. Highway 90 that connected New Orleans to the Westbank? And the sunsets on the I-10 twin-span bridge over Lake Pontchartrain were etched in his memory forever.

Now underneath the blue bridge, the Mississippi River stretched out, a deep greenish brown, the waves punctuating the surface into a million glittering diamonds. Fishermen bobbed in the current, casting and reeling with relaxed expertise. Despite his sudden ache of homesickness, Jude was comforted by this familiar water landscape.

Pettibone Park wasn't always in Wisconsin. In its early days, Houston County, Minnesota, claimed the land as payment for unpaid taxes. Early historical accounts described it as a harbor that catered to tough lumberjacks searching for beer and brothels. In 1901, Albert Pettibone purchased the land and designated it a public park. By 1918, President Woodrow Wilson signed a bill that authorized a border change between Wisconsin and Minnesota, and Pettibone Park became part of the burgeoning city of La Crosse, Wisconsin.

As he drove into the Pettibone marina, Jude noticed two old men fishing from a pier and multiple sunbathers lounging in the late September rays. A bare-chested college student ripped a frisbee into the air, enthused about a round of disc golf.

Jude parked in the shade along the blacktopped lot, unloaded the groceries from the car into the collapsible cart, and walked onto the third pier until he came to slip 67. The houseboat, though old, looked comfortable and clean. He stepped onto the deck, found the key under the empty flowerpot, and opened the door.

Inside, he got familiar with the layout of the tiny kitchen. Flinging open the small windows, a stiff breeze off the river evaporated the stuffiness inside. Pots, pans, and utensils began to appear as he created a light brown roux, then added carrots, onions, garlic, and peppers, the base of his famous gumbo. He stirred in chicken stock and prepared the fresh okra he'd found at the farmers' market. The shrimp, chicken, and okra would go in later. With the gumbo stock bubbling gently, he tackled a spring salad, tearing up iceberg and spring lettuces and adding cherry tomatoes, blanched asparagus, and hard-cooked eggs in a chilled bowl which he wedged into the refrigerator.

He cracked open a Spotted Cow beer and sipped it as he hummed happily under his breath. He prepared two chickens for roasting using olive oil, garlic, thyme, and lemons. He crisped some bacon, carmelized some onions to garnish the chicken later, and made an anchovy dressing for the salad, which he put in the fridge to chill. Then he stepped out on the deck of the houseboat again and found a warm spot in the sun, kicking back, relaxing in the beautiful harbor.

Jude Delaney was a study in contrasts. He was tall and lean, yet strong and muscled. He gave the impression of worldly accomplishment in his lavender silk shirt, casual slacks, and Doc Marten slip-ons, but the expensive clothes belied his simple beginnings. In his five-star establishment, he rubbed elbows with the rich and famous—the upper crust in New Orleans. Everyone raved about his food, and his culinary awards and recognition were hard-won and well-earned. His creative approach to Southern cuisine made his food timeless yet fresh and exciting. Jude was the impresario of the culinary world—an aloof king of cuisine. But secretly, he lived a life of insecurity and loneliness.

Beneath all the hype was a man who enjoyed simplicity and longed for the unpretentious pace of life before cell phones, Facebook, Snapchat, and the constant cultural hypervigilance that had invaded and plagued American society. He was so done with all the outrageous behavior and ridiculous attitudes.

His childhood was scarred by neglect and loss. His mother prostituted herself to feed her young son, and his father gambled away any respectability the Delaney name might have ever had. In the end, Lou Delaney died destitute in a New Orleans back alley without ever having had a relationship with his only son. His mother died when he was in his teens from ovarian cancer. By the age of fourteen, Jude Delaney was alone in the world.

While his mother turned tricks in his childhood, he spent hours lingering at the back door of the classic Louisiana café *C'est Bon* in the French Quarter. He'd lived in a slouching, rickety walk-up with his mother that faced the alley behind the restaurant. The alley became his childhood playground. He'd romped among garbage cans and delivery trucks, learning to look out for himself while playing with his Hot Wheels collection in the shade of a couple of beautiful linden trees. Beneath their heart-shaped green leaves, he listened to the talk that drifted from the restaurant's back door. The convivial atmosphere of the staff left him with a deep-seated longing for family and authentic relationships.

The head chef, Amado Cormeir, took a liking to him and fed him classic Southern cooking on white dinner plates with white dinner napkins—gumbo, grits and eggs, po'boys, sweet potato pie, and a variety of other classic Southern fares—which enlivened the boy's tastebuds and curiosity about food. Cormeir became Jude's surrogate father and his cooking mentor.

Gradually, Cormeir incorporated him into the culture of the diner, first as a busboy, then as a sous chef, and then as a classic Southern cook. Singlehandedly, the portly chef adopted him into the cooking family of *C'est Bon*. Cormier loved him and taught him the rules and etiquette that governed the cooking world. Jude learned the business from the bottom up. He adored the man and never forgot what Amado had done for him.

Waiting for DeDe to arrive at the houseboat, his stomach clenched anxiously despite the cool calm of his exterior. DeDe was the only person he'd ever met who had figured him out. She understood his real needs hiding behind his steely reputation. But then, DeDe should understand—she was an orphan just like him. DeDe wasn't a knockout goddess like many women who had strolled in and out of his life over the last twenty years. Rather, she had a subtle beauty that came from within—a rock-solid knowledge of who she was meant to be—something she'd credited to Hettie and Lorenzo Deverioux, her now-deceased grandparents.

"Don't pull any punches with me," she'd told him when they started dating seriously. In her low-country dialect, she crooned, "I knowed yo' from the minute I laid eyes on yo'. Yo' just like me." When she looked at him, her brown eyes seemed to see every wound he'd ever experienced—the loss of his mother, the embarrassment of her prostitution, the absence of a father, the insecurity of being alone and abandoned, the need to belong somewhere.

DeDe became Jude's nail in a sure place. She had the gift of getting to the essence of a person almost from the moment she met them. No prodigious crowing, no phony baloney, no braggadocio, thank you very much. And out of that honesty came trust. Trust. Such a simple word but laden with so much meaning. Trust was the reason he'd spent three weeks hunting her down when she'd inexplicably disappeared from his life three months ago.

Now when he thought about it, she'd been totally honest with him, and he'd sent her into overdrive by trying to hide every questionable thing about his life. Maybe she had good reasons for running away. After she'd left so suddenly, he realized he'd committed a grave error in not returning her honesty with some of his own. Now he was praying she'd let him back into her life.

Jude finished his beer, belched loudly, reclined with a waterproof pillow behind his head, and closed his eyes. His thoughts continued tumbling around in his head, and finally, the last three weeks caught up to him. He fell asleep in the warm sunshine, his beer bottle tucked between him and the boat cushion.

35

The early September afternoon was warm and balmy. Sam and Paul drove beside the Mississippi River along Hwy. 61 thirty miles into Winona, Minnesota. Winona took its name from the Dakota word Wenonah which embraced the legend of Princess Wenonah, the daughter of Chief Wapasha (Wabasha) III, who inhabited the site of the Native American village named Keoxa. The Native Americans who settled Winona were of the band of the eastern Dakota called Mdewakanton.

The picturesque bluff country was stunningly beautiful in the fall sunshine. Approaching the city, Sam noticed Sugar Loaf, the five-hundred-foot towering limestone pinnacle that watched over Winona like a finger pointing into the sky at the junction of U.S. Route 61 and State Hwy. 43. The name was given to the rock because it resembled the conical loaves of sugar that used to be packaged in Winona and sold throughout the U.S.

Driving through Winona into the historic district of Windom Park, Sam pulled up to the Blackman home on Third Street. He killed the engine. He noticed Paul had been subdued on the drive over.

"Hey, you okay?" he asked Paul.

"Yeah. Fine," Paul sighed, although Sam knew otherwise. Not

wishing to intrude, Sam grabbed his file folder of information off the seat and stepped out of the Jeep. Paul climbed out and joined him on the sidewalk.

The neighborhood was filled with historic homes that people affectionately called the lumber mansions. They were not unlike the ones found in the city of La Crosse. Lumber money had built them, and ingenious architects designed these Victorian castles with splendid attention to detail, making each home unique and memorable.

Sam and Paul stood in front of the Blackman home, a blue-sided two-story Victorian dwelling that featured doorways and windows wrapped with white stylized molding and a rambling front porch. A dark red front door was accentuated by a dome-shaped transom window.

Walking onto the broad porch, Sam rang the bell and waited. A young woman with dark hair and eyes came to the door holding a toddler in her arms.

"Hello. We're from the La Crosse Sheriff's Department," Sam said. They flashed their IDs. "We're here to talk to Doris Blackman."

"Oh, that's my mother-in-law. She lives in the carriage house out back," the young woman pointed behind her. "Just go down the driveway, and you'll see the separate entrance. I believe Doris is home. She doesn't drive much anymore," the woman said. The toddler stared wide-eyed at the detectives, his thumb stuck in his mouth, his hair tousled and curled around his face.

"Thanks. Sorry to bother you," Paul said, smiling at the child. They turned and walked across the lawn down the driveway to the rear of the house. The carriage house had the same blue siding and white trim. Another bell. Another wait.

A rustling at the door alerted them, and Mrs. Doris Blackman appeared. She was an attractive, elderly woman with beautiful white hair stylishly cut. Her smile was friendly, her eyes intelligent. She wore deftly applied makeup, making her seem younger than her seventy-five years.

"Hello. You must be the detectives from La Crosse," she said, opening the door wider. "Please come in."

Inside, the apartment was impressive. Gorgeous maple wood floors gleamed, and trim around the windows and pocket doors hinted at an elegance from an earlier time. Mrs. Blackman led them into the small living room decorated with modern leather furniture. Sam noticed a pot of coffee and cups resting on a silver tray on the coffee table. Watercolors of Winona cityscapes and Mississippi River scenes were hung on the neutral ivory walls. A floor-to-ceiling bookshelf filled one wall, and Sam noticed the wide variety of reading material—everything from fiction, geography tomes, ancient classics, and how-to books.

"Coffee, gentlemen?" Doris asked politely. It smelled wonderful and made the room seem warm and welcoming.

"That'd be great," Paul said, rubbing his hands together. They found a seat on the leather sofa.

While Mrs. Blackman poured the coffee, Sam began filling her in on the events surrounding the Kratt murder and its possible connection to the Yelski abduction.

"When we discovered the photo of Christina in the locket at the Kratt murder scene, we began to reexamine all the evidence that had been collected surrounding the cold case. That's why we're here. We'd like to ask you a few questions about the evening of the Yelski abduction," Sam finished.

"Well, I have a question of my own, actually," Mrs. Blackman said, lifting her blue eyes to meet Sam's. "Do you really believe that Mr. Kratt was killed because some vigilante sought revenge or wanted some kind of delayed justice? That seems pretty incredible to me. After all, it's been forty years since the abduction." She raised her cup to her lips and sipped politely. "Most people today wouldn't even recognize the Yelski name and probably know little if anything about the case."

"We know it sounds like a stretch," Paul spoke up. "But there doesn't seem to be another explanation for the locket and note found at the Kratt murder scene."

"What is it you think I can help with?" Mrs. Blackman asked.

"Did you know Eric Osgood?" Sam asked, watching Mrs. Blackman's reaction carefully. She looked surprised at a question that, at first glance, seemed unrelated to the topic they were discussing.

"Eric Osgood? Oh, yes, I knew Eric. He was a member of our church—First Lutheran, over on Glendale Avenue on the south side of La Crosse. He was an honor scholar—a Rhodes scholar, I believe. And a very nice young man," she answered. Her puzzled look continued.

"Were you aware that someone saw him entering your home on the night of the abduction at about six-thirty?" Paul asked.

Mrs. Blackman lowered her coffee cup to the saucer on the table, and her eyes widened noticeably. "Really? I didn't know that. That is rather disturbing, isn't it?"

"We're just wondering if there would have been some reason he came by your house at that time of night when you were gone, and Christina was alone," Sam told her.

"I know of no reason why he should've been there. Christina knew we didn't approve of any visitors while she was watching Dorian. It was a standard rule for all the babysitters we hired. She was always so honest and straightforward. This is such a surprise," she said. Mrs. Blackman's shocked reaction seemed genuine.

"I take it you were not aware that Eric had been in your home that evening?" Sam reiterated.

"No."

The interview continued for some time as Sam and Paul took Mrs. Blackman back through the events of the evening when the abduction of the young Yelski girl had taken place. But nothing in her recollection provided any new information they didn't already have in the original interview notes.

"Do you know what happened to Eric Osgood?" Paul asked.

Mrs. Blackman frowned. "I heard some years back that he went to Vanderbilt and became an ornithologist, but since then, I've lost track of him. Sorry I can't be of more help," she finished weakly.

"More coffee?"

"No, thanks. We appreciate that you talked to us. If you remember anything more, please contact us," Sam told her, standing up and handing her his card. "We'll let ourselves out."

The ride back to La Crosse was pleasant, but Sam wondered about Paul's withdrawn demeanor. Usually, they never lacked things to talk about—sports, marriage, kids, crime, sex, technology, politics. You named it, and they could talk about it. When they were almost back to the law enforcement complex on Vine Street, Paul opened up.

"Had a talk with Jones this morning," Paul started.

"Jones? Why?" Sam asked, his eyebrows coming together in a frown.

"Well, I might as well tell you. Higgins and I broke into Maddog's boat last night over at the municipal harbor and got caught on a police surveillance camera." There was a long silence.

Glancing at Paul, Sam let out an audible groan. "What in the world were you guys thinking?"

"Well, believe it or not, we did think about it and plan it. But we got caught."

"Not to mention it was totally illegal," Sam stated emphatically.

"Yeah, there's that, too. Believe me, the meeting with Jones wasn't pretty, but I scraped my pride off the wall after he let me have it, and I came out of his office with a letter of reprimand in my file. It could have been a lot worse." Paul rubbed the side of his face, then let his hand plop into his lap. The dark circles under his eyes hinted at a sleepless night.

"I can't believe you guys did that!" Sam said in an irritated tone, trying to understand. By now, he'd swung into the parking lot and shut off the Jeep. He turned and leaned against the driver's door.

Loosening his tie, he fixed a stare at Paul.

Paul continued to gaze out the window. "Listen, you don't have kids yet. This threat involving Lillie is really eatin' on Higgins. And I've got to admit that if it was my family, I might have done the same thing. He asked me to help him, so I did. Got my ass in a sling over it, too."

"Ah, don't beat yourself up. Everybody screws up once in a while. The important thing is—was it worth it? Did you find anything?"

"Yeah. Maddog's been watching Higgins' family with binoculars in those rocks behind his house. Higgins found pictures stashed in a drawer on the boat that the Dog had taken of Lillie. The infamous drug dealer seems intent on getting her back." Paul's face was intense and serious.

"That's not good," Sam said. His stomach flip-flopped. "That's really not good."

"No. No, it's not. And I have no idea what Higgins intends to do about it," Paul finished. "He wouldn't tell me, but he's probably planning some Lone Ranger thing."

"Well, there's one thing you can be sure of. He won't let this go without a fight," Sam replied, his forehead creased with hard worry lines.

"Yeah, I know. That's what worries me," Paul whispered.

"This may call for an intervention," Sam said overconfidently, "and I'm going to need your help."

"I was afraid you were going to say that."

36

By six-thirty Friday evening, the party on DeDe's houseboat was in full swing. Everyone had arrived around six o'clock, and the cool beautiful weather held steady, making the night on the Mississippi River magical. Dragonflies hovered over the water's surface, darting in jerks, their iridescence glowing in the evening light. Across the water, conversations from other boaters floated on the slight breeze, and smoke from grills in the park drifted into the evening atmosphere, the tantalizing smell of steaks and hamburgers fueling everyone's hunger.

Jude and DeDe were spectacular hosts in the tradition of Southern hospitality, passing drinks and food continuously until everyone was thoroughly satisfied. Recovering from the surprise of DeDe's secret husband, the team enjoyed a bayou-inspired feast—gumbo with okra and shrimp, corn on the cob, roasted chicken with bacon and caramelized onions, iceberg salad with anchovy dressing, and DeDe's wonderful dirty rice. Jude Delaney proved to be the marvelous cook that DeDe had claimed. Everything was fresh, delicious, and tastefully seasoned.

Jim watched the team relax and wished he could do the same. *If you don't quit this brooding, you're going to go into overdrive and have a heart attack, and you won't do anybody any good,* he thought. Lillie sat beside him on the deck, watching everyone with curious eyes. Her hand found its way into his, and he talked quietly with her as she watched the crowd. Somehow, she seemed to sense Jim's angst and had taken it upon herself to keep him company.

Carol and Ruby watched Henri and Melody toddle on the forward deck. Jim caught snippets of conversation that revolved around pregnancy. Ruby had blossomed and expanded since Jim had seen her a couple of months ago, but her beauty was just as seductive as ever. DeDe listened to the reproductive talk with enthralled wonder, adding vignettes about her grandma Hettie who used backwoods potions to help infertile women conceive. Some of it sent the girls into uproarious laughter. Paul, Leslie, and Jude were engaged in a lively exchange, and their easygoing banter floated across the water.

Sam wandered over and sat down next to Jim.

"So, I hear you and Paul had some extracurricular activities last night. Like clandestine type stuff which got you in hock with Jones," he began. He crossed his legs and sipped on his vodka-spiked watermelon punch. Jim thought he looked ridiculous with a pink drink in his hand, although it didn't seem to bother Sam in the least. *Whatever,* he thought.

Breaking his gaze away from the activity in the harbor, he turned to face Sam. "You heard right," he said simply. "You on a fishing expedition?"

"You might say that. If you need help, Chief, you know where I am, right?" Sam's hazel eyes were warm with alcohol-induced emotions.

"Sure, I hear you. I've got you on speed dial." He wasn't sure if Sam's concerns were authentic. Did he really want to get involved in a scheme that might go south? It didn't matter. *You'll never know what I've got planned,* he thought.

"Don't do anything crazy, Chief," Sam said. "Remember, two's company and three's a crowd does *not* apply in this instance. If you need the cavalry, we'll be there. Remember the Grandad Bluff escapade." Sam shuddered involuntarily. "Just call if you could use some help."

"Thanks. I appreciate it," Jim said, but he knew that would never happen. Confronting Maddog was his odyssey—a personal and solitary one. Defending his family and protecting them was nobody else's job but his.

"So, what are your plans, Jude?" Jim asked when the chef wandered over. "New restaurant in town?" Jim sipped a Leinenkugel's and took in the essence of the man. Although Jude had been nervous at the start of the dinner party, now he seemed loose and relaxed. His culinary prowess was evident in the delicious fare he'd shared with joy and abandon. Jim liked him very much.

"I hear there's a lot of European tradition in the area—Norwegian, German, a little French, some Bohemian—so I'm not so sure a true Southern restaurant would be a hit. But Midwest cuisine is coming into its own. Maybe a marriage of Southern sensibilities combined with great Midwest produce? What do you think?" He cocked his head and studied Jim and Sam.

"If the food is anything like we had tonight, it'll be standing room only. That's my prediction," Jim said, smiling enthusiastically. "You already have fans." He waved his arm over the crowded boat.

"Here, here. I totally agree," Leslie said, sliding in next to Sam. She looked amazing in a white linen shirt accentuated with lace across the bodice and a tight pair of jeans that played up her shapely figure. Sam tenderly wrapped his arm around her shoulders. "This food tonight was incredible. So when are you going to open your restaurant?" she asked, squinting up at Jude.

He smiled broadly, and the smile reached his eyes. Then he became serious. "It's a lot of work setting up a dining establishment. Finding a location with good traffic, creating a menu and marketing image, hiring staff, designing a decorating scheme, and equipping a kitchen and dining area. A huge amount of work," he repeated.

Rubbing his hands together, he continued. "Plus, it takes mega dollars. But I'm impressed with the high-quality local food scene. The farmers' markets are phenomenal. Beautiful river city. The nice vibe from the locals, plus the college population, is a good draw, too. There's a lot to like."

DeDe walked over. Jude pulled her close and kissed her cheek. "Here's my girl," he said sincerely, his demeanor softening with sentiment.

"What? Y'all fillin' these folks with yo' hoodoo?" she asked. "Don't believe a word he says," she teased, reverting back to standard English. Jim noticed her eyes shining when she looked at him.

After another half hour of animated conversation, Carol captured Henri, who had started to fuss and cry. "Jim, I think we should go before the whole evening goes up in smoke," she said. With that, everyone took their cues and started saying their goodbyes.

After everyone had gone, Jude and DeDe cleaned up the party mess. Jude boxed the leftovers and crammed them into the small refrigerator. Cleaning up the dishes and wiping the counters took another half hour. DeDe swept and bagged up the garbage, taking it to the dumpster at the end of the pier. Finally, the job was done, and they retreated to the forward deck cuddling together under a blanket in the growing darkness. A wispy fog hung over the surface of the water, and the air had a chill to it.

The sun had slipped below the bluffs, but the sky continued to glow with ethereal orange and pink clouds punctuated by the undulating black silhouette of the bluffs along the horizon. A few stars began to prick the darkening sky overhead, and a couple of boats floated on the river like bobbers on a fishing line. Lights from houses began flickering along the shore, reminding Jude of fireflies blinking in the night.

"It was a nice party. They're decent people, DeDe. Simple people," Jude said. "They seem like common, ordinary folks. Not out to impress anyone." Her head rested lightly on his shoulder while she wrapped her arm through his.

"Yes, they're very likable, aren't they?" DeDe commented dreamily. "They seem so *normal.* They've made me feel very welcome."

Jude held her hand, relishing the moment. "I missed you, baby ... a lot," he said softly, his eyes serious. DeDe turned her face up to his with a tenderness that filled Jude with hope.

She thought about the advice Leslie had given her. *Hold love loosely like sand in your hand,* "Oh, JuJu, I missed you, too." She leaned against him, placed her hand on his chest, and kissed him tenderly. "Bed?"

"You don't have to ask twice, sweetheart," Jude said. They stood up and walked into the houseboat, shedding their clothes as they went. Lying naked on the bed, Jude caressed DeDe, kissing her fervently all over, whispering, "Now this is what I'm talkin' about."

"Shh. Quit talkin' for once, will ya?" DeDe said, her breath quickening, returning his kisses eagerly.

"My lips are sealed, baby."

37

SATURDAY MORNING, SEPTEMBER 14

Sam was sweating profusely as he jogged along on the Bicentennial Trail in Hixon Forest north of the duplex on Cliffwood early Saturday morning. The soles of his shoes slapped the gravel-covered trail and mixed with his huffing breaths in a comforting rhythm. Occasionally bird song penetrated the foggy morning. The smell of decaying wood and leaves reminded Sam of the nights he'd spent camping with his family. The earthy smells activated his memory of places he'd been—the Black Hills, the Boundary Waters Canoe Area, Wisconsin Dells, and Devil's Lake. Good times, fun times.

Paco woofed enthusiastically, coming up behind Sam in a dead run in a futile chase with a squirrel who had hightailed it up a nearby tree. The black lab was beginning to show gray on his muzzle and eyebrows, and he had a little white on the tip of his tail, making him look like a quirk of nature—a black body with random splotches of gray and white as if an artist had stood back and splattered him with paint.

Despite his eight years of age, he was in remarkable shape. Sam figured all the morning runs and frisbee-catching exercise in the backyard had helped him keep his edge in the canine world. His eyes were clear, his hearing phenomenal, his intelligence keen, and his loyalty to Leslie unquestioned. Their missions together in the deserts of Iraq sniffing out IEDs had bonded them for life. That he'd finally accepted Sam into his circle of trusted friends after almost three years was rewarding. Sam had come to love the big brute as if he were his own.

Now, nearing the end of the trail, Sam slowed to a brisk walk, cooling down as he headed for the Jeep. Clipping Paco onto his leash, the dog panted happily next to him as they walked into the parking lot near the golf course. Opening the vehicle door, Paco leaped up in the front passenger seat, covering it with his slobber and drool as they headed home.

Sam rolled the Jeep to a stop in the driveway on Cliffwood. The neighborhood was shuttered and quiet for a Saturday morning. Random leaves from the oak and maple trees that lined the boulevard were beginning to flutter onto the driveway, a sure sign that fall had arrived. They went around to the back entrance, and Sam unlocked the door. Paco made a beeline for his water dish and kibble. Sam headed for the shower.

Walking into the bedroom with just a towel around his waist after cleaning up, Sam quietly rummaged through his dresser, digging out boxers, a yellow T-shirt that said U of N – LAS VEGAS, and a practically new pair of gray L.L. Bean hiking shorts he'd bought at Goodwill for five bucks. Leslie stirred when he sat on the bed to pull on a pair of socks.

She rolled on her back and let her arm flop lazily above her head. "What time is it?" she asked sleepily. Her golden hair fanned out on the pillow, and Sam looked at her over his shoulder.

"A little after six," he said, pulling on his sock.

"You run already?"

"Yep. I took Paco up to Hixon."

"That was some food last night, wasn't it?" Leslie said, staring at the ceiling.

"It was mighty tasty. Fantastic, actually," Sam said, standing. He walked to the closet to find his athletic shoes.

A sudden thud on the front door startled them, and they both looked at each other quizzically. Paco let out a series of deep barks and barreled to the door, then stood there whining, cocking his head from side to side. Sam heard a vehicle taking off from the curb, revving its engine as it went down the street.

He walked to the bedroom window peering through the blinds but couldn't see the front porch from that angle. But looking farther down the street, he noticed a black pickup moving fast, heading away from the duplex in a hurry.

"What the … ? Can't be UPS this early," he muttered. "Besides, it's a Saturday. You order anything from Amazon, honey?" he said distractedly. He walked into the living room, not waiting for her answer, carrying his shoes in one hand. He dropped the shoes on the floor and headed to the front entrance in his stocking feet.

Flinging the dead bolt aside, he swung the door open, but a heavy weight pushed on the door, catching him off guard, making him trip backward.

Marcellus Tate Brown lay crumpled like a wet noodle against the door's threshold. He was unconscious, his face battered and bruised, dried blood staining his nostrils, mouth, and forehead. Sam noticed his clothes were filthy, covered with blood, vomit, dirt, and mud like he'd been mauled in a gladiator's ring by a lion. Paco sniffed and snuffled with curiosity, then growled ominously, the hair standing up on the back of his neck.

Sam knelt next to Marcellus and felt for a pulse in his neck. Faint, barely there. "Oh, jeez!" Sam croaked to himself. "Lez! Get out here! Now!" he yelled over his shoulder. He heard Leslie race from the bedroom and stop abruptly behind him.

"Oh, my Lord!" Leslie exclaimed, leaning over Sam. Her eyes widened at the sight of the crushing injuries, and she wondered how anyone could still be alive after such damage.

"Call 911 for an ambulance, then call Higgins!" Sam ordered briskly. He leaned over Marcellus, rolled him on his back, and lifted his eyelids. No response. Pulling his shirt up, Sam was shocked at the bruises and contusions on his chest.

"Man, someone really worked him over," he said, tamping down the panic rising in his chest. "His pulse is very faint."

"So obviously, this is some kind of message?" Leslie asked, wincing at the condition of the man. Then another question. "Who's *they?*"

"Probably Maddog and his thugs," he said under his breath. "Marcellus! Marcellus! Can you wake up?" Sam shouted, patting his cheeks. Paco barked urgently. Sam heard Leslie giving the 911 operator the address of their duplex and the type of emergency.

"Ambulance is on its way," she said crisply.

A faint groan escaped the mangled body. Leslie watched in horrid fascination as Brown's tongue crept out of his mouth and moved over his cracked, blood-encrusted teeth and lips. Eventually, with great effort, Marcellus opened his bruised eyelids and squinted up at Sam.

"Marcellus, who did this to you?" Sam asked, leaning down close to his face. "Tell me." His nose crinkled at the scent of vomit and feces, and he pulled his head back, suppressing the urge to gag.

"Mad ... dog," he whispered. "Tell Higgins . . ." But he was out again, unconsciousness.

Farther up the street, Leslie heard the whining scream of the ambulance siren echoing down the maze of streets surrounding their duplex. Screeching into the driveway, two EMTs jumped out and ran up the stairs to assess Brown's condition. They ran back to the ambulance and returned with a stretcher and oxygen. One of the technicians gave him a shot of morphine for pain.

"Where are you taking him?" Sam asked. They continued monitoring his condition as he watched them work.

"St. Francis. It's closer, but he might not make it. He's very badly beaten, his vital signs are poor, and he's in severe drug withdrawal.

His condition is precarious, to say the least," the EMT said brusquely. Noticing Sam's confused look, he explained. "We've had him in the ER before. Why's he on your doorstep?"

Sam shrugged as he continued to stare down at Marcellus. "Somebody's sending me a message, I guess."

"Well, that's a comforting thought, eh?" the blonde attendant sneered.

The two EMTs maneuvered Marcellus onto a stretcher, lifted it, walked down the driveway, and loaded the patient into the back of the ambulance. The door slammed, and they took off, the siren wailing its obnoxious warning throughout the quiet neighborhood. Doors began opening, and people appeared on their porches and sidewalks in their pajamas and sweats to get a look at the commotion.

Sam looked Leslie up and down. "You need to get dressed. What about the chief? You call him?"

"I tried. Couldn't get an answer, so I left a message," she said. Turning quickly, she hurried into the bedroom and threw on a pair of jeans and a sweatshirt. Sam whipped on his shoes, fumbling to tie his laces with his shaking hands.

"Never mind, I'll call Higgins," he hollered down the hallway to Leslie. He punched Higgins' number in his phone and waited. Leslie appeared next to him in the living room. "Damn, he must have shut his phone off. I'll keep trying. You ready?" he asked.

"Yeah, let's go," Leslie said as she headed for the front door. Sam locked the door and ran to the Jeep. The traffic was light, and he roared down side streets until he came to Jackson. Driving rapidly to St. Francis Hospital, he whipped his vehicle into the emergency parking lot. He was about to get out of his Jeep when his phone buzzed.

"Birkstein."

"Sam, did Leslie call?" Higgins asked. "How come she's not answering her phone? What's going on?" He fired the questions rapidly, sounding irritated like he'd just gotten out of bed.

"Somebody dumped Marcellus Brown, one of my informants, on my steps this morning at six. He's been beaten to within an inch of his life. He managed to tell me it was Maddog. The EMTs don't know if he'll survive. We're at St. Francis, and we're just walking into the emergency room now."

"I'll be there in twenty minutes," Higgins barked. The line went dead.

38

The ER physician in the emergency room at St. Francis Hospital looked like he was about twelve years old. His skin was flawless with just a shadow of dark whiskers, and his eyes were as clear as a mountain stream. He had an innocence about him that Jim found depressing because it made him feel old. He didn't have so much as an ounce of fat on him. His name tag dangled from his smock next to his stethoscope—Dr. Tenny Lindstrom. Despite the multiple crises facing him in the ER, Dr. Lindstrom looked fresh-faced and chipper as if he were having a normal conversation instead of passing judgment on someone's chances at life. After Jim had given him the once over, he zeroed in on what he was saying. Dr. Lindstrom stood in front of Sam, Leslie, and Jim and gave his dire verdict.

"I'm sorry, but Mr. Brown has been drifting in and out of consciousness since he was brought in. We've patched his jaw together as best we can—he's not in good enough condition right now to make it through surgery, although he needs it. He's suffering from severe drug withdrawal. His injuries are extensive—a broken jaw, loose teeth, cracked ribs, a bruised liver and kidneys. We've done the best we can right now. But his biggest problem is the drug withdrawal. We've administered some medications to ease some of his symptoms, but whoever did this made him go cold turkey which would have been a short trip to hell. As it is, his existence is teetering on the brink. His major organs are threatening to mutiny and shut down."

Jim rocked uneasily on his feet. "He's a very important link to a major drug kingpin that we're trying to apprehend," he began explaining. "If he regains consciousness in the next few hours, we really need to talk to him." Jim handed the physician his card, as did Sam.

"Sure, I understand. We'll call if his condition improves and he can communicate," the doctor said briskly. He turned and waved, rushing to his next emergency case.

"Since when are doctors twelve years old?" Jim asked gruffly.

"Not twelve. Maybe thirty," Leslie suggested.

"Are you going to be home today in case we need to reach you?" Sam asked as they headed to the lobby entrance stepping around someone being pushed in a wheelchair and another patient teetering on crutches.

"Thought about taking *The Little Eddy* out on the river and heading south to where the Bad Axe dumps into the Mississippi. We'll be back toward evening."

"I'll handle anything that comes up with Marcellus," Sam offered. They stopped on the sidewalk out front.

"Thanks. I'll have my phone, so call if you need something," Jim said. He turned and waved as he walked to his Suburban.

Leslie looked after him, mumbling under her breath, "I worry about him."

"You aren't the only one," Sam replied, grabbing her hand. "Breakfast?"

"Sounds great," she said as they returned to the Jeep.

When Jim arrived back at his house on Chipmunk Coulee Road, he was greeted with squeals and giggles. Henri and Lillie were chasing each other naked through the house, screaming up a storm. Jim scooped up Henri as he scurried past him. He carried him into the bedroom, rummaging through the dresser for clothes. Henri squirmed and tried to wriggle out of Jim's grasp.

"No, you don't, you little bruiser," Jim warned. "You want pancakes and sausage?"

Henri stopped squirming and nodded his head vigorously, his brown eyes serious and focused.

"Then let's get dressed, little guy," Jim finished, his voice no-nonsense.

Once Henri was dressed and Lillie had found some clothing, Jim walked down the hall and peeked in the bathroom. Carol was in the shower.

"Honey?"

"Uh-huh," she said patiently.

Jim opened the shower door about six inches. "Are you up for a little trip on the river?"

"Absolutely. I'll be out in a minute," she said.

Jim headed back down the hallway to the kitchen. Lillie and Henri had settled down and were playing with Legos in the sunshine on the dining room floor. Jim started browning the sausage links in the pan, then threw together some buttermilk pancake batter. Within minutes the children were wolfing down the fluffy pancakes, dripping syrup and melted butter on the table and down the front of their clothes. They were finally quiet, and Jim could take his first sip of coffee. He stood by the counter, relishing the peace that had finally descended, however brief it might be.

Carol appeared, dressed in jeans and a long-sleeved light blue polo shirt. Her feet were bare, her hair was damp, and she wore no makeup. Jim thought she was lovely, although she would have argued with him about that.

"Coffee?" Jim asked, kissing her lightly on the lips.

"Absolutely. Mmm, pancakes and sausage. You're showin' me

up, buddy," she said, smiling happily, wrapping her arm around his waist. "Where'd you run off to this morning? Breaking into another boat?"

Jim frowned and untangled himself from her hug. "No. I'll fill you in later," he said sourly, pointing to the children.

"Got it," she said, picking up her plate of sausage and cakes.

By eleven o'clock, Jim was piloting *The Little Eddy* out of Pettibone Harbor, heading south toward Lock and Dam #8 near Genoa, Wisconsin. Henri cuddled in Jim's lap at the wheel of the boat, his little chubby hands tightly gripping Jim's large ones as they navigated the current. Lillie ran from side to side up on the front deck with Carol, pointing out a bald eagle soaring above the bluffs. Carol's eyes met Jim's, and she mouthed, "Thank you." Her tanned face was relaxed, her brown eyes smoky and captivating.

Once they were through the lock, the Mississippi River opened up, wide and glorious. Jim leisurely piloted *The Little Eddy* through the rapid current, enjoying the sight of the soaring bluffs and the comforting warmth of sunshine soaking into their bones. Eventually, he navigated into an area of scattered inlets and islands where the Bad Axe River emptied into the Mississippi. He found a deserted sandy beach on a small, secluded strip of land.

Running the boat up on shore, Jim jumped off and tied up to a small clump of paper birch. A chipmunk ran the length of a weathered, fallen log on the sandy bank, its tail aloft in the air like a miniature flag. Lillie hopped off the boat, pointed excitedly at the little animal, and proceeded to hop back and forth over the top of the log, trying to find the chipmunk's burrow.

They set up a little camp, arranging blankets and pillows for napping under a weeping willow, unfolding lawn chairs around a campfire area, and organizing a small grill and a cooler that held their food and drinks for the day.

Carol followed the children deeper onto the small island exploring the wildlife and admiring the birds. The fresh air and warm temperatures invigorated them, and they spent a good hour hiking and investigating every inch of the little world they'd landed on. Carol felt like the cruel, evil threats of Maddog Pierson were a thousand miles away. While they explored, Jim drank in the beauty of the river scenery, sipped on an iced tea, and leaned back in his lawn chair, watching dragonflies dart among cattails along the shoreline, thinking about the Kratt murder. The little chipmunk came back during the quiet interlude and chirped a warning in Jim's direction.

Eventually, Carol emerged from the woods, the children following her like a pied piper. She looked bright and happy. Lillie ran to Jim, holding something behind her back.

"Bapa! Guess what I found?" she asked breathlessly, her blue eyes shining with excitement.

"A treasure map?" Jim's eyes twinkled, and his face creased in a dimpled smile.

"No. That would be silly on this uninhabited island," she said, her expression turning serious, her eyes flashing.

"Do you even know what uninhabited means?" he asked.

"Yes, I know what it means. It means no humans live here." She sighed impatiently, irritated by Jim's question. "Now, guess what I found," she said again, hiding her hand behind her back. Carol raised her eyebrows and tilted her head in Jim's direction.

"An acorn?"

"Nope."

"A snail?"

Lillie shook her head.

"A bear cub?"

"Bapa! Only good guesses," she complained, stomping her foot in the sand.

"I give up. I don't know," Jim said, raising his hands in a hopeless gesture.

Henri stood next to Lillie. His blond curls shone in the sunlight, and he fixed his brown eyes on his sister. Very carefully, she withdrew her hand from behind her and thrust her surprise at Jim. A tiny painted turtle clawed his limbs in the air, frantically looking for an escape. Henri reached out his fingers and stroked the shell gently.

"A tootle, Daddy," he said quietly.

"Well, look at that. What are you going to do with him?" Jim asked.

"We're just going to pet him and watch him, and then we're going to let him go," Lillie informed him seriously. "He needs to be free." Jim nodded in agreement.

Carol found an ice cream bucket on the boat, and she put about an inch of water in the bottom. Walking up to the children, she said, "Here you go. Why don't you watch him in the bucket?"

"Hey, great idea, Mommy," Lillie said. The children grabbed the bucket, dumped the turtle in, and scooted off to sit on the blanket under the willow. They chattered happily, tilting their heads over the pail to observe the baby turtle. Jim patted the chair next to him, and Carol sat down. Jim noticed her scrutinizing gaze.

"So, are you going to tell me what happened this morning?" Carol asked. He'd been secretly hoping she'd forget to ask. He hesitated, fearing the carefree atmosphere they'd been enjoying would evaporate and blow away like an empty rain cloud.

"Marcellus Brown, one of Sam's drug informants, was thrown on Sam's doorstep, beaten and in severe drug withdrawal. He managed to tell Sam that Maddog was responsible for his condition. The ER doc isn't sure he'll live."

Carol leaned back, tipping her face toward the sky. She stayed silent for a while. Jim leaned over and gently took her hand.

"I knew I shouldn't have told you. Don't let it ruin our day, honey."

"It's pretty hard not to," she said disgustedly.

"Well, now we know what this jerk is capable of. He's paying me back for going on his boat and stealing those pictures of Lillie. If

Marcellus' beating is any indication, the guy is cruel and inhuman. We may have to initiate our plan sooner than we thought." Jim looked at Carol, and the happiness she'd displayed a few minutes ago vanished. He waited a few minutes. "What'd you think of Jude? Quite the character, huh?" he asked, trying to lighten the conversation and recapture the mood.

"Jude? Handsome devil, isn't he? Fantastic chef. Very personable and definitely has some chemistry going on with DeDe. Guess that would explain their marriage, huh? What's not to love?" Carol leaned around Jim, checking on the children.

"They're fine, honey." A few more moments of silence followed. Then he turned to her and said, "Let's just leave the world behind and enjoy today. This day. Right now. Right here. Let's just be in the moment," he finished. Carol stared at him with wide eyes.

"Boy, you're starting to sound like a millennial," Carol chuckled. Jim placed his hand around the back of Carol's neck, pulled her over to him, and gave her a deep kiss. When he pulled away, he looked into her eyes. "We're going to be fine. Just fine."

"I'm going to hold you to that. If the kids weren't here right now, we could be doing something else," she said seductively, the corners of her mouth lifting in a subtle grin.

"Well, I'll remind you of that later tonight," Jim said, grinning.

"Mommy, we're hungry. When are we going to eat?" Lillie asked, frowning as she watched Jim and Carol kiss again.

Carol jumped up, and soon she had organized a snack of ham and cheese sandwiches, chips, and cubed melon from the cooler with brownies as a special treat. The afternoon unwound in a lazy reverie of golden sunshine, deep restful quiet, and the beauty of the flowing river at their feet. The kids slept under the willow while Carol and Jim indulged in some rare daytime reading and a glass of wine.

Toward evening, Jim baited Lillie's fishing pole and helped her cast into the calm on the leeward side of the little island. The heat of the day was fading. It was wonderfully quiet, and a floating haze had appeared over the water, creating a haunted, ethereal effect. A blue heron poked his way along the opposite bank, his neck hunched into his shoulders, freezing in a statuesque position now and then. Suddenly he squawked harshly and flew away, his wings beating in slow rhythmic flaps. As they fished, Lillie spoke up.

"Bapa?"

"Yeah, baby. What's up?" *More questions—always more questions.*

"Why did Sara have a dark cloud over her head today?" Lillie asked, ceasing her fishing efforts and focusing an intense gaze on Jim.

Jim frowned, pointed to her bobber, and said, "You've gotta watch your cork, or you'll miss the fish, honey." Jim thought about what Lillie had said. *What the heck was that supposed to mean?*

Lillie remained quiet, but when Jim looked over, tears were rolling down her cheeks. She laid her pole in the sand and stood facing him.

"What's wrong, kiddo? Tell me," Jim said, laying his pole aside, kneeling, and gathering her in his arms.

"I just told you. You didn't listen. Sara has a cloud," she said into Jim's shoulder. Her arms were wrapped around Jim's neck in a tight squeeze. He could feel her heart beating against his chest. "Will she be safe?"

"Well, Sara is pretty good at taking care of herself. Do you want me to call her and check?"

Lillie pulled back so she could look into Jim's eyes. She nodded her head up and down while Jim wiped her tears on his sleeve. He pulled his cell phone out of his Bermuda shorts pocket, speed-dialed Sara's number, and waited.

"Dad? What's up? I thought you were on the river," Sara said cheerfully. Lillie was studying Jim's face, easing closer to hear Sara's response.

"We are. Lillie was worried. She said you had a dark cloud over you today."

"Hmm, really? Did I forget to say my prayers or something?" she chuckled. "Let me talk to her."

Lillie listened carefully for the next couple of minutes while Sara reassured her that she was just fine. "I'm camping at Goose Island. You probably went right by here on your way down the river. We could've waved to each other. Are you listening?"

Lillie responded by nodding her head.

"She's listening," Jim said into the phone.

Sara continued. "Lillie, this is an order. You have fun with Bapa, Carol, and Henri, and don't worry about me, okay?" she counseled. "I expect a fish when I get home, kiddo."

Jim knew things were better when Lillie broke into a huge grin. But underneath, he was uneasy. It would be simple to dismiss Lillie's perception of a cloud as a bunch of childish mumbo-jumbo, but that would be a big mistake. He knew that the things she perceived could be a warning. More than once, they'd been bang on. Take the other day, for instance. She'd seen Maddog at St. Ignatius School. What had she said? *The man was dark like night.* That was a pretty good description of a criminal like Maddog. Now she'd seen a dark cloud hovering over Sara. Did that mean Sara was one of Maddog's targets, too?

That night as Jim unloaded the day's camping equipment in the garage and cleaned out the Suburban, he thought about Lillie's prayer at bedtime. Despite Sara's reassurances over the phone, Lillie's concern for her was still front and center.

"... and dear God, you know everything, and you see everything, so please watch over Sara. Help her be safe. Amen."

Now Jim stopped his organizing and stood stock still in the garage. He was having a sudden revelation of his own. Was Maddog targeting Sara for some reason? After Marcellus' beating, Jim knew he was capable of anything, including murder. He quickly finished his unpacking and headed into the house.

Entering the den, he plopped in his black office chair and punched Sara's number on his cell. It rang four times and went to message. After listening to the message blip, Jim said, "Sara. It's Dad. Listen.

Be careful and be aware of your surroundings while you're camping. If you get this in—"

A voice interrupted. "Dad? What now?" Sara asked, obviously piqued at this further interruption.

"Oh, hi, honey. It's nothing urgent. I was just thinking about you. Who's with you at Goose Island?"

My Dad, the detective, she thought. "Sandy Matson, Father Knight, and Bobby Blake. The guys have their own tent. Listen, Dad, I know you and Carol are really anxious about this threat, and I understand why, but don't worry about me. I'll be fine. Really, I will. I should be home by about noon tomorrow. I'll see you then."

"Sure. I trust you. Love you. Have a good night," Jim said more confidently than he felt.

The line went dead. But Jim's anxiety had not eased. *What about prayer?*

He sat in the darkened room and whispered. "God, you know how worried I am. Give me the kind of simple faith that Lillie has ... faith like a little child."

39

SUNDAY, SEPTEMBER 15

The Sabbath Day dawned stormy. Bruised purple clouds hung in the eastern sky, and soon flashes of heat lightning were followed by low, growling thunder that rattled the windows and sent vibrations through the wooden floors of the house on Chipmunk Coulee Road. Sheets of rain pounded the roof, and the trees whipped angrily in the swirling wind currents. Amazingly, Lillie and Henri continued sleeping.

Carol lay awake, listening to the rain on the roof. She knew that by tomorrow morning they would be residing with Gladys Hanson at her farm up on County Road K north of Chipmunk Coulee Road. Their beautiful home, which had been so full of happiness and joy, would be empty and vacant. The discussion about the move had been contentious but necessary, in Jim's view.

"Can't we wait another day or two?" Carol asked, whispering against Jim's chest.

"Nope. We've already risked their safety by waffling and not deciding. Today's the day, honey. I'm sorry." What he really wanted to say was that he was sorry that a criminal had jeopardized their family's security and happiness. But Carol already knew that, so he saved that pitch for some other time when it might be more desperately needed.

"You're going to stay every night so you can see the kids?" she asked softly.

"Absolutely. You know I will."

"Lillie's going to have a fit. She's going to ask a million questions."

"I know that, too. We'll deal with it."

Carol rolled away from Jim, put her feet on the floor, and rose in one graceful movement. She turned and faced Jim, looking down at him lying in bed. Her silky nightgown hung loosely over her figure, draping in folds around her hips. Her hair was tangled, and her face was drained of emotion. When she spoke, her voice was flat and cold.

"I hate what he's doing to us, Jim. If I had a gun, I'd be tempted to shoot him dead."

Jim shot her a withering glance. "You don't know what you're talking about, Carol. I've shot people, and believe me, it's always the last resort, something you avoid at all costs. It lives in your memory and haunts you forever. It changes you. Don't ever say that again." His voice was like an arctic wind, and when she met his gaze, his eyes were like pieces of cold, blue flint.

Carol looked away, and Jim could see tears blooming in her eyes. He reached for her hand and pulled her back down in bed. Caressing her to his chest, he rubbed her back. "I know this is tough, but when everyone's safe, and we come back home, we'll celebrate. This is just temporary."

"I feel like we've been violated," she said, a muffled sob escaping.

"You feel that way because we have been violated. Maddog's trampled on our privacy and sense of safety. He knows what he's doing. But so do we. We understand that this threat's serious, and we're taking steps to protect our children. It's what most normal people would do, and I hope we're normal. I think we are." Carol heard the doubt in his voice.

"We are," she said, trying to reassure him. She lay with her head on his chest, memorizing his smell and warmth and strength. After some moments, she said, "Okay, I'm with you. I hate this, but I'm with you. Besides, all that really matters in this life is who you love and the memories you make with them. And I love you and the kids, and I'll always remember Saturday and that sweet day on the island in the Mississippi. The kids were so happy, and that stupid little turtle . . ."

Jim smiled and kissed the top of her head. "It's not turtle; it's tootle."

Carol giggled. "Right, tootle."

"I'll make breakfast after I hit the shower."

40

The Delta jet banked sharply over the Mississippi River as it approached the La Crosse Municipal Airport on French Island Sunday evening. Professor Margretta Martin squirmed uncomfortably in her seat, peering down at the snaking river below her. Although full darkness was a half hour off, she could still make out the familiar soaring bluffs, the islands and inlets of wildness within the boundaries of the river, and the beauty of the hardwood forests flanking its shores. As the view materialized through the floating clouds that drifted past the tiny passenger window, Margretta was filled with a tender nostalgia. At the same time, she was gripped with apprehension, leaving her with a jumble of conflicting emotions.

When she'd talked with Lt. Higgins over the phone about the renewed investigation into Christina's abduction, she was hopeful that the current interest in the cold case would conclude the nightmare she'd been living all these years. Assisting Lt. Higgins in solving the forty-year-old mystery of her sister's disappearance was a responsibility she couldn't sidestep. It was long overdue. She needed to pay homage to her sister's memory.

When her husband, David, had died ten years ago of a sudden brain aneurysm, she'd lost her focus in keeping the search for

Christina's killer alive. Lieutenant Higgins' call jump-started her resolve again. Her heart beat wildly when she thought of visiting the city where she'd spent the early years of her life and where her sister had disappeared at the age of fifteen.

The flight attendant made one last pass with a garbage bag encouraging passengers to keep their belts buckled and their seats in an upright position. The seatmate next to her, a buxom middle-aged woman with frizzy red hair, had been sloshing back gin and tonics since Kansas, and now she hurriedly chugged the rest of her drink and threw her cup in the garbage. She groaned ominously, and Margretta hoped she wouldn't vomit.

Slowly the airplane descended over La Crosse and landed safely. The plane taxied up to the terminal at 9:37 p.m. Margretta unbuckled her seat belt, stood in the aisle, and worked the kinks out of her back and neck. Traveling light with just a carry-on, she grabbed her bag from the overhead bin, then waited patiently for the passengers ahead of her to deplane. Once in the terminal, she headed to the rental car counter, and in an hour, she had arrived at her air B&B cottage on Lake Onalaska, just a ten-minute drive from the airport.

She entered the five-digit code in the combination lock box and removed the key. Walking into the cottage, she felt an overwhelming sense of Midwestern hospitality and cheerful optimism. The décor of the small one-bedroom cabin was a combination kitchen/living room, a decent bath, and one large bedroom, giving the cottage a small but comfortable footprint. It was better than a hotel room, and she had access to the dock where she could sit and take in the river scenery if she felt like it.

Flipping the lights on in the kitchen, she went to the bedroom and put her bag on the queen bed. Her phone beeped in her jacket pocket.

"Hello. This is Dr. Martin," she said pleasantly.

"Margretta. This is Jim Higgins. Just checking to make sure you arrived okay."

"Yes, thank you. I just walked into my cottage. I'm getting settled."

"Flight good?"

"Just fine. I didn't anticipate hearing from you tonight, but that was very kind."

"No problem. I just wanted to inform you there have been a few developments since I last talked to you. How about if I fill you in over breakfast tomorrow morning?"

"That'd be great."

"There's a Perkins near George Street by the big locomotive. Do you remember where that is?"

"Sort of. I'll find it. Time?"

"How's eight o'clock sound?"

"Great. See you then."

Margretta laid her cell phone on the nightstand and wandered through the house to the kitchen.

Rummaging through the cupboards, she found a hotpot and a selection of tea. She filled the pot, flicked it on, and put a peppermint tea bag in a mug with a spot of honey.

After a brief phone call from the hostess of the cabin, who confirmed her arrival, Margretta poured boiling water over the tea, took the mug into the small living room, and sat on the couch. The tea relaxed her wired nerves, and she felt a weariness washing over her.

She had no idea what lay ahead. Clutching to an irrational hope, she prayed the investigative team would be able to discover what had happened to Christina. Would the agony and uncertainty of the last four decades finally be resolved? Who had committed this vile act? What were the last moments of Christina's life like? Margretta wondered if she'd ever be free from the guilt and shame of not being able to prevent this tragic crime.

She shivered with insufferable doubt. She felt as if she had lived the last forty years in the shadow of this moment, waiting for the truth to crawl out from under a rock. Still, she remembered her hope had been shattered in the past by the passage of time, the lack of evidence, the death, and the disinterest of witnesses. Then she chided herself. *That's normal,* she thought. *People move on with their lives.*

Margretta sighed deeply and carried her mug to the kitchen sink. She flipped off the light switch and walked into the bedroom. She'd only been in La Crosse for an hour and was already exhausted by the weight of the past that swirled in her head. She closed the blinds. Stripping off her clothes and laying them on the overstuffed chair by the window, she slipped a nightgown over her head. Pulling back the sheets, she crawled into bed, turned on her side, and fell into a restless, churning sleep.

Her dreams that night were soaked in fear. Unsavory characters who had no faces drifted aimlessly before her. Her sister, Christina, floated in and out, always eternally young and dewy. Margretta knew they were hallucinations, and she tried to awaken, but the dreams were like a movie clip that repeated itself over and over in a sickening loop. Finally, near dawn, the nightmares stopped. She sat up abruptly in bed near daylight, her face wet with tears.

"Oh, Christina. What have I gotten myself into?" she whispered in the predawn darkness. "Will I ever find out what happened to you?"

41

MONDAY, SEPTEMBER 16

Very early on Monday morning, Jim stood in the door frame of the bedroom gazing at his children, who were oblivious to danger, enjoying peaceful, undisturbed sleep. Lillie and Henri were tangled together in a double bed upstairs in Gladys Hanson's farmhouse next to the bedroom Jim and Carol had slept in overnight. At this moment, things were quiet, and Jim and Carol's children were safe. Most people took their security for granted; they thought it would always undergird their way of life. But Jim knew it was fleeting—something that was hard to describe and live without and could disappear quickly in the blink of an eye by a hapless encounter with a deranged, evil individual.

He walked back into the bedroom and let his body sink into the cushion of an old, comfortable wingback chair in the corner of the bedroom. He spent some moments in undisturbed prayer and read through some of his favorite Psalms. From the chair, he watched the sun's rays spreading out in golden shafts, illuminating the tiny farmstead. Carol tossed and turned restlessly until she finally opened her eyes. She stretched her arms over her head and pushed her toes downward until they touched the bed's footboard.

"Morning," she said sluggishly. Jim noticed her bare shoulders peeking from beneath the bedclothes. "These sheets smell so sweet. I'll have to ask Gladys what she does to them to make them feel so soft and smell so good."

"They're probably fifty years old and made of cotton," Jim said quietly. "And I think she makes her own soap from goat's milk." A few moments of silence followed. Then he said, "Listen, I'm going to go in to work early, but I'll be here for dinner tonight. I may bring Margretta Martin here for the evening. Will you warn Gladys?"

"Sure. I'll take Lillie to school and Henri to daycare. Sara promised to bring Lillie here right after school." She rolled over in bed, propped her head on her elbow, and looked at Jim sitting in the chair. "You know, I think this plan might work," she said calmly.

"Good. It's important we have a unified front. Lillie will sense if we're in disagreement."

"I know. You're right."

Jim got up from the chair. He'd already shaved, brushed his teeth, and dressed. Now he grabbed his lightweight wool suit coat and pulled it on. He walked to the bed, leaned over Carol, and kissed her tenderly. "I know this is hard, but remember, we're doing the right thing to protect our kids."

"I know. Now go before I start to cry." She held his face in her hands and kissed him again. Jim turned, grabbed his shoes, and tiptoed down the stairway into the kitchen. It was quiet, and he was surprised Gladys was not already up messing about. *Just as well,* he thought. *Thank you, God, for friends like Gladys.* He let himself quietly out the side door to the farmyard, walked to his Suburban, and drove into La Crosse.

Jim rolled into the Vine Street parking lot half an hour later. Steering his Suburban into a space near the front entrance, his footsteps echoed on the damp pavement. He used his key card to enter the building. On the third floor, everything was dark and eerily quiet.

Jim glanced at the wall clock—six-thirty. He walked down the hall and entered his office, flipping on the lights and hanging his suit jacket on his office chair. He spent an hour reviewing the points he wanted to make with Margretta Martin, plus a few important questions he needed to ask her.

At seven-thirty, he slipped on his jacket and said a quick good morning to Emily as he hurried out to his Suburban. His early arrival at the office and sudden departure before working hours had even begun sent Emily, his secretary, into an uncharacteristic spin.

What in the world is going on? she thought. *Jim is acting so strange lately. Was it his marriage? The kids? The job? What?*

Driving across town to the north side of La Crosse, Jim Higgins rolled into the Perkins parking lot and entered the restaurant. Feeling foolish, he realized he had no idea what Margretta looked like. He stood by the counter until a friendly waitress came up and asked, "Booth, table, or counter?"

Jim apologized. "I'm sorry. I'm meeting someone, but—"

"Lt. Higgins, right?" the waitress asked, picking up two menus from the counter.

"Yes. How did you know me?"

"I've seen you in the paper and on TV once in a while. The lady you're meeting is right this way," she said, leading him across the open, sunny dining room to a booth along the wall.

Margretta looked up from the menu as Jim approached. Curly brown hair highlighted with blonde overtones framed an oval face that still had the scars of teenage acne. She had large, hazel eyes that were friendly and intelligent. A shy smile greeted him. Despite her seemingly pleasant demeanor, Jim noticed the dark circles under her eyes.

"Lt. Higgins. So good to finally meet you," Margretta said softly, offering her hand.

Jim worked his way into the booth, shook her hand, and ordered a cup of coffee while they looked at menus. After they'd ordered their food, Jim spent some time bringing Margretta up to speed on the investigation.

"... so that's where we're at, but I have a couple of questions for you," Jim proposed.

"I'm all ears," she replied.

"I'm wondering if you've ever seen this necklace before?" Jim asked, scrolling through his phone to a photo of the locket left at the scene. Handing the phone to her, Margretta studied the image as the waitress set their breakfasts in front of them.

"No, it's not familiar. When my parents died, I was given Christina's jewelry, but I've never seen this necklace. Is this the one that was found next to the murder victim?"

"Yes. We thought you might recognize it. I also wanted to show you the photo we found inside the locket." He handed his phone across the table again and watched her reaction as she inspected the picture of Christina and Eric Osgood.

Margretta sighed tellingly. "She was such a pretty girl. Intelligent. Sensitive. Driven."

"Do you recognize the man in the photo with Christina?"

"Vaguely. After forty years, it's hard to remember. I was already in college by the time this was taken, but I'm assuming it's Eric Osgood. It looks like him. Is that right?"

"That's right. That's him. What can you tell me about his relationship with your sister?" Jim asked.

"My sister shared her feelings about Eric with me. I vaguely knew him from high school. He was a sophomore when I was a senior, and I had my own set of friends, so our paths didn't really cross. He was very intelligent, studious, polite, and had a big thing for my sister. But the relationship didn't really heat up until they were juniors, and I had already taken off for college."

Jim watched Margretta carefully. She hadn't seemed surprised about the photo of Christina and Eric, which he found interesting. "Were the two of them serious?"

"You mean, were they having sex?"

"Well, serious doesn't necessarily mean people are having sexual relations, does it?" Margretta was quiet for a moment. Then Jim asked, "Were they having sex?"

"My sense of things was that they hadn't been intimate, but it was just a matter of time before it was going to happen. I gave a lot of sisterly advice about birth control." Jim's eyebrows shot up at this comment, and he looked up at her as he took another bite of scrambled eggs. Margretta crunched on a piece of toast and continued.

"It's just that Christina was a very gifted scholar, and she had big plans. Her interest was in space, specifically the application of physics in space. A real cutting-edge field at the time. Through some of my dad's connections with NASA, she got a scholarship to spend the summer of her senior year at a space camp at Cape Canaveral for eight weeks. That was a really big deal, especially for a girl. And as her big sister, I didn't want to see her do something stupid—like getting pregnant—that would interfere with her plans and career." Margretta stirred her coffee absentmindedly, took a sip, and then looked at Jim over the rim of her cup.

"I understand," Jim commented. "So where do you think the locket came from?"

"Maybe Eric gave it to her. That seems logical since it had that picture of them together in it."

"It's quite expensive. I'd find it surprising that a high school student could afford such an extravagant gift." Somewhere in the restaurant, the sound of crashing dishes made Jim jump.

"Eric's family had money. If my memory serves me, I think his dad was a CEO at Trane Company, and his mother was a cancer specialist at Gundersen. I don't think money would have been an issue for him."

"But I'm still struggling with where the locket came from. Who had it in their possession and brought it with them to the murder

scene? If we knew that, we'd know who may have murdered Kratt."
Jim decided to turn a corner in the conversation. "Two of my
detectives interviewed Mrs. Jewel Loiselle a few days ago."

"I should know that name, but it's been a long time," Margretta
said, a puzzled look crossing her features.

"The Loiselles were neighbors to the Blackmans. They called the
police when they heard the screams and couldn't get into the house."

"Yeah, I remember that now." Margretta pointed her finger at
Jim. "That's why that name sounded familiar."

"Jewel claims she saw Eric enter the Blackmans' home at six-
thirty the night of the abduction and leave again at seven-thirty.
They kissed at the door about seven-thirty; Christina was alive and
well. Did anyone ever tell you that?"

"No. Really? I've never heard that before," she said. Jim nodded
assertively. "You don't think Eric had something to do with the
disappearance of my sister, do you?"

"It's a new piece of information that has just come to light forty
years after the fact. It expands the possibilities surrounding the case.
Whether he was involved or not, the fact that he was at the
Blackmans' home the night of the abduction brings a lot of other
questions to mind," Jim said.

"Like what?"

"Was Eric involved in the planning, or was he the one who
abducted your sister? After he left the house the first time, did he
return later? If he returned, did he witness the abduction, but was he
too scared to report it for fear he'd be considered a primary suspect?
The list goes on."

"That does open some new avenues of investigation, doesn't it?"
Margretta said.

"Yes. Do you know anything about Eric's life since the abduction?"

"All I know is that he wanted to be an ornithologist. And I've
heard through the scientific grapevine that he was involved in some
major landmark bird studies in Alaska. But other than that, I don't

know his whereabouts. But I would certainly be willing to investigate his past. I have a lot of connections in the education and scientific worlds. I'd be glad to see what I can find out," she offered.

"That'd be great. Why don't we meet tomorrow at my office at about one o'clock? It's on the third floor of the law enforcement center on Vine Street." Margretta noticed Jim's piercing blue eyes, salt and pepper blond hair, and deep dimple in his left cheek. For the first time in many years, she felt hope blooming in her heart despite a part of her brain that reminded her that the chances of finding out what happened to her sister were slim.

"I have to tell you," Margretta said, covering Jim's hand with hers, "you've given me some hope in this whole morbid affair. I've agonized over my sister's fate for an awfully long time."

"Well, we're working hard to try and figure out what happened. But I don't want you to get your hopes up, although we're trying our best to resolve your sister's abduction and the murder of Sylvester Kratt at the same time," Jim said, gracefully pulling his hand away and picking up the check. He stood up, shook Margretta's hand again, turned, and said, "See you at one tomorrow. Hopefully, you'll find out something about Eric Osgood."

42

O n Monday afternoon, Eric Osgood leaned back in his swivel chair and gazed out the large office window overlooking the Root River in Houston, Minnesota. Below him, a netted enclosure contained three owls who were recuperating from minor surgeries. The weather, though cloudy, was warmer than usual, and the humidity had been climbing throughout the day. Puffy cumulous clouds were stacked in the blue sky, and the river in the distance was deserted except for a power boat pulling a water skier who churned up a wake of white foam.

Lacy, the barn owl, had been brought in after she'd been hit by a car. She hopped gingerly along the ground, her broken wing tucked against her body with a strip of veterinarian's gauze wrapped around her middle. Eric was hoping she would make a full recovery and be able to be released back into the wild. Two others, a northern saw-whet and a barred owl, had been found injured and starving when they could not hunt for food. He watched as an assistant entered the enclosure with the day's meal of field mice.

Eric's brown hair was flecked with gray and hung over his wide forehead, and his gray beard added a distinguished look. His full lips and wide nose didn't make him handsome in the traditional sense, but his empathetic eyes burned with an intelligence that was mesmerizing. He thought about the journey that had finally brought him home to the Coulee Region less than six months ago.

After graduating from Logan High School in La Crosse in 1978, he went on to earn a bachelor's degree with a double major in biology and zoology from UW–La Crosse. After earning his master's degree in avian conservation and management at Vanderbilt, he pressed on and was awarded his doctorate in raptor ecology at the University of Pennsylvania in Philadelphia.

Since then, he'd spent his middle-aged years making a name for himself in the avian world. Numerous field studies observing birds in their natural habitats had taken him to remote locations around the world, and now he was considered one of the world's foremost experts on owls. His study of the snowy owls in Utqiagvik, Alaska, thrust him into the desolate landscape of the tundra where he'd lived for almost five years. His groundbreaking discoveries of the climate changes taking place in the arctic environment and the impact on snowy owls made headlines in the worldwide bird community. When a recruitment call came for a director of the International Owl Center in Houston, Minnesota, he stepped down from the rarified world of research and writing to direct the activities at the center. He was near retirement and thought the slower pace and less demanding work would be an easy transition. He was wrong but for reasons that had nothing to do with owls or the work at the center.

His broad shoulders slumped as memories swirled in his head. Sometimes he swore he could still smell Christina's soft hair and feel the warmth of her lips. Although they'd never consummated their relationship in sexual intercourse, he'd made love to her many times in his mind. He sighed loudly. In the quietness of his office, he closed his green eyes, tilting back in his chair, daydreaming about things that might have been. Christina. Marriage. Children. None of that had happened when the abduction had taken place at the beginning of their junior year in high school.

Eric wondered at the wisdom of returning to his stomping grounds. Nothing but sorrow and disappointment had stalked him here. In order to deal with Christina's disappearance, he'd left the area and lost himself in the intellectual and scientific world. His dedication to his profession and his work ethic alienated him from his parents, who were now deceased, and his brother, who only called once a year as a polite gesture at Christmas. Most of the time, Eric's family hadn't even known where he was or what he was doing. But that wasn't their fault.

His attempt to drown his sorrows by winging his way across the globe studying birds, their habitats, and the threats facing them in the twenty-first century had challenged his mind and fulfilled his sense of adventure, but it did nothing to heal his broken heart. He'd loved Christina deeply. It was as simple as that. And since her disappearance, no matter what he'd tried, nothing had filled the void when she'd vanished on that October evening in 1977.

Regrets. They seemed to follow him, poking and haunting him. It was a poor way to spend a lifetime. Unfortunately, it was the only way he knew how to live.

43

Early Monday afternoon, Paul Saner and Sam Birkstein pulled up to the Wet Your Whistle bar just south of Victory on Highway 35 along the Mississippi River. As taverns went, it was a typical Wisconsin institution. The siding on the front of the bar was faded to a tired, dull gray, but a new front awning covered in green steel extended over the entrance door, which had recently been updated and painted a brick red. The parking lot was empty except for two cars. After a phone call to Rollie Gander, Paul and Sam agreed to meet him at the bar to talk about information he had concerning the Yelski abduction and disappearance. As Paul and Sam stood on the sidewalk, a huge Harley motorcycle roared by the tavern, followed by an equally huge dual-wheeled tractor.

Walking into the darkened atmosphere of the tavern, the men found a booth, and Sam ordered coffee. Rollie Gander reminded Sam of Gandolf from *The Hobbit,* minus the full beard. He had white fly-away hair, perceptive eyes, a prominent nose, and a hunched physique that suggested years of arthritic joint damage. Gander slid into the booth and got comfortable. He wore a pair of khakis, a faded denim shirt, and a well-worn cotton cardigan layered over the top. After introductions, he began telling what he knew.

"I used to own a bar in Readstown—The Thirsty Turtle," he began, placing his elbows on the Formica tabletop and crossing his arms. "That was before my conversion to the Jehovah's Witnesses. In June 2007, I was tending bar in the afternoon. We'd just had a suicide in town about two days before. A couple of guys came in and ordered a beer. I was busy washing glasses and keeping a few other customers happy, so I wasn't really listening to these two guys' conversation."

"Did you know these men?" Sam asked. "Could you describe them or identify them?"

Rollie shook his hand in front of him. "No, that was a long time ago, and they hadn't been in my place before. They weren't from the community. Anyway, the suicide in Readstown came up in their conversation, and for some reason, I tuned in. You know, one ear on their conversation while I was doing my work."

The waitress came with a carafe of coffee, creamer and sugar, and three cups. Sam poured the coffee and passed the steaming cups around.

Rollie continued. "I overheard the one man say that the suicide victim was involved in "that Yelski" thing back in '77. I perked up my ears because I've always been interested in that unsolved crime, but I tried to be discreet while I listened in. The guy who committed suicide was Howard Lake, and he worked for the power company. See, at the time of the abduction in '77, Dairyland Power was upgrading their lines from Westby to Richland Center, and he worked on the line installing new poles and wire."

"And how does this tie into the Yelski crime?" Paul asked, wondering where this rambling conversation was going.

"I'm getting to that," Rollie said, shifting in the booth. He leaned back and adjusted his legs. His eyes seem to visualize something in the distance.

"Go ahead," Sam said, rolling his hand in a circle. "We're with ya."

"In the conversation, the two guys hinted that this Lake guy had buried the Yelski girl somewhere along this new power line. Made sense to me. He was on the crew, and he knew where they had cleared brush and dug up ground, so finding a place to bury a girl would have been easy for him."

"What else did they talk about?" Sam asked, writing some notes in his small pocket notebook.

"Nothing, really. I didn't interrupt," Rollie said.

"Why'd this guy kill himself? Did he leave a note or something?" Paul asked.

"Not that I know of. I read about it in the paper. Hung himself in the barn. But he was a good friend of Sylvester Kratt. I'm wondering if those two guys carried out the abduction, and then Lake took care of getting rid of the body." Rollie stopped and gazed at the two detectives with an attitude of superiority. "Doesn't seem like that big of a stretch, does it?"

"And you never figured out their names—these two guys?" Paul asked.

"I went in the cooler to get some more beer. In the afternoon, I always got more stock on the shelves before the evening got busy, and when I came out of the cooler, they were gone." He shrugged his shoulders. "I just thought it might be helpful for you to have this information, that's all."

"What did you know about Sylvester Kratt? You linked Kratt and Lake together. Why?" Paul asked.

"They were high school buddies—you didn't see one without the other—and they led a pretty wild life. Kratt put his family through hell with his addictions, porn, and booze. It wasn't a stretch to imagine he might take advantage of an attractive young girl to carry out his fantasies."

"Were there rumors to that effect?" Sam asked.

Gander paused. His eyes had suddenly become hard and uncompromising. "They both tried to come on to my daughter when she was only seventeen. I threatened them to within an inch of their lives, and they never bothered her again."

"Really? Well, that's interesting. Listen, we appreciate you meeting with us, Rollie. Here are our cards if you think of anything else and need to contact us," Sam said.

They finished their coffee, exchanged some weather observations, and finally got up from the booth and walked out into the sunshine. The river was hazy with humidity. A few fishing boats were bobbing in the current. Gander strolled to his car. He'd seemed offended that his story hadn't created more of a stir with the detectives. Sam and Paul stood in the parking lot for a moment, enjoying the late fall sunshine. Sam stuck his hands in his pockets and turned to Paul.

"Whaddya think?" Sam asked.

Paul shrugged and made a wry face. "It could be true, but we don't really have any way to verify the information."

"That's always the problem," Paul said. "Witnesses who can't identify the people they talked with, no addresses or phone numbers, and they don't come forward to tell police for years. Pretty hard to follow up on that."

"Well, Lake probably still has family around here. Be interesting to find out why he killed himself," Sam said, "although that could be another wild goose chase."

"We've been on convoluted hunts before."

"Yeah. Let's go."

By the time Paul and Sam got back into La Crosse, the afternoon was almost gone. They conferred with Jim about the Gander interview.

"Doesn't sound too helpful to me," Jim said, running a hand through his hair. "We're not really into recovering bodies that have been buried for forty years, although this suicide of Howard Lake could prove useful. Keep digging on that. See if you can find a more solid link between Lake and Kratt. I'll get the girls to investigate the Dairyland information."

"Did you meet with Margretta Yelski?" Paul asked.

"Yep. She's all in. She's going to try to track down this Eric Osgood. We're meeting here tomorrow at one. Maybe we can put all this stuff together into a coherent theory. I'm going to talk to Heather again."

"Heather? Who's that? Refresh my memory," Sam said, his brow crinkling with a frown as he loosened his tie.

"Kratt's daughter. See if she remembers this Lake guy."

"Right. Well, tomorrow then," Paul said, turning to leave.

"Hey, Chief. You'll let us know if you need anything, right?" Sam asked, the worry reflected in his hazel eyes. "If Maddog shows up?"

"Sure. Right now, all's quiet on the western front," Jim said, reaching for his cell. "I'll catch you tomorrow."

44

Margretta Martin spent the rest of Monday morning and the early part of the afternoon investigating the whereabouts of Eric Osgood. From acquaintances she called in La Crosse, she discovered Eric had been gone from the area for many years living in places as far away as Jamaica, the Galapagos Islands, and Alaska. It wasn't until she called another ornithologist she knew in Eugene that she discovered he'd recently returned to Houston, Minnesota, to direct the activities at the International Owl Center.

"International Owl Center, Jennifer speaking. May I help you?" a friendly voice said over the line.

"Yes, I hope you can," Margretta replied. "I'm looking for Dr. Eric Osgood. Would it be possible for me to speak with him?"

"What is this concerning, ma'am?"

"Oh, I'm an acquaintance from the past, and I was hoping to reconnect with him."

"Is this of a personal nature?" The voice didn't seem so friendly now.

"Not really. I'm a science colleague, and I wanted to see if I could pick his brain on a couple of subjects," Margretta explained, hoping her ruse would placate the suspicion of the receptionist.

"Oh, well, you should have said it was business. Let me see if he's in his office."

Margretta tried to calm the sudden anxiety she felt while she waited. The only thing she really had in common with Eric was Christina. She'd only met him a couple of times, and that was over forty years ago when they were both teenagers. She wasn't even sure he would remember her, but she hoped he could shed some light on the abduction. However, she'd been disappointed with other leads before. She wasn't holding her breath.

A deep voice resonated over the phone. "Hello, this is Dr. Osgood. How can I help you?"

"Hello, Eric. It's Margretta Martin—Margretta Yelski. I've been searching for you," she said.

There was a long pause. "Margretta? Christina's sister? Really? Well, what a surprise! How are you?" She was surprised to hear the excitement in his voice. Then without letting her answer, he asked another question. "What're you doing these days?"

"I'm in La Crosse because there have been some new developments surrounding Christina's disappearance. Apparently, some clues were left at a recent murder scene in La Crosse on the north side that indicated the murdered man may have been involved or knew something about Christina's abduction. The police—well, Lt. Higgins and his team—believe the two crimes may be connected in some way. Pretty amazing, huh?"

"That *is* amazing, but I'm not sure I know anything that will make a difference. Besides, it doesn't bring Christina back, does it?" His voice was tinged with sadness, but beneath it, there was a bitterness and resignation that Margretta understood well. She had fought her own battle with disillusionment for many years.

"No, it doesn't bring her back. And I can understand your feelings. But the detectives working the case would really like to speak with you."

"Why?" His voice was raspy with frustration.

"They believe you may have some information that might help them. Possibly something you may have heard or seen could give them a new direction in the case." For a long moment, there was an uncomfortable silence. Margretta wondered if she'd miscalculated in contacting him and soliciting his involvement.

"Well, I guess I could do that," Eric said in resignation. "But I really don't think it will make any difference."

"It will make a difference to me," Margretta said softly.

Eric was surprisingly moved by her simple statement. He reconsidered and then said, "Well, if it's that important to you, then I'll do whatever I can to help."

"Great. How does one o'clock tomorrow afternoon sound? At the law enforcement center in La Crosse? Someone will interview you about the abduction."

"You can count on it. I'll be there," Eric said. His hands began shaking as he laid his cell phone on the desk. He closed his eyes briefly. *I can't believe this. Someone is still pursuing the abduction after all these years. Who would've guessed?*

45

Early Monday evening, Leslie huffed and blew a stray strand of hair away from her sweating face. Moving boxes and random pieces of cast-off furniture in the spare bedroom of their duplex was harder work than she'd anticipated. Her back ached, and she'd bruised her foot when she'd dropped the corner of a broken-down dresser on it. Paco stood next to her, panting and whining, his saliva dripping on the floor.

"Hey, boy. What's the matter?" she said sympathetically. Paco's tail hung limply. His dark eyes studied Leslie. She leaned down and thumped his side while he licked her face enthusiastically, enjoying the saltiness of her skin. "I know this isn't your idea of fun, but I can't play frisbee right now. Just a little while longer. Then we'll go out and play some catch. I promise," she explained as if he could understand. He barked several short barks, whined, and looked toward the bedroom window.

"Go lay down now," Leslie ordered, snapping her fingers and pointing to the hallway. Paco turned and padded obediently to his dog bed at the end of the hall. Groaning loudly, he plopped into it, laying his massive head on his paws.

Working quickly before Sam got home, Leslie assembled the

SUE BERG

easel she'd bought at a local craft store and set it in the corner of the room near the window. A small stool and a wooden TV tray that held brushes and acrylic paints sat in front of the easel. Placing a blank canvas on it, she stepped back, suddenly intimidated by the brilliant whiteness of the empty surface. Her inner voice clamored to life.

What makes you think you can paint? What an arrogant assumption. Are you for real? The teasing, taunting thoughts seemed to poke at her. She shook her head to clear her mind and stop the agitating chorus.

"Dr. Turner said I needed an outlet to ease my anxiety," she said out loud, trying to dissipate the feeling of foolish incompetence that had come over her. "So shut up. In fact, go to hell!" she said intensely. "Besides, I won't know if I can paint if I don't try."

"Try what?" Sam asked, making Leslie jump and grab her throat. "Who're you talking to, honey?" He stepped into the doorway and stood there. *What's going on now?* he thought.

Leslie took a deep breath. "I'm giving myself a pep talk, I guess," Leslie replied defensively. "Don't sneak up on me like that! It triggers a lot of bad memories." Her hair was disheveled, and her jeans were covered in dust. She looked sweaty and tired.

"I'm sorry. I didn't mean to startle you." Sam's hazel eyes took in the changed atmosphere. "Wow! I see you've rearranged the room." The room seemed bigger now that it was organized and straightened. A new bookshelf in the corner held some of Leslie's and Sam's trophies, memorabilia, and family photos. His eyes focused on the easel and blank canvas.

"Well, I'm glad you noticed. It was hard work."

Sam walked into the room and stood before the easel. "Painting? Well, with your interest and knowledge in art, that's a great choice for a hobby. Good for you, babe. I bet you'll be really good at it." He turned to look at her and noticed her subtle smile. "Does this mean that other forms of therapy will diminish?" he asked, smiling more broadly now.

"Not in the least. Painting is therapy, but it's totally different."

"Better than making love?"

"Making love with you is in a category all by itself, Sam. There's nothing to compare it to." Suddenly she burst out in an infectious giggle. Sam joined in.

"Oh, that's good. That's very good," he said, feeling secretly validated. He walked over to her and kissed her. Then turning serious, he said, "I'm proud of you, you know. And I hope you'll be a raving success. Maybe by this time next year, you'll be having your first show."

Leslie placed her hands on his chest and played with his loosened tie. "I'm just doing it to relax, but thank you for always believing in me, even when I do something goofy, like painting," she said softly.

Sam grabbed her hands. "Having an interest in something other than work and me is very healthy." His hazel eyes were intense. "You're taking charge of your life. That's good. And I'll always believe in you. You know that. That won't change."

"That's why I love you." She kissed him tenderly.

"So, what's for dinner?" he asked.

Leslie's face crinkled in a grimace. "Oh, shit. I got so wrapped up in my project that I forgot to cook."

"Olive Garden?"

"Sounds good. Let's go."

Olive Garden was moderately busy for a Tuesday night, but Sam and Leslie were able to get a table immediately. Once seated, Sam ordered a bottle of their best red wine. They studied the menu, and the waitress brought their salad and breadsticks.

"Tell me what you found out about Howard Lake. Did he work at Dairyland in the late seventies?" Sam asked, crunching on his salad. He took a swig of wine and waited.

"Well, we dug into the records at the main office, and he was employed at Dairyland Power from 1974 until his suicide, mostly as a lineman. He worked on the Highway 14 upgrade during the late seventies and early eighties. So that part of Rollie Gander's story can be confirmed. I also wondered if the two men in Rollie's bar could have been other Dairyland employees who worked with Lake. A girl at the office is getting a list together for me. The other question is whether Lake knew Sylvester Kratt. When you talk to Lake's relatives, that would be something to ask them."

"They did know each other. They were classmates and apparently drinking buddies. Gander told us they had a pretty wild reputation, and they even had the balls to try and come on to his seventeen-year-old daughter," Sam told her.

"Bet that didn't go over well."

"No, it didn't. Gander threatened them, and they backed off." They concentrated on their food for a few moments.

Leslie paused a moment and chewed on a breadstick. "But I have another question that probably doesn't have an answer ... yet," Leslie said. "And it's kind of a wild tangent."

"Gotta think outta the box. That's what Higgins always says," Sam said, slurping up a couple of spaghetti noodles. "Go ahead. Shoot. I'm always up for original thinking. Anything to help untangle this mess so we can figure out what might have happened."

"Who had possession of the locket after the abduction? Do we know at this point?"

"No, we don't know," Sam asked his fork in mid-air. "But I don't understand what you're after." His brow was scrunched into a frown.

"Well, someone had the locket. That's why it appeared at the crime scene. So who had it before Kratt's murder? If we could figure that out, we might be able to find the killer."

"What about this Eric Osgood? Maybe he had it," Sam suggested.

"Possible, I suppose. But why would he have had it if he had given it to Christina? Of course, we don't know that he gave it to Christina, but maybe by tomorrow afternoon, we might. Higgins showed Margretta the locket, and she didn't recognize it. So if Kratt was Christina's killer, maybe she was wearing the locket the night she was murdered. But then how did it appear at the murder scene? You'd think they would have disposed of it when they buried her. You know, get rid of the evidence. Bury it with her, or whatever they did with her."

"I see what you're thinking, but maybe Kratt kept it as a souvenir. Some killers do stuff like that. Anyway, whoever left the locket at the murder scene had to have known the significance of it and had access to it. Who would that have been?"

Leslie dug into her plate of ravioli with renewed enthusiasm, ravenous from her afternoon redecorating activity. They ate silently for a while as Sam thought about this new theory.

Finally, he said, "As I see it, we can't eliminate Eric Osgood as Kratt's murderer yet since we haven't talked to him. We don't know whether he has a decent alibi for the night of the murder, but I can understand Eric Osgood's motive in killing Kratt—revenge for stealing away his love and future with Christina. Margretta has a definite alibi. She was leading a symposium at Eugene for 500 biotech engineers the night of Kratt's murder. Nothing like five hundred witnesses to validate your alibi."

"According to Higgins, she loved her sister dearly. Besides, why would she go to all the trouble of murdering Kratt after forty years? How would she even know he was involved?"

"Hey! I'm letting the evidence lead me to some logical conclusions; that's all. Isn't that what I'm supposed to do?" He sighed loudly and twirled some more spaghetti on his fork. "You do realize we've got very little to go on."

"You'd have to be living under a rock not to know that. But here's another idea. What if there was a third person involved in the abduction who's still alive? Howard Lake committed suicide, and the third member of the trio whacks Kratt. With no other witnesses left from the original abduction, the third member goes to his grave with the secret of the crime, and it's never solved." They were silent while they thought about that. Then Leslie asked, "Who else would have motive and opportunity to kill Kratt? We're missing someone who's right under our noses."

"I don't know. My brain's on overload, and I'm stuffed."

"Dessert?" Leslie suggested as the waiter began clearing away their dishes.

"Sure. But not that kind. I'll collect dessert later," he said, grinning wickedly.

"Sam!"

46

TUESDAY, SEPTEMBER 17

Sara Higgins reveled in the luxurious quiet that saturated the house on Chipmunk Coulee Road. Usually, by six-thirty on a weekday morning, she could hear the rumble of feet upstairs and the creaking of the floor joists as the Higgins family prepared for work and school. That was one of the disadvantages of living in a basement apartment.

Now at six o'clock, it was serenely still. With the entire family residing at Gladys Hanson's farmette, she was the solitary occupant at the Chipmunk Coulee house. After an intense argument with her dad, who had insisted on her moving to the farm, too, she'd convinced him she would be vigilant and careful. He'd conceded but was still uneasy about the arrangement.

Over a year ago, the arrival of two children to the Higgins household within two weeks of each other—Henri's birth and Lillie's surprise arrival from living on the street—made the need for Sara's presence obvious. Jim and Carol asked her to move into the basement apartment, paying minimal rent in exchange for regular babysitting. Lately, it seemed she was needed more than ever, but it had worked well so far.

Lounging in bed on a weekday seemed like an unearned indulgence, but Sara sighed with satisfaction. *Enjoy it while you can,* she thought. She rarely had a weekday morning to relish a slower pace and take her time preparing for school, except when a snowstorm hit and school was canceled. Without the responsibility of picking up Lillie for the ride to St. Ignatius, she felt like she had all the time in the world.

Sara watched some squirrels gather stray acorns that had fallen on the patio during the night. The sun was just brushing the sky with a pink hue along the edge of the woods in the backyard. Somewhere nearby, a couple of crows cawed raucously in the early morning.

Sara stared at the ceiling, her mind wandering over the last three years since her mom's death. Sometimes she wasn't sure how she really felt about her dad's new lifestyle. Losing her mom had deeply affected her. Despite their obvious age difference, Sara had treasured her mother's companionship. She'd spent many hours with her, shopping, painting her nails, talking and discussing life's ups and downs, sharing the rewards and pitfalls of dating, and walking along the country roads that surrounded their home. When her mom was diagnosed with advanced breast cancer, Sara tried to put on a brave face for her dad's sake, but privately she'd been devastated. She often wondered what her mom would think of her dad's life now.

Sara truly loved Carol. She had a generous spirit and seemed well-matched to her dad's quirks, personality, and the demands of his job. She was quite capable of standing up for herself when the situation demanded it. It was obvious watching the two of them that their love was passionate and joyful. Her dad seemed genuinely happy with his new family, but she wondered what the aging years would bring. Keeping up with a two- and six-year-old was no easy feat for someone in mid-life. She hoped that everything would work out.

This latest threat from Maddog Pierson had taken its toll on her dad. She could see his gray hairs increasing by the week. His face was haggard with uncertainty, and he was distracted and distant.

"Dad, everything okay?" she'd asked him on Sunday afternoon as she lounged on the patio reading a book. "You seem like you're somewhere else."

Jim stopped his work on the rose bushes near the patio and gazed at her. "That sounds like something your mom would've said."

"You didn't answer my question."

"Well, no, everything's not okay until we resolve this idiotic situation with Maddog. What a degenerate!" Sara could hear the irritation and frustration in his voice. "That he would even think I would let Lillie have any contact with him tells you something about his moral code and thought processes. I'm sure his brain is saturated with every kind of alcohol and drug known to man."

"Undoubtedly. Maybe you should go see Vivian. She might be able to give you some good advice."

Jim stared at her, tamping down a surge of anger. He waved his hand in frustration. "Vivian?" He let out what sounded like a snort. "Honey, Vivian is a great gal and runs a wonderful counseling service, but I don't need any counseling."

"How's Gladys adjusting to the plan? She's been invaded. She okay with that?" Sara asked.

"She's a trooper, and she doesn't seem to mind. She truly loves our family and is willing to step up to the plate and deliver. You can't ask much more than that of a friend."

Sara stood up and faced Jim. "I worry about you, Dad," Sara said, the tears beginning to mist in her eyes.

Jim laid his shears on the rock wall, came around, and stood in front of her on the patio. He put his hands on her shoulders and gave her an intense blue-eyed gaze.

"Listen, I don't say it enough," he said, "but you have been such a ray of hope in this miserable affair. Thank you for watching over Henri and Lillie when you might have wanted to do other things with people your own age. I know Carol appreciates it, too," Jim said, wrapping her in his arms. "Love you, honey," he said softly into her hair. She basked in the warmth of the hug for a moment, then she pulled away but stood close to him, looking up into his face.

"When this all gets resolved, I think I'm going to move on," she said, not sure his reaction would be positive.

"Really?" Sara could see the effort it took for him to remain impartial.

Sara nodded. "Yeah, really. Father Knight thinks I should go to graduate school and pursue a master's degree in education. I think it's a good idea. I have the money you and Mom put away for me, and it's grown over the years. I won't accumulate a lot of debt by going back to school, and the payoff in a higher salary and better positions will be worth it."

"Where are you going to go?"

"Not sure yet. Still looking at some good Catholic colleges. Maybe St. Catherine's in St. Paul, but Viterbo here in La Crosse would be a great choice, too," she said, shrugging. "It won't be til next year anyway."

"Well, honey, it's your choice, and it sounds like you're determined. More education is never a bad idea." He stared at his daughter, realizing suddenly that they were relating adult to adult. It shocked his parental sensibilities, but then he'd raised his children to be independent and make their own decisions. It was gratifying in a certain sense, but in his heart, she would always be his little girl.

Recalling the conversation, Sara groaned and rolled out of bed. After showering and dressing, she ate a leisurely breakfast, drank a cup of coffee while she watched a segment of *Good Morning America* on TV, and organized her school papers in her briefcase. Locking her door, she climbed the stairs, exited the garage, and got in her Ford Escape.

The drive down Chipmunk Coulee Road was beautiful. Autumn was settling across the landscape like a beautiful canvas painted with vibrant colors. The hardwood forests were saturated with fall colors—swatches of red and orange mixed with the deep green of the evergreen trees on the steep hillsides. Leaves drifted across the road, and Sara braked when a wild turkey jumped from the ditch and tentatively made its way across the blacktop. The musky smell of humus and dying vegetation wafted into the partially opened window.

Turning south on U.S. Hwy 35, Sara drove through Stoddard, a sleepy little river town. A few locals wandered across the main street into the River Road Café. From somewhere, the smell of cinnamon rolls drifted on the breeze, and Sara's stomach cramped with hunger. The Burlington Northern wailed its warning as it passed an intersection, clattering down the tracks, the click-clack of its wheels echoing against the bluffs in the cool morning dampness.

As Sara approached Genoa, she noticed a woman standing outside her car on the shoulder of the road, looking anxious. The amber flashers on her vehicle blinked steadily in the morning sunlight. She looked cold with her arms wrapped around her chest in the cool September air.

Against her better judgment, Sara slowed, pulled onto the shoulder, and came to a rolling stop behind the woman's car. She powered down her window, leaned her head out, and asked, "Do you need some help?"

The woman hesitated, made a helpless gesture with her hands, and then said, "Well, I must have run out of gas, but I'm not really sure if that's the problem. Do you know anything about cars?" Her voice seemed shaky, and she looked scared.

Sara nodded. "Well, I probably know more than most women my age. Let me take a look," she said confidently. She got out of the car and walked to the stranger's vehicle. When her hand reached the driver's door handle, she looked in the back seat. A large man with long stringy hair abruptly sat up. He seemed to fill the car with his menacing presence. The Glock pistol pointed at her chest made her breathing stop. The little "o" of the barrel drilled a hole in her, and she felt herself shrink inside. All the warnings and concerns of her dad raced through her mind in a blink of an eye. *Be aware of your surroundings.*

"We've been waiting for you," the man's raspy voice squawked. "Now, walk around the front of the car and get in the front passenger seat. Don't try anything stupid, or you won't live to tell about it." His eyes were like hard granite pellets, and his muscular hand gripped the handle of the pistol firmly and confidently.

Sara whispered a short prayer and woodenly stumbled to the other side of the car and got in. The smell of human sweat and pot inside was strong and nauseating. The woman got behind the wheel, shut off the flashers, started the engine, and pulled carefully onto U.S. 35.

"Turn left up there on Highway 56. Find a place where we can pull off the road," the man in the back seat ordered. Sara began shaking. Fear threatened to overwhelm her, and tears began snaking down her cheeks. She wondered if the man was Maddog Pierson. When she thought of the implications of his threats on her family, her terror knew no bounds. She kept praying. When she closed her eyes, she could see her dad standing before her, his blue eyes blazing. That seemed to stabilize her and give her strength. *You don't know it yet, but you'll never get away with this,* she thought. *My dad will hunt you to the ends of the earth. He will never give up until he finds me.*

The woman turned on a less-traveled gravel road, found a field road, and drove the car a short distance until the overhanging trees obscured a view of the vehicle. The man got out of the back seat, opened the front passenger door, and grabbed Sara's arm, pulling her out of the car. She jerked her arm away and stood in front of him.

"Turn around," he ordered gruffly. Sara turned to face the door. "Gimme your wrists."

Sara pushed her wrists behind, and he expertly duct-taped them together. He roughly grabbed her arm, directing her into the car's back seat, but not before he tied a blindfold over her eyes.

"Now, lay down and shut up! That's the only way you'll ever see your family again," he threatened as he pushed her into the back seat.

Sara did as she was told. Her heart thumped with such force she thought it would jump out of her chest and run away down the road. She struggled to calm herself, to take in as much as she could of her surroundings, and to learn anything about her captors that might help her stay alive. But her hopes began to fade as the car traveled farther afield over the twisting, curving country roads. The two kidnappers in the front seat wisely stayed quiet, avoiding conversation.

After a brief half-hour journey, the car pulled onto what Sara thought must be a service road for agricultural machinery or maybe a hay field. Something that sounded like rustling grass seemed to be brushing up against the sides of the vehicle. After a short distance, the car came to a stop. The car door opened, and the man leaned in.

"Sit up," he ordered. He helped Sara out of the car and dragged her into a building, his hand biting into her bicep. Once inside, he led her to a hollow empty-sounding room, rebounded her hands in front of her, and then pushed her into a rickety overstuffed chair that smelled like dirt and rodent pee. Once she was seated, he taped her ankles together. "We'll check on you later." Sara heard the door to the room slam shut, and for the first time that morning, prayer failed her, and her tears flowed freely.

Dad, can you hear me? I'm scared. Silence. Then another thought. *God will never leave you nor forsake you.* She leaned her head back on the soft chair and remembered Father Knight's soothing voice. Then she thought about Lillie—her piercing blue eyes, her probing intellect, her tender heart—and her vision of a black cloud hanging over Sara's head. *She has a gift.*

Sara was beginning to wonder if she would be the pawn that would be exchanged for Lillie. Was that Maddog's plan? If that's what he thought was going to play out, he was badly mistaken. *My dad would die before any harm came to me or Lillie. You have no idea who you're dealing with. This will never work.*

SUE BERG

For a moment, the thought gave her strength, but when she envisioned losing her father in a reckless gamble—one that could easily become violent—the tears came again. She cried for what seemed like hours until exhaustion and worry overtook her, and she fell asleep.

47

By nine-fifteen on Tuesday morning, Jim was downtown near the Lowe, Pritchert, and Hanson Law Office on Pearl Street. The historic neighborhood in downtown La Crosse retained its aged brick storefronts. Many of the buildings had preserved their original 1930s details—the high narrow windows and doors and Victorian trim work. Until recently, the brick streets were a unique feature, but even they could not withstand the modernization of the downtown district and had been replaced with blacktop paving. The businesses were small and specialized—an ice cream parlor, a hotel outfitted for wedding parties featuring a ballroom, a mercantile general store, and a funky establishment highlighting Wisconsin products and souvenirs, especially cheese. Several bars and taverns peppered the downtown district as well. Third Street in La Crosse had the same reputation as Bourbon Street in New Orleans, except on a smaller scale.

Jim found a parking spot and walked along the street until he came to a brick facade with dark windows tucked between a bar and a nail boutique. Entering the law office, he was immediately greeted by a pert, energetic receptionist who exuded confidence and efficiency. *Another Emily,* Jim thought. Then feeling guilty, he thought about how often he'd taken Emily for granted and made a mental note to bring her flowers one day this week. Her continual foresight, planning, and preparation ensured his success in fulfilling the bureaucratic side of his profession. He couldn't do his job without her assistance.

"Good morning. May I help you, sir?" the receptionist asked, broadcasting a friendly smile.

Jim flashed his ID. "I'm wondering if I could speak with Heather Lovstad?"

"Did you have an appointment?"

"Well, no. Something's come up in our investigation of her father's murder, and I was in the neighborhood, so I thought I'd visit with her a few minutes if she's available." Jim gave the woman his best smile.

She lifted her hand to her hair and fluffed a few curls. "I'm sorry, but she's up in Holmen at her counseling session right now."

"Oh, that's understandable considering what she's gone through the last few weeks," Jim said sympathetically.

"Oh no. You misunderstand, sir. She regularly sees her counselor every month. She's done that ever since she's worked here. It's a standing appointment—the third Tuesday of every month without fail. Just like clockwork." Then she said sotto voce, "Of course, no one else gets to do that around here."

"I see," Jim said. A little alarm bell began clanging in his brain. "I'll just stop by another time. Will she be back by noon?"

"Yes. She has a number of cases that she's prepping for court which need her attention."

"Maybe I'll give her a call this afternoon."

"Should I tell her you stopped?"

"No, that's not necessary," Jim explained. "What I have to ask isn't that urgent. But thanks for your help," he finished as he turned to leave.

"My pleasure," the receptionist said, giving Jim a coy smile.

As Jim strolled back to his Suburban, his thoughts zeroed in on Heather's counseling appointment. What kind of problems could require a standing counseling appointment with no end in sight? Didn't most counseling preclude the idea that it would no longer be necessary at some point, that your emotional state would improve, and that you would develop strategies to deal with your problem so you didn't need the services? Who stayed in counseling for twenty-some years? *Probably more people than you realize,* Jim thought. It was a question that begged for an answer.

Jim thought back to his initial interview with Heather. She had admitted to an uneasy relationship with her father. Was that because of some sexual abuse or possible incest? Jim hated to jump to that conclusion, and Heather claimed she hadn't been abused. Still, who'd want to admit that? Hiding it would be a common defensive reaction for someone who didn't want to admit to the horror, especially if it involved her father. And Kratt's sexual appetites could have extended to his daughter, especially with his pornographic tendencies.

Jim wasn't sure what he'd stumbled upon, but in every case he'd investigated in the past, he could look back and isolate a piece of information on which all other clues hung. One revealing fact could open a door that had previously been closed. He wondered if this might be the moment when things began clicking together. On a whim, he decided to call Vivian, Carol's psychologist sister, who owned and operated a successful family counseling practice in Holmen, north of La Crosse.

"Jensen Family Counseling Services. How may I direct your call?" a calm voice said.

"Yes, I need to speak with Vivian Jensen, please," Jim said pleasantly.

"She's quite busy, I'm afraid," the receptionist said.

"She'll speak with me. Tell her Lt. Higgins is calling," Jim said, toughening his tone, his impatience growing.

"I'll try, sir," she said.

SUE BERG

Presently Jim heard Vivian's familiar voice.

"Jim, anything wrong?" Her voice sounded tight.

"Well, something's always wrong in the world I work in. But no, Carol and the kids are fine if that's what you're wondering. Don't worry."

"Good. So, what's up? Something you need professionally?"

"Yes. I know you can't divulge any information about a patient's specific problems because of confidentiality, but I was wondering if you could tell me if you have a certain person as a patient at your practice."

The line was silent for a moment. "Yes, I can tell you that, but that's it. I can't reveal anything else about the nature of the actual counseling. That would destroy our confidentiality with patients and shred their faith and trust in us as professionals."

"Yes, I understand that. So, do you have a Heather Lovstad as a regular patient?"

"Yes, she's a client here, but she counsels with Adam Standing Horse, not me."

"Right. Thanks, Viv," he said.

"That was a little too easy. Are you sure that's all you want?"

"Oh, I'd love to pick that counselor's brain about Heather, but that would be illegal and unprofessional, and I've gotten myself embroiled in enough sticky situations lately. Carol will have my hide if I get my butt in another sling."

"That sounds too interesting to pass up. We need to have lunch soon," she said, giggling.

"You've got it, Viv. I'll call you," Jim said hanging up.

Jim arrived back at his office at about ten-thirty and set to work summarizing and preparing the theories, evidence, motives, and suspects they'd be looking at for the afternoon meeting at one o'clock. He reviewed the case notes in the Yelski file, skimming the records he's already read for what seemed like the hundredth time. The Kratt evidence seemed straightforward, but it told him nothing.

They just didn't have enough dots connected yet, but he knew the murder on George Street and the disappearance of Christian Yelski were inextricable. They were tangled together somehow.

Sitting at his desk writing on a yellow legal notepad, he heard a commotion in the lobby. A moment later, Carol appeared at the door to his office. She looked upset. Her eyes were large and panic-stricken, and her demeanor hinted at some kind of crisis. Normally, Carol was a fastidious dresser; now, her business suit was rumpled, and she looked uncharacteristically disheveled.

"Honey, what're you doing up here?" Jim asked. "Did you need something?"

"Father Knight called from St. Ignatius about half an hour ago." At the mention of the school, Jim stood up, waiting for the other shoe to drop. "Sara hasn't shown up for work, Jim."

"Sara?" he repeated, like someone who just woke up from a nap. Then his face crinkled in confusion. "So where is she?"

"She doesn't answer her cell. I've tried for half an hour. About ten minutes ago, 911 got a call from someone at the Citgo station in Genoa. When the guy at the station got to work about eight, he noticed Sara's car alongside the road on Hwy. 35. When it was still there after nine o'clock, he walked across the highway and found her keys, her phone, her briefcase, and her purse still inside it. He called it in. She's gone, Jim." Carol watched his reaction. Jim stood bolted to the floor. "Jim, did you hear me?"

"What'd ya mean ... she's gone?" Jim felt his eyes dilating and his breathing coming in short rasps. He rubbed the side of his head as he searched Carol's face for some kind of explanation. He could still recall the fragrance of Sara's shampooed hair from Sunday, the warmth of her body as they'd hugged on the patio, the determination in her blue eyes when she'd talked about furthering her education. There must be an explanation for this.

At that moment, Sheriff Davy Jones appeared at Jim's door, looking serious and focused. "Jim, a deputy from Vernon County found your daughter's Ford Escape down on 35. It seems to have been abandoned with her belongings still inside."

Jim brought his fist down on his desk, startling Carol and Jones. "That perverted degenerate!" he yelled loudly. Jim lifted his eyes to the ceiling, stood there briefly, then ran his hand through his short-cropped hair. "I've been waiting for him to make a move. How could I have missed this? Then he thought, *Lillie was right again.* "Where's Lillie now?" he barked brusquely, looking at Carol.

"Father Knight is in her classroom, and Sheriff Clancy from Vernon County sent an officer to guard the outside entrance of the school," Carol informed him.

Jones interrupted. "I've issued a BOLO to a full arsenal of law enforcement personnel from here to Madison over to Eau Claire and back to Wausau. They'll be looking for anyone who may have a woman in tow who fits Sara's description. We'll find her, Jim."

"Fat chance, Davy," Jim said. "Not happenin'. BOLO or not, the guy's been planning this for months. He's eluded cops all over the state before. He'll do it again." His eyes blazed with anger. Maddog's bold move made him feel like he'd been punched in the gut. "We won't find him, but he'll find me when he's ready. Sara isn't the one he wants; it's Lillie. She's the prize. Until he gets her, Sara will probably stay alive, and we have a chance at a good ending." The weight of his words made Carol gape at Jim with an open mouth.

He suddenly became aware that Carol had gone completely pale, and her eyes seemed glazed over in shock. She leaned against Jim's desk, covering her eyes with one hand. Jim rushed to her side, pulled her to his chest, and held her closely. She wrapped her arms around his waist and hung on.

"He won't get away with this," he whispered in her hair, looking over at Davy. Sam and Paul appeared in the doorway. One look at the trio and they knew the news about Sara was true.

Jim's phone burred, indicating he'd received a text. He opened his phone, and his stomach clenched in a small hard ball of anger: "Want Sara back? Stay tuned, sucker!" the text snarled. Jim handed the phone to Sam. As he read the text, his jaw rippled in apprehension.

"Whaddya need us to do, Chief?" Sam asked, his voice hard and determined.

Jim led Carol to a chair near his desk. "Everybody grab a chair and sit down," he said. Nobody did. "First, under no circumstances are we answering or responding to any kind of electronic communication. We can't afford to give him that kind of power. If he wants Lillie, which he does, we're going to make him work for it."

Carol sputtered, "At whose expense? Sara's? That doesn't seem to make much sense, Jim."

"I know, honey. But texting with him will just contribute to his feelings of power and control," Jim told her.

Sheriff Jones interrupted. "He's right, Carol. But I'll assign a couple of my staff to follow Facebook, Instagram, and Snapchat for possible posts, although I doubt he'll go public. We'll keep an eye on those," he said. "We may even be able to locate him if he continues to use the same cell."

"I doubt that he will. He's got a system in place, but I agree. We have to monitor any communication he might release over the web. Maddog will contact me when he's ready. I anticipate he's planning an exchange. He wants to trade Sara for Lillie," Jim said. "He can only do that if Sara stays alive."

"That's not happening, Jim. No trades," Carol said firmly. She'd seemed to have recovered from her shocked state, and now her brown eyes burned ominously. Her face had become like chiseled marble, the determination in her eyes familiar—The Tiger Mom. The men in the room took stock of her. "He has no idea what he's set into motion," she finished, making eye contact with Jim. "Sara is not going to be a pawn in some power game."

"She already is," Jim reminded her softly. "Some negotiations will have to be made at some point. We have a hostage situation now." He turned back to the team in front of him and continued.

"We're going to carry on with business as usual, as hard as that might be." He held his hands in the air as if to calm everyone standing in front of him. "I want a lid on this. No press, no news releases. The more normal we appear, the more we impress upon Maddog that we are rational-thinking adults who will meet him head-on. Any off-the-wall comments or behavior by us will be interpreted as a psychological victory. A victory in intimidation. That's not happening," Jim said firmly. "We're not playing mind games."

Davy Jones stepped toward the door, then turned before heading back to his office. "Jim, can I take Paul and use him as a liaison between your family, your staff, and the sheriff's department?"

"Yeah, that sounds like a good move," Jim said. He locked eyes with Paul. "Thanks, buddy."

"I'm on it, Chief," Paul said.

"One more thing," Jones said, holding up his index finger. "Everybody needs to get a disposable phone from Walmart. As this scenario plays out, we'll use burner phones when we need to communicate about the abduction. Maddog may be sophisticated enough to be able to monitor our cells. So let's go dark with this. Use your regular cell for your normal contacts but the disposables for any abduction updates or plans."

Jim turned to Sam. "Sam, you go to Walmart right now and get the phones. Bring them back here so we can get organized. And listen, we're still going ahead with our one o'clock meeting. I want everyone there."

The day was bright outside with golden sunshine, but a moody darkness had already descended inside. As Jim poised dramatically behind his desk, Carol thought he resembled a soldier preparing for battle. When she thought about it, she supposed that's exactly what it was like. *He is a lieutenant, after all,* she thought. *And he's in the battle of his life.*

48

Gladys Hanson had been a farmwife and social worker all her adult life. She had a no-nonsense personality that could be mistakenly construed as domineering, bossy, and insensitive. Nothing could be further from the truth. A heart of gold beat within her. Her work with adoptive parents at the La Crosse County Courthouse for over thirty-five years had given her plenty of experience in coping with seemingly impossible situations accompanied by volatile emotions.

As she began supper preparations, she prayed that Jim and Carol's children would come to no harm. "And deliver us from evil," she whispered quietly under her breath.

In her opinion, two more lovely children did not exist anywhere on earth. Henri's curly blond hair and fair skin hinted at Jim's Nordic ancestry, but his brown eyes were a gift from Carol. He seemed bright, although somewhat clumsy. But after all, he was only eighteen months old.

Lillie was a unique little soul. Gladys worried that her intelligence and precocious curiosity would overshadow Henri in the coming years. A firm hand and loving discipline would be needed to keep her from becoming spoiled and bratty, and her mind would need continual challenges to develop her keen intelligence and curiosity. However, Gladys was certain that Jim and Carol were up to the demands of parenting an exceptional child.

Forming a pie crust with floured hands and a rolling pin, she hummed distractedly under her breath. She'd never had the privilege of birthing her own children, but she'd spent plenty of time fostering and loving those who'd had a rough start in life. Her husband, Leo, now deceased, had fully supported her endeavors. In her old age, she still frequently received letters and phone calls from the many children she'd nurtured as they coped with their chaotic childhoods.

Filling the pie crust with plump juicy blueberries, sugar, lemon juice, and butter, she formed the crust with a scalloped edge, set it on a cookie sheet, and popped it into the oven. Then she turned her attention to the pork roast resting on the counter. Sprinkling the surface with sage, thyme, salt, and pepper, she nestled it in a blue roasting pan with peeled carrots, onions, and garlic bulbs. When the pie was finished, the roast could go in.

The telephone on the buffet rang and broke into her thoughts. She walked slowly across the room, her arthritic hips creaking.

"Hanson residence. Gladys speaking," she said.

"Gladys. I have some news," Jim said.

By his impatient tone, Gladys could tell something was up. "Go ahead, Jim. I'm listening."

"Sara was abducted on her way to school this morning."

"God in heaven!" Her voice caught in her throat, and then she reined in her emotions. "How can I help?" she asked, pushing a silver curl away from her face, then resting her hand on her chest.

Despite the dire circumstances, Jim smiled. Help. That's what he'd always gotten whenever he confided in Gladys. "We're deciding on a plan, but it's not totally in place yet. You can expect a few extra mouths for supper. Father Knight will be bringing Lillie home from school. Leslie is picking up Henri from daycare, and Carol should be driving into your yard within the next few minutes."

Gladys heard Carol's vehicle come to a crunching stop on the gravel driveway. Then a door slammed. She looked out her window to see Carol walking quickly toward the house. "Yep, Carol just rolled in. Anything else?"

"We need a lot of prayers, and we want to keep the commotion over this event as low-key for the kids as possible."

"Totally understandable, but you and I know that Lillie will figure out something's wrong quickly. My advice is to be honest about the situation without scaring the pants off her."

"Right. We'll deal with it. Listen, I've got some other stuff on my plate. I'll try to be home by six."

"Everything's under control here," Gladys said, raising her hand in greeting as Carol walked through the door.

"Good. I'll see you later," and the phone disconnected.

Gladys hung up the phone, then opened her arms. Carol walked into them, cried softly for a few minutes, and tenderly pulled away to look into Gladys' hazel eyes. Eyes full of kindness, empathy, and grit. An odd combination but one that comforted Carol immensely.

"Now listen here," Gladys began, sounding like the practical soul she was. "The Lord knows everything that is going on. He knows all about this situation, and he's on our side. We need to have some food ready for these people who are coming. Let's have a cup of coffee, and you can tell me what's happened and what the plan is," she said, offering a thin smile. "And then we're going to cook up a storm."

"Okay. I can do that," Carol said, her voice wobbling. "I think."

"Sure you can. You'll do that and more than you ever thought possible. As your day is, so shall your strength be," Gladys said as she wrapped her arm around Carol's shoulder and guided her to the wooden kitchen table. "Coffee in a minute, and then some praying and cooking."

49

The meeting on the third floor of the law enforcement center on Vine Street convened at one o'clock sharp on Tuesday afternoon. A sense of foreboding and a contentious attitude seemed to hover in the room. Jim was familiar with that mood; it usually came when frustration and lack of clues converged in a perfect storm to discourage and thwart the solution of a crime. *Must be the devil workin' overtime,* he thought.

Now with Sara's abduction complicating things further, Jim wondered why he was even here. He should be coordinating a statewide search for his daughter. But he knew technically, according to police procedure, no one is considered missing until forty-eight hours has passed. Instead, he stood in front of a whiteboard in a stuffy, claustrophobic classroom and gazed at his team, whose eyes were fixed on him.

The team had been expecting Jim to be tense and nervous. His outwardly calm demeanor in the face of Sara's abduction seemed unnatural and disconnected from reality. As they began discussing the two crimes, the tension in the classroom ramped up. The theories about the Kratt murder, the Yelski abduction, and the evidence to support a link between them were discussed, reimagined, and rearranged. Jim spoke in a slow, deliberate manner, but underneath his words, an unspoken challenge cut through the atmosphere like a knife.

Jim looked tellingly at each member of his team. They were scattered around the room. Paul was perched casually on a stool at the side of the board, and DeDe and Leslie were seated at a white table in front of the board. Davy Jones was standing behind the table where the women sat, listening carefully, monitoring the mood of the investigative team, trying to keep abreast of the Kratt investigation and the Yelski cold case. Jim noticed the look on his face. *He probably wonders how this team ever solves anything.*

"Okay, let's summarize what we've got so far. Based on our interviews and the existing evidence that's available from the cold case and the stuff we've uncovered, we have three basic theories to consider. First, the murder of Kratt and the Yelski abduction are two separate incidents that are not related despite some of the evidence that's come to light."

"None of us really believes that, Chief," Sam said, crossing his arms over his chest. Jim looked at him, stupefied, while Sam reviewed the evidence. "What about the newspaper articles about Yelski we found in Kratt's possession? We already agreed it suggests a connection that's more than a coincidence." He was standing at the whiteboard, filling it in with the current evidence and possible motives.

"Point taken," Jim said curtly.

"And the fact that we uncovered a person that visited the Blackman home the night of the abduction is an important piece of evidence we didn't have before," DeDe spoke up. Shrugging, she added, "We just don't know if it ties in with the Kratt murder yet."

"True," Jim said. "We haven't interviewed Eric Osgood, but he's supposed to be here this afternoon sometime. He could be an important link."

"Then there's the infamous pothole clue," Paul said. Jim rolled his eyes. "But the theory that the two crimes are not related is still a possibility."

Jim started again. "The second theory is that someone knew Kratt was involved in the Yelski abduction. Someone murdered him to eliminate the possibility that he would go to the police, admit his involvement, and clear his conscience."

Everyone stared at Jim, wondering where he'd come up with that idea.

Jim squirmed uncomfortably. "That may become clearer as we continue to gather evidence, but we also have to be prepared to accept the fact we may never fully discover the link between the two crimes, if there is one."

"That's a lot of mays and mights and ifs," Paul said.

Sam held his marker aloft, trying to synthesize what he was hearing. However, no one challenged Jim's second hypothesis.

"That's still the most plausible theory, don't you think?" DeDe asked.

"Maybe. Do you have something to add or subtract?" Jim said.

"No. No, I don't," DeDe said. Jim moved on.

"The third theory is that someone who is unknown to us at this time committed the murder of Kratt for reasons totally unrelated to the Yelski abduction and for motives we don't understand yet. Whoever it was tried to make the two crimes look like they were connected, possibly to lead us in a different direction," Jim finished. Everyone remained silent. "Now, I'd be interested in anything you've discovered that supports or negates any one of these three theories."

Sam, who'd been writing the theories on the whiteboard under three columns, looked uneasily at the members of the team.

"Leslie has another theory, Chief," Sam said. Everyone looked in her direction.

"Go ahead. We're listening," Jim said, feigning patience. He rolled his shoulders to ease the tension in his neck and upper back. He had a splitting headache and wondered what his blood pressure reading might be. It took every ounce of concentration to keep his mind on the task at hand and not let his brain form images of Sara bound, raped, and thrown in a ditch somewhere. He was still hoping she would be used in some kind of exchange; therefore, she'd have to be kept alive, which didn't preclude her from being beaten or sexually assaulted by the most notorious miscreant in Wisconsin. Sipping from his coffee cup, he looked at Leslie over the rim. He knew he was failing miserably to maintain a relaxed, in-charge demeanor. From the expressions on their faces, he knew his team was onto him. Still, he made a noble effort to listen as Leslie unwound her theory.

"What if the Yelski abduction was carried out by three people? We know, based on the conversation between the two guys at the bar in Readstown, that Howard Lake was believed to be linked to the Yelski abduction. He was a good friend of Sylvester Kratt's. Lake committed suicide, although we're not sure why. Kratt was strangled by someone. Could Kratt's murderer be another member of the abduction team who decided to get rid of the last person who could rat on him, leaving him the last man standing, so to speak?" Leslie watched Jim and noticed his jaw working furiously.

"Yeah, and actually, Jim's last idea is the same as the one DeDe had—that someone involved in the Yelski abduction may have eliminated Kratt because his conscience was telling him to go to the police and confess the crime," Paul reminded everyone. DeDe cast him an appreciative glance.

Jim had a faraway look in his eyes, stared into space, and said, "Anything is possible in a murder investigation, but not everything is probable. Distinguishing between the two is the balancing act in any investigation."

"I'm not sure I understand the difference between the two, Chief," Leslie said, looking confused by this philosophical rabbit trail.

Listening to the discussion, Davy Jones prepared himself for another wandering metaphysical explanation of the crazy things criminals did when in reality, many were just plain stupid and frequently acted impulsively without forethought or planning. He crossed his arms over his chest and stared at the floor. He had to admit that Higgins was not shy about making himself a target of ridicule and verbal abuse. *Here we go again,* he thought. *How many times have I heard this broken record?*

"Let me put it this way," Jim continued. "If you say something is probable, you are expressing more confidence about it than if you say it is possible. In other words, all things that are probable are possible, but not all things that are possible are probable. For example, today, many things could happen to me. I could be attacked by a shark, struck by lightning, hit by a car, or take a walk. All are possible, but only one is probable."

The team looked at Jim with something close to incredulity. *Was the guy cracking up?* thought Paul. *What about the possibility your daughter has been abducted by the biggest meth dealer in Wisconsin? How does that theory stack up in the probability game?*

"We need to figure out which of these scenarios or combinations of them are probable, even though any one of them or a combination of them could be possible?" DeDe asked tentatively.

"Exactly," Jim said, pointing an index finger at DeDe. "The question is this: What is the most probable theory we have of the crimes which is supported by the evidence we've uncovered? That's our challenge, people," Jim said with finality.

Silence. No one moved. Jim was flummoxed. Frustrated with a lack of response, he continued.

"Okay, let's back up the train. You realize that we still have a lot of legwork to do before one or a combination of these theories begins to look probable, right? We don't have enough evidence yet to arrest someone. So, we need to go back to the drawing board." Jim turned and pointed. "Sam, I want you to contact Heather Lovstad, Kratt's daughter, and schedule a formal interview here downstairs as soon as possible. Tomorrow morning would be great, but something needs to be scheduled for the next day or two. If she's not willing to come here, ask her to choose a location. We'll come to her. It's imperative we interview her again. I've discovered something about her that needs to be confronted."

"Yeah? Like what?" Paul asked, resting his head on his fist.

"Apparently, she has a counseling appointment every month, has had for the last twenty years, at a counseling service in Holmen. She readily admitted that she had an uneasy relationship with her father due to his pornographic interests. So, I'm thinking she may not have been totally forthcoming about her relationship with her father when I talked to her. She must have some ongoing issues of some kind," Jim explained.

"You're suggesting incest or sexual abuse?" DeDe asked.

"It's a distinct possibility, one she may not want to admit to," Jim said.

"Do you suspect she might have murdered her father?" DeDe asked.

"Although it's rare, kids kill their parents more often than we like to admit, especially when abuse is involved," Jim answered. "Possible? Yes. Probable? Don't know yet. Need more information."

"I'll schedule the interview, Chief," Sam said.

"DeDe and Leslie, you're going to talk to Eric Osgood. He's probably already arrived. Be thorough. Get a good history, and check his alibi on the night of the Kratt murder. Ask him about the locket." Jim checked his cell for the time. "Talk to Emily. He was supposed to be here at one, but maybe he didn't show. If he didn't, go find him."

The two women stood. "We've got it," Leslie said.

Davy Jones interrupted. "Wait. Before everyone leaves, you're all aware of the threat Jim and Carol are facing with Sara's disappearance. We all need to be ready at a moment's notice to help in whatever way we can."

"Goes without saying, Davy, but thanks," Jim said. "The threat is far from over. It's a parent's worst nightmare, and my daughter, Sara—" Jim suddenly choked on his words, and his eyes misted up.

His fists opened and closed at his sides. Leslie walked over and stood in front of him.

"Just call, okay?" she said quietly. Jim nodded, embarrassed by the sudden overwhelming show of emotion that had blindsided him.

After the women and Sheriff Jones left, Jim turned to Paul.

"I know you're helping Jones on the Maddog thing," Jim said to him, regaining control, "but in the next few days, I want you to find Howard Lake's relatives—parents, siblings, wife—and see if you can find out why he killed himself … or if he killed himself."

"No problem." Paul paused. "Now, will you take some advice?" he asked, locking eyes with Jim. "Go home. You look like shit. Get some sleep if you can. Sam's going to sit in the driveway tonight—"

Jim interrupted in a loud voice. "Like hell he is! Besides, you don't know where we're staying. And anyway, that's not necessary," he argued.

"Like hell it isn't! We're all taking shifts until this thing is over. You may be chief, but that's the way it's going to be," Paul shouted emphatically, poking his finger at no one in particular, his eyes flashing. "Gladys Hanson on County K, right?"

Jim sighed. Realizing how exhausted he was, he acquiesced. "I guess there's no point in arguing."

"You got that right. On this team, we take care of each other, remember? Now go home," Sam finished, squeezing his shoulder.

Jim turned, waved, and walked down the hall to his office.

Sam turned to Paul. "Is the tracking device working?" Paul asked.

"You betcha. She's on, and I'll be monitoring it. Of course, with us sitting in the driveway every night, I doubt that he'll try to skip out when Maddog calls."

"Then you have totally underestimated his desire to go this one alone," Paul said, watching Jim leave his office and walk down the hall. "You know how stubborn and bullheaded he can be."

Sam crinkled his nose. "Yeah. I know all about that."

Eric Osgood sat across the table from DeDe Deverioux and Leslie Birkstein in an interrogation room on the ground floor of the law enforcement center. He seemed relaxed, even friendly. He was dressed in a casual plaid cotton shirt open at the neck and a pair of well-worn blue jeans. His graying hair was neatly combed, and his beard trimmed. He scrutinized the two detectives with a detached scientific air, noting their demeanor and carefully watching their preparation for the interview. DeDe noticed his observational skills and wondered, *Who's interviewing who?*

Leslie checked the closed-circuit camera, did a test run, and when she was satisfied the equipment was working properly, she began the questioning.

"So, Mr. Osgood," she began, but Eric interrupted.

"Oh, please, let's not be so formal. Eric is fine with me, if that works for you."

"All right, Eric. Can you tell us about your relationship with Christina Yelski?" DeDe started.

"Sure. We attended Logan High School together from 1975 to 1977, but we didn't really get to know one another until our freshman year when we both joined the Science Explorers Club. It was at those meetings that I really got to know Christina well." He paused, but neither woman interrupted with another question.

He gazed at the wall over the head of the women as if he were visualizing her. His face softened as he talked, and his voice deepened and took on a soothing intonation. "She was lovely, beautiful, really. And her mind was extraordinary. She was a physics whiz and had dreams of one day working at NASA. I have no doubt that she would have succeeded. She had a fierce independence and will to achieve. Of course, I loved the avian world, but we found common ground in our interest in flight; she in space flight, me in bird flight. That's really when I fell in love with her. When we shared our dreams about what we wanted to accomplish in the scientific world, you couldn't help but love her. She would have been the perfect mate for me—physically beautiful, disarmingly polite and charming, and intellectually gifted. Of course, I may be characterizing her unfairly. She wasn't perfect. No one is."

"Did she feel the same way about you?" Leslie asked, her curiosity aroused.

Eric stared at Leslie, and a flash of offense crossed his features. "Well, from all indications, I believe she loved me as much as I loved her. What are the chances that two prodigies could find each other and fall in love?"

"I imagine that is a rather rare event," Leslie agreed.

"It's come to our attention that you visited the Blackman home on the night of the abduction. Could you tell us about that?" DeDe asked, leaning forward and resting her arms on the table.

There was a pause, and DeDe was about to repeat the question when Eric began to explain.

"We'd been working on a project for biology class, and Christina had written some text for our presentation that she wanted me to read. She knew she wasn't supposed to have any visitors while she babysat, but we talked about it, and although it might seem pretty innocuous now, back then, we felt like we were getting away with some kind of clandestine, adult activity. I know it sounds stupid forty years later, but at our age, it was kind of thrilling to break the rules. Especially for us. We never broke any rules." Eric smiled at the thought. "If I remember right, I came about six-thirty and left about an hour later."

"Why didn't you tell the police about your visit?" Leslie asked.

"Would you have? I never told anyone because I thought I'd be accused of being involved somehow. So how did you find out I'd been there?" Eric asked, his eyes perceptive, sharpened with curiosity.

"A neighbor lady saw you come and go. She didn't tell the police either, so we consider your presence at the house a primary piece of new information in the case." Leslie watched Eric carefully.

"Am I a suspect in the abduction?" he asked, his demeanor

serious. He leaned forward in his chair and clasped his hands on the table.

"Let's just say you're a person of interest," DeDe stated. She went on. "Did you notice anything unusual about the situation that night?"

"No, not really. Christina played with the little boy." He rubbed his forehead. "Can't remember his name," he said.

"Dorian," Leslie reminded him.

"Yes, Dorian. Cute little kid. She gave him a snack and carried him up to his crib shortly before I left. That's it, really."

"Then what happened?" DeDe asked, her eyes studying Eric's face.

"We chatted a little more, she walked me to the door, I kissed her, and well, I gave her a locket—quite an expensive one. We'd gone to Homecoming together, and in the wisdom of sixteen-year-olds, we knew we were in love, so I wanted to give her something to symbolize our relationship. That was the last time I saw her alive." His shoulders slumped, and his face collapsed with sadness at the thought.

Leslie asked, "So you had no sense that Christina was fearful or was feeling insecure in the situation at the Blackman home?"

"No, not at all. She seemed perfectly normal."

"Any phone calls while you were there?" Leslie asked.

"No, none."

"Did you walk to the Blackman home?" DeDe asked.

"Yes, I only lived about five blocks away."

"You didn't notice any cars parked along the way that were unfamiliar?" she continued.

"No. I wasn't a motorhead like most kids my age, so I doubt that I would have noticed a strange car anyway. Most guys my age were interested in cars, but I was looking at birds. I was the odd man out—obviously."

Leslie smiled and continued. "Did you return to the Blackman home later in the evening for any reason?"

"No."

"So the last time you saw Christina alive was when you left the Blackman home at about seven-thirty. Is that correct?" Leslie asked, trying to verify Eric's story. Eric nodded in the affirmative. "Was Christina wearing the locket when you left?"

"Yes, she put it on right away. She really loved it. When I left, she was wearing it."

"Anything inside the locket?" DeDe asked.

"Yes, a photo of us together in front of her parents' house. I had to cut it way down to make it fit inside," he said.

"Where were you a few weeks ago on Saturday evening, September 7, between 9 p.m. and 12 p.m.?"

"Hmm. Let me look at my calendar." Eric pulled his smartphone from his shirt pocket and scrolled until he found his calendar. "Oh, yes. I should have remembered. There was an international symposium in Minneapolis at the Millennium Hotel on the Nicolet Mall about climate change and how it is impacting bird populations around the world. I was asked to be a guest speaker and talk about my work with snowy owls on the Alaska tundra. Very interesting conference." He looked up expectantly at the two women. "I can give you the name of the chairman of the event in case you'd like to contact her."

"Yes, we'd appreciate that. Thank you, Eric. You've been very helpful." Leslie said.

"Is there anything else you'd like to tell us?" DeDe asked, still feeling depressed they'd had no real breakthroughs, except the fact that Christina was wearing the locket when Eric left.

"Only one thing. I loved Christina. I believe we eventually would have married and had a family. Someone stole that opportunity from me when they abducted and snuffed out Christina's life. I'll do all I can to help you solve this cold case," he said emphatically. "Christina wasn't the only one who lost her future that day—I did, too." Leslie noticed the determined look on his face and thought, *We need all the help we can get.*

"Thanks, Eric. We appreciate your cooperation," DeDe said, rising from the chair. They shook hands and gave Eric their business cards. After he left the room, Leslie strolled beside DeDe as they left the interrogation room. DeDe stopped in front of a soda machine that was humming erratically in a vestibule. Turning to Leslie, she said dejectedly. "Well, that was a dead end." She popped some quarters in the machine and punched a button for a Pepsi. The can clanged noisily into the bottom of the machine.

"Higgins won't be too happy," DeDe added. "But I don't think Eric has the grit to kill someone."

"Yeah, I hear you. Like Higgins says—everything is possible, but not everything is probable."

50

By early Tuesday evening, Sara had been held captive for twelve hours. She was none the worse for wear. During her isolation, she exerted some self-control and reined in her emotions. *Crying and hysteria will get you nowhere,* she thought.

She reviewed her options. None of them looked promising. She had no idea where she was. Well, that wasn't exactly true. She knew she was within an hour of La Crosse. Using an average speed of 55 mph, she figured they'd only traveled about a half hour. Using that as a guideline, she estimated she was within thirty or thirty-five miles from where she'd left her car. In her mind, she could visualize a Wisconsin map and a ring extending around the city of La Crosse. No matter how you sliced and diced it, the area was huge, heavily wooded in some areas, and sparsely populated in other places. With a growing sense of frustration, she realized plenty of isolated areas surrounding La Crosse could be used to hide someone who'd been abducted.

She hadn't been raped or beaten, for which she was truly thankful. No one had tried to extract knowledge from her about her father or family. Whether her luck would continue to hold, she wasn't sure. She was alive, and she assumed that was the only option available to Maddog if she would be used as a bargaining chip for Lillie.

Maddog had taken a huge gamble tangling with someone like her dad. Sara shook her head when she thought of the impending confrontation between these two men. It would be ugly. In fact, it would be a fight to the finish, not dissimilar to something that had happened at a place called the O.K. Corral.

Still, in some ways, she thought philosophically, Maddog Pierson and Jim Higgins had a lot in common. Both were used to commanding a team and giving orders. They valued loyalty and the ability to carry out a plan. Both were bullheaded, focused, and determined. But there, the similarities ended, and the stark differences began.

Her dad worked tirelessly fighting wrongdoers who preyed on the unsuspecting public. He'd seen the price that victims paid for the violent behavior of the scumbags of the earth. In most cases, no amount of redress in the courts or prison sentences could repay the victims for their injuries, loss of innocence, and damage to their sense of security and well-being.

Sara loved her dad for his belief in the all-encompassing goodness of God—the benevolence He graciously extended to his flawed children, his involvement and influence in human affairs that ended on a wooden cross at Golgotha. She was beginning to understand that evil cannot be explained or rationalized away. Evil was evil purely for its own sake, and anyone that got in the way, whether innocent or complicit, paid the price it demanded, and they were forever changed. That's what motivated her dad to excel in his job. He did his best to love his family, provide them with security and comfort, and would ultimately give his life for them if he had to. These were the foundational blocks that were a part of Jim Higgins' moral code. Sara chuckled to herself when she recalled her dad's famous statement: The best thing a father can do for his children is to love their mother. That was the Jim Higgins that Maddog would confront. And even though her dad hadn't succeeded in winning every battle, nonetheless, he had stacked up an amazing record of solving difficult crimes and bringing the perpetrators to justice.

Maddog, of course, operated on the dark side. Listening to her father enumerate his long list of criminal activities, Sara concluded that Maddog lacked a moral compass and the stabilizing effect of human love. It sounded as if he regularly threw caution to the wind and risked his life and the lives of others to deliver drugs to as many customers as possible. In the process, he seeded addiction, chaos, and violence with every transaction. Lacking familial love did not bode well for him as a father. From what her dad had told Sara about Maddog's early years, it sounded like his young life had been a continual whirlwind of abuse, violent chaos, and drunken pandemonium on a hardscrabble farm in central Wisconsin. A mother who drank to endure a marriage of physical violence and abuse. A father who could not show affection to his son. Sara thought the Dog's heart must be like a shrunken, withered apple hanging on a dying tree. In analyzing both men's lives, the effects of their actions would be felt for generations to come.

Sara squirmed uncomfortably and winced. The duct tape on her ankles and wrists was beginning to cut off her circulation. She'd had nothing to eat or drink the entire day, and now her stomach growled in protest. She felt weak and hungry, and her bladder was bursting. She hoped she'd be given the chance to relieve herself. Thankfully, it wasn't hot in the building where she was being confined. Wherever this place was, it had been very quiet all day. In the distance, she'd heard a tractor running earlier, but since then, there had been no traffic noise nearby which led her to believe she was hidden away from main highways and county roads.

Finally, as dusk was falling, she heard an ATV pull up next to the building. The engine stopped. Footsteps clomped across the outer floor of the porch, there was a fumbling of the lock, and someone halted outside the room. Sara's heart rate ramped up. A key was inserted in another lock, and the door squeaked open on its hinges. Heavy boot steps echoed across the floor until they stopped in front of her.

Someone grabbed her wrists and cut the duct tape, then did the same to her ankles. Her blindfold was loosened and taken off. Even though it was almost dark, she squeezed her eyes shut against what little light there was. Slowly she opened them. A man she assumed was Maddog pulled a hardback chair over, turned it backward, and sat down in front of her. She smelled pizza, and her stomach cramped with hunger pains.

She studied the man sitting before her. He was unkempt; his shirt was wrinkled like a crumpled newspaper and was stained with sweat beneath the arms. His hair, dark with grease, was tied back in a ponytail. He reeked of cigarette and marijuana smoke. His blue jeans were full of holes, the bottom edges encrusted in mud. He wore a pair of square-toed leather boots. Startling green eyes looked at her from a handsomely rugged, unshaven face, but his stark flat countenance was like marble, cold and lifeless. Still, Sara imagined that he would clean up pretty good with a little soap and water and a razor.

She rubbed her wrists, trying to get the circulation moving.

"Maddog, I take it?" she asked, meeting his vacant gaze.

The corners of his mouth lifted imperceptibly. "Hungry?" the man asked, leaning over and plucking a piece of cold pizza from a box on the floor.

Sara nodded, took the pizza, and began wolfing it down. After a moment, he offered her a bottle of water. She drank deeply, the liquid dribbling off her chin, and then took another piece of pizza when he offered it to her.

She assessed him with a cold blue stare. "What's your plan?" she asked him, chewing energetically on a piece of chewy crust. When he remained silent for several moments, she continued, "You must have some kind of plan that I'm sure involves Lillie and my dad. Otherwise, you wouldn't have risked kidnapping me from the side of the road in broad daylight on a U.S. highway."

He remained silent until Sara wondered if he was mute, stupid, or both.

"You look like your dad," he said, stating the obvious.

"Well, since I'm his daughter, I suppose that stands to reason," she said, wiping her lips with the back of her hand.

"Are you making fun of me?" he asked, frowning, leaning forward, propping his hands on his knees.

Sara shook her head. "No, not at all. I'll take your statement as a compliment, but most people would say I'm more like my mom than my dad." Her friendly chatter seemed to put him at ease, but inside, her heart was tripping to a rhythm of its own. "Thanks for the pizza. I guess I was hungrier than I thought."

He grunted and continued to assess the creature he'd captured. Sara returned his gaze. She felt a shiver of trepidation crawl up her spine when he looked at her as if she were a rabbit in a cage. She didn't like how he ran his eyes up and down her body. *Distract him,* she thought.

"Any chance I can go outside and pee?" she asked, meeting his curious stare.

He lowered his eyes. "I guess," he said. He pushed himself off the wooden chair he'd been sitting on as Sara rose stiffly from the dirty overstuffed rocker. "Come on," he said as he led her outside. After the staleness of the cabin, the freshness of the evening air smelled wonderful. Sara drew several huge gulps into her lungs. The scent of evergreens and bracken ferns reminded her of hiking and camping.

"Over there," he said, pointing to a bank of high grass. Sara walked tentatively toward the grass, waded into it, then turned and faced him. She squatted and relieved herself. As she did her business, she took stock of her prison.

The cabin was a simple crude structure, probably an abandoned deer hunting shack, made of two-by-fours, treated plywood, and a roof covered with cheap shingles that had begun to peel and flake. It was small but had a tiny porch, one small window, and a wooden door with a hasp and padlock. Inside were two rooms. One seemed to be sleeping quarters, and another had probably been a kitchen. It was on the edge of a huge tract of agricultural land which had been planted with corn. The towering stalks bordered the cabin on one side in a field that seemed to go on as far as the eye could see. The wind rustled the drying corn stalks and reminded Sara of a yellow ocean rippling with waves. More tall foliage around the cabin's edges almost completely obliterated it from sight. An oak, a couple of maples, and a white pine partially shaded the cabin. A steep hill rose behind the cabin blocking the sunshine and keeping it in the shade. In the final analysis, the cabin was almost undetectable from land or air. Maddog had planned carefully, and Sara's heart sank when she realized this place would keep her hidden for a very long time if need be.

"This your property?" Sara asked as she walked back toward Maddog.

"No. I'm just borrowing it," he said with a grin. Then his expression turned sour and angry. "Why the hell do you care? Get inside," he barked, pointing his arm toward the cabin.

Sara looked up at the sky as they trekked back to her prison. The stars were just beginning to prick the velvety purple of the night sky. Rustling gently in the night wind, the trees were dark, and their silhouettes etched sharply against the horizon. The fragrant scent of pine jostled memories of nights she'd spent with her dad and mom and her twin brother, John, camping on isolated islands in the swirling current of the Mississippi River. They would lie back on their sleeping bags and point out the constellations they knew. That seemed like a thousand years ago now. Tears misted her eyes. *I'm okay, Dad. I know you're looking for me. I'm not worried, but I am a little scared. I love you all.*

51

Gladys Hanson's house on County K was finally quiet now at ten o'clock, but throughout the early evening, it had been noisy, filled with friends and family who'd come to lend support and comfort to Jim and Carol. Father Knight had prayed a lovely prayer before the evening meal. Leslie had pitched in and helped Gladys serve some delicious food. Sara's twin, John, and his wife, Jenny, arrived looking harried and tense, wide-eyed with shock. Hugging Jim and Carol, John did his best to reassure everyone that Sara was smart and tough. Carol's sister and brother-in-law, Vivian and Craig Jensen, had driven down from Holmen to offer whatever support was needed. And, of course, Lillie and Henri entertained everyone with their childish innocence and antics, temporarily relieving the angst of the situation.

"I don't need to remind you, Jim, of what this moron is capable of, do I?" Vivian asked as they stood off in a corner of the dining room, sipping a beer. "As a father, you're going to feel some pretty intense emotions until this is all over."

"Got it, Vivian. I just hope my predictions of a tradeoff for Lillie will keep Sara relatively safe. And yes, I'm very aware of what he could be doing to her this very moment," Jim said woodenly. "On the bright side, Davy Jones has called out law enforcement in three counties to scour the countryside for Maddog and Sara." His face looked haggard, and he stared zombie-like into a space somewhere outside the window. He took a sip of beer.

"Well, let's hope she's not hurt too badly. The psychological damage alone could have serious ramifications down the road," Vivian said. Grabbing Jim's elbow, she continued. "Keep praying. That's something that most psychologists won't admit helps, but it does."

Jim's eyes met her concerned gaze. "No use in praying unless you have faith, Vivian."

"And you do. You and Carol and Lillie," she said comfortingly.

Jim's eyes misted over. "Carol and I appreciate you being here more than we can say," he said tenderly.

"Hey, what's a family for anyway?" Vivian said weakly.

Hovering in the background, Sam had uttered his own prayers for Sara's safety. He remembered all too well the hostage situation Leslie had found herself in over a year ago when her boyfriend had beat her and locked her in a plywood box in subzero temperatures. Sam shivered when he thought of the conditions that Sara might have to endure before she was rescued.

Jim and Carol were emotionally ragged and exhausted from the intense uncertainty of their daughter's disappearance. The headache that had plagued Jim in the afternoon became a roaring crescendo behind his eyes in the evening. He'd finally resorted to taking some migraine medication to ease the throbbing pain and sensitivity to light. Carol was calm now, even though her heart fluttered wildly with crazy palpitations during the day. But when everyone began arriving, she was buoyed by the hope, comfort, and love of family and friends.

Now in the quietness of the house with Henri securely tucked in bed sleeping, Carol sat on the edge of the double bed and listened to Lillie's questions.

"Why do we have to stay with Grandma Gladys?" she asked

tearfully. "I wanna go home," she whimpered softly. "When are we goin' go home, Mommy?"

"You love Grandma Gladys. She's helping us until we can get Sara back home," Carol explained patiently. They'd decided not to shield Lillie from the news of Sara's abduction, but they left out the disturbing details.

"Will Sara be safe?"

"We hope so. Bapa has a lot of people who are trying to help find her."

"But will she be safe?" Lillie persisted.

"We don't know, honey. But we can pray for Sara, can't we?" Carol leaned over Lillie and tenderly kissed her cheek. Lillie's eyes seemed a brighter blue against the white of the pillowcase. She continued to hold Carol's gaze, her face a unique reflection of childlike faith and innocence that now seemed tainted by the realities of evil.

"You close your eyes now and go to sleep. We'll be close by if you need us," Carol reassured her. "Right across the hall."

"You stay by me now?"

"I'll stay by you now."

Carol moved to the rocking chair in the corner of the room and quietly waited until Lillie had fallen asleep. Then she stumbled to bed, the exhaustion and drama of the day melting into the night.

Meanwhile, Jim and Sam had parked themselves on the front seat of Sam's Jeep Cherokee. The night air was chilly, and the yard light near the barn created an orange halo on the gravel. Night bugs flew in random patterns under the light, their nervous energy fueling their erratic flight. Parking his Jeep under the sprawling branches of a huge soft maple, Sam had pointed the hood toward the barn so he had a good view of the road and driveway.

"You don't have kids yet," Jim said, breaking the silence, "but when you see them for the first time, and they look into your eyes … well, it's a moment in your life you never forget."

Sam hesitated to tread on Jim's reflections, so he stayed quiet.

"We never expected twins, you know. Margie didn't suspect anything was out of the ordinary. When we got to the hospital, and the doc delivered John, we thought that was it. We had a beautiful son, and we breathed a sigh of relief. But Margie's pains wouldn't let up. The next thing we knew, she'd delivered another baby—our precious Sara. We were shocked and happy and scared all at the same time." Sam glanced at Jim, and he could see tears wetting his cheeks.

"She's got a good head on her shoulders, Chief." Somehow, he felt like his dad, the pastor, listening to people's confessions. It was a delicate balance, knowing when to talk and when to listen.

"I know. She's a great kid. I just hope she can hold her own with Maddog."

Sam wondered at his statement. *Must be fatigue talking. There weren't too many who could go toe to toe with Maddog and come out unscathed on the other side.* He thought about Marcellus Brown, who'd died late Saturday afternoon, and once again, a weariness came over him like an unexpected ocean wave that hits you broadside and leaves you breathless.

"I do know one thing," Sam stated quietly.

"What's that?"

"You need to go inside and get some sleep. This could go on a while, and you'll be no good to anybody unless you rest."

"You're right. Thanks, Sam," Jim said, reaching across the seat to squeeze Sam's arm. "You're a good kid and a good cop." He fumbled his hand across the door until he found the handle. He pulled it and stepped out of the Jeep. Leaning into the open window, he watched Sam silently.

"I'll be fine. Go to bed, Chief."

"Right," Jim replied.

Sam watched him walk to the house. He stumbled once as he approached the door, then he turned and waved to Sam, disappearing inside. Sam's Walmart burner cell vibrated in his pocket.

"Birkstein."

"Just checking in. Everything okay?" Paul asked.

"Yep. Higgins just went in the house, and hopefully, he'll get some sleep."

"Good. See you in the morning."

"Right."

Sam replaced his phone in his jacket pocket. Another few minutes went by. His own cell phone buzzed, making him jump.

"Hey, love."

"I miss you," Leslie said wistfully. "Our bed isn't the same without you."

"Hmm. Yeah, I miss you, too, honey."

"Anything goin' on out at Gladys'?"

"Nope, dead as a rock. But that's good. Everybody's tucked in bed except me."

"Poor baby." Sam could imagine her subtle smile and capricious eyes.

"Well, don't worry. If this thing goes on for a while, you'll be takin' your turn in the driveway, too."

"This is true. Hey, just called to say good night. Love you," Leslie said, her voice soft and seductive.

"Night, honey. Love you, too."

The darkness and quiet ganged up on Sam after half an hour of trying to stay awake. He caught himself drifting off a couple of times. He turned on the radio, but he couldn't stay awake. As he dozed, flashes of Leslie's abduction blew across his memory. Then he thought about Sara being molested and beaten. He caught a breath, its intake like frozen winter air, and he suddenly jerked awake. He tuned in to an all-night radio talk show. Maddog's cruelty and depth of depravity were evident in the beating of Marcellus Brown that had cost him his life. He couldn't imagine the price that would be extracted from him if he hurt Sara. *That's not a place you want to go,* he thought.

52

WEDNESDAY, SEPTEMBER 18

DeDe Deverioux jostled along in the cab to the George Street neighborhood, where the driver dropped her off near the Kratt residence. Stepping out of the cab, she leaned into the front passenger window and made arrangements with the cab driver to be picked up in two hours. That would give her the opportunity to canvass the area and re-interview the neighbors in the blocks adjacent to the Kratt residence. She had reviewed the police notes of the initial contacts they'd made on Sunday, September 8, the day after the murder. That was before she'd been hired. Could another set of eyes discover something that had been missed? Maybe, but the chance of uncovering new information was doubtful. Still, she hoped something would come to light.

She began with the closest neighbors, the Sloans. Walking up to the front door, DeDe rang the bell and waited. The two-story house was old but well-kept, with a couple of monstrous soft maples shading the front stoop. When no one answered, she turned around and was about to move on to the next residence when the door scraped open.

Turning back, DeDe flashed her ID and said, "Hello. I'm Detective

Deverioux from the La Crosse Sheriff's Department. I'm wondering if you could answer a few questions."

Mrs. Sloan, a petite woman with dark hair cut in a classic wedge, eyed DeDe's ID badge nervously. "We already talked to the police about the murder," she said defensively, her eyes nervously zeroing in on the Kratt residence next door.

"Yes, I know that. But we're hoping people may remember something else they didn't mention before. Did you notice any cars in the alley behind your home on the night of September 7?"

Mrs. Sloan looked over DeDe's head, and a puzzled expression crossed her features. "Cars? You mean like cars that weren't normally parked around here?"

"Yes, that's right. Something out of the ordinary, maybe?"

"We're not allowed to have any vehicles parked in the alley. That's a city ordinance, you know."

"Oh. I didn't realize that. But go on," DeDe encouraged.

"Well, our vehicles have to be parked in our garages off the alley or out front here on George Street. That's what the ordinance says, and the police check, believe me."

"I understand," DeDe said, growing impatient with the woman's focus on parking laws.

"I don't recall any strange cars parked around here that evening, though, if that's what you're asking."

"Is there anything else you can recall that stands out from that night?"

"No, nothing really. Kratt was a quiet guy, kept to himself. Other than that, there's nothing else to report—at least from my end of things. I didn't see anything out of the ordinary. Sorry," Mrs. Sloan said.

"Well, thanks for your time. Here's my card in case you think of something."

Mrs. Sloan reached for the card, looked at it, and put it in the pocket of her faded apron. "People around here are pretty nervous since that murder. It's not something that happens every day, you know," she said.

"Yes, it's always upsetting when these things happen, Mrs. Sloan," DeDe responded.

"Well, goodbye then," she said, quietly closing the door.

DeDe was just getting started, and she was already discouraged. She continued moving through the block of homes that made up the city block that surrounded the Kratt residence. Most people were at work, but after an hour of walking the neighborhood, she'd talked to four people who had seen nothing unusual the night of the murder.

An hour later, she approached a large two-story home on the back side of the block and across the alley from the Kratt home. The front porch floor was being replaced with a new one. Carpenters were hammering and sawing, removing the rotted planks and replacing them with new pine ones. The sharp, pleasant scent of sawdust filled the air. Pieces of two-by-fours and other scraps of wood littered the lawn and steps around the porch. A nail gun punched the boards with loud bangs, and a circular saw's piercing squeal filled the air.

"Is it safe to step on this?" DeDe shouted above the racket.

"What?" the carpenter asked once he saw DeDe, and his saw stopped screaming. He took out one of his foam earplugs and held it mid-air.

"Can I step on the porch?" she asked again, pointing to the old worn boards that were being removed.

"Sure. It's safe," he said. He replaced the ear plug and returned to work, revving his saw.

DeDe rang the bell, uncertain that it could be heard over the construction hubbub, but soon the front door opened. A young man with a mop of unruly hair stared at her. He pushed a few curly locks away from his face. He was dressed in a UW–La Crosse sweatshirt and faded blue jeans. His feet were bare.

"Help you?" he asked politely.

Over the buzz of the saw, DeDe yelled, "Could I ask you a few questions about the Kratts?" as she pointed across the alley to the Kratt home.

The young man's eyes drifted to DeDe's credentials, and he said, "Why don't you come in, so we can get away from all this noise?" He opened the door wider and stepped aside, indicating she should come in.

"Thank you," DeDe said, enjoying the muted quiet and the absence of the screaming power tools when he closed the door. He turned, and DeDe followed him into the main living area of the home.

"Let's sit in the living room. My parents are at work, and I have class at the U at one-thirty. Make yourself comfortable," he said, pointing to the couch. "Now, what can I help you with?" he asked, sitting in a leather recliner.

"Oh, this is nice. Thank you. Your name?" DeDe asked, pulling out her small memo pad from her shoulder purse.

"Morgan Olson. I live here with my parents and a younger sister who's still in high school. I'm assuming you have questions about the Kratt murder, right?"

"Yes, I do. I'm just re-interviewing all the neighbors. I'm wondering if you were home the night of the murder. That would have been Saturday, September 7?"

"No, my girlfriend and I were at Long John's Pub off George Street with some friends having a pizza and a few beers. Later," he stopped and looked at the ceiling, "probably about eleven-thirty, we walked through the alley behind Kratt's." His eyes came back to hers. "It's kind of a shortcut to our house through the alley."

"Did you see anything unusual in the alley?"

"Well, what do you mean by unusual?" Morgan asked, cocking his head to one side.

"Strange cars, people hanging around, a stranger who seemed in a hurry," DeDe said, shrugging. "I don't know. Anything out of the ordinary."

"Now that you mention cars, there was an SUV parked on Kratt's lawn under that big row of trees that borders the house on the north side. Kinda hard to see unless you knew it was there. The branches of that soft maple tree hang down low. It was sitting partially hidden under the branches. It was a dark color, maybe dark green or navy blue. Some kind of Forester or something."

DeDe felt a chill. "Really? You're sure of the time?"

"Yeah, my girlfriend and I were hoping we'd come home to an empty house," he lifted his eyebrows suggestively, "but my parents walked in right behind us. Kinda killed the romance for the evening. Know what I mean?"

DeDe smiled. "Yeah, I understand."

Morgan continued. "They'd been over to my uncle's playing cards. I remember it was between eleven-thirty and midnight. Maybe closer to midnight. But they came down Livingston and then parked in the garage. They didn't come through the alley, so they didn't see the SUV."

"Do you think your parents could confirm the time?" DeDe asked.

"Probably. Want me to call them?"

"That'd be great," DeDe said, smiling again.

Morgan slipped his cell out of his pocket. "I've got them on speed dial," he said confidently, brushing a wisp of hair away from his face. "Don't tell anybody that," he whispered, smiling. DeDe liked his sense of humor. When his mother answered, he asked if she'd talk to the detective. Mrs. Olson said she would, and she confirmed the time.

"This is great," DeDe said to Morgan after she'd hung up. "This could really help in our investigation. One more question. Did you notice if any lights were on in the house?"

"I think the house was dark, but I'm not sure about that," Morgan said.

"What about your girlfriend? Would she remember?"

"Maybe. She's in class right now, but I don't think she'd mind if I gave you her cell number. I'll text her that you'll be calling," he said.

Morgan and DeDe exchanged numbers. Standing and walking toward the front door, DeDe turned and said, "Thanks, Morgan. You've been a big help."

DeDe walked briskly to the place where the taxi had dropped her. The driver was waiting for her. When she arrived at the law enforcement center, she went straight to Jim's office. Knocking on the door frame, Jim waved her in, holding up a finger.

While he finished his conversation, DeDe looked at him carefully. He looked exhausted, his face tight like a piece of brittle paper. Worry and anxiety seemed to add years to his actual age. The calm demeanor he usually displayed was conspicuously absent. He seemed distracted, but he was clean-shaven and wore a pale yellow dress shirt which was tucked in a pair of navy chino dress slacks. He'd loosened his navy tie and rolled up his sleeves. Still, the anxiety in his eyes and his mussed gray-blond hair screamed stress. He nervously twiddled a ballpoint pen as he talked. He looked up at DeDe and rolled his eyes. When the conversation ended, he laid his cell on his desk, threw the pen down, and looked up at her.

"Where've you been?" His eyes focused on her after flitting around the room.

"Canvassing the George Street neighborhood again. I think I might have something."

"Tell me." Jim pulled his shoulders back, tucked his chin but kept his eyes on her face.

DeDe filled him in on the details of the interview with Morgan Olson. "The kid was sure about seeing the vehicle and seemed to have a good memory for details. On the way over here, I called his girlfriend. She confirmed the vehicle information, and she was sure the lights were off at the Kratt house when they walked by. Then I called the DMV. Heather drives a 2017 Subaru Forester SUV, dark green in color."

Jim rubbed his hands together. "This is good. I can use this in our interview at three. By the way, I want you to watch behind the glass when we interview Heather. Have you done many interviews of sexual abuse victims?"

"Are you kidding? Working at NOPD? Way too many, I hate to tell you."

Jim nodded. "We'll talk about your impressions afterward."

"Sam interviewing with you?"

"Nope. He's home sleeping. Paul'll be there," Jim explained.

"Three o'clock?" Jim nodded.

"I'll be there, sir," she said.

The day, which seemed longer than any other in Jim's recent memory, continued to play out like a high-flying kite on a taut string that was about to break. Uncharacteristically, Carol had called him twice on his cell. She was distraught about Sara's absence, keyed up about Lillie and Henri's safety, and feeling guilty about imposing on Gladys' customary calm existence. Jim spent several minutes listening to her vent, trying to reassure her gently.

"We'll be fine. Waiting for him to contact us will be the hardest part, believe me," Jim said.

"Isn't there anything we can do to draw him out, to get him to contact you so we can get this thing over with?" Carol asked.

"Nope. It's a waiting game now."

"Well, it stinks," she said sarcastically.

"It's the only game in town, unfortunately. I need to go, honey."

"I hate this," she said.

"So do I, babe," he said.

By two-thirty, Paul and Jim were preparing an interrogation room, checking the recording equipment. Heather Lovstad, Sylvester Kratt's only daughter, was scheduled to arrive at three o'clock. DeDe had yet to show up, but Jim expected her shortly. She would monitor the interview from the one-way glass in the room that adjoined the interview cubicle.

"So, what are we after exactly, Chief?" Paul asked, setting a couple of bottles of water on the table. "What's the goal here?"

Jim punched the recording button and saw the green light glow. He turned to Paul with a distracted expression on his face. "The goal? How 'bout the truth? As fickle as that concept may be in this world of shifting morality, I believe the truth has yet to be discovered concerning Ms. Lovstad. She readily admits she had a wary, distrustful relationship with her dad—that's by her own admission." Jim cracked open a bottle of water and took a long drink. He continued.

"When I thought back on the initial interview and reviewed my notes, something bothered me. I just got the feeling something was hinky. Is she a victim of incest or some other kind of sexual abuse?" Jim shrugged and shook his head. "Don't know. Maybe we'll find out, but we need to be careful. Anything she tells us needs to be viewed with a healthy dose of skepticism. Victims of sexual abuse often suffer horrible feelings of rage and helplessness, but they lock themselves in a prison and wear a straight jacket of self-imposed silence that makes everything worse. If that's Heather's story, then she could be a deeply disturbed individual."

"You gonna mention the counseling?"

"Maybe, maybe not. We'll see how things play out. You've read my interview questions and areas of interest, so jump in whenever you want to," Jim said glancing at the wall clock in the tiny room.

DeDe poked her head around the door. "I'll be in the next room, sir," she said. Jim nodded.

At 3:02 p.m., a police officer escorted Heather to the interrogation room. She was attractively dressed in a dark blue pencil skirt, navy pumps, and a conservative white blouse with lace accents on the shoulders and bodice, and her outfit was overlaid with a dark brown lush-looking leather jacket. Her makeup was tastefully applied, and her hair had been professionally cut, colored, and styled. She exchanged handshakes with Paul and Jim, removed her jacket, hung it on the back of the chair, and then sat at the interview table, fidgeting nervously. Her appearance surprised Jim. She'd seemed much more vulnerable when he interviewed her at home. Today, beneath her polished image was an attitude of confidence and authority. Jim wondered what the interview would reveal.

He kept his baritone voice reasonable and evenly modulated, leaned his elbows on the tabletop, and clasped his hands casually in front of him.

"So Heather, some new information has been discovered as we've investigated your father's murder. In our last talk, you said you had a rather unsettled relationship with your dad. Could you tell us about that again?"

"When you talked to me the first time, I believe I told you that he was addicted to pornography. Because of that, I became very uncomfortable in his presence," she said. "Is that what you're referring to?" Jim found the edge in her voice interesting.

"Yes, but could you elaborate? Were you afraid of him? Did he threaten you or hurt you in any way?" Jim probed gently. Suddenly, Heather looked confused, and her eyes seemed to turn darker as if a shade had been pulled across her face. Jim continued.

"We realize this may be difficult for you. Take all the time you need," he said softly. Instead of being completely present during the interview, he could feel his mind going to the dark side, wondering what was happening to Sara. *How would you want your daughter to be treated if she'd been sexually assaulted?* Then his stomach clenched painfully as his mind wandered to some very vile places he'd seen as a cop. He couldn't imagine Sara in those places. The pictures forming in his brain of Maddog sodomizing his daughter filled him with a rage he couldn't describe. He felt the rebirth of his headache igniting at the back of his brain, the slow, pounding tension building behind his eyes.

"I don't know what else you want me to say," Heather said after some moments of silence. Jim was embarrassed he'd tuned out for a few moments. She feigned innocence about her original statements, but Jim wasn't fooled.

He felt tension in his jaw, realizing he'd been biting down on his back teeth. A bitter taste of bile filled his mouth. He started speaking again, attempting to leave the disturbing daytime nightmare out of the present discussion. "I got the impression that there might have been something you were afraid to admit when I talked to you the first time. Is that true?"

"Admit? You mean like something weird between my dad and me?"

"I don't know. You tell me," Jim said.

"My father was a sick man," she said. Jim could see her hastily constructed walls of denial being thrown up like a roadblock—walls she'd used in the past to distance herself from questions and suspicions.

"What do you mean by that?" Paul asked.

Heather gave Paul a duplicitous look. "Come on. Are you for real? I know La Crosse is a small town, but I'm sure in your police work you've seen the effects of pornography on the human soul, let alone all the victims it gathers in its web. What do you think the basis of all human trafficking is?" She lifted her eyebrows and shook her head. "You must certainly deal with victims who've been in human trade." She paused as if waiting for them to approve of her knowledge of police activities and disapprove of her father's reprehensible behavior. She gave each man a cold, calculating glare, but Paul and Jim stayed quiet, making no comments.

"Well, since you asked, let me fill you in. Pornography is addictive and feeds a lust most people wouldn't ever want to admit having. It wrecks any natural sexual drive. The hope of a normal, loving sexual relationship is all but destroyed. That's what it did to my mom. She was sacrificed on the altar of some ideal sexualized woman—some floozy who only existed on the pages of my father's pornographic magazines and in the disgusting images in the videos he spent time watching."

Her face reflected hard angles, the soft pinkness of her cheeks was gone, her initial attractiveness blighted by her scorn and fury.

"We're all too familiar with the sex industry. We see its effects all the time. I'm sorry to hear how it ruined your family. But how did it affect you?" Jim asked, bringing the conversation back on point.

"Well, what do you think? It's part of the reason my marriage didn't work." Despite her attempts to maintain an outwardly calm disposition, her anger was forming like a tsunami picking up speed as it raced to shore.

"I thought you were talking about your parents' marriage. Why would it affect yours?" Paul asked.

Heather looked at him like he was an obtuse adolescent. "And you're in law enforcement? God help us! Kids are like sponges, detective. They absorb their parents' problems. Besides, when I was older, my mom told me about the hypocrisy of trying to love someone who couldn't even see you. When my dad looked at my mom, he didn't see her; he saw all the sleazy, gut-wrenching sadistic girls he'd chosen to spend his time with—women in chains and leather. He never appreciated the beauty of my mom once he started down the porn trail. It ruined any chance she had to have a healthy, happy marriage."

Jim's headache, kept at bay throughout the day with Tylenol, reared its ugly head again until it felt like a band of steel gripping the sides of his temples. His eyes felt like they'd been scraped with sandpaper. "Have you ever received any kind of counseling?" Jim asked, blinking rapidly several times.

"Yes, I have. So what? Lots of people get counseling," she sneered. Heather's eyes snapped with frustration, and her voice sounded tinny and thin. Her head jerked back and forth between Paul and Jim like a bobble head in the back window of a car. "What are you after here?"

Jim held Heather's gaze. "The truth. Somehow, I still don't think we've heard it when it comes to you and your father."

SUE BERG

"The truth about my father is staying right where it's always been—within our family. Out of sight and out of mind," Heather said brashly, tapping her index finger on the top of the table. "It's not something I'm proud of, and I don't wish to relive the pain of our relationship, especially with two people I don't know from Adam." Her neck and upper chest had turned bright red.

"You might not want to discuss it, but it's never really out of your mind, is it? It's never more than a blink away. That's why you've been in counseling for over twenty years," Jim said. Jim knew bringing up the length of her counseling was a gamble, but he had nothing else to use to break through her denial.

She leaned forward, her large hands clasped together in front of her. Jim was struck once again by the burly nature of her body—her thick, manly hands, her muscled, defined biceps, and her broad back and hips. "Don't jerk my chain, Lieutenant," she whispered hoarsely. "Counseling is protected by privacy laws."

"I'm well aware of that, ma'am," Jim said. He decided it was time to turn the corner. "Do you know Howard Lake?"

Heather leaned back, sinking into her chair, her shoulders slumping inward. "Howard Lake? I don't specifically remember him. Was he one of Dad's high school chums? Did he work at Dairyland Power?" Her eyes had become little pieces of hard, glittering stone, her face a taut mask.

"So you do know him?" Paul said.

"I didn't say that. Why do you people keep putting words in my mouth?"

Answering questions with questions. The liar's oldest trick in the book, thought Jim. He shifted the questioning again. "What kind of car do you drive?"

"A 2017 Subaru Forester."

"This morning, I reread your statement you gave during your interview the day after your father's murder. You told me the night your father was murdered, you were with friends downtown drinking until eleven o'clock, and that you came home immediately afterward and went to bed. In checking with the three friends you were with, they all testify that was what happened. Where were you between eleven o'clock and midnight on that same night?"

"Lt. Higgins, why is this an issue? I was in bed, as I told you."

"That's a bold-faced lie, ma'am. A witness has come forward and will testify that he saw your Subaru parked underneath your father's trees in his yard between eleven-thirty and midnight the night of September 7. What were you doing at your father's house at that time?"

The silence that followed was prolonged and intense. It was so quiet Jim could hear the ticking of the wall clock directly above his head. Finally, Heather lifted her chin and looked down her nose.

"I refuse to answer any more questions without my lawyer present." She seemed wooden, devoid of feeling. Jim met her unrepentant gaze and felt the inhumanity of her stare send a chill up his arms.

"Ms. Lovstad, be very careful that the thing you despise the most in others doesn't become the credo you use to define your own life. It's like trying to sell snake oil to a snake oil salesman, ma'am." Jim paused, but Heather sat silent, glaring somewhere above Jim's forehead. "Let the record show that Ms. Lovstad has refused to answer further questions and has requested her lawyer be present before we proceed further. Interview terminated at 3:24 p.m.," Jim stated flatly.

"You may expect to be scheduled for another interview within the next couple of days," Jim told her. She nodded imperceptibly. She stood, grabbed her jacket, strolled to the door, and clattered down the hallway in her pumps, hurrying to the end of the corridor where she turned the corner and disappeared. Jim and Paul exchanged a perplexing glance.

"I'm going to ask city police to put surveillance on Ms. Lovstad beginning this evening," Jim stated. "And I'm going to get moving on a search warrant for her residence.

"They may not be able to assign officers on such short notice," Paul said.

DeDe's voice came over the loudspeaker. "That was very interesting, sir," she said. "She's got a boatload of skeletons in her closet, and they're banging on the door to get out."

Jim tipped his head to the ceiling speaker. "No kidding. Any other insights?" he asked, aiming his comments at the speaker.

"She's full up on the baggage, all right. She's used to stuffing it. Kids abused by their parents, whether sexually, physically, or emotionally, have intense feelings of animosity and hatred for the one person who is supposed to protect them but ends up using them for their own selfish appetites. They trade in power; hence, torture and murder are familiar ways for them to grab the gusto and hang on. Those are mighty motivations for criminal activity. Payback time, so to speak."

"Thanks for your input, DeDe," Jim commented.

"No problem, sir," she finished.

Paul opened the door for Jim and accompanied him down the hallway. "I'll see you tonight. I'm going home to get a little nap in," Paul said.

"See you later," Jim said. He walked down the corridor and continued to the office of Police Chief Tamara Pedretti, which was located on the first floor of the law enforcement center. He knocked quietly, negotiating his way past a secretary outside the chief's door. Tamara was turned away from him, talking on her phone, gazing outside at the traffic rushing by on Vine Street. The trees were undulating in the gentle breeze, leaves drifting haphazardly onto the carpeted lawn surrounding the center. Hearing the knock, she turned and waved Jim in. He took a seat across from her. She finished her conversation and looked up expectantly, laying her phone on the desk.

Jim didn't quite know how to interpret her expression. Disappointment? Pity? Irritation?

"Hey, I've been meaning to get down here and apologize for the screwup with Maddog's boat down in the harbor. I didn't realize your team had your sights on him. It was totally my fault—very unprofessional. I apologize," he said. Tamara stared at him, but her eyes were soft.

"No problem, Jim. We all slip up once in a while. Frankly, it was an indicator that we needed to improve our interdepartmental communication. It was a much-needed springboard for some changes. So even though it was unfortunate, something good will probably come out of it. What can I do for you?" she asked, moving the conversation along.

"I just finished interviewing Heather Lovstad, the daughter of Sylvester Kratt," he started. Seeing Tamara's blank expression, he said, "The murder on George Street back on the seventh?"

"Oh, sure. Sorry. I'm with you now. Go ahead."

"We're not sure yet, but based on the evidence from our investigation, we believe she's somehow involved in her father's death. She walked out of our interview this afternoon and refused to answer questions about her whereabouts the night of the murder. I'd like some surveillance on her—the sooner, the better. After our interview today, she may run. I don't want to lose her and end up chasing her through six states. Any possibility we can put a couple of officers on her for a few days until something pops loose?"

"I think that's reasonable, except our budget looks like a Mack truck drove through the middle of it. I'll see what I can do, but it's pretty short notice," Tamara said.

"Fair enough," Jim said. "I'd appreciate it."

"How're you and Carol doing with Sara's disappearance?" she asked.

Jim leaned forward, resting his elbows on his thighs, his hands hanging limply between his legs. "Truthfully, it's a parent's worst nightmare, but we're holding it together … I guess." He sat up again and ran his hand over his face nervously.

"Anything I can do?" she asked, her eyes sympathetic.

"I don't know. Pray?" Jim said, sighing loudly. "I just wish Maddog would make his move so we can get this thing over with."

"Well, for what it's worth, we're all behind you. If you need something, you just call," Tamara said.

"Thanks, Tamara. I appreciate it. Are we okay?" he asked, moving his index finger back and forth between them.

She held up her palm. "We're fine, Jim. Let me know if you need anything," she said as her phone buzzed. She gave him an offhand wave as she answered her call.

Jim took that as a dismissal but a friendly one. He stood, waved, and walked to the elevators out in the hallway. Several officers greeted him, wishing him well. He rode the elevator alone up to the third floor, all the while wondering what event might have triggered Heather Lovstad's repressed feelings for her father to explode on the night of September 7. Was the discovery of the necklace a reminder of the abuse she'd experienced, and it tripped her trigger? Who had the necklace in their possession on the night of the murder—Heather, Eric Osgood, or Kratt himself? Or did something else happen? An argument? A threat? Some out-of-control event. He had no clear answers. Who knew? He certainly didn't.

His phone buzzed in his pocket. He was tempted to ignore it but answered, thinking it might be Carol.

"Higgins."

"Lt. Higgins. It's Margretta. Anything new in the investigation?"

"Nothing significant enough to make an arrest, although we have had some interesting interviews. And we're pursuing some leads about some guys who worked at Dairyland Power."

"Well, that's something, isn't it?"

"Maybe. We don't know yet," Jim answered. "Something I can help you with?"

"No, not really. I'll be in town a few more days, then I'll take a flight back to Eugene on Sunday, so if you have any questions, you can call my cell," she explained. "I'm visiting some long-lost cousins I haven't seen in almost forty years. It's given me a sense of kin, so even though you may not solve the mystery of my sister's abduction, at least I've reconnected with family again, and that's been really good. Plus, Eric Osgood has promised to keep in touch with me. All is not lost."

"I'm glad to hear that."

"Please keep me in the loop, Lt. Higgins. I'd really appreciate it," Margretta said.

"I can do that, and thanks for your help."

"Sure, no problem. I hope you can find some answers."

"I do, too."

Margretta hung up. Jim thought her trip to Wisconsin was an exercise in futility, but that wasn't his problem right now. He was weary to the bone. After retrieving his suit coat from his office, he flicked the lights off, thanked Emily for her help, and rode the elevator down to the main lobby. Walking outside to his Suburban, the weather seemed heavy with moisture despite the bright sunshine. The humidity had spiked, and the smell of ozone was in the air. Noticing the leaves on the trees were showing their undersides, Jim thought a storm was beginning to brew. The clouds were darkening underneath the cotton ball clouds, building into layers of metallic gray edged in black.

He opened his vehicle and climbed in, glancing at the dashboard clock—4:46 p.m. He dialed Carol, then waited for her to answer.

"Hi, honey. What's up?" she asked. Her voice sounded thick and clotted, like she'd been crying.

"How're you doing?"

"Well, I have my moments, but right now, I'm helping Gladys make chocolate chip cookies. Chocolate in any form eases stress. What's up?" she asked, more insistently this time.

"Just wondering if you need anything from the store before I head home."

"Oh, that's nice, but I stopped when I came home from work and picked up some stuff for Gladys even though she insisted we didn't need to worry about anything while we're with her."

"Sounds par for the course. I'll be home in an hour or so."

"See you then," Carol finished, clicking off.

53

WEDNESDAY EVENING

The deer hunting cabin was cooling from the heat of the day. Sara could hear the rumblings of thunder in the distance, like bowling balls bouncing haphazardly down an alley. After the oppressive silence that stretched throughout the day, she welcomed anything that told her the world still existed beyond the flimsy walls of her prison. The air in the cabin was stale with the smells of wool hunting jackets, gun oil, and rodent droppings. She hoped she'd be allowed another trip to the grass patch to relieve herself.

She was hungry, she could smell her own odor, and the urge for a hot shower was almost overwhelming. Last night she'd had trouble sleeping. Without physical activity, she wasn't tired. As she sat in the oppressive darkness, her mind went into overdrive, thinking of the possibilities that lay beyond the bend. The emotional roller coaster she'd been on the last few days was taking its toll on her spirit, and her self-confidence had slipped. She wondered if she'd ever feel safe again. When she'd finally drifted off to sleep, disturbing dreams of hands reaching for her, groping at her body, caused her to wake with a jerk. She was sweating, and yet she was chilled. No one had given her a blanket or sleeping bag, and her school clothing provided little warmth against the cool night air. It had rained earlier, but now it seemed clear.

The moonlight through the small window created a square of white on the rough plywood floor of the cabin. Sara stared at it dumbly, her mind racing with the possibility of escape. She'd reviewed her options and decided that any attempt to break out of the cabin at this point was futile. She was no longer blindfolded, but her hands and feet were duct-taped together, making any movement impossible. She didn't have a weapon to cut the tape with; the cabin was virtually empty except for the recliner and wooden chair. No one guarded her at the moment, but that seemed immaterial in the overall scheme of things.

Maddog came and left at odd hours, bringing convenience food and water to quench her hunger and thirst. He refused to engage her in conversation, despite her efforts to connect with him on a personal level. She wasn't sure if that was what she should be doing. Maybe she was leading him on and giving him grandiose ideas, stoking his sense of control. Whatever. All she knew was his eyes studied her like a wolf might study a rabbit caught in a snare, and when he focused his attention on her, she felt her skin crawl as if insects had penetrated her clothes.

Throughout the past two days, as she observed Maddog's behavior, she concluded that trying to predict his actions was impossible. His goal seemed to be keeping everyone off guard. Apparently, successfully eluding the police included never developing a pattern of behavior that could be studied or predicted. *So far it was working,* Sara thought. *Why would he mess with it?*

At some point in time, she'd fallen asleep again, only to jerk awake when she heard the ATV approaching the cabin. The sky was lightening in the east with a pink glow that seemed to flow over the horizon like an ocean wave washing over the shore. An owl hooted nearby. The cabin door banged open, and Maddog stomped across the floor. He looked refreshed. He'd showered and changed his clothes. Even his hair was clean and combed back away from his face.

Once again, he cut the tape on her wrists and shoved a Kwik Trip breakfast sandwich at her, which she grabbed and hungrily devoured. Several swigs of water later, she asked to relieve herself. Instead of cutting her ankle tape, he sat in front of her, his eyes quiet, deep, and dark like a pool of stagnant backwater on the Mississippi. His silence confounded and terrified her. Leslie fought the urge to question him, to try to relate to him on some level. *What do you think you're doing?* she thought. Then she chided herself. *Quit trying to appeal to his humanity. He doesn't have any.* After listening to her dad's accounts of his experiences in law enforcement, she finally understood something. There were just as many criminals running loose who'd never been caught as those who were rotting in prison. A prime example of that axiom sat in front of her now.

"You ever made love to anybody?" he asked quietly, a slick grin lighting up his face.

Sara was dumbfounded at the question. Her stomach cramped with fear; his question conjured up her worst fears like a genie escaping a bottle. "That's kind of a personal question, don't you think?" she asked. Her lips parted slightly, and her eyes stared at the wall above Maddog with a faraway look. "I'm not about to share that with a complete stranger."

"I'll take that as a no." Another shit-eating grin. "A virgin. I should be so lucky."

"Would you mind telling me what your plan is? I'm sure my dad and Carol are very worried about me."

"Well, now that you brought that up, I think it's time for a selfie." Maddog reached into his jean pocket and pulled out his smart phone. He got out of the chair, knelt down next to Sara, and placed his arm around her neck. She cringed when his skin touched hers, and a feeling of dread coursed through her as he tightened his hold, pulling her head close to his. Maddog held up the phone at arm's length and snapped the photo. He released his hold, stood up, and reviewed the photo. "Perfect. Let's hit the grass for a pee. Then it's time to get a message to your dad."

Sara flexed her ankles when the tape was removed. They went outside, she did her business and began walking back to the cabin.

"No, no, little missy. We're into stage two of the plan." He chuckled noisily to himself. He walked to the ATV. "Climb aboard and hang on."

Oh my Lord. What now?

54

THURSDAY, SEPTEMBER 19

Jim woke suddenly, his dreams dissolving into thin air. Carol's arm rested on his chest, her fingertips lying lightly on his skin. He kept quiet, not moving, trying to give her a few more moments of slumber. The events of the week had left them strung out and exhausted, but thankfully his headache seemed to have disappeared overnight.

Lillie and Henri were grouchy and irritable these last few days, not sleeping well in an unfamiliar bed. The absence of their normal surroundings and the interruption of their daily routines had upended them. Last night tantrums erupted, filling Gladys' house with screams and tears. Jim and Carol wrangled the children into the bathtub, then dressed them in their pajamas. While Carol helped Gladys clean up the evening meal, Jim sprawled his lanky frame across the double bed in the children's room, propping himself against the headboard as he read them their favorite stories, trying to keep Lillie's unrelenting questions at bay. Winnie-the-Pooh, Laura Ingalls Wilder, and Frog and Toad did nothing to alleviate the continuing crisis of Sara's absence.

"Who took Sara?" Lillie began her cross-examination between stories. *Here we go. The inquisition,* Jim thought. *The kid's probably going to be a lawyer.*

"Someone who thinks it will solve his problems," Jim whispered. Henri was almost asleep, cuddled against Lillie's side, his soft curls still damp from his bath, his eyes at half-mast.

"Will it?" her little voice squeaked.

"Will it what?" Jim asked, confused.

"Will it solve his problems?" Lillie turned her head slightly so she could peer into Jim's eyes.

Jim squirmed uncomfortably. "His problems are just beginning, but for reasons you don't understand, honey. The important thing is that you're safe here. And I want you to remember that God watches over us," Jim counseled.

"Like he watched over Grandma Juliette and me when we lived in the park, and we didn't have a house?"

"Yes, like that. Exactly like that," Jim said. He reached for her hand and clasped it tenderly. He was surprised that it gave him so much comfort. He kissed her hand.

"Bapa, what about—"

"Shh. No more questions. It's time to go to sleep. Let's say your prayers."

Lillie closed her eyes, clasped her hands together, and began. "Dear Jesus, thank you for Bapa, and Henri, and Sara, and Mommy, and Gladys, and God's angels, and . . ." Her prayers continued for several minutes until Jim intervened.

"We need an Amen," he said quietly, leaning toward her.

"Amen," Lillie whispered. She looked about to start up again, but Jim laid a finger on her lips.

"Shh. For real now," Jim whispered. He pulled the blankets up around her shoulders as she turned on her side. "You need to shut your eyes and go to sleep, toots."

Toward morning, Jim had a dream. It was so real that when he woke up, the familiarity of the soft bed and cool sheets confused and disoriented him. The wetness on his cheeks left him feeling empty and hollow.

In the dream, Sara was with him on a skinny island in the Mississippi River in the early rose-tinted light of false dawn. The quiet was exquisite—the kind that touches your soul and makes you believe the world is a beautiful place. They were fishing for walleye, the current swirling around them. He'd cast his rod and watched the jig hit the water. They'd been using grubs and minnows like they always did, but Sara changed her tactics and rigged her pole with a buckshot rattle spoon. She reeled slowly, giving her pole a few light lifts and a shake now and then. A great blue heron was perched in the marshes down the beach, sitting motionless, his neck hunched back onto his shoulders, his beady eyes watchful.

Jim noticed Sara's luminous blonde hair and her steady blue eyes. She was tall like him and had a lanky yet feminine profile. Looking over at him, her eyes softened with affection. Suddenly a floating mist came between them and blocked her view. She spoke his name softly with an edge of concern lacing her words.

"Dad? Dad? Where'd you go?" she asked, panic creeping into her voice.

He tried to answer her, but his voice failed him. His feet had gotten tangled up in some brush by the shore, something that never happened in real life. Then he stupidly dropped his pole. The current seemed like a writhing snake that ensnared his feet, and he felt himself topple sideways, go under, and come up far from shore. He was stunned at his ineptitude and the pernicious strength of the river's current.

He watched Sara appear and then fade away in the smoky haze, her expression inscrutable. She called to him again. He tried to answer, but it felt like someone had stuffed a sock down his throat. He fought the current, but it sucked him under. He took a huge gasp of air and woke up in bed next to Carol.

He stared at the ceiling in the early morning light, remembering the dream, sweating, disturbed by its possible meaning. He wiped the wetness from his face with the back of his hand. Carol mumbled in her sleep. She threw her leg over his thigh, and her arm jerked, her fingertips resting lightly on his neck. Then she was still again, her breathing slow and steady on his shoulder.

Despite the disturbing dream, these moments when the world hadn't intruded yet were becoming more precious to him all the time. He watched the treetops move gently in the breeze out of the second-story window, the colored leaves floating listlessly in a dizzying dance onto the green lawn. The coming of the morning calmed him down, escorted him back into the real world, and slowed the irregular beating of his heart. He heard the rooster that Gladys kept in the yard crowing raucously, his *doos* penetrating the serene atmosphere of the farmstead.

Sara, where are you, honey? he thought, studying the cracks on the farmhouse ceiling. He knew the abduction of his daughter was just a precursor to another round of senseless violence and threats. It made him think some thoughts he didn't like—thoughts about his profession. Maybe it was time to get out of police work. The violence of the criminal world was inserting itself into his family life, and the danger, worry, and stress it caused them disturbed him at a visceral level. It was like watching a lake after it had been churned up by violent storm winds bouncing with flotsam that drifted and bobbed on the surface and finally washed ashore.

His home had always been his fortress, the place where he could recreate and renew his commitment to resisting the evil in the world. It was a place of peace and love built with a woman he loved deeply. Now they'd had to leave their home on Chipmunk Coulee Road, an event he could never have foreseen even a month ago. The chaos of the week had sent everyone, including himself, into a tailspin. He felt intensely discouraged and vulnerable.

Carol breathed deeply, raised her head, then blinked rapidly in the early light. Her face was puffy with sleep. Jim turned toward her, and she cuddled against his chest. With her hair mussed and her skin a radiant pink blush, Jim was aware once again of how very blessed he was.

"Mornin', love," he whispered, cupping his hand behind her neck and kissing her cheek lightly.

"Seemed like an awfully short night," Carol said under her breath. "How's your headache?"

"Gone like the wind, and in its place . . ." He pushed his hips next to her and pulled her closer to himself.

Carol's eyebrows lifted suggestively. "Yeah, I got the message."

"Are you up for it?" he asked provocatively in her ear.

"Well, obviously you are," she said, pulling back to look him in the eyes. "But since you're asking. Yeah. Yeah, I am up for it." She kissed him tenderly and whispered, "I love you, honey."

Jim leaned over and kissed her lips. They were soft and warm and seemed to melt into his. Carol ran her fingers through his graying hair, then kissed his eyes and mouth. She rolled on top of him, sitting upright, pulled her nightshirt off over her head, watching Jim's expression change from worry to pleasure, his blue eyes softening with desire.

"You're so beautiful, babe," he replied softly, reaching for her.

Afterward, they lay tangled together, reveling in deep contentment and satisfaction, embracing the peace and quiet before the kids woke up. Their early morning reprieve was comforting, although that usually wasn't a word Jim would have used to describe their conjugal relationship. Still, today he'd take comfort over anything else the lovemaking offered.

Carol finally spoke. She said what they both were thinking. "Day three, honey. Do you think we'll hear from Maddog today?" Her voice sounded far away, tense, and hesitant.

Jim felt the weight of her question in his chest like an intense burning coal that radiated its heat outward to his skin. How could one repugnant individual exert so much influence over their lives? Even the pleasure of making love to his wife didn't lessen his anxiety. Instead, it reminded him of what he had to lose if everything went south. He hoped he was right about his assumption that Maddog had kidnapped Sara so she could be used as a bargaining chip in exchange for their daughter Lillie. But why hadn't he called?

"He might call today. Who knows what the chump is thinking," Jim said, suddenly feeling off-kilter and grouchy, the elation of the sex evaporating.

"Well, we'll find out today," Carol said confidently, rolling on her back, pulling the sheet over her breasts. She tucked her arms beneath her head on the pillow and stared at the cracked ceiling in the cramped bedroom.

"How do you know that?" Jim asked, turning toward her, watching the side of her face.

"Just a feeling. Woman's intuition. A sixth sense. Whatever. He's going to make a move soon, and I think it's going to be today."

"A self-fulfilling prophecy? Don't go there, honey," he warned as he laid his arm over her stomach. "Newsflash: never try to predict a criminal's movements. You'll end up disillusioned, beat up, shot, or dead."

Carol glanced over at him and raised her eyebrows. "Well, you predicted it, big guy," she reminded him in an accusatory tone. "You said he'd be contacting you."

Jim rolled over and sat up on the side of the bed. "Yeah, I know what I said, and I still think I'm right about that. But when is the question. He could play this out a long time. It's an odds game, and we're on the short end of the stick."

Carol grumped, slapped her hand against the mattress, and rolled from bed. Digging through her open suitcase on the floor, she grabbed a pair of panties and a bra. She walked from the bedroom, crossed the hall, and quietly closed the bathroom door. In another minute, Jim could hear the dull pinging noises of water sluicing against the metallic shower stall. He sat naked on the edge of the bed, said a silent prayer, and walked into the bathroom. The smell of lavender steam hit him as he opened the door. He stepped in and joined Carol in the shower.

As they soaped up, Jim thought of the lyrics to a Don Williams song: *Lord, I hope this day is good. I'm feelin' empty and misunderstood. I should be thankful, Lord, I know I should. But, Lord, I hope this day is good.*

55

Jim stepped onto the farmhouse stoop and surveyed the morning. Everything was hushed. Damp humidity hung in the trees, and condensation dripped on the vehicles parked beneath them. He stepped down from the porch and stood silently on the gravel driveway, his mind turning over what Carol had predicted. A cardinal sang a solitary song in the huge white pine that shadowed the north side of the house. Jim noticed Paul stretching his arms over his head, rubbing his eyes. He gave him a half-hearted wave and walked down the gravel driveway to the maple tree where Paul had parked his Ford F-150 pickup near the driveway's entrance onto County K, where he'd spent the night on sentry duty. Paul rolled down the passenger window as Jim approached.

"Hey. All's quiet on the western front. You want me to stay awhile yet?" Paul asked, his hair tousled and unruly, his eyes outlined with black circles from lack of sleep. He rubbed his unshaven jaw with the heel of his hand. Reaching over the seat, he poured a cup of coffee from his thermos.

"As soon as the kids and Carol leave, take off. Go home and sleep awhile. I'm going into the office. I'll see you later, bud." Jim tapped the passenger door with the flat side of his hand. "And, thanks."

"No problem."

Jim climbed into the Suburban that was parked by the barn, cranked the engine, and pulled out of the driveway. The road was damp with rain that had not evaporated last night, and the air was heavy with the smell of earthworms and rotted leaves. Farther down the road, a field of plump pumpkins lay on their sides, their brilliant orange color punctuating the vines' dry, desiccated stems and leaves. When he reached Hwy. 35, Jim aimed the truck into La Crosse.

The Great River Road was quiet now before the rush of morning commuters. Wisps of low fog drifted in and out of the trees along the roadsides, and the rolling bluffs had turned shades of burnished gold, orange and red. An ethereal mist floated above the surface of the river, forming wispy shapes that looked like smoke from a campfire.

Jim swung into the Kwik Trip on Mormon Coulee Road for a Karuba Gold coffee and cinnamon crunch bagel with cream cheese. Carol wouldn't approve, but she'd given up trying to control his on-the-run breakfast habits.

Walking onto the third floor of the law enforcement center from the elevator, Jim stopped to chat with Emily, who was chipper and smiling at her desk.

"Some messages, Jim," she said, reaching for a stack of yellow Post-it notes that she placed unceremoniously in his hand.

"Should I thank you for this?" Jim frowned, thumbing through the stack. Emily shrugged. "More insignificant minutia that will clog up my day. Most of these people won't answer my phone calls, and the vicious circle will start again. I hate phone tag."

"It's part of the job, sir," she said, glancing down at her stack of documents and papers clipped together. She began sorting and prioritizing with an efficiency that Jim found fascinating but, at the same time, intimidating.

"Sorry. I do thank you, Emily. You're the best," Jim said. She flashed him a high-wattage smile. Then she stopped and really looked at him. "Are you feeling all right? You seem awfully stressed lately."

"Lots of crappy stuff on my plate right now. I apologize."

"Not a problem, Chief. I'm here to serve," she said, smiling.

Walking into his darkened office, Jim laid the pile of messages on his desk, set his coffee down on the blotter pad, and hung up his suit coat. He fished his cell from his pocket and dialed the City Police desk.

"City Police. How may I direct your call?"

"Could you connect me with Tamara Pedretti's office, please?" he asked as he twirled a paperclip in circles on his desktop.

"One moment."

In the time the call was transferred, Jim got up and walked to the narrow window in the office. Observing the early morning traffic on Vine Street, he noticed a lone bicyclist pumping energetically as he zipped along the main thoroughfare, ducking and weaving through the light traffic. *The guy's inches from death,* Jim thought, shaking his head. *Colliding with a truck or car, a biker had about as much chance of survival as an ant under a size twelve shoe.* An older Hmong couple had set up a stand on the corner where they were hawking pumpkins, squash, melons, and various multi-colored gourds and Indian corn under a blue plastic tarp. An empty school bus rumbled by, and a mud-splattered cement truck honked impatiently when a car hesitated at a stoplight that had turned green.

"Chief Pedretti. May I help you?"

"Tamara. Jim Higgins. Wondering what we've found out about the surveillance on Heather Lovstad? Anything interesting?"

"Haven't talked to the officers yet. Do you want me to send them up when they get here?"

"That'd be great. Thanks."

With a prolonged sigh, Jim glanced at the messages, walked to his desk, and began sorting them. His phone buzzed.

"Higgins."

"Morning," Sam said. "Get some sleep?"

"Very little and what I did have was sketchy. What's up?" Jim asked gruffly.

"Getting back to you about Howard Lake. Do you want it now, or should I walk over?"

Jim was confused. He thought that was DeDe and Leslie's assignment. "Walk it over. I'm sorting through my messages, and I'm expecting some other calls."

Five minutes later, Sam strolled into Jim's office. He held a file folder in his hand with a yellow legal pad crammed with notes. Sam took it out, and Jim pointed at it.

"That Lake's info?" he asked.

"Yeah. DeDe and Lez spent some time yesterday poking around Readstown and at the Vernon County sheriff's office. I was just reading through it." Sam's hair was combed but had fallen in a gentle cascade of curls around his neck and ears. He wore a light pink dress shirt, navy Dockers, and a coordinating navy tie with pink elephants. *More Goodwill finds,* Higgins thought. Sam found a chair and pulled it over in front of Jim's desk.

"And? What'd they find out?" Jim asked impatiently.

"Well, since they're not here yet—" Sam started, opening the file folder. There was a rustle at the door.

"No need, Sam. We'll take over," DeDe said as she and Leslie strolled into the office, taking the folder and legal pad from his hand. DeDe's cheeks were flushed pink as if she'd been exerting herself. Leslie stood next to her and threw Sam an annoyed expression. She raised her eyebrows when he looked like he was going to protest.

"Could we get on with it, people?" Jim asked, noticing the subtle nonverbal cues being exchanged.

"I agree," DeDe started, referring to her notes on the yellow legal pad. "Howard Lake was a high school classmate of Sylvester Kratt at Kickapoo High School. They played Legion baseball together, went to the same parties, and dated many of the same girls. Neither had a criminal record, although they catted around the saloons and taverns in the Readstown and Viola area after high school, picking up girls, partying, and being your average run-of-the-mill knuckleheads. A few fist fights here and there, a couple of DUIs—nothing serious, or at least nothing with seemingly criminal intent. Then Sylvester married. It seemed for a while, his life took a more conventional turn, and he straightened out, taking his role as a parent seriously when his son and daughter arrived on the scene. During those years, Howard didn't play a major role in Sylvester's life; they kind of drifted apart. This is according to Lake's sister, Genevieve Petronski, whom we interviewed yesterday." DeDe stopped briefly, and Leslie took over.

"According to Genevieve, Howard never married. He stayed on the family farm and ran it with his dad. Genevieve said Howard always felt his dad took advantage of his physical strength to do the backbreaking labor on the farm—baling and stacking hay bales in the barn, mucking out the manure, harvesting several acres of tobacco, plowing and planting the corn and soybean crops. After a while, Howard wised up and got a job at Dairyland Power up on the river."

"Could we get to it?" Jim asked impatiently. He felt a tightening in his chest—anxiety of some kind. His patience was skating on very thin ice. Sam flashed him a look of concern.

"The upshot is when Howard began working at Dairyland, he hooked up with a hardscrabble drifter, Dan Stern, from Owatonna, Minnesota, who also had been recently hired there. Stern had a similar background. Farm kid, grew up poor, had a tendency to drink too much, picked up a lot of different girls, was never in a serious, committed relationship. The two began carousing in the La Crosse area, barhopping and hustling coeds at the university, even though they were in their late twenties. Somehow on the party circuit, they hooked up again with Sylvester, who had started frequenting the bars on Third Street. As we know, there are no shortages of drinking bashes to choose from. Those kinds of guys seem to find each other somehow, and they became inseparable drinking buddies, according to Genevieve. But they garnered the attention of the La Crosse cops when they began cruising the Third Street bars trying to pick up coeds from the U. Stern had a charge filed against him for assault, but it didn't stick or wasn't investigated seriously. The three of them got involved in a brawl on Third Street with some college guys and cleared out a bar. And the trio was also frequently seen coming out of an adult bookstore on Division Street on the south side of La Crosse."

"This is according to whom?" Jim asked grumpily. He'd leaned back in his office chair and locked his hands behind his head.

"Police records from the La Crosse Police Department and friends and acquaintances who were interviewed by detectives from the Vernon County Sheriff's Department at the time of the Yelski abduction," DeDe said.

"Why were they persons of interest in the first place? None of this explains how they would have become acquainted with Christina Yelski," Jim said, feeling lost, not getting the connections. "Their activities and their minor scrapes with police don't warrant the attention of a murder investigation." He sat forward and rested his elbows on his desk.

Leslie shrugged and continued. "John Daines, a Vernon County investigator, wrote that a denim jacket and a pair of work trousers were found a few months after the abduction by a deer hunter along a side road off Hwy. 14 called Stenslien Lane. They were covered with blood stains, which matched Christina Yelski's blood type. Farther down, along this same road, a pair of brown workboots were found that were similar to the casts of the prints that were discovered near the basement window of the Blackman home. The jacket fibers and threads matched fibers found in a nail on the basement window of the Blackman home. The investigators believed the jacket and trousers belonged to someone who spent time in a harness—someone who might be a lineman repairing and stringing lines from pole to pole," Leslie finished.

"Why a lineman?" Sam asked.

"The underarms of the jacket were well-worn from some kind of apparatus he wore. They concluded that the clothes belonged to someone who worked from heights and wore a safety belt of some kind," DeDe said. "They could never narrow it down to discover the perpetrators, although they interviewed numerous companies who did aerial work. But remember, sir, Dairyland Power was constructing new power lines in Vernon County where Christina's clothes were discovered, and these men's clothes were found. Stringing high line poles would have involved a safety harness of some kind."

"Okay. That's a weak link, but I think I'm following. So Stern and Lake could have conceivably used harnesses in their line of work, and when the jacket and work boots were found, investigators became suspicious of them because of their interest in young coeds and their employment at Dairyland. Dubious at best, but go on. So what about Howard's suicide?" Jim probed.

"Ten years ago, according to his sister, Howard seemed to have some kind of guilt crisis about something he'd done or knew about, although he never shared with his sister what that was. He asked her if God could forgive any kind of sin. She didn't know what to make of that, so she brushed it off as some kind of mid-life crisis. About three months later, on a weekend when his parents were gone, he drove to the farm and apparently hung himself in the barn. His dad found him Sunday evening when they returned from a fishing trip up north," Leslie said.

"Was an autopsy performed?" Jim asked.

"No, the family didn't request one since the method of death seemed pretty straightforward and suggested suicide," Leslie said. "With the odd questions he'd asked his sister, the family figured he'd come to some crisis point in his life, and when he couldn't resolve it, he took his life."

"Did he leave a note?" Jim asked. Both women shook their heads in the negative. Jim's eyebrows cocked together in skepticism. "What about this Dan Stern? Where's he at?"

DeDe looked up from the report, locking eyes with Jim. "Drowned in a mysterious boating accident over by Lake City, Minnesota, about five years ago."

"What was mysterious about it?" Sam asked, getting back in the fray.

Jim groaned. "This just gets worse and worse," he mumbled.

"According to witnesses who were interviewed after the accident, Stern was in his boat, sitting—not fishing—and when they looked again, he was gone. Just fell in, jumped in, whatever. No life jacket, probably couldn't swim. He was found about two hours later, with no signs of trauma. However, the autopsy found abnormally large amounts of Versed in his system, and he'd also been drinking, which may have contributed to his confused state."

Jim leaned back in his swivel chair, which creaked ominously under his weight. "So our timeline looks like a suicide by hanging ten years ago, then a suspicious boating accident about five years ago, and now Sylvester bites the dust by strangulation," Jim said. "That's about it in a nutshell?"

"Yep," DeDe said.

"What a mess," Jim said, but he was thinking *serial killings.* Something connected the three drinking pals, and it probably led to their deaths. His cell buzzed.

"Higgins," he said curtly. He listened, then said, "Send them up." Shutting his phone, he focused on the trio in front of his desk. "Ladies, go down to Davy Jones' office and catch him up to speed on this newest information. Sam, the officers who did surveillance on Heather are coming up. I want you to hear this."

In a couple of minutes, Officers Steve Thorsen and Mike Leland, both city cops, appeared in Jim's doorway. Mike Leland had been with the city police department for about five years and was studying at Wisconsin Technical College to earn his investigative license. He also had been along when a take-down of a dangerous criminal went wrong near Avalanche a couple of years ago, in which Paul had been seriously injured. Steve Thorsen was a new recruit.

"Tell me. What is Heather up to?" Jim questioned.

Mike told Jim what they'd observed during the surveillance. "Heather spent the evening at her home. Then about ten o'clock, she got in her vehicle and drove south to the airport in Viroqua. They have a landing strip and a couple of hangers there. She spent time in one of the hangers. She had a key to get in and was there for about an hour. Got in her car, drove back to her house, and reappeared this morning dressed and ready for work, where we dropped her at about 8:30 a.m."

"Interesting," Jim said. "Nobody else was with her?"

"Nope. She was alone," Steve said.

"Was she carrying any luggage?" Jim asked.

"Nothing that we saw," Mike said.

"Huh. Okay. Thanks, guys. We'll catch up with you later," Jim said.

When DeDe and Leslie returned from the sheriff's office downstairs, Jim laid out a plan.

"Ladies, I want one of you to call down to Viroqua and talk to whoever is in charge of the municipal airstrip. Find out why Heather would be there. Maybe she has a plane or is trying to hire somebody to fly her somewhere. I don't know, but it sounds like she's getting ready to run."

"We're on it, Chief," Leslie said as the women turned and left the office.

Watching the traffic outside his window, Jim spoke to Sam, his voice quiet yet strained. "Get some photos together of Dan Stern and Howard Lake. We're going to pay a visit to Heather at the law office. It's time to turn her crank," Jim said sourly.

While Sam was getting the photos together, Jim opened the file of information they had collected on the Kratt strangulation. He combed through the handwritten notes from his team, the crime scene photos, the information about the necklace and note, the summaries of interviews from neighbors and other witnesses, and Luke's forensic findings. Then he looked at the notes about Stern and Lake. He knew he was probably reading something crucial, but it eluded him. He was pretty sure the disappearance of Christina Yelski tied the three men together in some kind of conspiracy, but hard physical evidence was still largely absent.

This new information on the Readstown trio was interesting and seemed to confirm friendships and activities that bordered on predatory and irresponsible behavior. But nowadays, how unusual was that? Not very. The information of wear on the clothing seemed significant and could be useful down the road, but they still had no firm indication that Heather Lovstad knew Lake or Stern.

He thought about Heather again. From all indications, she had been a reliable employee at the Lowe, Pritchert, and Hanson Law Office for the past twenty-one years. But the comment from the receptionist the day Jim visited the office still struck him as peculiar. What had she said? "No one else gets to do that around here." What was that all about?

Jim leaned back in his chair and studied the ceiling. *Well,* he thought, *maybe it was time to rattle her cage.*

SUE BERG

56

By ten-thirty in the morning, Jim and Sam were driving out of the parking lot on Vine Street, heading to the law office downtown where Heather Lovstad worked. Finding a parking space, they walked down Pearl Street past mid-century brick buildings and entered the law office. The receptionist who had greeted Jim at his previous visit was at her desk. She looked up expectantly and flashed them a friendly smile when the door opened, and Sam and Jim entered the reception area.

Jim and Sam flipped open their IDs. "We'd like to talk to Heather Lovstad, please," Jim said evenly.

"Just a minute. I'll see if she's available," the woman said.

"No, ma'am. You don't understand," Jim interrupted. "Being available has nothing to do with it. This is an official police visit. She has no choice in the matter. We *will* talk to her either here or downtown." Jim waited a moment, watching the friendly smile of the secretary disappear, replaced by a confused frown. When she failed to respond, Jim went on. "I can send a cruiser over to pick her up and take her downtown, but I doubt that she would want to create that kind of scene." Sam stood at Jim's elbow and exchanged a feisty look with the secretary, his mouth set in a hard line.

"I see," she said, her eyes bouncing back and forth from Jim to Sam. "I'll see what I can do. Just a moment, please. You may sit in the reception area while I find Heather."

"Thank you. We'd appreciate that," Jim answered.

After the receptionist exchanged a hushed conversation with someone on the other end of the line, she stood up from her swivel chair behind the desk, crooked her finger at Jim and Sam, and led them into the interior of the office complex to a small break room. The lounge was furnished with a couple of plastic tables, molded chairs, and a five-foot length of lower kitchen cabinets with a counter covered with a stained Formica top. Parked in the corner next to the wall was a coffee pot, a stack of Styrofoam cups, and a hotpot for tea. Jim walked over and poured coffee into a foam cup as the secretary quietly closed the door. Sam found a chair and fished out his phone to check his messages and texts.

They waited, and a few minutes later, Heather came into the room accompanied by Dale Pritchert, one of the law firm's founding partners. They remained standing. Jim and Sam stood up. Heather looked coldly from Jim to Sam while introductions were made, and they flashed their IDs.

Pritchert looked the part of a lawyer—a conservative gray suit, a red tie imprinted with a subtle check design, and a crisp white shirt with large gold cufflinks. His curly hair was professionally cut, and his face gleamed from a recent shave. An air of superiority rolled off him as his green eyes roamed over the two detectives. Heather wore a sleek black shift with a gold chain and gold earrings. Her hair was soft and luminous, her makeup flawless. *Obviously, I'm not the only one who dresses for success,* Jim thought.

"Good morning, Ms. Lovstad," Jim said. "We have a couple more questions concerning the investigation into your father's death. We'd like to know if you recognize these two men." He pulled two four-by-six-inch photos from his suit coat pocket and laid them on the table, pushing them toward her.

Heather leaned over the table, picked up each photo, and examined them carefully. Then she laid them back down, shuffling them nervously under her fingers. She glanced uncertainly at Pritchert, who nodded imperceptibly.

"I believe I know this person," she said, tapping her finger on the photo of Lake, "but I haven't seen him for a long time—maybe ten years or more. Howard Lake, right?" She looked up at Jim, but he kept his eyes flat and non-committal. She turned her attention to the other photo. "This other person I don't remember ever meeting." When she looked up, her eyes were hooded, and her demeanor was cautious. Little wrinkles had formed at the corners of her mouth, and she stared unblinking at the two detectives. Jim noticed a faint throbbing in her neck.

"You're sure, Ms. Lovstad?" Jim asked. She nodded but stayed mute. What Jim said next was a total shot in the dark, but he said it anyway. "We have reasons to believe you've met the other gentleman in the photo." Jim took his index finger and pushed the photo of Stern toward Heather. She nodded in the negative. "You're sure you've never seen this man before?" Jim repeated.

"Never," she said more firmly this time.

"Well, frankly, I don't believe you, but thank you for your time. You don't have to meet someone to know who they are, do you?" Jim said, still standing in the cramped room. Heather's face darkened with anger, and Pritchert leaned closer and touched her elbow gently—a subtle reminder of some confidential matter they seemed to share on another level—a secret they'd kept hidden until now. Sam shuffled uncomfortably next to Jim and tugged nervously on his tie.

"Don't leave town, Ms. Lovstad," Jim reminded her. "We haven't finished our investigation into your father's murder yet, and we may need to talk to you again."

Heather looked down her nose and remained silent. Sam felt strangely intimidated by her.

"Could I have a word with you in private, Mr. Pritchert?" Jim asked, shifting his blue-eyed gaze to the lawyer.

Pritchert turned to Heather and laid a hand on her arm. "I'll go over those depositions for the Carney case with you when I finish here," he said. Heather smiled shyly at Pritchert, glared once more at Jim and Sam, then pivoted and left the room. Pritchert watched her leave and then turned back to Jim. "Now, what is it that you need to talk to me about?" he asked.

He tipped his clean-shaven chin up and looked down his nose at Jim and Sam. His attitude spoke volumes. A high-handed impatience had seeped into his voice, and it exuded from his pores as if he was shooing away a pesky fly. His attitude that cops were in a category on par with the floor sweepings was palpable, and Jim felt his anger growing. *Back it up, buddy,* he thought.

"How long has Ms. Lovstad been employed at your firm?" Jim asked Pritchert.

Pritchert seemed to relax a bit, and his shoulders dropped slightly. "Since she graduated from high school over twenty years ago. She worked her way up the ladder while she got her degree as a paralegal at WTC. She's one of the best we have on our staff," Mr. Pritchert said, his tone bordering on nonchalance.

"Most law firms have a focus of some kind. What's your specialty here?" Jim asked, ignoring the condescending attitude.

"Corporate law and, most recently, we've been expanding into violation of employee working conditions and employee rights," Pritchert told him. His eyelids were at half-mast, and Jim felt him taking inventory, checking off his character against some master list of culturally acceptable traits.

Slipping his right hand into his pants pocket, Jim continued. "How many employees do you have here?"

"Including the partners, we have a staff of three lawyers and twelve support staff," Dale said. "Could you get to whatever it is you're fishing for? I've got a busy day ahead of me."

"Sure. Describe your relationship with Ms. Lovstad," Jim said seriously.

Mr. Pritchert pulled his head back as if he'd been slapped, and his lip curled in a sneer. "You're kidding? My relationship with Heather?" Pritchert asked, holding his hands out with his palms up. "Your suggestions cast aspersions on our work relationship and creates suspicion where none should exist, officer."

By now, Jim was ready to spit in his face. He reined in his irritation. "That was a nice little piece of legalese. Now answer the question, sir. How would you describe your relationship with Ms. Lovstad?" Jim asked again, biting off his consonants in frustration.

Pritchert parked his hands on his hips, leaned toward Jim, and snarled, "I resent the tone of your question, Lieutenant."

"The question wasn't meant to offend. If you're offended, then please explain the source of the offense. I'm all ears," Jim said, leveling his gaze to meet Pritchert's brusque response. Jim was sure by now that he was coming up woefully short in the lawyer's eyes.

"She's an employee and a damn good one," Pritchert barked.

"Might I remind you that this is an official police investigation. You would be wise to cooperate to the best of your ability, sir," Jim said, and the challenge in his eyes was unmistakable. "I will turn over every rock until I start getting some truthful answers from Ms. Lovstad and your firm. I think you'll find it to be to your advantage to cooperate," he finished. "News travels fast in a small town like ours."

Pritchert stuck his index finger between the collar of his shirt and his neck. Pulling at his collar, he stretched it as if it were cutting off his air. Then he straightened his tie and took a deep breath. "Understood," he said, although his antagonism still bristled below the surface.

"One of your staff insinuated to me when I was in the office earlier this week that Ms. Lovstad seems to have privileges that have not been extended to other employees here. For instance, her standing appointment during working hours at Family Counseling

Services in Holmen on the second Tuesday of every month. Is it true that she receives special consideration in this regard? Does it center around her time off, or are there other perks we don't know about?" Jim's blue eyes drilled in on Pritchert's face, and he held his stare.

"We try to accommodate our employees' requests, especially when it pertains to maintaining their mental health," he said. Little beads of perspiration were breaking out along his hairline, and he nervously opened and closed his right hand and shifted on his feet.

"So Ms. Lovstad suffers from mental health issues?" Jim asked.

"I didn't say that. You did," Pritchert responded. Jim raised his eyebrows. Pritchert briefly closed his eyes, then opened them and leveled a stare at Jim.

Jim continued. "Look, taking into consideration Ms. Lovstad's standing counseling appointment, someone would have to be incredibly naive to think that—"

But Pritchert was through with suggestions of favoritism and insinuations of clandestine relationships. "What are you suggesting, Lieutenant? That Heather is a basket case? That her mental condition is less than stable? That she isn't capable of leading a fulfilling life and having a rewarding career just because she needs counseling? I have news for you, Lieutenant—that's half the population of the United States!" By now, his words were snapping like an angry flag in a brisk wind. "You're incredible! What is it with you people?"

Jim suddenly stepped close to Pritchert, close enough to smell his coffee breath spewing into the air, blowing on his face. Pritchert took a step backward. "In case you aren't aware of it—which I highly doubt—Ms. Lovstad is a primary suspect in the strangulation death of her father on September 7. She is also a possible suspect in the previous deaths of two other men we believe may have been involved in a forty-year-old cold case," Jim said. "That will not change until we get some answers that satisfy our questions and either corroborate the evidence we've uncovered or negate it. Are we clear on that?" Jim asked, his words clipped and precise. He tipped his head, straightened his tie, and waited for an answer.

Pritchert met Jim's stare with a mundane glance that one might give to a hired servant. "Perfectly, sir. Now get out of my office," he snapped.

"Not until we clarify a few facts. You admit that Heather sees a counselor on a regular monthly basis, and her counseling time is taken during the working day. Is that correct?" Jim asked, putting some bite in it.

"Yes, that's correct."

"Do other employees get the privilege of those perks? Isn't it standard procedure to schedule personal appointments after regular hours are completed for the day?"

"She uses her PTO, which is perfectly acceptable," Pritchert said, smiling uneasily. "Nothing wrong with that."

"Does Ms. Lovstad own a plane?" Sam asked out of the blue. The corner of Jim's mouth barely registered a slight upturn. Leave it to Sam to pick a moment to catch the lawyer off-guard.

A frown crossed Pritchert's face, and he stared at Sam as if he was just first noticing him.

"Try to keep up with the conversation, sir," Sam said, his tone clipped. "Does Heather own a plane?"

"No," Pritchert said. His eyes flicked around the room, eventually landing back on Sam.

"Do you own a plane?" Sam asked, pointing his index finger at the lawyer's chest.

"Yes." Pritchert straightened his shoulders, but his sullen look changed imperceptibly to one of panic.

"Where do you store it?" asked Sam.

"In the municipal hanger down in Viroqua," Pritchert answered. "Their monthly rental rates are cheaper than La Crosse."

Jim jumped in. "Are you planning to help Heather escape this investigation by whisking her off somewhere in your plane? Because if you are, I'm here to tell you—"

"That is blatantly ridiculous!" Pritchert shouted, pumping his fist up and down. "We have nothing to hide!"

Jim's gaze bored into Pritchert's face. "Do you talk to your clients like this?" He held up his hand. "Don't answer that. Let me say this again. Ms. Lovstad is the primary suspect in the murder of her father. Your association with her will necessarily involve further inquiries from our department. You may be called downtown to the law enforcement center to answer more questions in a formal interview, and you may be served with a search warrant. I'm reminding you that we will be investigating the nature of your relationship with Ms. Lovstad and her relationships with other personnel in your firm."

"Your point?" Pritchert asked.

"Keep your powder dry," Jim answered, his eyes like brittle blue glass.

"What?" Pritchert asked, his brows crinkling in a frown, confused by the challenge.

"Think about it," Jim said. "We'll see ourselves out."

The crisp autumnal breeze outside revived Jim and blew the stale smell of the law office and Pritchert's hostility and superiority out of his nostrils. Out on the street, as they walked to the Suburban, Sam commented, "It was interesting that she mentioned ten years in relation to the photo of Howard Lake. That's as long as he's been dead."

"Yep. I noticed that, too. And she knows Dan Stern, I'm sure."

Suddenly Jim heard footsteps behind him. A hand gripped his arm and spun him around. Sam moved closer to Jim's side, his arm coming up in a defensive pose.

"Listen, you jerk! You can't come into my office and threaten me and get away with it!" Pritchert snarled as he poked his finger in Jim's chest, his face hard, his nostrils flaring.

"If you touch me again," Jim said, "I'll have you hauled in for assaulting an officer of the law."

Pritchert swore a string of profanities as he worked his way into a full-blown harangue. "You leave Heather alone! She doesn't deserve the charges you're trumping up against her. If you arrest her, you'll have to deal with me!" Pritchert's jaw chewed on his back teeth, and his face had hardened like a piece of brushed tin.

Jim held his ground, his posture tense and alert. "Isn't that what I've been doing? Dealing with you? Get this, Pritchert. You've been warned. I mean it when I say if you ever threaten me again, you'll be looking for your ass up your sleeve." Jim could feel Sam studying the side of his face.

Pritchert stared at Jim for a long moment, his nostrils flaring, a thin trickle of sweat sliding down the side of his face. Then he turned and walked briskly down the sidewalk, his tie swinging back and forth.

"Whoa, Chief. What's his problem? Did I miss something?" Sam asked, his hazel eyes wide with surprise.

"Well, if you missed something, then so did I because I never saw that coming. His protection of Heather is interesting, wouldn't you say?" Jim asked, watching Pritchert whip open the door of the law office. "Somehow, I think we uncovered something that sheds a whole new light on Heather Lovstad."

"Interesting doesn't begin to describe it," Sam said sullenly, wondering about the hornet's nest they'd stirred up.

"Right now, I want you and Paul to head up to Lake City and see what you can dig up about Dan Stern. Find out about the day he died. Talk to the coroner, rescue squad, police. See what conclusions they came to or what their inclinations were about his death. Take a picture of Heather and flash it around. See if you get any bites."

Paul got to the office about noon after his night surveillance at the Hanson farm. He was at his desk wading through some paperwork he was sure would never see the light of day once it left his basket. His head was stuffy from lack of sleep, and as he worked, he listened to Sam espouse his opinion about the morning's events.

"... and I think Heather is shackin' up with Pritchert—probably has been for years. Think about it; she's his mistress on weekend flings, that kind of thing."

"Well, until you come up with hard evidence, that's all bullshit conjecture, and we've already done plenty of that."

Sam's phone buzzed in his pocket. He checked caller ID and noticed the unknown number flashing on his screen.

"Birkstein," he said.

A raspy voice that sounded as if it had been scraped raw with sandpaper came over the line. "Fuzzy Bursell here. How ya doin', Sammy boy?"

Fuzzy Bursell was a small-time con man who hung out on the south side of La Crosse, but his criminal tendencies spread throughout the Tri-State area. Currently, he lived in the upper half of a seedy two-story walk-up on Losey that he occasionally shared with a nurse's aide who worked at the Benedictine Care Facility close to the river.

In the past, he'd dealt drugs and had been involved in a number of illegal scams and flimflam operations in the immediate La Crosse vicinity. These included selling non-binding, fraudulent burial insurance to the elderly, fronting a lawn and home care service which charged exorbitant fees to those who could no longer care for their properties, and running an employment agency that hired out ex-cons who were supposed to be electricians, plumbers, and carpenters. These and several other rackets were just a few of his many forays into the world of small-time crime. Even though his employees had virtually no blue-collar skills in the construction trade, he'd done a bustling business targeting the poor, handicapped, and elderly until a small home on the north side of La Crosse burned down due to faulty wiring and severely burned the occupant who was in a wheelchair. When the investigation and trial were through, Fuzzy had stacked five years at the state prison in Boscobel. He'd completed his sentence two months ago. Now he was back in La

Crosse relatively free to create more criminal havoc as long as he checked in often with his parole officer.

"Fuzzy, what's the haps?" Sam asked, slipping into the lingo. Paul looked up. Sam stood next to his desk, making a talking mouth with his hands and rolling his eyes as he listened to Bursell.

"The word out on the street is that Maddog's holed up with some hostage he grabbed down on 35. He's got some hideout places back in the hills around Romance, where he meets some of his drug clientele. Might be there. I hear the gal's quite a beauty. She may be a little worn out before he's through with her, though, if you get my meaning. I'll bet he screwed her every which way—"

"Hey! Shut your face and watch your language," Sam said, his cheeks flushed with anger. Paul looked up from his paperwork. "Take it down a couple of notches. Remember who you're talkin' to. Anything other than Romance? That's a lot of territory, and it's woody and hilly."

"That's all I got. Later." And he was gone. Sam stared at his cell, then walked down to Jim's office and knocked. Jim looked up, irritated.

"What now?" he asked, leaning back in his creaky office chair.

"Got a tip from Fuzzy Bursell that Maddog may be holed up around Romance somewhere. That's the talk on the street, anyway."

"Fuzzy? Really? He's got a brain the size of a walnut. The odds of finding him in that neck of the woods are almost nil. It's rugged terrain—steep hills, deep valleys, and dense woods with lots of creeks crisscrossing the coulees. A lotta acres to cover and not enough manpower to do it."

Sam ran his hands through his hair. "He claims Maddog has several hiding spots in the hills. Just thought you might want to know. I'll put out the word to some of my contacts and see what I get. It's worth a try," he said, shrugging. When Jim didn't respond, he said, "What about checking out four-wheeler trails? And I think there's a bike trail around there somewhere, too, that was converted from an old, abandoned railroad bed. Leslie and I have thought about doing a weekend down there."

"No time or personnel, Sam. Right now, you and Paul need to head to Lake City. See what you can find out about this Dan Stern guy."

"We're on it, Chief," Sam said, turning and leaving the office.

57

The morning had flown by after Jim met with DeDe, Leslie, and Sam. Their discussion about the Kratt, Lake, and Stern trio made them all wonder if they were dealing with a serial killer bent on delivering vengeance for a crime committed forty years ago. But three murders stretched out over fifteen years seemed unlikely, although crazier things had happened. When dealing with criminals of questionable intelligence and brains shrunk to the size of peas by alcohol and drug use, anything was possible. Go figure. Then with the visit to the law office, Jim had to adjust his schedule and modify his theories again—and this was all before lunch.

As it turned out, Carol's prediction of a phone call from Maddog that dayhad come when he was up to his eyeballs in paperwork that seemed to bring him no closer to a solution about the murders in front of him. He'd been making phone calls, playing catch-up, when his phone pinged, alerting him to a text message. He was distracted when he opened his message, but that didn't last long. The text included a photo of Maddog and Sara and a short message: "Seas Branch Quarry off County Y. Vernon County. 10:00 tonight. Bring Lillie. Come alone. Mddg"

Gripping the cell phone in his hands, Jim whispered to himself,

"I'll take you down if it's the last thing I do." His stomach turned over, and a hard ball of anger solidified deep in his gut. The photo of Maddog gripping Sara's neck and pulling her into a tense selfie filled Jim with hatred and a cold, hard fear. His heartbeat clanged in his chest like a gong. In the photo, Sara neither smiled nor grimaced; she just looked genuinely petrified. Jim could understand why. *What kind of things had he already done to her?* Jim wondered. Closing his eyes, he tried to erase the images in his mind of what she might have already experienced.

He sighed and sagged in his chair. All the restless nights of interrupted sleep and his waking nightmares were catching up to him. He felt used and spent, but at the same time, his nerves were jumping like an electric wire pulsing with current. His stomach growled, and he realized he hadn't eaten anything since early morning. Even Lillie had noticed his preoccupied stare at breakfast. He looked like a walking zombie wrapped up in a cloak, his haunted eyes fixated on an invisible point behind Gladys' hutch.

"Bapa? You're not listening," Lillie had whined at the breakfast table. "What are you lookin' at?"

Jim jerked and lowered his eyes to Lillie, who sat across the table from him. "What? I'm sorry, Lillie. What were you saying?"

Carol sent him a sympathetic glance as Lillie sighed, the disappointment on her face stabbing Jim with guilt. "Never mind," she grumped, taking a bite of toast, avoiding Jim's stare, her eyes like the wash of a blue-green ocean wave.

Jim glanced at the clock—3:30 p.m. If he was going after Maddog tonight, he needed to return to the house on Chipmunk Coulee Road to pick up a few supplies. He debated putting his ATV on his trailer and dragging it along to the quarry, but after some consideration, he decided against it. It could only be justified if he could keep the vehicle upright through the woods. Slipping and sliding down unfamiliar muddy trails at night was asking for more trouble, and he already had enough. His skill set, or lack thereof, would probably result in a rollover. *Don't tempt fate.* Then he thought, *KISS: Keep it simple, stupid.*

At four o'clock, he strolled past Emily's desk and waved casually as the elevator door closed. He walked to the Vine Street parking lot and climbed in the Suburban, driving south until he reached U.S. Hwy. 35. He breezed along the river to his residence, feeling strangely liberated by the text from Maddog. As he drove, he put all the scenarios out of his mind that had stolen his sleep and peace of mind for the last week. All they did was distract him from what he had to do—rescue Sara, neutralize Maddog's threats, and come home in one piece. That was a formidable game plan in anyone's book.

Weaving through the busy traffic on the river road, the silence at his house saddened him. His home had always been his haven. Now everything was locked and shut up tighter than a drum. The familiar sounds coming from the house when he walked inside from a day at work were absent—the smells of dinner, the noise of the kids playing, Carol's sweet kisses. His eyes welled up with tears when he realized what Maddog had stolen from him. *It's ending tonight*, he thought, gritting his teeth.

He spent some time in the garage searching through his black tote bag, which held his emergency stash—his Maglite, a first aid kit, a track phone with prepaid minutes, a couple of hundred dollars in cash, and his Leatherman tool. He'd never needed it before, but now he grabbed the flashlight, the first aid kit, the Leatherman, and a sweatshirt from the back hook in the hallway. Then he remembered that Sara had left her jacket in her car, so he went into the bedroom and rummaged through Carol's shelves until he found one of her sweatshirts. He rolled the shirts up and jammed the other things into the worn black tote, which he threw on the front seat of the truck. His Kevlar vest was in a locked tool chest in the back of the truck, along with his department-issued Sig Sauer 9 mm pistol and ankle holster.

He sat in the driveway and thought about what he was facing. How do you negotiate with a drug-addled idiot when the prize in the exchange would not even be there? Very carefully. On top of it, he wondered how he was going to slip away from Carol without tipping her off to his plan. But he'd worried for nothing. Carol provided him with a perfect excuse.

After the evening meal, Jim played on Gladys' living room floor, scuffling and wrestling with Lillie and Henri while they crawled on his back and stomach and squealed with childish delight. Gladys and Carol cleaned up the kitchen from the evening meal. Baths and story time occupied another hour, and soon it was almost nine o'clock. In the meantime, Leslie had arrived in the yard at dusk and parked in her position under the enormous maple tree in Sam's Jeep Cherokee. Jim knew he would have to get past her, too.

After the kids were in bed, Carol hunkered down on the couch to watch the early nine o'clock news on FOXX. When Jim came into the room, she looked up from the television and said, "I forgot to tell you. Pastor Berge called and wondered if you could come and see him this evening at the parsonage. He's been very busy with hospital visits, but he said he's been thinking of you and praying for all of us. I didn't commit one way or another, so I guess it's up to you whether you want to drive up there or not," she finished.

Jim tried to tamp down his enthusiasm for the excuse she was giving him on a silver platter. He thought a moment as if he were considering it, then said, "Well, I've been wanting to discuss this whole sordid affair with him, so maybe I'll just run up there for a while—if you don't mind."

"I'm fine with it. I'm going to shower and read in bed for a while. You'll be home by ten?"

"Yeah, probably. It shouldn't take too long." He felt a pang of guilt at his deception, dismissed it as necessity, leaned over her, and kissed her lightly on the lips. He memorized the image of her sitting on the ancient tan couch, her bare feet crossed over one another, clutching a throw pillow to her chest, looking up at him with her deep brown eyes.

"I'll wait up for you—" she started to promise, but Jim interrupted.

"No need. Berge can get long-winded and go down some complicated theological trails, so don't worry if I get home a little later," he told her. He leaned down and kissed her again.

"Are you all right?" Carol asked, her voice reflecting suspicion, her eyes clouding.

"Yeah. As good as I can be, I guess, considering the circumstances," Jim said nonchalantly. He turned and stopped, looking back at her. "Don't worry."

"Never does any good anyway, does it?" she asked. The sadness in her eyes made Jim swallow hard.

"Nope, it doesn't. See you in a while," he said, lifting his hand in a half-hearted wave.

Carol nodded, twiddled her fingers at him, and then re-focused her attention back to the news.

At ten-thirty that night, Carol was awakened by the sound of muffled crying. She thought she was dreaming, but when she fully awoke, she groped in the dark feeling for Jim's warmth in the bed. Then she felt the coolness of the sheets and realized he hadn't come home. At the same moment, she noticed a small figure huddled next to the bed. She reached over and turned on the lamp that sat on the bedside table.

"Lillie? What's wrong?" she asked. "Come here, baby," she said, holding out her arms.

Lillie grasped Elsa, her *Frozen* doll, firmly under her arm, her eyes squinting in the brightness of the lamp light. She scampered up on the bed and crawled into Carol's lap. She could feel Lillie's heartbeat racing inside her chest.

"Did you have a bad dream?" Carol asked, kissing the top of her head.

Lillie began softly crying again. "Bapa's with Sara. They're in trouble. Someone's going to hurt them. We have to help them, Mommy!" she whimpered. "They're in trouble," she repeated, looking into Carol's eyes with an unnerving gaze. Her voice was getting louder the longer she talked.

"No, no. Bapa's up to see Pastor Berge. He's just fine." Carol tried to reassure her.

Lillie shook her head beneath Carol's chin. "You're wrong, Mommy."

Suddenly, footsteps creaked on the stairway. Carol turned her wide eyes toward the door. She thought about Henri, sleeping innocently in the next room—alone. The bedroom door swung on its hinges, and Leslie appeared holding Henri, whose eyes were cloudy with confusion.

"Sorry to disturb you, Carol, but we've got a problem," Leslie said soberly.

Carol clutched her hand to her chest, cradling Lillie to her. "Oh, really? What's going on? Is someone here?" Then she caught herself and held up a finger. "Let's all go down to the kitchen and have a cup of hot chocolate."

Leslie slowly shook her head back and forth. "That won't solve our problem, but you need to come downstairs and talk to Gladys. We've got a plan that we think will work."

Everyone tramped down the narrow staircase and into the bright fluorescent lighting of the kitchen. Gladys stood next to the square oak table, her ample figure engulfed in a pink cotton terrycloth robe, her feet made ready in crew socks and wide athletic shoes. Rumpled by sleep, wisps of white hair stood out on her head, and her expression was one of mild irritation. A .22 shotgun lay on the kitchen counter next to the sink.

"Sam texted me about ten minutes ago," Leslie began. "Apparently, he and Paul attached a tracking device to Jim's truck this week so they could monitor his movements. He's northwest of Viroqua, moving along County Y. They think he's going to meet—"

she stopped abruptly and caught Carol's eye, "to meet someone, and they're following him. Sam thinks it would be wise to move to a different location until everything is resolved."

"Okay. We can do that," Carol said. "Just let me get a few things—"

But Leslie butted in. "No, there's no time. We need to move now. We can go to my place. We'll make beds on the couch and floor. We'll be fine with Paco there."

Carol glanced at Gladys, who silently shook her head.

"I'm not going. I'm staying here," Gladys said. "Nobody's running me out of my own home. Don't worry your pretty little head. Got my .22, and I know how to use it. Besides, what are they going to do with a worn-out old woman like me, huh?" Gladys tipped her head forward and looked over her glasses.

"You need to come along!" Carol argued. "You can't stay here alone."

Gladys placed her hands on her hips in a gesture of defiance. "Time's a-wastin'. Get going now," she said, shooing them all toward the door.

Carol turned and hugged Gladys.

"Godspeed, love," Gladys whispered in Carol's ear. "I'll be praying."

Leslie picked up Henri and carried him down the driveway as Carol and Lillie hurried behind her into the velvety dark night. They all climbed into Leslie's Jeep. Carol sat in the back and buckled the kids in. Leslie fumbled with her keys, hit the ignition, and started down County K, twisting and turning on the road as the trees swayed in the black night breeze.

58

FRIDAY, SEPTEMBER 20

Sara's wild ride on the ATV through the wooded hillsides above the hunting shack earlier Thursday morning was just a memory now. The jaunt on the four-wheeler at dawn gave her a brief flash of hope. Then she checked her gullibility at the door, realizing it was a ridiculous frame of mind when you were in a situation with someone as desperate as Maddog.

As soon as she'd swung her leg over the seat on the four-wheeler, Maddog had bored through the woods like a bat out of hell. The muddy track was full of rain puddles from the night before, and as he drove through swales and small creeks, the ATV kicked up showers of softened silt, sludge, and fecund brown water that splattered Sara's back and head. Weaving in and out of shaded areas, Maddog handled the ATV with the confidence and skill of a true backwoods expert. Hank Williams' song lyrics floated into Sara's memory as Maddog tore along rough trails thick with undergrowth and careened around corners and up steep hills. *A country boy can survive.* Obviously, he'd done this before and survived. Sara desperately hung on until her knuckles turned white from gripping the aluminum frame on the back seat.

SUE BERG

They rode for about half an hour until they came to a clearing where an abandoned house trailer sat beneath a huge gnarled white pine. A copse of overgrown arborvitae formed a backdrop behind the trailer, and discarded bottles and cans littered the weed-infested clearing. The trailer became the prison where she was unceremoniously dumped early in the morning. Like before, she was bound with duct tape and strapped to a broken-down filthy lime green chair. Despite the cool temperatures outside, the trailer warmed quickly in the stifling afternoon sunshine. As the heat expanded the rusting sheets of corrugated tin, the metal of the trailer roof cracked ominously.

Evening fell over the abandoned clearing, and Sara's stomach cramped in hunger. She was sure she'd never be able to get the grungy perspiration and dirt off her skin again. She dreamed of hot water, soap, and shampoo. It was quiet inside the broken-down trailer except for the nocturnal skitterings of mice and rats who'd become active as the sun went down.

Maybe by tomorrow, the exchange will happen, she thought. Then a wave of guilt came over when she realized she'd given little thought to Carol, Lillie, or Henri since the abduction. Maddog had effectively diminished her concerns for her family by feeding her fears of this hopeless predicament. The only person she'd been thinking about was herself.

She steamed with anger at her selfishness. Deep down inside, she had to admit that her confidence in her dad's ability to rescue her was waning with each passing hour—her attempts at positive thinking were wearing dangerously thin. She tried to remember all the past situations in which her dad had fought for those who had been innocently hurt and psychologically damaged or killed at the hands of insane, irrational lowlifes. She'd agonized about her dad's safety, and in her fevered supplications, she prayed that God would protect her and bring this crisis to a good end.

But as the hours wore on, and she struggled alone with her thoughts, she felt abandoned. Her prayers seemed ineffectual and pointless. She thought of the thirteen-year-old girl kidnapped last year after her parents were shot point blank in their northern Wisconsin home. *How had she survived for almost three months chained under a bed?* Sara thought. *I've only been held for three days. God, help me.*

She'd drifted in and out of troubled sleep. Dozing in the chair as dusk settled on the trees outside, she heard the ATV engine roaring up the trail. It skidded to a stop in the weed-choked yard where the trailer sat. The motor idled noisily, rattling, missing on a cylinder, and blowing smoke. The door was yanked open, and Maddog appeared in front of her, jittery and keyed up. His eyes reflected an alcoholic sheen, his cheeks bloomed with a red flush, and his breath was ripe with whiskey. Sara could see the determination in his eyes. They were impassive and hard as obsidian.

"What's going on?" Sara asked, her eyes wide with concern. His glassy-eyed stare shook her confidence, and for the first time since the ordeal began, she was truly terrified.

"Time to come to Daddy," Maddog said, bending down and cutting the duct tape on her wrists and ankles. He grabbed her arm roughly and jerked her out of the chair. "Come on! Outside!" he ordered gruffly.

They climbed on the four-wheeler again and thundered down rough paths filled with potholes. They traveled through the darkening woods until they came to an abandoned railroad track that had been converted to a bike trail. It was pitch black now, but the trail was smoother with a hard-packed pebble surface. As they sped along with only the ATV headlights for illumination, Sara realized she had no idea where they were or what Maddog's destination might be. They came to a junction where the bike trail crossed a gravel township road. Maddog stopped the ATV abruptly.

"Get off," he ordered, his voice thick with agitation. He spat tobacco juice carelessly in the weeds along the trail.

Sara climbed off the ATV and stood next to the road where a late model Ford Expedition was parked on the shoulder. Maddog maneuvered the four-wheeler into some tall undergrowth next to the trail, grabbed Sara's arm, and dragged her across the road.

"Get in the truck!" he said, pushing her across the front seat of the vehicle.

"Are we meeting my dad somewhere?" she asked, sounding braver than she felt.

Maddog looked over at her as he grabbed the steering wheel, his eyes glittering with predatory rapture. "You better hope he brings Lillie, or you won't live to tell about it, and I'd like nothing better than to take you apart, little missy. It'll be an experience you'll never forget."

Propping herself against the passenger door, she stared silently into the dark, her breath coming in short rasps. Her blonde hair was greasy with sweat and mud. Her shoulders slumped forward, but just as she was about to close her eyes, a visage of her dad wavered in front of her just beyond the windshield. She could see his tall, lean frame, his piercing blue eyes, and his winsome smile. She risked a second glance at Maddog's face. When she looked back, expecting the ghostly image of her father to be gone, he was still there, smiling at her.

"Did you say something?" Maddog barked.

She shook her head and stayed silent, but inside, her heart burned with hope. *You're in for the surprise of your life,* she thought. She allowed herself a momentary smile.

Maddog's testosterone-laden sweat and nervous energy infused the atmosphere of the Expedition with a stench that made Sara want to gag. He started the engine and rammed the truck into gear as gravel sprayed into the ditch when he pulled out on the road. His mad alcoholic gaze and the look of mean-eyed grit on his face led Sara to believe the worst was about to happen, and she couldn't do a thing to stop it. She gaped through the dark windshield at the road, but she could feel Maddog's eyes boring a hole in the side of her face. *Don't let me down, Dad,* she thought.

59

"Where the hell are we?" Paul asked, gripping the steering wheel until his knuckles turned white. His face was bathed in the green reflected light from the dash, his brow crinkled in agitation. In the passenger seat, Sam fumbled with his laptop, trying to get a handle on where Jim was headed. Throughout the week, he'd been regularly checking the tracking device they'd placed under Jim's Suburban.

Tonight, Sam logged onto his laptop at six o'clock and then rechecked again at nine-thirty. It was then that he realized Jim was on the move south on U.S. Hwy 14, which he found suspicious, especially since Leslie was supposed to be sitting in his yard doing surveillance. After a call to Paul, they headed toward Viroqua in Paul's Ford F-150 pickup. The situation reminded both men of other instances they'd been in together in which the best-laid plans had gone south, and as payment for their participation, they got their clocks cleaned.

"Why does he always have to do this Lone Ranger thing?" Paul asked. "Where's all the 'Let's hear it for the team' crap now?"

"I don't know, but forget all that stuff and listen," Sam said. "We're coming up to County Y. We need to go east and drop into the valley toward Avalanche."

Paul turned left on County Y and continued driving as they dropped into a long narrow coulee following the curving road through rolling hills where a yard light illuminated a broken down, weathered barn and a small farmhouse that stood next to it, dark and still. Farther down the road, a mobile home crouched next to a creek, and a couple of weekend cabins appeared to be unoccupied. Suddenly, a white-tailed doe leaped across the road, forcing Paul to brake hard. Twenty feet behind her, a buck followed, hesitating on the edge of the road. Tiptoeing cautiously onto the gravel, the buck snorted and put his nose to the ground, his bone-colored rack gleaming in the headlights. He leaped off into the ditch in a mad scramble to find his mate, his nose sniffing the air for estrus. Paul blew out a sigh of relief and accelerated.

Suddenly Sam blurted, "Wait a minute. Jim's turned onto Seas Branch Road, heading north. He's stopped—he's not moving."

Paul came to Seas Branch Road, turned north, traveled a few hundred feet, and stopped in front of a small cabin where a single light illuminated a small window in the house. Inside, a television flickered in the darkened interior. Next to the cabin, a hedge of lilacs swayed gently in the night breeze. Paul killed the engine, listening to the motor ticking through the cab's open window.

"What's on Seas Branch Road?" he said.

"Don't know yet, but it's too weird to be a coincidence," Sam said.

"Enlarge your map. Maybe it'll show us what's up ahead."

Sam fiddled with the laptop for a few minutes, the light from the screen illuminating his face inside the cab. "Oh, there's a quarry up ahead—a pretty big one. Could be where Maddog's meeting the chief," he said, squinting his eyes at the screen. "It's only about a half mile ahead. Let's pull ahead off the road, and then we'll hike up to the quarry," Sam suggested.

"Then what?" Paul asked.

"I don't know yet. We'll have to scope it out."

Paul leaned over and gazed at the image on the screen. "Easier said than done," he said, "especially in the dark." He pulled the truck ahead ten feet, then shut the engine off. He grabbed a black duffle bag he'd stored on the floor of the truck, opened it, and brought out a Maglite. "Is this another one of those convoluted chases you talked about the other day?" he asked, looking over at Sam in the dark.

"Looks like it. Let's dud up, partner," Sam said, softly closing the laptop and laying it on the seat.

The two men stepped outside the Ford pickup onto the asphalt road. They strapped on their Kevlar vests, clipped their handcuffs on the back of their belt loops, and holstered their pistols. Paul zipped a waterproof Golf rain jacket he'd bought at Dick's sporting goods store over his vest and walked around the truck where he waited for Sam in the shadow of a clump of sumac that grew along the edge of the road. Pulling a black Badger sweatshirt over his Kevlar vest, Sam grabbed his night vision goggles off the floor of the pickup and walked out on the road to join Paul.

The evergreen trees hanging over the road looked like dark paper cutouts against the navy night sky. A gentle wind caressed the needles, and they made a wisping sound perfuming the night air with a potent scent. The two men walked toward the quarry without speaking, their boots quiet underfoot, the tips of the trees lit by a moon that had risen above the horizon and hung like a yellow-orange ball in the velvety coal-black night.

After walking about a hundred feet, they caught sight of Jim's Suburban and another dark vehicle parked on the shoulder of the road on the opposite side. Jim had pulled his truck over into the ditch as far off the road as possible. Paul grabbed Sam's arm, pointed at the truck, and then pointed toward the rising bulwark of limestone that formed a natural ring around the huge blasted hole in the earth— Seas Branch Quarry. A deep dry run formed from past flash floods ran parallel to the steep wall next to the road. Sam climbed down into it, scrambled over several small boulders, and climbed up the other side through immature sumac, willow, and poplar. He worked his way upward slowly over the steep incline of the wall pausing every few seconds to listen for the sounds of voices. Pebbles skittered down the slope as he climbed, but he didn't hear any other sounds. Paul followed him.

They climbed steadily in the night air planting their feet carefully in the tall grasses that grew along the edge of the quarry until they were able to see the deserted floor stretching below them in the rising moonlight. Paul's foot worked a stone loose, and it clattered noisily down the embankment. Both men froze, but everything remained eerily quiet. Throughout the quarry, crushed gravel was randomly stockpiled on the exposed limestone floor, the piles resembling small mountain ranges lit up in the moonlight.

Sam stopped suddenly, pushed his hand backward toward Paul, and quickly lay prone on the ground, slipping on his night vision goggles. A terrible foreboding settled over the scene, a silence that sometimes comes before a catastrophic event like a tornado or hurricane—black, ponderous, and evil. Sam used his hand to clear away the grama grass. Far below them, he could detect movement, and he realized it was Jim walking toward the far side of the quarry. A pinpoint of light bobbed unsteadily but slowly advanced forward. Sam removed the goggles, turned to Paul, who lay next to him, and pointed in the direction of the light. Paul nodded and used the goggles to observe Jim's movements.

A second later, he whispered, "Whaddya think? Should we go down and follow him? Or should we hike the rim of the quarry til we're right over them?"

"We'll be no help if we're above him on the rim," Sam said. "Those gravel piles are huge. They'd be good cover, but we'll have to be awfully quiet. Let's get closer if we can."

"Sounds good," Paul whispered. "Besides, I don't want to slip and fall two hundred feet to my death."

"Ditto that. I hear you, brother."

They scuttled backward away from the edge of the quarry, got up from the ground, and climbed back down as rapidly as they could until they were again at the quarry's entrance. It was blocked with two steel cattle gates secured with a chain and padlock. Paul shone his flashlight on a small blue sign with white lettering that said, "Private Property, Stay Out."

They climbed silently over the gate, worked their way up a steep embankment, and walked quietly into the immense open air of the deserted quarry. The moonlight illuminated the scene and reminded Sam of an old Western movie, blue with dark shadows that shifted in the light.

Sam headed out across the quarry floor in the shadow of the gravel piles, with Paul following close behind. *Let the chips fall as they may,* Sam thought.

60

Earlier that evening, after making his excuses to Carol and Leslie, Jim had driven steadily south on Hwy. 14, the moon rising in the night sky until it looked like an orange orb hanging in space. The air was crisp and clean, the road humming beneath the tires. He suddenly realized that he welcomed this moment; reality couldn't be worse than the constant nightmares he'd seen playing on the movie screen of his mind—of what Maddog had done to his daughter, his beautiful Sara.

Bring it on, you pervert, he thought, gritting his teeth, his lips pulled back in a sneer. He caught a glimpse of himself in the rearview mirror and was shocked that he could possess such a look of hatred.

He parked his truck near the quarry and got out. Standing next to his vehicle, he took in the vibe of the place—the smell of lime dust and the fluttering of birds in the trees surrounding the quarry. Jim could imagine the frenetic activity of the quarry during the day, with crushers, loaders, and dump trucks moving in the choking yellow lime dust. Now at night, the quarry became an amphitheater of dark shapes and silent hulks of monstrous machinery. He swallowed the bile that had flooded his throat and spat in the gravel by the Suburban. He sensed a certain drama in the air, wondering how the night would unfold.

He grabbed his Maglite off the seat, walked around the truck, climbed the steel gates that blocked the entrance, and began walking across the flat quarry floor. He passed huge piles of purple-shadowed gravel that reminded him of ancient pyramids looming in the ambient moonlight. The shadow of his body moved along the ground like a blue bruise. Walking along the limestone floor, he passed huge piles of quarried blocks stacked like a child's set of building toys. His footsteps crunched underneath, making him feel exposed as if he'd unconsciously stepped into the glare of a blinding spotlight on a deserted catwalk. As he approached the far side of the quarry, a deep voice called out, "That's close enough, Higgins. Stop right there."

"Dad? Is that you?" Sara called out.

"Yeah, honey. It's me. Are you okay?" Jim asked loudly. His throat was dry and prickly, and his tongue felt shriveled like a prune against the roof of his mouth. He coughed and cleared his throat self-consciously. He nervously opened and closed his hand next to his side. The weight of his gun strapped to his ankle felt like a omen of disaster, and he fervently hoped he wouldn't have to use it. He flicked off his flashlight. In the darkness, he reached down and unfastened his pistol, then stuffed it inside the waistband of his jeans.

Jim heard the scraping of footsteps in the gravel as Maddog and Sara approached him. His eyes had adjusted to the darkness, and he watched them tenuously walk in his direction. A fetid odor of sour sweat and unwashed clothes wafted in the air as they came nearer. A lantern was switched on, and suddenly a small area lit up in front of Jim like the lights at the foot of a stage. He stared at Maddog, who was holding Sara clenched to his chest, his thick hairy arm wrapped around her neck. Sara's eyes filled with tears when she saw him. Jim was shocked at her appearance; her hair was stringy, and her clothes were dirty and wrinkled. She looked vulnerable in a way that made his heart ache.

"Do you really need to restrain her in such a demeaning way?" Jim asked, his eyes boring into Maddog's. "Where do you think she's going to go?"

"She's been very cooperative so far, but I wouldn't want her to get any ideas about running off in the dark," Maddog replied. A grin tickled the corners of his mouth, and he lifted his chin toward Jim. "Where's Lillie?" he asked.

Jim noticed Maddog's eyes gleaming like chips of black granite. A breeze blew out of the south and ruffled the trees at the edges of the quarry, and the night wind carried scents of drying corn and ripening vegetation in the last throes of the growing season. Despite the coolness of the night air, Jim could feel sweat trickling over his rib cage inside his shirt.

"After we've agreed on our terms, I'll call for her," Jim said.

Maddog jerked his head back. "What're you talkin' about? Terms?" He spat the word out of his mouth like a piece of rotten meat. "Apparently, my reputation has been lost on you. I've never given anything up to the enemy, and I don't plan on starting now."

"Well, then, this will be a first for you, won't it?" Jim clenched the back of his teeth, the muscular ripples erupting along the outline of his jaw. His blue eyes blazed with a determination that seemed to make Maddog shrink back in uncertainty.

Sara squirmed. Maddog bristled with contempt and tightened his grip around Sara's neck, lifting her feet a little higher off the ground so she had to stand on her tiptoes. She gripped his arm, her face flushing with confusion. Jim noticed some kind of pistol tucked inside Maddog's jeans, and he felt his rationality eroding, replaced with a wave of anger and hostility. *What a bunch of bullshit,* he thought. "So, let's talk," he said. "There must be something you want out of this exchange."

"Don't complicate it, old man. You already know what I want. Let's keep it simple. I get Lillie, and you get Sara."

Despite the seriousness of the situation, Jim let out a subtle chuckle. "That's not going to happen. You missed your opportunity to step up to the plate and be a father six years ago. You abandoned Lillie when she needed you most. You walked away from her when she was born, and I walked into her life when she was found homeless, living in a park with her grandmother. I have two daughters—Sara and Lillie. You can't just waltz in here now and reclaim your parental rights."

"Don't preach to me," Maddog snarled. "I don't need you to remind me of the mistakes I've made."

"Fair enough," Jim responded calmly. "When I talk about an agreement, I'm talkin' about you, partner. What are you going to give to get Lillie? Because you're going to have to kill me to get what you think you want. Are you willing to do that?" Jim asked. Noticing Maddog's expression collapsing into a flat mask, he continued. "Are you willing to kill a cop to achieve your goal? You'll pay a heavy price if you do, believe me. Maybe you better reconsider your proposal."

Maddog seemed to lessen his grip on Sara for a moment as he absorbed this new set of facts. Behind them, Jim saw a flicker of movement at the edge of the lantern light. Sam and Paul peered silently around a pile of gravel.

"What if I'm not willing to negotiate? What then?" Maddog asked, but his voice lacked the bravado he'd had just a minute ago. As with all bullies when confronted, his veneer of braggadocio began crumbling and disintegrating in the face of an immovable challenge.

Jim continued. "I hate to tell you this, but you've already lost, buddy. You're going to prison for a very long time. Marcellus Tate Brown died in the hospital Saturday morning. Before he died, he identified you as the person responsible for his injuries. He admitted that to one of our police officers. So, you're up on a murder charge, and now you'll also be charged with aggravated assault and kidnapping. Those are the unpleasant facts, Maddog. You can either give up this whole idiotic scheme, or I'm going to have to arrest you. I don't want to hurt you, and I certainly don't want to kill you." Jim's voice took on a sarcastic tone. "But believe me when I say that I want you to be in a position to appreciate the full weight of the law. In case you hadn't heard, prison is like nothing you've ever experienced."

Maddog laughed raucously. "You're kidding, right? You didn't tell me your dad was a comedian, Sara. Prison or death? That's not negotiable—that's not even a choice!" he spat. "This is the biggest bunch of bullshit I've ever heard."

What happened next could only be described as a split-second decision in Sara's mind made by the grace of God. At the very instant Sara felt Maddog's attention wane, he stepped forward, and she caught him off balance and rammed her elbow into his stomach hard. Then she hooked her foot around his ankle, causing him to trip and fall backward. He made a *woof* sound as he went down, hitting the ground hard. She wrenched herself out of his grip, rolled on her side, sprang to her feet, and ran into the darkness of the quarry.

In the free-for-all, Maddog fumbled for his gun, pulled it out, and began shooting wildly at Jim. Two shots went wide, but the third hit Jim in the shoulder, sending him reeling backward and knocking him to the ground.

By this time, Paul and Sam came barreling out from behind the pile of gravel. Scrambling forward, Sam tackled Maddog, repeatedly pummeling him with his fists while Paul wrenched the gun from his hand. The three men rolled in a ball of kicking feet and punching fists until Paul finally forced Maddog over on his stomach. Sam cuffed him face down on the ground, where he continued spewing violent obscenities and threats.

"Shut up!" Sam yelled as he kicked him with his boot. Paul continued to secure his feet together to prevent him from running.

"Call the sheriff and get an ambulance down here!" Paul yelled to Sam. He ran to Jim's side and leaned over him, sweat pouring from his face. "We got him, Chief. We got him. Hang on. Help is on the way," he said, kneeling beside him.

Jim's shoulder was burning up. He rolled on his uninjured side and held his arm still, but he began shaking, and his legs quivered uncontrollably. He could feel the blood soaking his shirt, puddling underneath him in the gravel. In the chaos, the lantern had tipped on its side, and its light spilled into the vastness of the quarry. Out of the darkness, Sara appeared at his side. She knelt and talked to him quietly, right next to his face. Sam suddenly appeared and hovered over him, looking scared and wide-eyed with adrenaline. He aimed his Maglite at Jim's wound.

"Ambulance is on the way. Hang on," Sam said softly. He tore his sweatshirt off over his head.

Jim was drifting on the edge of consciousness, and his pain was ramping up. He groaned and clenched his teeth when Sam pressed the sweatshirt on his wound.

"I knew you'd come, Dad," she said, stroking his hair.

"That was quite the move you had back there, honey," he mumbled, gritting his teeth.

"Teachers of fifth graders have some awesome skills," she said, smiling.

Paul interrupted. "You need to lie on your back, Chief." Jim rolled over and let out a moan.

"Did he hurt you?" Jim asked her, his eyes searching her face for a clue. She quit smiling, and her face became a mask of some inscrutable private emotion.

"Later, Dad. Really, I'm fine," she said as she clasped his hand. She leaned over and kissed his cheek. "You be quiet now. Everything's going to be okay."

In the distance, the pulsating whine of the ambulance and police car sirens split the night air. The tops of the trees reflected the glow of moonlight, and Jim noticed the stars blazing in the sky above the quarry. He stared at the glittering pinpricks of light in the curtain of the darkness, but he couldn't stay awake, and he drifted into the black velvet of unconsciousness.

SUE BERG

61

SATURDAY, SEPTEMBER 21

Jim dreamed he was underwater and swimming to the surface for air. Suddenly he gasped a gulp of air and opened his eyes to an IV bag dripping silently into his arm, the smell of lingering antiseptic in an unfamiliar room. The sun was shining brightly outside, and when he turned his head, he saw a couple of floral bouquets arranged on the wide ledge below the window that gave a view of the Mississippi River and the blue-green bluffs in the distance. He heard the clatter of a meal cart outside in the hallway and the rustle of a nurse's uniform making crinkling sounds next to his bed. The blood pressure cuff tightened around his arm. With his good hand, he felt beneath the hospital gown to the bulky bandage on his shoulder. He closed his eyes again, letting his hand drop back on the sheet, the chaos in the quarry flooding back into his memory.

The ambulance had taken an hour to get to the Seas Branch quarry, administer first aid, load him on a gurney, and rush him to Gundersen Lutheran, where he was immediately prepped for surgery. In a haze of morphine and loss of blood, he vaguely recalled seeing the tense, worried expression on Carol's tear-stained face above him as she held his hand and kissed him. Then nothing, until now.

He still didn't know how Sam and Paul had found out about Maddog's plan, but he knew one thing—he was going to get his butt chewed by any number of people for his display of arrogance and independence, to say nothing of his crass disregard for his partners' concerns.

He drifted off to sleep again and must have dozed for another hour until he woke again to muffled voices in his room. He wiggled his feet, lifted his arm, and laid it across his forehead. He recognized the familiar scent of sunflower perfume in the room. Opening his eyes, he saw Carol leaning anxiously over the bed rail.

"Hey, how're you feeling?" she asked quietly, stroking his hair while she talked. He grabbed her hand.

"Sleepy. What time is it?"

"Two-thirty in the afternoon. You've been out awhile."

"Yeah, I figured. Who's here?"

"Sara, John, Vivian, and the kids. Sam and Paul are home sleeping."

"Who's holding down the fort?"

"Probably Leslie and DeDe, but don't worry about that right now."

His eyes were half closed, his lips felt numb, and he knew he sounded thick-headed. "Did Sam and Paul get hurt?" He blinked rapidly, trying to ease the vertigo that made the room rock slowly from one side to the other.

"A few bumps and bruises in the scuffle," Carol informed him. She brushed her fingertips across his cheek. "You could have told me about meeting Maddog. What did you think I'd do? Try and stop you?"

Jim shook his head slowly. "I'm sorry. I think I'll be repeating those words a lot in the next few days." Carol smiled sadly.

"I think you're right," she said. "I'll wait 'til later to chew you out."

Sara came into view above him. Her eyes had a strange faraway look despite the tentative smile on her face. She grasped Jim's hand, tears beginning to shine and escape onto her cheeks.

"How you doin', Dad?"

"I don't know yet. I'll know when I move, and I'm sure when I do, it's gonna hurt like hell. Did you sleep?"

"Only after I stood under a hot shower for about an hour. I think I sent the water heater into convulsions."

Jim heard some commotion by the door. Lillie and Henri walked slowly toward the bed, their eyes wide with worry and wonder. Henri clutched his favorite blanket under his chin as Lillie led him closer to Jim.

Vivian lifted the children onto the bed only after she cautioned them to be careful and quiet. Lillie folded her hands in her lap and stared at Jim, her blue eyes like a snippet of sky. Henri began softly crying. He reached for Carol, and she picked him up and went to the window, pointing out the tiny cars in the parking lot below.

"Bapa, are you okay now?" Lillie asked, her mouth quivering slightly, her eyes shiny with tears.

"I'm going to be just fine, toots."

"Are you mad anymore?" Her face was somber, trying to gauge Jim's current mood. A wave of guilt shadowed Jim's face when he realized she'd absorbed a lot more of the emotional depth of the crisis than he'd given her credit for. Vivian watched him, lifting her eyebrows slightly as Lillie grilled him. She fired more questions at him. "Is that bad man in jail? Can we go home now?"

Jim returned a glazed stare at Vivian and Sara, noticing their furtive glances. "I'm not mad anymore, and besides, I was never mad at you. I'm sorry about that, honey."

"That's okay. You caught that bad man who tried to hurt Sara, right?"

"That's right, baby. He's locked up, and he can't hurt us anymore. And to answer your other question—we're going to go home now."

Lillie's eyes popped open wide, and a huge smile creased her face. She clapped her hands excitedly in front of her. Jim motioned to her with his good arm, and she crawled carefully up the side of the bed along the railing and laid her head on his chest. He grimaced slightly with pain, then smiled weakly.

"I love you, Bapa."

"I'm countin' on it, toots," Jim said, tears welling in his eyes.

The afternoon passed quickly with a slew of visitors and a brief meeting with the doctor and physical therapists. Jim could feel himself falling off a cliff of exhaustion and pain. The gunshot in his shoulder had torn through the upper left pectoral muscle, shattered the clavicle, tore the brachial blood vessel, and exited the deltoid, all of which contributed to considerable blood loss, bone shatter, and muscle tear and rupture. Jim had been lucky. He was sure if Maddog had not been off balance when he'd squeezed off the shot, his number would have been punched. As it was, he had a serious recovery ahead of him and extensive therapy to regain the mobility of his shoulder joint.

All this information was delivered in a rather dry, formal discourse at the side of Jim's bed by the attending surgeon whose wiry gray hair and deep brown eyes reminded him of a college professor delivering a lecture to interns who seemed intellectually challenged, their pens poised above empty notebooks.

The doctor exited the room with his worshipful entourage fluttering around him. A few minutes later, Carol, Vivian, and Sara left with the kids to go home to Chipmunk Coulee so Jim could rest. After eating some dinner on a tray and another dose of morphine, Jim slept soundly until midnight when he woke up and noticed Sam hunkered down with his laptop in the reclining chair in the corner.

"Hey. I thought visiting hours were over. What're you doin' here?"

Jim slurred. He hated the effects of the morphine, that unpleasant sensation in which he barely hovered at the edge of reason and comprehension.

Sam shut the cover on his laptop, which he laid on the floor, hoisted himself out of the chair, and walked over to Jim's bed. He stood casually next to him with his hands in his pockets. He wore gray and black plaid shorts, an orange University of Florida sweatshirt, and Doc Marten sandals.

"I sweet-talked my way in with the nurses using police business as my ticket." Sam grinned and winked. "They just couldn't resist the Birkstein charm." Then he became serious. "The rest of the crew stopped, but you were out of the country."

"I believe it. Those drugs really do a number on you," Jim said. "How do addicts even function on this stuff?"

Sam looked at Jim out of the corner of his eye and said, "I hate to tell you this, Chief, but our case surrounding Heather Lovstad is about to dry up and blow away."

Jim swallowed self-consciously and tried to focus his eyes on Sam's face. He felt the room spin precariously. "What happened? What about the search warrant for her place? Did somebody follow through with that?"

"That's in the works right now, but she seems to have disappeared overnight."

"We waited too long. Anybody know where she went? What about Pritchert?"

"Last time we checked at four this afternoon, he was slaving away at the law firm in the service of his clients. We have no idea where Heather is. Surveillance was dropped without notice, probably from lack of funds. Guess the department couldn't afford the overtime."

"Do Heather or Pritchert own any property around here where she might go to hide out until the smoke clears?" Jim asked. "What about the river? Maybe Pritchert has a boat, and he took her to one of the islands."

"That sounds like drugs talking," he said, pulling the corners of his mouth downward in a look of doubt. He chewed on a hangnail on his thumb and then said, "Don't know, but we'll check into it."

"You do that. We'll get her, Sam. I'm breaking out of here tomorrow, according to the doc, and I'm on leave for a while—maybe a couple of weeks—but I want you to call me every day, and keep me in the loop."

Sam turned his head slowly and looked at him. He shook his head and lifted his chin, seeming to have a silent argument with himself. After a few quiet moments, he straightened his shoulders and gave Jim a hard gaze.

"What?" Jim asked. "What's the matter now?"

Sam's mouth dropped open, and he dipped his head in Jim's direction. "Keep you in the loop? Kinda like you kept us in the loop with Maddog? Really, Chief?" His normally mellow hazel eyes had a fire in them that looked like the reflection of a candle flame inside an amber glass. He turned toward Jim and parked his hands on his hips in a gesture of defiant impatience.

Oh, boy. Here we go, Jim thought. He blew his breath out of his nose and shifted uncomfortably in bed. "Well, I knew that was coming, and I deserve it. I apologize."

"You apologize? Like that makes everything copacetic?" Sam said, shaking his head from side to side. He pointed his index finger at Jim and wagged it up and down. "You and Sara could have been killed out there. And not to sound like a friggin' hero or anything, but if we hadn't shown up, your family might be planning your funeral instead of your homecoming! Sara's, too!" Sam brought his hand down on the bed rail, his face flushed with a pink hue, his nostrils flared. He looked away and stared at a point on the opposite wall waiting for Jim's response.

A heavyset nurse popped her head through the door. "Everything okay in here?"

Jim flopped his hand in her direction. "We're fine. We're just having a discussion."

"Keep it down, guys," she cautioned with a scowl. "It's after hours."

After she left, Jim asked Sam, "You tail me or what? How'd you know where I was going?"

"We fitted a tracking device on your truck at the beginning of the week."

"Well, I guess we might as well get it out in the open, huh?" Jim said, a challenging undertone to his voice. "So much for my privacy. Anything else I should know?"

"Don't lay this at my feet, Chief. You made your decisions, and we made ours, but the point is we should have made them together."

The room had suddenly become stuffy. In the uncomfortable silence that followed, Sam moved to the window and stared into the night.

"Let's not do this," Jim said softly.

Sam's back was hard and uncompromising. He rubbed the back of his neck with his hand, turned, and walked back to the side of Jim's bed. Jim cringed when he saw his determined expression.

"Chief, when I joined the investigative team, you made a big deal out of supporting each other and having each other's back. Didn't you tell me that?" His tone bordered on belligerence.

"Yes. You're right. I did." *Don't argue. You know he's right.*

"So what's changed? And don't give me this macho bullshit that protecting your family is your job and no one else's. We're public servants hired to safeguard our citizens no matter the situation. That includes you, too."

"You're right. Let's not be this way, Sam. Can you ease up on your partner a little?" He was hoping a soft answer would calm him down.

Sam cocked his head and bit his lower lip with his teeth.

"Come on, Sam. Ease up, buddy," Jim said quietly. "We're all okay."

Sam didn't say anything, walked to the chair, picked up his

laptop, and left the hospital room.

"Sam! Sam!" Jim shouted after him. He stared at the empty chair, feeling useless and spent, then flopped back on the pillow, his face a mask of pain and disappointment.

62

The wide dark planks of the barn's loft floor shone with an oiled sheen that could only be produced by age, dust, and the sweat of farmhands who'd unloaded hay bales in the sweltering heat of a Wisconsin July afternoon. Shafts of sunlight streamed through the four-paned windows in the peak of the barn and created yellow polygons on the wide planks. Dust motes danced in the swirling beams of light, and the air was infused with an earthy smell of old hay and pungent mold. Pigeons cooed softly in the peak, the rafters splotched with their white excrement.

DeDe Deverioux and Jude Delaney stood gazing upward at the soaring roof of the barn, imagining the amount of money, energy, and sweat it would take to reconstruct and conform the barn's image into the upscale restaurant Jude envisioned. In his meanderings around the area, he'd discovered the property on the southern edge of La Crosse just off Hwy. 35 and was immediately smitten with the spectacular views of the Mississippi backwaters to the west and the blue-hunched bluffs that rose dramatically along its banks.

"I'm trying to understand what you see in this property, JuJu," DeDe lamented. "It's going to be awfully expensive to remodel."

Jude grabbed DeDe's hand, turned her toward him, and placed

his powerful hands on her broad shoulders. She wore a pink cotton sweater, pearls, and a tight pair of blue jeans with sandals. Her hair was glossy and fell softly around her face. "I know you're practical and realistic, but right now, I need you to believe in me and my dream, De. I don't have anybody else in this world who understands me like you do. Can you trust me on this?" Jude's dark eyes searched her face, and she saw his intense need for acceptance and understanding.

"Well, keep talkin', baby. Unveil your vision. Tell me what you're thinkin'," DeDe said.

"Come on. Let's look around," he said, grabbing her hand.

They climbed down from the hayloft and began inspecting the sprawling interior of the dusty hip-roofed barn. Jude patiently explained his plan, which involved gutting the interior and decorating everything in a modern rustic theme using recycled materials. Adding floor-to-ceiling windows to the west and south would let in plenty of natural light. In addition, they would expand the dining area in the summer months with an outdoor attached pergola surrounded by perennial gardens and build an addition that would include a state-of-the-art kitchen.

DeDe had to admit that as Jude walked throughout the property articulating his vision, she was beginning to see the potential of his expansive design. She stood in the half door, looking out at a view of the river and the surrounding bluffs. The faint odor of cow manure wafted on the breeze, and goldenrod and purple aster bloomed in yellow profusion on the sloping bank. The vantage point above the scenery toward the river probably explained the price point the realtor had quoted to them.

"Back here," Jude said, grabbing her hand and pointing emphatically, "we'll have a smokehouse and a firepit. Oh, and over here," he gestured in a different direction, "we can extend the patio and pergola to include casual dining at lunchtime. We'll use recycled tin, shed board, and old barn beams to construct the new areas, and of course, everything will have to be wired and insulated. We'll make it as energy efficient as possible—the millennials should love that." Jude sighed loudly. "This needs to be *the* destination dining experience in La Crosse and the Tri-state area with the emphasis on the rural charm of Wisconsin coupled with a farm-to-table theme."

"It's a lot of work, honey. What's your target date for opening?" DeDe asked.

"Well, I was hoping May 1," Jude said, raising his eyebrows. "Think that's possible?"

"Possible, but you have to have a crew that will be here every day to complete it by then." Charging forward, DeDe asked the dreaded question. "What about money?"

"There are already three interested parties in the property on Canal Street in New Orleans. It's listed at $2.7 million. They might even get into a bidding war. That reminds me—I have to call Levina when we get done here."

"I think it can work, but I'm really only going to be playing an advisory role, you know," DeDe said. "I've got my career at the sheriff's department to think about. And you've got to be sure this is a move you really want to make." DeDe locked eyes with Jude. "Are you sure about this? Because building a restaurant business from the ground up says permanence to me. Like this is where you really want us to put down our roots. Am I reading that right, JuJu?"

"Absolutely, but you think it's feasible, right?" His deep brown eyes reminded her of a little boy begging for an ice cream cone before supper.

"I think your design is great, and once your cuisine hits the scene, I'm sure it'll be *the* nightspot in town. What about a name?"

"Don't know. What about *Si Bon?*"

DeDe smiled. "*So good* in French. I like that. And it will be ... so good."

He grabbed her hand and pulled her to his chest, kissing her tenderly. "There are a couple of bales of hay upstairs in the loft.

We could break this place in good—bring us some good luck for the future." He kissed her on the lips again, moving his hands across her back, moved down and kissed her neck, then pulled her toward the hayloft ladder. His brown eyes focused on her face.

"You gonna make it worthwhile, *mon cheri*?" DeDe smiled in anticipation.

"Oh yeah. It'll be *si bon*," Jude chuckled, stepping up the ladder.

"You willing to meet me at nine tonight and check out Heather's place?" Sam asked Paul. His face was scrunched up in a scowl, and his mouth was turned down like he had a bad case of indigestion. "I hate to wait until Monday to use that search warrant."

Leslie and Sam had just finished breakfast at Paul and Ruby Saner's home on Market Street. The air was thick with the smell of burning leaves. In the neighborhood, bloated pumpkins sat on porches and sidewalks like flaming orange lanterns, and multi-colored leaves floated to the ground, their descent lazily falling in random, helter-skelter fashion. Neighbors were out cleaning up their yards and bagging leaves for pickup on Monday. Ruby and Leslie were busy cleaning up the kitchen. Sitting in the back screened-in porch, Paul and Sam watched Paco and Melody as they played in the enclosed yard.

"What do you hope to accomplish, Sam? Heather's flown the coop, and she's not likely to return on a Saturday night. Any evidence she had that might prove her involvement in the murders is probably long gone by now." Paul propped one leg on his knee and sank deeper into the padded lawn chair.

"Well, I don't know what else to do. I can't believe we lost track of her. Any hope we had of putting this one to bed has pretty much been flushed down the toilet. I know she's involved somehow in these murders, but I just can't get it right. Damn! It's so frustrating," Sam complained.

"Settle down. We'll figure it out eventually," Paul said, staring at Melody as she tumbled down the slide in the backyard. He looked over at Sam, noticing his agitated state. "There's something else in your craw. What's wrong? You seem pretty tense."

Sam ran his hands over his face in frustration. "Higgins and I had words, but he didn't get to use his," Sam said sourly. "I crawled all over him about his caper in the quarry. You know, the old grind about not including us, how he could have been killed. On and on and on. God, I ripped him a new one and huffed out of the room like a spoiled brat. I'll probably be lucky to still have a job come Monday morning."

Paul waved his hand in the air. "Take it easy. Higgins is always more than willing to admit when he's wrong. Did he apologize?"

"Yeah, he did, but like my dad always says don't apologize if you're not willing to change your behavior. And really, how much change have we seen?" Sam asked, continuing his harangue. "Remember his caper up on Grandad Bluff when he was going to catch the mad bomber by himself? He's still running around the country trying to be the big hero, trying to rescue everyone without any assistance from anybody, including us. Why the hell does he keep doing that?"

"Whoa! Who put a load of judgment up yours, Sam? Where's all that grace and forgiveness I always hear you spoutin' about? You and I both know that hostage situations are notoriously unpredictable. Maybe he thought his chances to get Sara back were better if he met Maddog alone."

"Yeah, right. Not." Sam remained sullenly slouched in his chair, his feet crossed at the ankles, his arms clasped behind his neck. Leslie appeared in the doorway. She raised her eyebrows tellingly in Paul's direction.

"Ready to go, hon? The laundry's calling our names," she said.

Sam rose to his feet. "Sorry for the sermon. Thanks for breakfast. Call me if you change your mind." He whistled for Paco.

"Sure. Not a problem."

As Leslie and Sam climbed in the Jeep, Paul stood on his front porch steps, wondering at the intensity of Sam's frustration. His immaturity and impulsive nature were well-known throughout county law enforcement, leading to frustration and misunderstandings over the past couple of years. But in the end, Sam was a talented detective with unusual insights that helped them put miscreants away.

What had they missed about Heather Lovstad that made Sam so sure she could kill three people, including her own father? Paul shifted on his feet as they pulled away from the curb. He'd have to spend more time reviewing all the evidence they'd collected so far. They were missing something.

Paul felt Ruby's presence at his elbow. She stared down the street at the receding Jeep.

"Trouble with Sam?" she asked.

"He's got something up his butt. I'm just not sure what it is yet."

"That's the time you better watch him. He might do something crazy."

"Yeah. I know. Don't remind me."

Jim's arrival at home on Chipmunk Coulee Road from the hospital Saturday afternoon triggered a celebratory mood in Carol and the kids, but Jim was feeling anything but victorious. When he saw the birthday cake on the buffet and several brightly wrapped packages, his morphine-soaked brain suddenly remembered that yesterday had been his fifty-fourth birthday.

"Bapa! Bapa! Happy birthday! We've been getting ready for your party," Lillie shouted as she ran to greet him. Her eyes were bright with excitement, and Henri clapped gleefully and hung onto Jim's leg. They'd strung the dining room with crepe paper streamers and balloons and set the table with a brightly colored paper tablecloth and matching paper plates and napkins. Lillie and Henri jumped up and down excitedly in front of Jim. He noticed a couple of crude handmade cards in the center of the table.

Carol pumped her palms up and down in front of the kids. "Easy, guys. We can hear you, and we know you're excited, but Daddy is still hurting. Remember that talk we had about being quiet and gentle for a few days?" Carol said, her brown eyes serious and reflective.

Lillie's face fell, and her smile disappeared. Seeing a disaster brewing, Jim intervened. He knelt in front of Lillie and Henri, gathered them both in his good arm and placed a kiss on each one's head. "I can't believe you remembered my birthday, and I can't wait to have a piece of that cake."

Lillie turned and looked up at Carol. "See, I told you Bapa would be excited. Your cake has a big fish on it, and wait til you open your presents!"

Carol smiled. "Right again, Miss Lillie. Come on. Let's get washed up for supper."

She escorted the children down the hall to the bathroom as Jim wandered into the living room. The strap from his sling bit uncomfortably into his neck, and he tried to adjust it, but it didn't help. Being home felt foreign to him, but he knew he was still circling the airport and hadn't landed yet. Hoping the dizziness would diminish, he sat down in the swoopy black chair and pulled the lever, which popped his legs into the air. As he gingerly leaned back into the cushioning comfort, his heart swelled at the sounds of normalcy—Lillie and Henri's chatter, Carol giving orders, the unfettered laughter that had been missing these last weeks. He closed his eyes and murmured a prayer of gratitude.

Outside, dusk descended, flooding the trees and lawn with a rosy hue. In the last few weeks, the greenery in the backyard had begun shedding, and soon, in a month or so, Jim knew the trees would be bare, and cooler weather would prevail.

After the birthday hoopla was over, Carol corralled the kids for baths and bedtime routines. Once they were in their pajamas, Jim read to them softly in his deep baritone voice, and the tension and uncertainty of the last few weeks seemed to untangle. Walking down the hall after tucking them into their beds, he overheard Carol on the phone in the living room.

"… and it's so good to be back home."

Jim strolled to the kitchen for a second piece of birthday cake. Leaning against the counter, he listened to snippets of Carol's conversation. His shoulder was beginning to throb, and he opened and closed his clenched fist.

"It's just part of the job, Viv," Carol was saying. More listening, then, "I'll tell him, but it might not do much good."

After she hung up, she came into the kitchen and began making their evening tea.

"Raspberry okay?" she asked.

"Sure, that's fine. Is Vivian trying to get me to come to counseling?"

"Actually, no. She knows you'll get counseling with the department. But she is quite concerned about Sara. She thinks this whole kidnapping incident could result in some serious issues for her, and she's offering her services if we think Sara might benefit." Carol took their tea mugs from the cupboard, spooned a teaspoon of honey in each mug with a tea bag, and then poured the boiling water over the concoction.

"Well, that's up to Sara, honey. She's an adult, and she can make her own decisions," Jim said dryly, watching Carol fuss over the tea. He hated these discussions because he knew that, fundamentally, his daughter's life had changed forever. There was little he could do as a father to restore her confidence and security. He wasn't sure what would give her back her enjoyment and purpose in life.

"I know that, Jim, but she might need a nudge to get started. It's awfully easy to just keep saying you're fine when people ask and then still experience a lot of anxiety and angst and not know what to do about it. Our Midwestern sensibilities tell us to be tough and slog on until we get through it, but I know after my sexual assault, without Viv's help, I might still be wallowing in it. Your sense of security and safety goes out the window after an incident like this, Jim. Believe me," she finished. "I know." Carrying the tea and some slices of banana bread out to the living room, Jim followed her as she continued speaking over her shoulder. "Besides, Sara's my friend; she's one of the best people I know, and I love her."

"I know you've gotten close to her, and I'm glad about that. She misses her mom more than she'll ever admit, and you've filled a void in her life that Margie left. Still, let's just keep a handle on it and see what happens," Jim counseled. He sipped his tea and took his pain medication. His cell phone buzzed in his jean pocket. He set his mug down and pulled out his phone.

"Higgins."

"Jim. Davy here. I'm over on 1378 Cass Street watching Heather Lovstad's house burn up."

"What? How does this stuff keep happening?" Jim said loudly, sitting up suddenly and grimacing. Carol looked up, alarmed at the tone in Jim's voice, a wash of anxiety reflected on her face.

"We'll find out as soon as we can get in there. It could be intentional to get rid of the evidence; we're not sure yet. It's not a total loss, but it's a huge mess, and the warrant to look for physical evidence tied to the three murders probably won't turn up anything. It literally went up in smoke."

"I can't believe this," Jim said disgustedly. "Are we ever going to get a break in this case?"

"Our breaks are rapidly diminishing, my friend," Davy said. "On a brighter note, Paul and Sam are here, and as soon as they can safely enter the house, they're going to go over everything with a fine-toothed comb."

"That won't be until tomorrow, if then, but keep me in the loop," Jim said.

Davy clicked off, and Jim laid his phone down.

"What now?" Carol asked.

"The evidence we might have found in the Lovstad case probably just went up in smoke." Jim explained what had happened.

"Well, it's not your concern right now. You need to get into bed. You're starting to look a little pale." Carol took his mug, walked the tea things to the kitchen, and grabbed his hand. "Come on, big guy. You need some serious rest."

They walked into the bedroom, and Carol turned on the bedside lamp. She slowly and carefully helped Jim undress and slip on a pair of pajama bottoms. She laid back the sheets and carefully propped pillows around him until he seemed comfortable. Then she slipped on her nightie and shut off the light. When she crawled into bed, Jim reached for her. She snuggled up against him, enjoying the feel of his skin on hers.

"You know, you scared the liver out of me," she said quietly in the darkness. Jim could feel her shaking, and he grabbed her hand and kissed it.

"I'm sorry, babe. It's a hazard of my profession," he said.

"I thought about how I would raise Henri and Lillie without you. And I just couldn't imagine my life without you by my side," she said. By now, she was crying softly, partly from relief and partly from reliving the fear she felt in the waiting room when Jim was in surgery, "Promise me you won't leave me, Jim."

"You know that's a promise I don't have the right to make. Only God knows when our time on earth is over," Jim said. He rolled toward her, grimacing as he moved. "But I will tell you one thing that won't change. I'll always love you. And if I was in better shape, we could be doing something a whole lot more interesting than crying on a pillow."

Carol smiled weakly, took Jim's face in her hands, and kissed him tenderly. "Leave it to a guy to reduce a woman's anxiety to the need for sex."

"Do I know women, or do I know women?"

"Shh. Go to sleep before you get yourself in real trouble," Carol chuckled.

63

SUNDAY, SEPTEMBER 22

"**I** can't believe you burned up my house! Are you a flamin' idiot?" Heather shouted as she threw a pillow toward Dale. He was sprawled on the bed in his home on 14th Street, trying to convince Heather to settle down so they could have sex. It wasn't working.

"Listen! I had to create a diversion of some kind. Higgins was getting uncomfortably close to figuring out some stuff, and I had no choice," he whined, his hair disheveled, clumps sticking out from his head.

"Why didn't you burn down your own house? Why'd you have to use mine? I loved my house, and now it's ruined!" She swore passionately, then began crying, huge noisy sobs that shook her whole body. Everything was unraveling, and she had no idea where the two of them would end up. She stood in the middle of the bedroom weeping, her fists clenched at her side.

Dale climbed out of bed and approached her cautiously like one might approach a rabid dog. He stood in front of her, and when she didn't hit him, he decided it was safe to attempt a hug. Mistake. She roughly pushed him away.

"Get away from me, you housewrecker! I don't know why I stick with you," she said with a vehement hoarseness. "You're nothing but a loser!"

"Baby, listen! I'm sorry. You've got good insurance, and everything will be covered. Look at it this way. If you want to make any changes, now's as good a time as any," he said, leaning down to look into her eyes. "Look at the bright side of things, for once."

"The bright side! You are unbelievable! You're like a prognosticator of bad news. Being around you is like being around the devil himself," she said, but the wind was going out of her sails. She stepped around him and sat on the edge of the bed.

A good sign, he thought. *Easy does it. Don't piss her off any more than she already is.*

He reached for her hand, and she didn't pull away. "I'm sorry, baby, but the fire is going to give us some time to make another plan. Believe me. It will work. Higgins is shot up and off the case sitting on his sorry ass, recuperating at home. Now we can work on distracting those other bozos and make a plan to get out of here."

Heather looked over at him, and for once, he truly felt sorry for her.

"You'll see, baby. Everything's going to work out," he said tenderly.

"Promise?" she asked timidly, like a little child.

"Promise," he said, leaning over to kiss her.

"Prove it, big guy," Heather said huskily.

"My pleasure," he said, rolling her back on the mattress.

It was nine-thirty on Sunday morning. Sam and Paul stood inside the small Cape Cod-style bungalow on Cass Street that belonged to Heather Lovstad, scrutinizing the damage from the fire on Saturday night. Their eyes drifted from the blackened wallpaper in the living room to the scorched sofa and armchair to the water-soaked carpet that squished beneath their feet. Heather was still missing. Their last hope of finding evidence that connected her to the deaths of three men in a forty-year-old murder case seemed to have literally gone up in smoke. The fire department had loaded up their equipment in the early morning hours on Sunday. Now the La Crosse fire chief and arson officials from the State of Wisconsin were poking around the house, inspecting burn patterns and hot spots in a grim effort to determine the source and cause of the fire.

"Any hint at what caused the fire?" Sam asked one of the officials moving through the living room.

The burly man looked out from beneath his plastic face mask on his huge red helmet. "Looks like some kind of Molotov cocktail that came through the front window. Whatever it was worked." He shrugged and walked off into the depths of the kitchen.

"Well, we better get started," Paul said unceremoniously, holding the limp search warrant. "Where do you want to look first?" He snapped a mask over his nostrils and mouth and handed another one to Sam.

"You take the bedroom. I'll go to work in the den where the computer is. Those two rooms have the least amount of smoke damage," Sam said, trudging toward the hallway. "If we find anything, we'll probably find it there."

It wasn't until well after eleven o'clock in the morning that Paul came across a small greeting card box buried on the upper shelf of the bedroom closet behind a pile of sweaters. The edges were frayed and worn, and the picture on the top of the box had faded with time. Paul removed the stiff rubber band around the box and began shuffling through its contents. The photos at the top of the collection were of family events—Heather with her parents and brother at birthday parties and Christmas celebrations, seemingly innocuous records of innocent family gatherings and happy vacations. However, toward the bottom of the box, a photo caught Paul's attention. He stopped shuffling the contents and inspected the image before him.

In the photo, Heather stood ramrod straight, flanked on each side by Howard Lake and Dan Stern. Her face seemed cut from gray paper, her eyes like pieces of black coal. Her hands were clenched at her sides, and her body was stiff with latent aggression. The two cohorts who accompanied her leered at the camera as if they had some hidden secret, lewd grins pasted on their faces. Their expressions suggested an agreement of purpose and a complicity in evildoing that made Paul sick to his stomach. A chill prickled his spine. He got up and walked into the den, where Sam clicked through emails and documents on Heather's computer.

"Sam. Take a look at this," he said, thrusting the photo at him.

Sam took the photo and ran his thumb across the surface, removing particles of dust. "Huh. Heather claimed she'd never met Dan Stern. Guess that was a lie." He looked closer, his eyes squinting at the image on the paper. "Did you notice that necklace? Is that the one that was found at the murder scene? It sure looks like it."

Paul hovered over Sam's shoulder and reached for the photo again. "Gimme that," Paul said. Sam handed the photo to him. "Jeez. It's hard to tell, but it does look similar, doesn't it?"

"Let's run it over to the department and get Lucy to look at it. Maybe enlarge it so we can see more of the detail," Sam suggested.

"Nothing will get done today, but I'll bag it and take it over when we're finished here. We probably won't hear anything until late tomorrow," Paul said.

"Ask them to put a rush on it," Sam said.

"Yeah, right. Since when has anything with rush stamped on it actually been processed quickly?"

"I hear ya," Sam said. "Probably won't happen, but it's worth a try."

The two detectives continued wading through bags, boxes, drawers, computer files and emails, garbage in the wastebaskets and garbage in cans in the garage. Finally, at four o'clock, tired and stinking of smoke, they hung it up and bagged the mysterious photo. It was the only solid piece of circumstantial evidence that might link

Heather to the murders of Howard Lake, Dan Stern, and the murder of her father, Sylvester Kratt.

"You found a photo?" Jim said. "Of what?" Carol stood next to him, listening to the conversation, gauging the subject matter from Jim's responses.

"You need me to come in and have a look?" Jim asked. Carol shook her head in the negative, wagged her index finger, and mouthed, "No way." Jim scratched his eyebrow with his thumb and gave Carol a frown. He continued listening. Finally, he straightened his shoulders, grunted with discomfort, and said, "Yeah, that'll be great 'cause I'm hurtin'. We'll be home. Then I won't have to argue with Carol about leaving the house."

"You got that right, buddy," Carol whispered under her breath.

Half an hour later, Sam rolled into the driveway on Chipmunk Coulee Road in his Jeep. Lillie was pulling Henri up and down the paved driveway in his little Radio Flyer wagon. Sam hopped out of the Jeep, fist-bumped Lillie and Henri, walked to the front door, and was met by Carol, who hugged him and graciously invited him in. Crooking her finger at Sam, she began walking through the house, leading him to the porch that overlooked the backyard terrace.

"Jim's out here on the porch," Carol said as she walked through the living room. "Can I get you something to drink?"

"No, thanks. I'm fine," Sam said.

The sunshine was radiant—a glorious Indian summer day—and the leaves from the trees tumbled across the lawn with each gust of wind. Somewhere a cardinal whistled his cheerful song, and another answered. Jim breathed deeply of the musky autumn scents and stretched his legs along the chaise lounge, a pillow propped behind his back and under his sling.

"Hey, come on in, Sam," Jim said when he appeared at the patio door. "Sit down. What's up?"

Sam sat down and pulled the photo from his pocket in his suit coat. He handed it to Jim, then watched his face carefully.

"Well, it's definitely Stern and Lake," Jim said. "I knew she was lying about knowing Stern. It always makes it difficult to tell what the truth is when lies are mixed in. A lot of people are good at it. Heather knows Stern and Lake. Now what? What're you going to do next?"

"We need to find Heather," Sam said resolutely.

"That may be harder than you think but start with Pritchert. Roust him out of his lair. Rattle his cage. Get in his face because I can almost guarantee he's involved with her in this whole mess somehow, and he probably knows where she is. I got the distinct impression he would go to great lengths to ensure that Heather remains loyal to him."

Sam's brow crinkled. "What makes you think that?"

"They're in love or some kind of sexual tryst," Jim said as if it were fact. Then he began firing questions at Sam. "Remember how protective he was of her? Where would they hide out? Did you find out whether Pritchert has other property where she could stay? What about his marriage?"

Sam held up his hands. "Whoa, Chief! The only thing I know about Pritchert is that he's not married. The rest is up for grabs, but we'll get on all that tomorrow." There was an uncomfortable pause. Sam studied Jim's tanned face noticing the extra lines around his eyes and the pinched wrinkles at the corners of his mouth. Despite his interest in these latest developments in the case, he could see a bone-weary exhaustion just below the facial expression, like a deep and painful bruise.

"How're you doing, Chief? Everybody at the office downtown is wondering." Sam shifted in his chair, stretched out his legs in front of him, and crossed his ankles.

"Everybody? Really, Sam?" Jim gave a half-hearted chuckle. "I doubt that. But to answer your question, I'm stiff and sore, but it's really nothing compared to what could have happened. Thanks to you and Paul, Sara and I are still here."

Sam blushed with embarrassment. "How is Sara? She gonna be okay?"

Jim's eyes clouded with worry. "We don't know. She's very withdrawn. She's struggling, but we just don't know how exactly, and she can't seem to verbalize it yet. Father Knight has been supporting her, giving her extra time off from her teaching job, and we're trying to give her some space to work out the kinks, but that's not easy. Carol's been good for her. We're hoping that with time, she'll turn it around and get back to normal."

"I don't know about that, Chief. That might be a little too optimistic. You may have to accept that this is your new normal for a while. Recovery is a long road. I know. I've been there with Lez. Still am, for that matter."

"Well, then, I guess I'll have to lean on you, won't I?" Jim's eyes softened with emotion, and he looked away into the trees in the backyard. "I just feel so damned useless."

"Been there, too. I'd be honored if you'd count on me. Truly I would, Chief."

Carol interrupted them, stepping into the porch carrying a sweating pitcher of iced tea. She poured a tall glass of sweet tea with crushed ice and a lemon slice for Sam and Jim. Then she left quietly, sensing she was intruding.

"Did you uncover anything about Stern when you guys went to Lake City?" Jim asked.

"Paul went to the Lake City Police Department and read the report on Stern's death out on the lake and the interviews of witnesses who'd been on the lake and at the bar that afternoon. Then we visited the Hideaway Bar, where Stern was last seen before he went out on Lake Pepin. Nobody remembers much about that afternoon. The bartender who worked that day has since moved to the Twin Cities. Paul finally got his number and tried to call him but got no answer. He's going to try again tomorrow. Other than that, we haven't made much progress. Truthfully, it seems like a dead end."

"Keep digging. We're gathering some decent evidence. Who knows where it'll lead," Jim said.

Sam stood and stretched his arms to the ceiling, chugged the rest of his iced tea, and headed for the door. As he left, he turned and said to Jim, "You rest. Try to behave. I'll talk to you later."

"Thanks for stopping."

64

MONDAY, SEPTEMBER 23

Sara Higgins stood in her empty classroom, waiting for her rambunctious fifth graders to begin arriving. She desperately wanted to run away and hide somewhere, but her sense of duty to her students overrode her own needs. Outside, a gust of wind blew leaves against the large windows that faced the south. A bright yellow school bus pulled into the school parking lot. In the distance beyond the buildings of the tiny town, the Mississippi River sparkled brightly in the morning sun, and an eagle soared against a brilliant blue sky, the updrafts rising off the bluffs above the sleepy village.

Despite Father Jerome's encouragement, she was still apprehensive about her return to the classroom. Nothing was the same. She knew her world had shifted in a way she couldn't explain. The whole abduction experience had cracked the foundation of her worldview, and now events were divided along a line of "Before the Abduction" and "After the Abduction." That sounded simplistic to everyone except those who had lived through a similar experience—like Carol. She got it in a way no one else did.

Tapping at her door startled her. She turned and saw Father Jerome standing in the doorway, his hands in his pockets.

"Sorry. Didn't mean to scare you. Anything I can do for you this morning?" he asked. Sara noticed his deep brown eyes and kinky dark hair. He had a compact, dense body and a winsome personality that had won the affection and admiration of the entire parish at St. Ignatius. He was dressed casually in blue jeans and a sky-blue shirt with his Roman collar underneath.

"I hope I'm ready for this," Sara said, her eyes clouding with anxiety. "I'm not feeling real confident about my ability to deal with these little squirrels right now."

Father Jerome walked into the room and plopped his haunches on the corner of a student's desk and carefully folded his hands across his lap. He felt waves of apprehension rolling off her.

"Listen, if you get to a point today when you need to leave, just call my office, and I'll come and fill in for you," he suggested. "And if you decide you just can't do this right now and you need to take a leave of absence, I have some other options, so please let me know."

"Really? You'd do that for me?"

"Absolutely. Don't be shy. Just call me."

"You don't know how much that means to me. Thanks," Sara said, her eyes soft with tears. "I just feel so jumpy and nervous, like the first day of school when I stood in front of my classroom for the first time."

"That's totally understandable. Don't apologize for it. I'm here to help in whatever way I can. Just let me know."

"Thanks, Father."

"Please—call me Jerome."

"Oh, I couldn't." She noticed the disappointment on his face. She hurried on. "But you've been so good to me through all of this," she said. Her eyes locked with his. "I couldn't have a better friend." She smiled shyly.

He stood up and walked over to her. Grabbing her hand, he gently held it in his large one. "You didn't deserve this, nor did you ask for it. You survived it. God will help you understand this experience so that you can help others who've suffered as you have. I'm praying for you. I want you to remember that." His warm brown eyes seemed to envelop her, and Sara found her racing heart calming and her resolve strengthening.

"That is so unbelievably kind. It means so much to me."

And then Father Jerome did something that totally surprised her. He leaned over and very softly kissed her cheek. He looked deep into her eyes, smiled, turned around, and walked out of her classroom.

Sara stood stock still, and after a moment, she touched her cheek tentatively, wondering what had just happened between her and Father Jerome.

Later that morning, Paul was seated at his desk, the case file folders heaped in lopsided piles on the floor. Papers spewed out of them, and the mess surrounding his desk looked as if a wind storm had blown through the window scattering his work in every direction. He'd spent the last two hours reviewing each case, starting with the Yelski abduction and then the Kratt strangulation, trying to uncover some tidbit of relevance in a mountain of seemingly irrelevant information. Nothing they'd uncovered seemed important enough to shed new light on any aspect of the cases.

"This is hopeless," he said to himself. Maybe Pritchert had killed Kratt. He tipped his head at that new possibility, but then in frustration, he threw his pencil down in disgust and leaned back in his chair, hoisting his legs up on the top of his desk, crossing his ankles.

His phone buzzed. He groaned and picked it up, checking caller ID. "No rest for the wicked," he whispered. "Saner," he said into the phone.

"Hey. This is Tip Lawson—the former bartender at the Hideaway in Lake City. I got your text."

Paul sat up abruptly, shifted his legs underneath the desk, and leaned his elbows on the blotter. "Yeah, do you have something for me?"

"Well, that's why I called. I might. You sent me a picture of this Heather chick. But she was never in the bar that day, at least not when I was on duty. But there was a guy with Stern for awhile that afternoon. They sat together in a booth, and both of them were drinking pretty heavily, and they were having a serious discussion."

"Did you know this guy with Stern?"

"No, I didn't catch his name, but he stood out from the rest of the bar crowd."

"In what way?" Paul asked.

"Well, the way he dressed, for starters. This guy was in a blue-collar bar, but his clothes were anything but blue-collar. He wore a fancy long-sleeved dress shirt with an expensive tie and ironed blue jeans. And he wore gold cufflinks. Who wears cufflinks with jeans?"

"You said ironed blue jeans?"

"Yeah. I mean, there wasn't a wrinkle in them. It literally looked like the guy spent time ironing them, and he wore those tasseled loafers. I mean, they were fancy and spit-polished. You could've seen your bare ass in them."

"Okay. What else was different?"

"Well, I got the impression he was some kind of white-collar professional. He was jabbing his finger on the tabletop, and Stern couldn't get a word in edgewise. He seemed really pissed off at him for some reason. You know, leaning forward, getting in his face, threatening him. Now I'm no psychologist, but to me, it looked like he was trying to intimidate Stern. Every time I came to the table with their drinks, the conversation stopped and … well, there just seemed to be a lot of tension between them."

"How'd you remember all this? Seems like a lot of detail to recall after five years?" Paul asked.

"I reviewed it. It's on the surveillance tape from the bar."

Paul's stomach turned over. "What surveillance tape?"

"Well, Hideaway had a number of armed robberies a few months before Stern's death, and the owner installed a couple surveillance cameras as a deterrent. Seemed to work. They never had another robbery after the cameras were installed."

"But the owner didn't keep every tape, did he?"

"No, but when Stern drowned under suspicious circumstances, I dug through the tapes that were there and found the one that was recorded on the day of his death. My boss said I could keep it."

"You're telling me you still have it?"

"Shit, yeah. That's why I'm callin' you. When do you wanna see it?"

"This afternoon. Can we meet at Lake City?"

"Yeah, I guess so. It's my day off, but I live in Woodbury, so I can be there in an hour."

"How's one-thirty sound?"

"Sounds good. The Hideaway?"

"I'll be there," Paul said. "Oh, one more thing."

"Yeah, what's that?"

"You're in the wrong profession. Ever think about being a detective?"

65

By noon, Paul and Sam were traveling down U.S. Hwy. 61 heading northwest to Lake City, Minnesota, a scenic route that went through a string of small towns scattered along the western shore of the Mississippi River on the border between Wisconsin and Minnesota.

The day was overcast, and after fifteen minutes of driving, lightning flashed in the low-lying inky clouds, and thunder rumbled ominously. Soon the rain was pounding the windshield of Paul's pickup, coming in sheets that blew across the highway and, at times, obliterated a view of the river. Through occasional breaks in the rain, Sam could see irregularly shaped green islands floating in the waterway like pea pods in brown soup.

Paul slowed the truck as the windshield wipers slapped back and forth. The rain lashed the trees and scattered brown leaves across the surface of the blacktop road. Lake City came into view. The town was situated below the bluffs on a widening of the Mississippi River called Lake Pepin, a naturally occurring lake formed by the backup of water due to the sluggish current of the river and sedimentary deposits from the Chippewa River delta.

Paul passed the harbor filled with sailboats, their masts jabbing the sky like a bunch of toothpicks. The main street was lined with red brick storefronts and clapboard houses, and the steeple of city hall poked an angry finger at the sky. At the edge of town, the Hideaway Bar parking lot was almost empty. Only a few cars and trucks sat in it.

Paul parked the truck, and they made a run for the bar in the pouring rain. The interior of the Hideaway was typically dark, musty with the smell of stale beer and peanut shells, and decorated with neon beer signs and sports memorabilia. Along one side of the bar were several upholstered booths, and a pool table sat in a room toward the back. Paul asked the bartender if Lawson was there, and he chinned toward a booth without saying a word.

Tip Lawson had the burly make-up of a lumberjack. He was a compact man with a thick chest and hefty biceps. His dark mustache was flecked with gray, and it drooped beyond his full lips. Dark hair gathered in a long ponytail that hung down his back. He looked up expectantly when Paul and Sam approached the booth and slid into the seat opposite him.

"Quite a downpour," Lawson commented laconically.

"Yeah, it's a frog strangler," Sam said, holding out his hand and exchanging a greeting and handshake with Lawson as he brushed the wet drops from his shirt.

"You don't look old enough to be a detective," Lawson said to Sam with a snicker.

"I might look like a teenager, but it has its advantages when I go undercover," Sam said, lifting his eyes to meet Lawson's. "Dealers like to get the young ones hooked early—I try to catch them before they get their hooks in them."

"So, you've got the surveillance tape with you?" Paul asked, getting to the reason for the trip.

Lawson reached into his leather jacket pocket and produced the small disc. "It's from a closed circuit camera, and the images are pretty clear, although there's no audio."

"Anything else we should know?" Sam asked.

Lawson leaned forward and placed his elbows on the table. His beefy face took on a serious cast, and a deep furrow broke out between his heavy eyebrows.

"Toward the end of the tape, I thought I saw this guy make a movement that looked like he dropped something in Stern's drink. You know—some kind of date rape drug—like that. The gesture looked too planned to be casual. You might want to watch for that. Of course, I could be imagining things. When somebody dies under suspicious circumstances, you can find your logical reasoning running away with your imagination, and you start thinking weird thoughts."

"Don't worry about it. We'll go over this with a fine-toothed comb. If he fed Stern a drug, we'll find the point on the tape where that happened if it's there," Paul reassured him.

They talked awhile more until Sam and Paul made their excuses, got up from the booth, and walked to the parking lot, leaving Lawson sipping on his beer.

"Let's hope this tape gives us some kind of direction," Paul muttered as he drove back to La Crosse along the river in the steady rain.

"When we get back, I'm going downtown to talk to Pritchert and rattle his cage," Sam said. "You need to come with me and give me your impressions of the guy. And I might need your help if he decides to shoot me."

"Oh, boy," Paul said, rolling his eyes.

Back at the law enforcement center, Sam and Paul watched the surveillance video again.

"It's Pritchert all right," Sam said, squinting as he watched the two men arguing on the tape. "He's up to his eyeballs in Stern's suspicious death."

"Wait. Look at this section again," Paul said, rewinding the tape and hitting the play button. "I think this is where Lawson saw him slip the drugs into Stern's drink." They watched as Pritchert leaned over the table, poking his finger at Stern, distracting him, while his other hand passed briefly over his glass. His finger loosened slightly for a moment above the drink.

"There. Right there. Did you see it?" Paul asked, hitting the rewind button again.

"Yeah. He put something in his drink," said Sam, nodding his head. "Come on, let's go down to the law office and talk to him."

Sam stood abruptly, reached for his coat hanging on the back of his chair, and walked toward the door. Paul followed closely behind.

"We'll take my Jeep," Sam said. "Let's pump this guy and see what happens."

The law office on Pearl Street was still buzzing with activity even at four-thirty when Sam and Paul walked through the reception area and were shown into the office of Dale Pritchert. He was sitting at a massive oak desk piled with legal files and a couple of thick impressive volumes on corporate law. His tie hung limply around his neck, and his sleeves rolled to the elbows. He ran his hand through his gray-flecked hair and looked up with a sullen expression, his eyes hooded with suspicion.

"Afternoon, Mr. Pritchert," Sam said, lifting his hand in a slight wave. "This is Detective Paul Saner. We'd like to ask you a few questions." Sam stared at him, not breaking the eye contact. *Two can play this game, buddy,* he thought.

What is it that you're fishing for now, detective?" Pritchert asked, his lips turning upward in a slight smirk. "Why are you here? Again?"

"Do you know a Dan Stern?" Paul asked. He was in no mood for Pritchert's self-righteous attitude; he was tired, and his leg was aching. *Old wounds heal slowly,* he thought.

"Dan Stern?" Pritchert hesitated slightly, then recovered. "Well, I had a client named Dan Stern about two years ago. He's the manager of a credit union here in town. But somehow, I don't think that's who you're referring to, is it?" he asked.

"No. That's not the man," Sam answered. "This Dan Stern was an acquaintance of Heather Lovstad—maybe ten years ago or more. We know this because we found a photo in Heather's home that shows her with Dan Stern and another man named Howard Lake. It seems Stern drowned in Lake Pepin five years ago under suspicious circumstances. Do you know anything about that?"

"I don't understand what you think that has to do with me?" Pritchert sneered, his irritation building. He waved his hand in the air, seemingly unconcerned by the detective's pointed questions.

"We understand that Heather works in your office, and you have a close relationship with her," Paul stated. Pritchert blew air out his nose in a noisy show of arrogance. "If Heather knows Dan Stern," Paul continued, "then it's entirely conceivable that you know him, too. What did Stern do to Heather?"

Pritchert's lips parted in a conceited smile as he leaned back in his chair. "You people just never give up, do you?"

Paul continued, unfazed by Pritchert's rebuffs. "We've uncovered a surveillance tape that shows you with Stern at the Hideaway Bar in Lake City on the day of his death. We believe you put a drug in his drink, and as a consequence, Stern went out on his boat and fell overboard, drowning." Paul stopped speaking. Then after several moments of silence, he asked, "Tell us why it was so crucial for Dan Stern to be wiped out. What did he know that was such a threat to you? Or to Heather?"

"This is ludicrous! It's absolute total bullshit!" Pritchert snarled, lunging forward in his chair, bringing his fist down on the desk. "I've repeatedly told you people that my relationship with Heather is purely professional. And I repeat—I don't know this Stern guy! I'd be very interested in seeing this so-called surveillance tape!"

By now, Pritchert's voice had become loud, and Paul was sure it was drifting down the hallway. But he continued ranting.

"I know the tactics you people use to build a case, and I'm not going to be railroaded into becoming your so-called prime suspect! It sounds like the guy was a drunk and stupidly went out on a boat on a lake and fell overboard while he was plastered. He drowned. Duh. Are you surprised? Stuff like this happens all the time. I oughta know. I've represented families who've lost loved ones over some stupid accident that was totally preventable, and they pay me big bucks to find someone else to blame." By now, Pritchert had risen from his chair and stood, crossing his arms over his chest.

"You're right," Paul said calmly, nodding his head in agreement. "Idiots drink and then drive their cars, and people jump in a lake and swim and boat when they're totally hammered. Happens a lot. But that's not what happened to Stern. Yes, his blood alcohol level was .34—more than twice the legal limit—but an abnormally large amount of Versed was found in his bloodstream," Paul explained. "Versed that was put in his drink by you. But what I'm really curious about is what you two were discussing at the table in the bar. From the tape, you seem to be arguing intensely about something. What was it?"

"I have never been to Lake City. I don't know Dan Stern. And I will not continue this charade unless I have my lawyer present," Pritchert said emphatically.

"Fine. Call him. And you will come downtown to the law enforcement center for further questioning," Paul said. "You may have a lawyer present at the interrogation. That is your privilege."

Pritchert reached for his phone and turned away from Paul and Sam, staring out the window that faced the alley. The two detectives exchanged a glance. Sam rolled his eyes. Pritchert continued in a hushed conversation and then hung up. Turning back to Sam and Paul, he said, "All right. I've arranged for my lawyer to meet me at the law enforcement center at five o'clock, which is half an hour from now. Is that satisfactory?" Pritchert asked icily.

"No. We'll be escorting you to the center," Sam said brusquely.

"What? You don't trust me to drive six blocks? What do you think I'm going to do?" Pritchert whined.

"It's not negotiable," Sam said firmly. "You ready?" His eyebrows arched over his hazel eyes.

Pritchert's shoulders slumped. He reached for his suit jacket hanging on the back of his chair. "Fine. Let's go then," he snapped, resigned to the plan.

66

DeDe Deverioux and Leslie Birkstein were in traffic near the law enforcement center on Vine and were returning from a visit to the Dairyland Power corporate office. What they found was disheartening despite the fact that employee records existed for the three men they believed were involved in the abduction and murder of Christina Yelski.

"Too bad there wasn't a clearer record of their day-to-day activity as linemen," Leslie complained. "We know the general area where they worked, but you can't accuse someone of murder with those puny facts." Leslie's forehead creased with a frown, and she pushed a blonde strand of hair away from her face.

"Nope. Won't fly. We're basically striking out at every turn," DeDe said.

The stormy afternoon weather had cleared off, and now the evening sky in the west was painted with a hint of rose red streaked with bright oranges in a dazzling swirl of color that stretched across the autumn sky. A flock of Canadian geese flapped northward, honking noisily. The aroma of hot oil from a nearby Dunkin' Donuts drifted into the partially opened passenger window, and DeDe's stomach growled in hunger.

"I'm so hungry, and that smell is so tempting," she said, rubbing her stomach.

"But you're not driving," Leslie said, grinning. She pointed west. "Pretty sky. How're the plans for the restaurant going?"

"Jude is in New Orleans as we speak. He got a great offer for the restaurant, and he's hoping to close and sign within the week. Then we can really start to build a life here," DeDe said.

"How do you feel about that?"

"Good, although it might have been better if we'd both experienced the winter season before we made any permanent decisions."

"Well, the best advice I can give you about winter in Wisconsin is to get out and enjoy it," Leslie commented. "The winter season can be beautiful, and the really cold, cold days are usually few and far between. You've got to get your survivor attitude adjusted, and then you'll be fine. Skiing, sledding, skating, pond hockey, building snowmen. There are a lot of activities to choose from. And having some indoor hobbies doesn't hurt, either. Besides, you just have to remember the Norwegian philosophy of life," Leslie said.

"Oh yeah? What's that?" DeDe asked, turning to look at Leslie, her brown eyes filled with curiosity.

"There is no bad weather—only bad clothing." Leslie chuckled softly when she noticed DeDe's sanguine expression.

"I'll remember that when we're freezing our butts off," she said. Suddenly she sat up straighter in her seat, a puzzled expression creasing her forehead. "Hey! Look up ahead. That isn't Heather Lovstad's Forester, is it?" she asked as she pointed at a dark green SUV about five spaces in front of Leslie's Prius. It was stopped at a red light on West Avenue.

Leslie craned her neck to see. "Looks like it. I'll try to get closer."

When the light changed, Leslie gunned the engine, and soon she was bumper to bumper with the Forester. A large woman was driving and seemed oblivious to Leslie's traffic maneuvers.

"Looks like Heather. Let me get next to her," she said as she abruptly pulled into the left lane of traffic and brought the Prius parallel with the Forester. The car behind her laid on the horn and flipped her the bird.

"Deal with it, bud!" she shouted as she looked in her rearview mirror and noticed the gesture. "If it's her, get ready for a ride. I'm going to follow her. See where she's headed. Confront her and take her in for questioning."

"It's her," DeDe said, "but she's never met us, so she won't realize we're following her as long as you don't make it too obvious."

"Good point." Leslie fell back a few cars and continued to follow Heather through the streets near the university. Traveling south, the Forester turned into the Kwik Trip parking lot on Mormon Coulee Road. Leslie drove past and turned onto a city street farther down the road. She did a quick U-turn. They sat and waited as Heather filled her car with gas. Fifteen minutes later, her Forester crested the viaduct bridge over the train tracks and continued traveling south on U.S. Hwy. 35 along the river.

While she was following her, Leslie speed-dialed Sam.

"You're where?" Sam asked, confused.

"Following Heather Lovstad down 35. We spotted her in traffic on West Avenue. We're gonna see where she's going," she told him.

"I already know where she's going."

"You do?"

Yeah. She's heading to Higgins' place. You need to get off the phone and call him. Warn him that she's coming," Sam said, with an edge of grit in his voice.

"Right. I'll stay in touch," Leslie said as she snapped her phone shut. She dialed Higgins.

"Higgins' residence. Jim speaking," the familiar baritone voice said.

"Lt. Higgins. Leslie here. DeDe and I are following Heather Lovstad down 35. She may be heading in your direction. You need to get Carol and the kids out of harm's way. We'll back you up, but we have no idea of her intentions. You copy?" she asked.

"Yep. Loud and clear. I'll handle my end. Don't let her know you're following her. There's a turnout about five hundred feet beyond my driveway, where you can park your car. Double back to my house on foot. Go through the backyard and come up into the screened-in porch. I'll try to keep her occupied out front. Get your vests on and be prepared to take her into custody if things go south. I'll do the same."

"Right. On our way, sir," Leslie said crisply. Somewhere in the back of her mind, visions of Wade Bennett, her former boyfriend, came back—haunting her, tormenting her, chasing her. Feelings of terror, panic, and confusion threatened to overwhelm her even though she knew he was sitting in the Boscobel state prison some sixty miles southeast of La Crosse.

DeDe touched Leslie's arm, and she jumped involuntarily. "Are you—?"

"No, but that's not the issue right now. Right now, our job is to be sure we have Higgins covered. You up for that?" she asked.

"Absolutely. Bring it on," DeDe said through gritted teeth.

The interrogation room on the first floor of the law enforcement center was stuffy with the odor of cigarette smoke and sweat. Without windows, it was impossible to air it out. Instead, Sam flicked on the switch of a floor fan sitting in a corner, then he reached over and turned on the video camera.

"The fan doesn't help much, does it?" Paul asked. Sam shook his head.

"Talk to management. They're in charge of facilities, and whoever designed this building had their head up their—"

There was a faint knock on the door, and a police officer accompanied Dale Pritchert and his lawyer into the small room. Suddenly it seemed overcrowded to the point of claustrophobia.

Paul leaned against the wall, his hands resting behind his back, his feet crossed casually in front of him. Sam, Pritchert, and his lawyer seated themselves on opposite sides of the table.

Sam recited the Miranda rights to Pritchert and formally began the interview. He leaned over and started the video camera.

"This is Detective Sam Birkstein interviewing Dale Pritchert on September 24. The time is 5:32 p.m. Detective Paul Saner and Gus Hanson, Mr. Pritchert's lawyer, are also in attendance. Mr. Pritchert, I am going to show you the videotape from the Hideaway Bar in Lake City, Minnesota. After you've viewed the tape, I'll have some questions for you," Sam said.

Sam began the tape, and as the scenario from the bar unfolded, Pritchert became pale and withdrawn. He seemed to shrink inside his chair, his shoulders turning inward until he resembled a turtle tucking his head inside his shell. When the tape was finished, Sam turned his attention back to Pritchert.

"Once again, Mr. Pritchert," Sam began, "I'm asking you what the content of your conversation was with Dan Stern in the video you just watched." Pritchert pulled his lips over his teeth in a grimace. Finally, he looked up and briefly shook his head as if chiding himself that he'd been caught red-handed. Lying to police. Not good. He sighed loudly and began to speak.

"Well, there's no denying the videotape. I'm a lawyer, and I know you can't argue with that. That is me in the video having a discussion with Dan Stern."

"And what was the content of your conversation with Mr. Stern?" asked Paul.

"We were discussing his most recent threatening attempts to blackmail Heather Lovstad," Pritchert said.

"What threats specifically?" Sam asked.

"Over the years, Stern had repeatedly threatened Heather to remain quiet about the abuse he performed against her when she was a teenager," Pritchert said flatly.

"Please categorize the abuse. Are we talkin' sexual, physical, emotional? What?" asked Sam.

Pritchert gritted his teeth, looked down at his lap, then lifted his eyes to meet Sam's. "Heather was repeatedly raped and sexually abused in other ways by Stern, her father, and another man named Howard Lake over a period of about two years when she was in high school. The abuse continued randomly until she came to La Crosse to attend WTC. That's when she was finally able to escape from the influence these jerks had on her. She still suffers from the effects of it to this day, as you can imagine. Being police officers, I'm sure you can understand that." Pritchert reported this as if he were reading it out of a newspaper.

"And what were you discussing with Stern in the video?" Paul asked. "Did you threaten him?"

"I wanted to rip out his throat—and other parts of his anatomy— but instead, I told him if he ever contacted Heather again, I would come after his sorry ass and report all his activities to the police, and he'd never see the light of day and freedom again."

Sam's mouth had gone dry. He conjured up the image of Leslie the day she'd been beaten to within an inch of her life by her sociopathic boyfriend. He felt the anger well in his chest.

"Why didn't you?" he asked.

Pritchert blinked, confused. "Why didn't I what?"

"Report the abuse," Sam said.

"Heather was no longer underage; she was legally an adult. She said it would ruin her reputation, and if I reported it, she would have nothing further to do with me."

"How did Stern react to your threats?" Paul asked, getting back to the tape.

"He didn't have much to say, actually. He didn't get a chance because I was so pissed off I kept interrupting him whenever he tried to respond. I did get a sense that he was extremely worried about my threat to expose his activities with Heather. At the very least, he'd be up for statutory rape and looking at a long prison term if he was convicted. And I intended to convict him, but that would only happen if Heather was willing to report his activities to the police and testify against him in court."

"Which she wasn't willing to do?" Paul asked.

"No. Despite my encouragement, she's continued to keep her dark past a secret which is her prerogative, I guess," Pritchert said.

"So, did you put Versad in Stern's drink?" Sam asked.

"Listen, by the time we finished our drinks and conversation, Stern was in pretty bad shape. In actuality, he was scared shitless. To answer your question, I don't know where the Versad came from. Unfortunately for Stern, he made a poor decision to go out on the lake in a boat, drunk as he was, and he drowned. End of story. What more can I say?" Pritchert looked up with an expression that could only be interpreted as duplicitous.

Sam knew that without physical proof of purchase of the Versad—a receipt or the actual drug found in Pritchert's possession—they had little to hold him. And after five years, there was virtually no chance that any solid evidence still existed. If further irregularities were found in the suicidal death of Howard Lake, they could bring Pritchert in again as a possible conspirator in his death, but until then, they'd have to let him go.

"Where were you Saturday evening between eight and nine o'clock?" Paul asked.

Pritchert hesitated, but Sam could see it was well-rehearsed. "Heather and I went out for a drink downtown, then came back to my house and watched a movie."

"Any witnesses who could testify to that?" Paul queried.

Pritchert reached into his jacket pocket and pulled out a slip of paper on which he scribbled a name and cell number. "Check it out. They were with us at the Four Seasons bar downtown from about eight to ten." Pritchert slid the paper across the table, and Sam nodded, noticing his manicured nails. *Self-righteous little prick,* he thought.

"Somehow, I don't think this is the end for you, sir. We may contact you again for another interview as our investigation continues," Paul said, his eyes hooded with disappointment.

Pritchert got up from his chair, straightened his limp tie, and walked from the interrogation room with his lawyer in tow. Sam slumped over the table, holding his head in his hands.

"I could have sworn we had him," he said dejectedly.

Paul slapped him on the back. "Well, we found out about Heather's past. And there certainly is plenty of motivation for murder in that scenario."

Sam's cell buzzed. As he listened, his eyes widened, and his back stiffened with anxiety. He spoke briefly and hung up.

"Who was that?" Paul asked.

"A lab tech. The necklace in the photo of Heather is the Yelski girl's necklace," Sam said in a hushed tone. "They're ninety percent positive it's the same one."

"Holy cow," Paul whispered.

Sam's phone buzzed again. As he listened, he stood up and pointed his index finger at Paul. "Okay, okay. We're right behind you."

"Now what?" Paul asked, his eyes wide with alarm. "Who was that?"

"Lez. Get your vest and gun. The girls are following Heather Lovstad. She's come out of hiding and is driving down 35. It looks like she might be heading for Higgins' place."

Sam hurried through the door and began jogging down the hall, his tie swinging from side to side. "Come on! We've got to get to Higgins' place before all hell breaks loose!"

67

Back on Chipmunk Coulee Road, Jim shut his cell and hurried to the screened-in porch overlooking the backyard where Carol and the kids were playing.

"Carol! Carol!" Jim hollered. She looked up from raking leaves, alarmed at the urgency in his voice.

"What?" What's wrong?" she yelled back.

"Come here," Jim said, waving her into the house.

Carol dropped her rake next to a huge pile of leaves and sprinted toward Jim. She ran up the flagstone steps and slid the screen door open.

"What's going on?" she said, her face anxious as she walked rapidly across the living room. Jim was standing in the dining room, and he held up a finger when she parked herself in front of him.

"Leslie and DeDe are following Heather Lovstad, and they believe she's heading our way," Jim told her. Carol's eyes widened, and she tipped her head toward the ceiling in disbelief.

"When is this going to end, Jim? Huh?" she asked, the frustration building in her voice.

"I think it's best if you take the kids and go to Culver's for ice cream or to Vivian's 'til we see where this is going," Jim said rapidly.

"I don't believe this!"

Jim laid his arm on her shoulder. "I'm sorry, honey, but we'll talk about it later. Can you get the kids and go? I'll feel better if you're out of harm's way. I really don't know what she's capable of at this point. We can't take any chances."

Carol laid her hand on Jim's chest. "This is not over. We *will* discuss this later." She turned and stormed through the house calling the kids. Five minutes later, they were heading down Chipmunk Coulee Road for destinations unknown. Jim breathed a sigh of relief as he watched them drive away.

He muttered to himself under his breath. He desperately hoped that Leslie was wrong, that she was overreacting, that all of this was a false alarm. But he knew the animosity he'd generated in Heather was real when he tried to uncover her secret life of abuse. Now it might be coming due. Thank God his family was gone and would not witness this confrontation if it came to that.

He tried to calm the fluttering in his stomach. Walking to the kitchen sink, he poured a glass of water and drank it down, but he still felt jumpy and nervous. Suddenly, a dark green Forester SUV wheeled into the driveway. Jim could see Heather Lovstad inside the car. The vehicle stopped, the engine went dead, and after a moment, Heather stepped out onto the pavement. Jim watched her as she took in the environment of his home. Then she walked to the front door.

Just as the doorbell rang, Jim noticed Leslie's blue Prius roar by the driveway. Heather didn't notice and seemed unaware that she'd been followed.

The doorbell chimed its five-note melody. *Easy, easy,* Jim thought as he walked calmly to the door and opened it.

"Hello, Lt. Higgins," Heather said somberly. "I have some things I want to discuss with you." She wore tight blue jeans and a loose-fitting, cable-knit green sweater. She was calmer than he'd ever remembered her from their past meetings. Jim wondered what had happened to make her disposition so non-threatening. *Don't be fooled. She's not finished with this whole charade yet,* he thought.

"I'd rather we talk at the law enforcement center, but since you've driven out here, please come in," Jim said. He stepped aside as Heather squeezed past him. She looked around, taking in the features of his home. Then her eyes fell on his bandaged shoulder, and she met his stare with an uncompromising hardness.

"Nice place you've got here," she said, walking into the dining room and staring at an oil painting hanging above the maple buffet. "Paid for, I'm sure. I suppose you heard about the fire at my house," she said, turning and waiting for Jim to invite her to sit down.

"Yes, I was sorry to hear about that."

"I also understand your two minions were in my home searching for something. Did they find what they were looking for?"

"Why don't we sit in the living room?" Jim suggested, stretching his arm in that direction. Heather eyed the sling around his neck again, walked ahead of him, and found a place on the blue velvet sofa. Jim sat in the black swoopy chair facing her. He waited a moment and then began his explanation.

"Detective Birkstein and Detective Saner found a photo of you with Howard Lake and Dan Stern when they searched your home. Could you explain how you knew them?"

Heather was a big-boned woman, but Jim marveled at how small she looked at this moment. She seemed to shrivel into the cushions of the couch. She looked at Jim, and he was taken aback by the bitterness reflected in them. Then as quick as a flash in time, her mood changed again. She was somewhere else now—in the past, back before she'd lost her innocence. In truth, Jim wasn't sure she was even aware of his presence. The change in her was remarkable. *She's not what she seems to be*, he thought.

"It started when I was a sophomore in high school. I'd come home from a basketball game, and my dad was playing cards with Howard and Dan. They were pretty drunk, and my mom was gone to her sister's in Waterloo, Iowa, so they pretty much had free rein."

Jim's stomach constricted with the agony of the confession he was sure Heather was going to tell him. How many times had he sat in an interrogation and listened to the anguished accounts of women who's been sexually exploited, raped, and beaten or intimidated into silence, ground into an existence of fear, self-loathing, and animus toward men by the actions of a family member or friend?

"They did despicable things to me that night, and it didn't end for almost two years."

Jim stayed silent, knowing any response he might express would be an inadequate commentary.

"I didn't kill Dan or Howard. But I thought when they died that I'd feel some kind of victory. Instead, I just felt empty—empty and used up like a piece of driftwood that washed up on shore."

Jim waited a few moments, and when Heather stayed silent, he forged ahead.

"Heather, in the photo of you with Dan and Howard, you're wearing a necklace. Where did that necklace come from?" Jim asked. His blue eyes searched her face.

Heather frowned in confusion. "Necklace?" she repeated as if she were waking from a dream.

"Yes, you were wearing a necklace in the photo. Where did you get it?"

Heather sighed, and after more silence through gritted teeth, she said, "My dad gave it to me and always wanted me to wear it. I hated that necklace." Her expression became dark, as if an inky cloud was passing through her. She sat up straighter, and her body became stiff with tension. Jim thought about an octopus who shoots the water around him full of black ink to hide from his enemies.

"Do you know where your dad got it?" Jim asked.

"No, not exactly, but I have a pretty good idea." Her voice had become small and pinched. "I think it was something that happened a long time ago."

"But did he ever tell you where he got the necklace?" Jim persisted. By now, Heather had leaned back on the couch and kicked her feet out in front of her in a surly posture that reminded Jim of a rebellious teenager.

"He never told me where he got it, but I assumed it was maybe my grandma's or something. But for some reason, the necklace made me uncomfortable in a way I can't really explain. Maybe it was the way my dad looked at me when I was wearing it. I don't know. I always wondered if it belonged to some other girl he had abused like he abused me."

Jim debated how much he should reveal to Heather about Kratt's possible involvement in the forty-year-old abduction and homicide of Christian Yelski. He paused, thinking, feeling a terrible sadness for Heather. "Have you ever heard of Christina Yelski?" he finally asked.

"Yeah, my dad used to talk about that sometimes. Wasn't she the teenager who disappeared from La Crosse in the seventies?"

"Yes, that's her. We discovered a number of newspaper clippings about the abduction in some of your dad's papers. We believe that whoever killed your father knew about the abduction as well. There were indications at the scene of his death that suggested the murderer had knowledge of your father's possible involvement."

"So?"

Her flippant answer riled Jim. He felt his anger building.

"Why are you here, Heather? What is it that you want from me?" Jim asked impatiently. If this was supposed to be a confession, it was stranger than fiction.

Heather gazed at Jim with an unnerving calmness. "How did you know I'd been abused? I've only told a couple of people about that in my entire life."

"Experience. I've talked with plenty of abuse victims in my career. You learn to pick up the signs. Your intense denial that your father had ever touched you inappropriately didn't sit right with me. Plus, your latent anger and rage against him were pretty obvious. I have two daughters, and my instincts as a father and a parent kicked in. Sexual abuse is always heartbreaking. The victims never deserve it.

I'm sorry you experienced that. It should never have happened."

By now, dusk was falling outside. Jim stood and walked toward the porch pushing open a few windows. A fresh breeze blew in the room, and the musky smell of decaying leaves and vegetation carried on the wind. His shoulder began to ache again, and he wished this whole scenario was over and finished.

Walking back to his chair, Jim sat down and faced Heather, who had begun to cry softly. "You know who killed your father, Heather. Why don't you come clean?"

"You don't know anything," she said brusquely.

"Oh, yes, I do. It wasn't until I reviewed my notes from my first interview with you yesterday that I realized you asked me about the second item found next to your father on the kitchen floor. But I never told you there were two items. So when you asked about the second item, I knew you were aware of what the killer had left at the scene." Jim's blue eyes burned with a kind of righteous anger.

But Heather's response was cut short by the sound of a vehicle screeching into the driveway. Startled, Jim rose quickly and walked through the dining room. An unfamiliar car was parked at an odd angle on the blacktop behind Heather's Forester. At the same moment, Paul and Sam blocked the driveway and jumped out. Jim swung the front door open and stepped out on the sidewalk. Heather stood frozen behind Jim, framed within the doorway, her eyes wide with shock and apprehension.

Dale Pritchert stood in the driveway, brandishing a pistol. He waved it at Jim in a kind of desperate, threatening gesture.

"Give it up, Pritchert. Put the pistol down. No one has to get hurt," Sam said in a calm, low voice. At the sight of the pistol, Jim felt his heart rate ramp up, and a chill ran down his spine.

"What did you tell him, Heather?" Pritchert asked. His eyes were wild with agitation. His hand shook violently as he gripped the gun.

"Nothing. We just talked. That's all—I swear it," Heather said.

Jim glanced at her. She was frightened and intimidated by

Pritchert's presence and the gun he was wildly waving in the air. Around the corner of the garage, Leslie and DeDe appeared, their pistols drawn, assuming the position.

The whole cavalry has shown up, he thought.

In the last few moments, the puzzle pieces began falling into place for Jim. He drilled his gaze on Pritchert.

"When did you decide to kill Kratt?" he asked Pritchert. "Why did you do it? Was it to free Heather from her abuser so you could finally have full sway over her? So you could have complete control over her life and her choices?" Jim said.

"No. No. That's not how it was!" Heather said loudly. She had moved from the doorway, and now she stood next to Jim. He looked at her sideways. "Well, how is it then, Heather? Why don't you tell us," Jim said. "We'd all like to hear the truth."

"Shut up, Heather! Don't say anything!" Pritchert warned her. "You've probably already screwed it up and said too much!"

"Put the gun down," Jim said, taking a step closer to Pritchert. He locked eyes with Sam, then shifted his gaze to Pritchert again. "Put the gun down and let's talk," he said again, keeping his voice low.

In every confrontation, there's a moment in time when things are in limbo, when things can de-escalate, and rational thoughts and reasoning return to the participants. It's also the moment when the powder keg can explode. This seemed to be the moment. Jim was desperately hoping that Pritchert would recognize the futility of his threats and give up this last-ditch effort to save himself.

Sam and Paul eased up behind Pritchert. In a quick movement, Sam lunged toward Pritchert's wrist and wrenched the gun from his hand. Leslie and DeDe rushed forward toward Jim. Pritchert crumpled, resting his hands on his knees. Heather rushed past Jim and stood in front of Pritchert. They exchanged a glance while Paul slipped cuffs around the lawyer's wrists. Leading him to Sam's Jeep, he sat mute in the back seat, staring into the evening sky.

"We'll interrogate him again downtown and hold him overnight on the charge of assaulting an officer of the law and reckless endangerment. Hopefully, by that time, he'll tell us what's been going on," Sam said, standing in front of Jim. "The lab confirmed that the necklace in the photo of Heather was the Yelski girl's. I'm betting when we compare the fingerprints on the back door of the Kratt home, they'll be a match to Pritchert. We'll go over Heather's car, too. If he used her car the night of the murder, there might be physical evidence somewhere in the vehicle."

Jim's shoulders dropped, and he grimaced in pain. "Don't count on it. He's a lawyer, after all. He's well aware of the importance of admissible evidence in a court of law. And if he killed Kratt, he was careful. Thanks, Sam."

Sam turned toward the car. "We'll have someone come and retrieve the vehicles," he said over his shoulder.

"Sounds good," Jim said as he watched Heather climb in the front seat of the Jeep.

"We had you covered the whole time, sir," DeDe said, watching Jim carefully.

"We'll handle everything downtown. Don't worry," Leslie said.

"You're the best, you two," Jim said, a dimple creasing his cheek. DeDe and Leslie began walking through the backyard to Leslie's Prius, which was parked down the road.

Although Jim was sorry he wouldn't be at the interrogation of Pritchert, he was content to let Paul and Sam conduct the questioning. He watched the procession leave the driveway, then turned and wandered through the house, making himself comfortable in the swoopy black chair. He closed his eyes and felt an intense weariness wash over him.

Thoughts were swirling in his head. All of this started over forty years ago because someone was careless about what they decided to look at. Jim remembered a Sunday school song he'd learned as a child: *O, be careful little eyes what you see.* Boy, wasn't that the truth? Or was it?

Jim frequently questioned the current premise of American society.

Was everyone here just to become who they were meant to be? To have their needs met? By whom was the question. And for whom.

You couldn't argue with the fact that a secret glance of a licentious image by Sylvester Kratt had sucked him into a vortex of insatiable desires which had led to incest and the possible rape and murder of an innocent, gifted young woman whose talents and intelligence had been lost to the world.

And then there was Heather. Jim shook his head, trying to clear the images of her abuse that floated around in his head. The trail of murder, sexual abuse, and secrecy that had permeated her entire life seemed unbelievable. Impossible. Her life was a disaster, but not by her choosing. As in all sexual abuse, her innocence had been taken from her without her consent. Whether she could recover was up for grabs. Thoughts tumbled through Jim's head until sometime in his contemplation, exhaustion took over, and he fell asleep.

Someone tapped his arm. Jim jerked and opened his eyes. Lillie was staring at him while holding a chocolate shake. Her blonde curls cascaded down her shoulders, her blue eyes vibrant with reflected light.

"Here, Bapa. We got you a shake," she said softly. Henri stood next to her, looking somber and serious, his blond curls in a jumble.

Jim smiled and tousled his hair. "Hey, thanks. You know I love chocolate shakes. Where's Mommy?" he asked, slurping on the straw.

"Did I hear my name?" Carol asked, poking her head around the door frame. Her brown eyes were question marks wondering what had happened while they were gone.

"There's Mommy!" Henri shouted, pointing at Carol.

"I see you're none the worse for wear. Everything got resolved?" Carol asked.

"Sort of. I'll explain later," Jim said, winking at her.

"That oughta be good. Supper in an hour," Carol said, walking back into the kitchen.

68

TUESDAY, SEPTEMBER 24

Late Tuesday morning, Dale Pritchert posted the $50,000 bond required of him by the La Crosse Municipal Court. At his home on King Street, he began packing a suitcase. He thought back to his heated exchange with Judge Whitworth earlier in the morning. It had been risky, but it had paid off in his release from jail shortly before noon.

"You honor, I have been a trusted member of the La Crosse community for over twenty-five years. These trumped-up charges against my person happened when I tried to defend a coworker at our firm from a ridiculous accusation during an investigation into the tragic death of her father," he argued vigorously.

Sam and Paul stood at the back of the courtroom watching the procedure. Paul rolled his eyes in frustration. "This is total bullshit!" Paul whispered hoarsely. The interrogation had not gone as expected. Pritchert, his lawyer in tow, had admitted nothing. And without solid physical evidence of his presence at the scene of the crime, they could not hold him on a murder charge.

Sam laid his hand on Paul's arm and said softly, "Whitworth is no fool. He should see through his playacting, but you've got to admit our evidence is very tentative, so anything could happen, I guess."

Judge Whitworth folded his hands and looked peeved, his face in a conspicuous scowl. His white hair billowed from his head in an ethereal cloud, and he clasped his wrinkled hand on the trim of his wooden throne. "Mr. Pritchert, are you referring to the investigation by the La Crosse Sheriff's Department into the strangulation death of Mr. Sylvester Kratt?"

"I am, your honor. This is a miscarriage of justice. There is very little proof of Heather's involvement in her father's horrible death, and I am taken aback by the tactics the police have used to try and build their case. It borders on harassment," Pritchert said.

"I doubt that very much," Judge Whitworth said dryly, looking over his reading glasses. "Furthermore, Ms. Lovstad doesn't seem to be the only one being investigated. You also seem to be in the hot seat, sir. Threatening a police officer with a weapon is a serious criminal act. I will not be buffaloed by your dramatic and disgusting antics. Your bail is set at $50,000." His gavel made a resounding bang throughout the courtroom, and he asked, "Who's next, bailiff?"

"But your honor . . ." Pritchert whined.

"Save the histrionics for the theater," the judge said sourly. "You're excused."

Despite what seemed to be a failure, his dramatic appeal had been successful. He wrote a personal check for his bail and hurried out of court. He thought about the questioning the evening before. He'd survived the grilling without giving the two detectives a solid lead on the murder of Sylvester Kratt. In fact, he'd given them nothing to work with. Unfortunately, Jim Higgins had come alarmingly close to the truth yesterday during the confrontation on Chipmunk Coulee Drive. Now, the options available to him and Heather were narrowing rapidly. Their choices were extremely limited if they wanted to end up with their freedom intact.

"I'm picking you up in half an hour. Have you packed?" Pritchert asked Heather, his cell phone crammed between his ear and shoulder. The panic in his voice was unmistakable as he threw sweaters and jeans into his suitcase. Fortunately, they hadn't impounded his 2005 Chevy Silverado pickup.

"Are you sure this is going to work?" Heather asked. "Nothing else you've done so far has been too successful."

"Why wouldn't it work? Listen, Heather, this is probably our last chance to blow this place and start over somewhere else. Are you with me?" The silence on the other end of the line unnerved him. "Heather, are you there?"

"Yeah, yeah. I'll be ready."

Heather punched her phone and slumped in a chair, covering her eyes with her hands. How had her life come to this? Her house was in a shambles from the fire, she was scared, yet she was willing to run to destinations unknown with a man who had controlled her for over twenty years. What was wrong with this picture? *Plenty,* she thought. *None of it fixable.*

Getting up from the chair in the corner of her motel room at Super 8, she grabbed her clothing and stuffed it in her suitcase. She hated flying. Maybe it was the fact that someone else was at the controls, and she had absolutely nothing to say about it. Too late now. *The story of my life,* she thought.

In twenty minutes, Dale Pritchert pulled into the motel parking lot. He beeped the horn twice, and Heather appeared and ran to the truck. Opening the passenger door, she threw her suitcase into the narrow space behind the seat and climbed into the front. Pritchert leaned over and gave her an impersonal peck on the cheek.

"You look petrified," he said, his irritation palpable. "Stop worrying. Everything'll be fine." He rammed the shifter into drive and steered the truck to the parking lot exit. "The police have no solid physical evidence to tie me to the murder."

"Well, it's hard for me to believe you. Remember, you were the one who was going to commit the perfect crime." She laughed in disbelief. "I guess we know how that turned out." Heather stared out the front windshield.

"Hey! I did the best I could under the circumstances," Pritchert said, easing into the traffic on Rose Street. Noticing Heather's stoic expression, he turned his attention to the road. "Once we get out of the country, we'll be free to reinvent ourselves. False IDs, a new address, the works. You'll see. It's going to be fine."

"Once we start running, we'll always be looking over our shoulders," Heather reminded him. She crossed her arms and locked her eyes on the road ahead.

"Whatever," Dale said, his face dark with disgust.

Driving south on U.S. Highway 14, the countryside provided some brilliant fall scenery. The trees glowed with the height of fall color; oranges, reds, and browns reflected off the windshield and washed over Dale and Heather. Faded red tobacco sheds and dairy farms appeared sporadically throughout the hilly landscape, and a herd of Holstein cows grazed contentedly in a pasture. The weather was balmy, and the sunshine warmed the truck until they both began to feel drowsy. They didn't talk. There seemed to be nothing to say about the predicament they were in.

As they approached Viroqua, Dale turned right at the first stop light and drove through the gate of the small municipal airport. He drove up to a pole-type building where his 2010 Cessna Skycatcher was parked. Coasting to a stop in the parking lot, they got out of the truck and carried their bags through the hanger's service door. The single-engine two-seater plane was considered a light sport aircraft even though it cost Pritchert nearly $100,000. It was in good shape and should take them north to his isolated cabin in Lake of the Woods country in Canada, where they could regroup and make a new plan.

Pritchert opened the hanger door, and they climbed into the

aircraft. He cranked the engine. It coughed and sputtered briefly, then revved to life. The gas tank was full and would take them several hundred miles into Minnesota's Northwoods toward Warroad, where they would cross the border and enter Canadian airspace. Pritchert hoped to be at his cabin by sundown.

As he taxied the airplane out onto the short airstrip and prepared to take off, he looked again at Heather.

"It'll be okay. We'll be fine," he said, more to reassure himself than her.

"It'll never be okay. Nothing will ever be the same again," Heather said, slouching her large body into the cheap hard seat. "Let's go. I won't feel safe until we're as far away from Higgins as we can get."

Heather closed her eyes as Pritchert sped down the runway. She always felt nauseous when they lifted off. As the plane ascended, Dale reached for her hand and clasped it tightly. Then with a grim expression on his face, he veered north to safety.

69

FRIDAY, SEPTEMBER 27

In the few days since the confrontation with Dale Pritchert in Jim's driveway, the detective team worked feverishly to consolidate the evidence they had uncovered about the Kratt strangulation and Yelski abduction. The necklace found at the scene of the murder was definitely Christina Yelski's. The only thing Pritchert had admitted was that Heather had the Yelski necklace in her possession at the time of her father's murder. The photo that showed her wearing the same necklace as a young girl strengthened the suspicion that Sylvester Kratt was somehow involved in Christina's death.

Sam leaned back in his chair. The team gathered around morning coffee and collaborated and hypothesized about their current state of affairs. With the disappearance of Heather and Dale, the mood among them was dark.

"We should've arrested Pritchert when we had the chance," Paul said, his scowl reflecting his frustration. He pulled on the corners of his mouth with his fingers.

"We didn't have enough evidence to hold him," Sam said, "and he didn't give us any new facts when we interrogated him. Besides, I knew he'd never confess. He's a lawyer, for Pete's sake."

"Listen, guys, don't beat yourself up. We can still continue down the evidence road and get our ducks in a row," Leslie contributed. "The search warrant from Judge Whitworth should be ready late this afternoon. Maybe we'll find something at Pritchert's office or home. And don't forget. If or when authorities come through on the APB, we'll have solid evidence for an arrest that will stick, and neither of them will be able to slip out of our grasp again."

Everyone thought about that, then DeDe said, "Remember that the Canadian authorities just over the border have been notified with a description of their plane. They'll be looking for them, too."

They heard a faint knock on the outer door. Higgins entered the room looking refreshed in a crisp white shirt, burgundy tie, and dark gray flannel slacks. He seemed optimistic despite the sling that still hung around his neck. He walked across the room, grabbed a chair, and sat down facing the team.

"Meeting of the minds?" he asked, his eyebrows raised.

"I feel like my mind has gotten up and left the building," Sam said. He kicked his feet out in front of him and tucked his chin into the collar of his shirt in what could only be described as a pout.

"Don't give up yet. We've got a reputation to live up to. Just think of all the impossibilities that existed before this investigation began," Jim lectured.

"Yeah, and they still exist," Paul complained, locking eyes with Jim. "The whole damn thing is impossible."

"Now, now. Let's not be hasty," Jim said, pumping his hands up and down in front of them. "A forty-year-old abduction that was never solved and a strangulation in which the only physical evidence was a necklace and a note left us in very difficult circumstances. But Sam's discovery of the newspaper articles and Paul's work on the photo inside the necklace led us down some interesting paths. DeDe and Leslie uncovered the history of the drinking trio who most likely were directly involved in the abduction of Christina—although we really can't prove that."

"We may never be able to prove anything, sir," DeDe said, inspecting her fingernails.

The silence in the room seemed heavy and smothering. Jim continued. "You've all been working hard. I did come upon a discovery that I think you should know about."

Everyone looked up, hopeful that this piece of information would be substantial.

Jim continued. "When I went back and reviewed my interview notes of Heather's first questioning, I asked her about the necklace. She denied ever seeing it. But then she asked me what the second item was that was found on the floor by her father." He paused for effect. "But I never told her there was more than one item. So . . ."

"How did she know about the note unless she'd been there or knew who'd put it there," Leslie finished.

"Right. I was about to get to that issue when she was at my house, and Pritchert interrupted," Jim explained.

"So, Heather or someone she knows committed the murder?" Sam asked.

"I believe she knows who killed her father and probably had a part in planning the whole thing," Jim concluded. "I just didn't get a confession, unfortunately." He stopped and let that sink in. "You've all been working hard. Now we have to coordinate our efforts and pull this all together into a workable theory. It's falling into place. The possible is morphing into the probable." Jim looked at his young team of colleagues. He was so proud of them.

"Was that a compliment?" DeDe asked, a grin creeping into the corners of her mouth.

"It is what it is. I'll leave the interpretation to you guys," Jim said. "For my part, I believe that Heather has been held an emotional hostage in a controlling relationship with Dale Pritchert for a long time. Her ability to make her own decisions has been damaged beyond repair, and I think the rage she felt at her father's abuses gave Pritchert the permission he needed to strangle Sylvester in his kitchen on September 7. We'll see if the lab results from the cars and the fingerprints on the back door match Pritchert's, but I think they will. He left some physical evidence behind somewhere that will place him at the scene of the crime. And we're going to find it." He poked his finger emphatically at the team. "The lab is working hard to try and extract some DNA from the necklace, although I wouldn't hold my breath on that."

"If we're developing a timeline, let's get started," Sam said, picking up a marker and walking to the whiteboard filled with notes, photos, questions, and possible motives.

"October 8, 1977—the abduction and disappearance of Christina Yelski from her home in La Crosse," Sam said as he wrote the information on a long line that ran across the whiteboard. "What's next? Who's got a storyline?" he asked, eyeing each member of the team.

70

Tuesday evening, Dale Pritchert could see the shimmering reflection of Red Lake in northern Minnesota through the windshield of the small airplane. Their trip north had been uneventful, and Heather passed the hours perusing several magazines, sleeping, and occasionally engaging in discussions with Dale about possible future plans. They stopped at Park Rapids Municipal Airport in the late afternoon and refueled. When they were aloft again, Heather dug out sandwiches they'd gotten from a vending machine at the airstrip, and they had a snack.

Traveling over the northern regions of Minnesota, large tracts of piney woods appeared until they reached the Red Lake Peatland region. This area was a fifty-mile-long bog containing various islands, raised bogs, and ribbed marshlands. Caribou once used the trails through the vast swamp on their migratory route to their calving grounds in Canada. Pritchert flew over Big Bog State Recreation Area, which was peppered with sphagnum marshes, white cedar swamps, and lake beaches.

No sooner had he flown over the upper and lower Red Lakes and entered the bog region than the airplane's engine began sputtering and coughing. Alarmed, Heather's eyes widened. She gazed at the ominous flashing lights on the instrument panel. Dale frantically pushed buttons. Heather noticed a fine sheen of sweat popping along his hairline. The scenery below provided no place for an emergency landing—only marsh punctuated with jack pine, tamarack, and black spruce interspersed with open water. It spread out for miles.

"What's wrong?" she asked, her eyes wide with alarm.

Dale glanced over at her. "I don't know. I just had the plane serviced a month ago. There shouldn't be anything wrong." Heather noticed his hands were shaking as he worked with the controls.

The plane dropped precipitously in the sky. Heather's stomach turned over, and she began noticing the details of the scenery with alarming clarity below them—a couple of houses at a crossroads, some clothes whipping on a clothesline. A little farther on, a decrepit mobile home squatted in the wetlands, heaps of chopped wood piled up next to it. As the plane descended rapidly, the landscape was becoming uncomfortably large and close in the windshield.

"Are we going to crash?" Heather yelled over the spitting engine.

"Not if I can help it," Dale said tersely, his eyes wide with panic.

The plane wobbled and dipped as he tried to right its course. Nothing seemed to work. Suddenly, the plane began plummeting toward the earth in a dizzying spiral.

Heather screamed, "I don't want to die!"

Dale clung desperately to the controls, his muscles straining against the stressed airplane, trying in vain to level it out. The pine forest loomed ahead just below the undercarriage of the plane. When the first branch struck the fuselage, gasoline spewed from the belly onto the woods below, and soon an explosion ripped through the air, leaving an inferno behind them. The massive cloud of smoke would have been easy to see for miles. Regrettably, no one was there when the plane hurtled to the earth and was enveloped in a fireball of flames and black smoke.

71

SATURDAY, SEPTEMBER 28

The autumn sunset flamed crimson in the western sky like a burning ember, and the trunks of the trees in Higgins' backyard turned a darker shade of brown as the sun sank below the horizon. The wood fire in the ring on the patio popped and sent a flurry of sparks in the air.

Carol was inside finishing the children's baths and tucking them into bed. The ache in Jim's shoulder was a dull reminder that he wasn't healed yet. Returning to work would have to wait. More therapy was required. Jim groaned. He was never patient with the idiosyncrasies of the human body, and the aging process had seemed irrelevant to him until this latest incident. Now there were days when he felt older than his fifty-four years. He wondered if his shoulder would always cause him grief.

The basement patio door slid open, and Sara emerged. She had just showered, and the scent of something tantalizing drifted on the night air.

"I'm heading over to see Father Knight," she said cautiously, her hair still damp.

Jim looked up at her, not sure how to respond. "Sure. You have your cell?"

Sara frowned and sighed. "Of course, Dad. What millennial goes anywhere without their phone?"

Her answer came out harsh, and Jim shrunk back, surprised at the anger in her voice. Lately, it seemed she was mad at the world. It saddened him immensely to see his daughter suffering like this. Immediately after her response, regret washed over her.

"I'm sorry, Dad. That didn't come out right. Yes, I have my cell. I'll be home later."

"Okay. Be safe, honey."

Sara turned, waved over her shoulder, and said, "Try not to worry, Dad."

Fifteen minutes passed, and finally, Carol came down the flagstone stairs and plopped in a chair beside Jim. They sat quietly for a few minutes, enjoying the warmth of the glowing fire. Jim reached for Carol's hand, fighting to keep his emotions from spilling over.

"Everything all right?" Carol asked though she knew it wasn't.

Jim waited until he was sure his voice wouldn't betray what he felt bottled up inside. He lifted her hand to his lips and kissed it tenderly.

"No. Everything's not all right. At least not in Sara's world." Jim huffed through his nose and shook his head. "She's so angry, and I have no idea how to help her." His voice quivered, and his eyes misted over.

"I'm sorry about this, but don't you remember how gun-shy I was after my attack? I jumped at the slightest sound for six months," Carol said, her eyes sympathetic.

"Yeah, I do remember, but that was different. This is my daughter we're talkin' about," Jim said, his face resolute. "I'm supposed to be able to protect her from this kind of shit." They were quiet for a while, holding hands in front of the fire, each lost in their own thoughts. Then Jim said, "By the way, happy anniversary yesterday. I didn't forget, honey."

"I didn't want to seem petty, so I didn't mention it, but I'm glad you remembered. Marrying you was the best thing I ever did," she said, her face soft with emotion.

Jim leaned over and kissed her tenderly. "Our marriage is not in the category of anything that remotely resembles petty. When this case is over, and we clear up the messy details, we're going somewhere. Just you and me. I promise." Jim's cell beeped in his pocket. He stretched his legs out in front of him and dug the phone out of his pocket.

"Higgins."

"Is this Lieutenant Jim Higgins of the La Crosse Sheriff's Department?" a voice asked.

"Yes, this is Jim Higgins," he said as he sat up straighter.

"This is Sheriff Rodney Trefoil at Lake of the Woods County up in northern Minnesota. According to an APB issued by La Crosse County, we understand you're on the lookout for two fugitives who are possible suspects in a murder investigation. They were flying a small airplane. Is that correct?" he asked, his voice clipped and professional.

"Yes. They disappeared on Tuesday afternoon. The two suspects, Dale Pritchert and Heather Lovstad, left the Viroqua Airport around noon and were heading north to the property Pritchert owns somewhere up there. So, what's up?" Jim asked, feeling a tightening in his chest.

"Their plane was discovered late this afternoon north of the Red Lake Wildlife area. They must have experienced some engine trouble and crashed in a swamp near Big Bog State Recreation Area. A DNR official was doing a moose count and came upon the wreckage. Pritchert apparently died upon impact, but the woman survived. However, she's in very bad shape—multiple broken bones and some serious burns plus internal bleeding. She was flown to Rainy

Lake Medical Center in International Falls, where she's undergoing surgery right now. If they can stabilize her, they may med-flight her to Duluth for further treatment, but that won't be until later, no earlier than tomorrow morning."

"Will she be conscious in a few hours? Was she lucid at the scene?" Jim asked.

"There was no sign of brain damage. She talked briefly to the agent who found the plane. I would think by morning she may be able to respond to some questions," Sheriff Trefoil said. "But her prognosis isn't good."

They exchanged cell numbers. Trefoil promised to keep Jim updated about Heather's condition, but Jim already knew he'd be taking a hurried flight to International Falls as soon as he could arrange it. Trefoil signed off, and Jim laid his phone in his lap.

"What's happened?" Carol asked.

Jim filled Carol in on the details as he knew them, then punched in Sam's number.

He answered quickly. "Birkstein."

"Sam. It's Higgins. Pritchert crashed his plane in northern Minnesota. He's dead, but Heather is still alive, although she's very badly injured and is in surgery in International Falls as we speak. I need you to go with me to interview her. You won't need a bag. We should be home by tomorrow evening at the latest."

"Right. I'll be ready whenever you are. Just call when you have a flight confirmed." He clicked off.

72

SUNDAY, SEPTEMBER 29

By ten-thirty the next morning, Jim and Sam had endured a bumpy hitch on an American Airlines flight to Minneapolis. That was followed by a two-hour layover and another short flight north to International Falls, Minnesota. They arrived disheveled and bleary-eyed from lack of sleep. Jim's shoulder throbbed incessantly, something that even Tylenol didn't relieve. The air outside the regional airport was brisk and much colder than in southern Wisconsin.

Walking to their rental car, they slipped on their lightweight jackets, got into the car, and quickly drove to the hospital. At the registration desk, a young man gave them Heather's room number and pointed them to the second-floor critical care unit.

Flashing their IDs at the nurse's station, Jim said, "We're here to see Heather Lovstad."

A nurse glanced up from her computer. Her stethoscope hung limply around her neck and dangled on her chest. She looked tired, and her face was lined with concern. She quietly inspected the two men standing before her.

"Are you family or friends?" she asked.

"Neither. We're police officers from La Crosse, Wisconsin," Jim explained. "Ms. Lovstad is a suspect in a murder investigation we're conducting, and we were hoping to have an opportunity to question her."

The nurse's eyebrows flitted upward in uncertainty. "She's in very critical condition. I'm not sure you would get much of a response from her at this point," she said. Her eyes shifted to a figure behind Jim and Sam.

Suddenly a voice interrupted.

"It's okay, Stacey. Can I help you?"

Jim and Sam turned around.

"I'm Dr. Stengal Brewster. What questions did you have about Ms. Lovstad?"

Jim and Sam focused their attention on the physician. He was tall and lanky and met their stare with a brown-eyed gaze. His face was tanned and clean-shaven, his features arranged in such a way as to produce an attractive middle-aged man. His crisp blue shirt and red tie beneath his white coat gave him a look of authority and expertise. Jim guessed he was about forty.

After introductions, the conversation about Heather continued.

"You have to understand something. Ms. Lovstad's injuries are very serious. Life-threatening, actually," Dr. Brewster explained. "She's been put into an induced coma to help control some of her pain and to avoid possible swelling of the brain. Questioning her now would be useless. She wouldn't be able to respond."

"Well, I hope you can see things from our perspective, sir," Jim said patiently. "She is the only surviving suspect in our investigation of her father's murder, and she could have crucial information about another cold case from forty years ago. Without her input, both murders may go unsolved. That would be a tragic travesty of justice. Is there any way you can bring her out of the coma so we can interview her? We'll try to keep it as brief as possible."

Dr. Brewster stared at the tiles of the floor, deep in thought. Jim and Sam stayed quiet. After a few moments, he lifted his head and gazed down the long corridor. Clearly, he was feeling torn between his responsibility to his patient and the possible ramifications of what Heather might know about the murders. He sighed loudly and rubbed his forehead.

"Well, against my better judgment, here's what I'll do," he began. "I'll bring her out of the coma for a brief time." He held up his index finger and pointed at Jim. "But if her condition deteriorates in the slightest, I will stop the interview and ask you to leave. You have to understand that her condition is extremely precarious." He held out his palms and shrugged his shoulders. "That's the best I can do."

"Then that's what we'll have to run with," Jim said, glancing at Sam. "I appreciate it, sir,"

Sam fidgeted with the keys in his pocket. When Jim frowned at him, the jingling stopped, and he cleared his throat.

"How long will it take to bring her back?" Sam asked.

"Probably an hour or two at the most. It has to be done carefully," Dr. Brewster said. He turned and began walking briskly down the hallway. Over his shoulder, he said, "There's a family lounge down the hall to your right. Help yourself to coffee. Someone will contact you when she wakes up."

While they sat in the family lounge, Jim called Carol. She told him they'd been to church at Hamburg Lutheran. It had begun to rain there, and after lunch, she put on a movie for Lillie and Henri. They were eating popcorn and sprawled on the living room floor with pillows and blankets.

"Did Sara mention where she was going last night?" Carol asked Jim.

"Yeah, she said she was going to see Father Knight. Why?"

"She's not home yet. And I didn't want to call her. She'd probably accuse me of hovering. You know, that helicopter parenting thing."

Sara's unexplained absence sent a prick of fear through Jim's system, but he tried to keep his response reasonable. "Well, she's twenty-three years old, and I think we'll just have to cut the cord and let her figure out things without making her think we've totally abandoned her. I don't know how to do that, so if you have any ideas about that, just let me know."

Carol sighed. "I just wanted to warn you so you're not surprised when you get home. By the way, when will you be home?"

"We're hoping to interview Heather within the next hour. There's a flight out of here to Minneapolis at four-thirty. We're hoping to be on it. I'm guessing I'll be home by nine or ten tonight."

A nurse appeared in the door of the lounge signaling for Jim and Sam.

"Gotta go, hon. Looks like the interview is on. Talk to you later," Jim said as he stood and crossed the room.

"Good luck. I hope you get what you're looking for," Carol finished.

Jim hurried to catch up with Sam and the nurse, who were already down the hallway. They stopped in front of room #268. When Jim caught up, the nurse began explaining the protocol.

"Dr. Brewster is having a late lunch. He's on call if things go south. I'll be in the room by Heather's bedside the whole time, monitoring her vital signs. If she gets in any kind of trouble, the interview will have to end. Understood?" she asked, glancing back and forth between the two men.

"Sure, we understand," Sam said.

When they entered the room, the atmosphere felt heavy and ominous. The light in the room was dim, the shades drawn against the sunshine outside. Monitors beeped quietly, and the IV tube dripped steadily. Heather lay deathly still and silent, entombed in bandages, the sheets and thin blanket pulled up over her chest. Jim thought aboutall the trauma she'd endured during her lifetime.

Now she was on the precipice of eternity—the thin blue line between staying on this side of reality or crossing over. He wondered if she longed for release from the hell she had endured. Sam brought him up short.

"Do you think she knows how to get to heaven, sir?" he asked softly—a perfectly valid question coming from a Lutheran pastor's son. Jim looked at Sam. His face was warm with empathy and concern. Jim wasn't sure if his flushed cheeks were from the warm temperatures in the room or a sudden intensity of emotion. Sam crossed his arms over his chest, watching Heather's impassive face.

"I don't know, Sam. I guess that hasn't been my focus," Jim said sadly. "Now it might be too late."

Heather groaned quietly and shifted on her pillow. The nurse turned to the two men and wiggled her finger at them. They walked quietly to the bed, one on either side. Sam had his recorder out, and he laid it on the bed.

Jim leaned close. "Heather, can you hear me?" he asked gently, his baritone voice soft and expressive. He picked up a whiff of burned flesh and antiseptic.

A few seconds passed, then Heather turned her head toward the sound of Jim's voice. Her eyes opened slowly. They were filled with unfathomable pain and regret. Jim was familiar with these agonizing emotions. She recognized him, her eyes widened, and then she closed them again.

"Heather, we need your help," Jim continued. "Can you tell us who killed your father?"

Moments passed. Jim looked at Sam and shook his head. Then Heather whispered, her speech halting and slow. "Dale did. I didn't mean for it to go that far. But Dale wanted to move on in our relationship and blamed my dad for all my problems. He wanted to punish him." She groaned and gritted her teeth. "It's not what I planned."

"Who left the necklace and note in the kitchen beside your dad?"

"That was Dale's idea."

Again, moments flitted by until Jim wondered if Heather had passed on. But her chest continued to rise and fall with her shallow breathing. She opened her eyes, and this time, Jim thought she seemed to be looking past him at people who were no longer living. He'd read about accounts of dying people who talked to deceased relatives as if they were present. Maybe they were in some weird spiritual way. He felt as if ghosts had invaded the hospital room.

"Did your dad have Christina Yelski's necklace in his possession when you were a child?" Jim asked.

"Yeah. He had it when I was a kid," she whispered. "I didn't know whose it was, but I remember it lying on his dresser in his bedroom. I used to go in there and look at it. I always wondered whose it was."

Suddenly a machine close to Jim's head beeped ominously, and the nurse held up her hand. "You'll have to finish; this is very hard for her," she warned. "Her vital signs are not good."

"I'm so sorry this happened to you, Heather. I want you to know that what your father and those other men did to you was not your fault. You were a child, and you did nothing to deserve that. Do you understand?" Jim asked, clasping her hand. "Heather?"

Heather's eyes flitted open briefly, and a faint smile creased the corners of her mouth. "You're a good man. Thank you for coming."

The nurse shook her head. "That's it, I'm afraid. Her heartbeat has become very erratic. I'm sorry. You'll have to stop."

Jim leaned down and placed a tender kiss on her forehead. When he looked up at Sam, his eyes had misted with tears. He chinned toward the door, and they walked out into the corridor.

"You okay, Chief?" Sam asked, placing a hand on his shoulder.

"No. No, I'm not." He ran a hand through his hair in frustration and fatigue and wiped his eyes with the back of his hand. "Do you ever get tired of this sin-sick world, Sam?"

"Yeah, I do. I certainly do."

"Then that makes two of us. Let's go home."

The flight back to La Crosse was marred by nasty weather and turbulence. Before they left International Falls, they'd had a conversation with Sheriff Trefoil, who gave them the details of the Pritchert plane crash. The FAA had not determined the cause of the crash. They were still inspecting the wreckage of the plane. The whole scenario left Jim and Sam uneasy and jumpy.

During the flight, they looked at each other nervously every time the plane hit a rough patch. The flight attendants strolled the aisle and tried to reassure them that everything was fine. When a toddler behind them began to wail, it seemed like the icing on the cake.

Jim was driving up Chipmunk Coulee Road to his home by ten that night. The rain was falling in sheets, beating on the windshield, blowing across the road, and sweeping up leaves and debris. Jim switched the windshield wipers to high as the fierce winds buffeted the Suburban. Bursts of lightning in the night sky revealed the silhouettes of the bare trees, the sky glowing with incandescent shades of blue and white. When he drove into the safety of the garage, he let out a sigh of relief.

The house was dark and quiet. He slipped out of his shoes, hung up his coat, and headed to the shower. A few minutes later, Carol appeared at the shower door through the steamy fog.

"Hey. Did you just get here?" she asked, peeking in at him.

"Yeah. It's wicked out there. A real corker of a storm," Jim said, stepping out of the shower into a thick fluffy towel that Carol held for him. He kissed her tenderly. "Kids all right?"

"Yep. They went to bed early, and so far, they're oblivious to the storm. What happened with Heather?" she asked, her brown eyes sad.

Jim filled her in on the details of the interview while he dressed in a T-shirt and boxers. "Her condition is really rough. She may not make it through the night. She is probably one of the most tragic figures I've dealt with in my career. The way others abused her and threw her away like garbage. She's a damaged piece of goods, that's for sure, and Dale Pritchert used her fragile condition to control her and ultimately to justify taking the law into his own hands."

Carol's eyes softened with sadness. "I'm so sorry, honey. Truly I am." She turned and said, "I'll make some tea. Come out when you're done."

After Jim finished his nighttime rituals, he joined Carol in the living room for a cup of peppermint tea. A fire crackled in the little Franklin potbellied stove in the corner, sending warm light into the dimly lit room. Sipping the brew, Carol looked at Jim over her teacup. "I hate to bring any more trouble into your day, but Sara left a note for you." She reached over, plucked an envelope from the end table, and handed it to Jim.

"Did you talk to her?" he asked, wondering what kind of surprise the note might hold.

"Briefly. Just read the note. And remember, this too shall pass."

Jim frowned at her folksy advice. Breaking the gummed seal on the envelope, he fumbled with the letter, then began reading.

Dear Dad,

I realize you're probably confused by my recent behavior. Don't feel alone. I am, too. I've decided to leave for a while. It's nothing personal against you or Carol. I just feel like I'm suffocating under your concern. I need to get away and try to find myself again. Try to regain my true self—the person I used to be. I hope you understand. You have been the best Dad in the world. I will always love you. Please don't do your detective thing and try to find me. I need you to trust me on this. People who care about me know where I've gone. Try not to worry. I'm safe, and when I'm ready I'll call you.

Love, Sara

Jim was stunned, but then why should he be surprised with everything that had happened recently? He reread the note. Wasn't this the little girl who'd always been able to talk to him, to confide in him, to read his thoughts? Wasn't this the budding young woman who, despite the typical clashes between teenagers and parents, had always been respectful and loving and blossomed into a blonde beauty whose most endearing traits were her integrity and candor? Where was the woman who had held his hand after Margie's death, comforting him and putting his needs before her own?

When Jim thought about the changes in his daughter that had resulted from her abusive captivity by Maddog Pierce, his face darkened, and his blue eyes glittered with anger. As Carol watched him, the shadow of malaise and hurt on his face made her shrink inside.

"Jim, I can see you're upset. What's going on?"

Jim slowly folded the letter and handed it to her. He walked to the Franklin stove and adjusted the flue.

"Read it," he said gruffly. He walked out of the living room and down the hall to the bedroom.

As Carol skimmed the note, she groaned. *Fathers and daughters. Go figure,* she thought. Then, *this too shall pass.*

73

EARLY OCTOBER

In the early days of October, following the deaths of Dale Pritchert and Heather Lovstad, who died the morning after the interview, the team continued consolidating evidence. Still, no matter what they did, it all felt like a royal screwup.

"Did we accomplish anything at all?" Sam asked one morning, slouching in one of Jim's office chairs.

"Depends on how you look at it," Jim said. "Got a confession from Heather, and Dale Pritchert received some kind of delayed justice at the hand of God. So to answer your question, yes. I think we did accomplish some things, although it's not cut and dried like we wanted."

"It's a total rip-off, that's what it is," said Sam, his face set in a classic pout.

"In law enforcement, that's not all that uncommon, buddy," Jim sighed, his feet up on his desk. "It wasn't a total failure. We got Maddog." Sam continued to pout silently, his curly locks softly framing his youthful face. "You finish your reports yet?" Jim asked.

"Workin' on it."

During the days following the conclusion to the Yelski case, Sheriff Davy Jones had been fielding calls and texts from various news sources about the forty-year-old mystery, fending off the wolves who tried to lay blame or claim victory on the backs of the investigative team.

On a crisp October morning toward the middle of the month, when the scarlet and orange trees outside Jim's office reflected the brilliant sunshine, Jones walked into Jim's office and pulled up a chair.

Jim was feverishly trying to complete his reports before he and Carol headed for San Antonio on a belated anniversary trip. He looked up, gestured briefly with a wave, and finished the paragraph he was typing. After a few minutes, he swiveled away from his computer and faced Jones.

"Hey, what's up?" he asked casually, resting his hand on the thick file folder on his desk. Despite the intensity of his workload, he appeared relaxed and rested. He gazed at Davy with a calm, cool stare.

"Is that your evidence and conclusions in these cases?" Jones asked, his eyes drifting to the folder.

"Such as they are," he said, lifting his hands in a futile gesture and kept talking. "The Yelski case and the murder of Sylvester Kratt are inconclusive by any amateur's standard, let alone the letter of the law," Jim said, his voice thick with frustration. "Can't convict without solid physical evidence, and all we seemed to dig up was a lot of conjecture. Seems like the whole thing was just a stupid shot in the dark."

Jones frowned and shrugged nonchalantly. Then with a note of satisfaction in his voice, Jim went on. "But we did manage to capture Maddog. Alive. That's one predatory drug lord who's off the streets."

"True. He's sitting in Boscobel awaiting trial. As for the other cases that were dumped in your lap, you did your best, Jim. Sometimes, for reasons we don't understand, things don't work out."

Jim huffed. "Not acceptable, Davy. Christina Yelski deserved better. Her sister's waited forty years for answers. We were all hoping we could provide some for her."

"Well, it may be unacceptable in your world, but that's the reality of the criminal world until something else comes to light. And that may never happen."

They both sat in silence for a while thinking about that. Jones spoke up again.

"Ever figure out who started the fire at Heather's house?"

Jim made a wry face. "Probably Pritchert covering his tracks, but we're not sure. The fire marshall says it was something similar to a Molotov cocktail thrown on a trajectory from the front yard into the kitchen area. Who knows?" More silence. More reflection. "The fingerprints on the locket were inconclusive. You knew that, right?" Jim asked.

"Yep," Davy said. "But on a positive note, the fingerprints on the back door of Kratt's house were Pritchert's, and hair and fibers from his clothing were found in Heather's car, although that doesn't prove he was at the crime scene. But you have a deathbed confession from Heather that Pritchert committed the murder. That's something. Of course, he's dead, so it seems pretty pointless."

"Not pointless. We could push for a posthumous trial—"

"It'll never happen," Jones interrupted. "Too expensive and time-consuming. Besides, who'd benefit from it?"

"Heather's brother," Jim responded. "He deserves some answers. I'm going to try anyway. All Judge Whitworth can say is no. It's one way to provide justice for Heather. She has no voice now. That girl was tossed around from man to man like a dirty rag. She had a terrible life. At least, I'll know we did everything we could to bring this to some kind of closure, as vague as that may be."

Jones conceded the point and moved on. "Any word from Sara?"

"Nope. I don't want to discuss it," Jim said brusquely.

"Fair enough. When are you leaving on your trip?"

"Tomorrow morning."

Jones stood. "Enjoy it. You deserve some recovery time. How's the shoulder?"

Jim rotated his shoulder and arm in a circular fashion. "It's coming along with therapy. Should be eighty percent in a couple of weeks."

Jones turned and walked toward the door. "Catch you later. Enjoy the trip," he said over his shoulder.

"Thanks, Davy."

Jones waved his hand over his head as he exited, and Jim was left pondering the bizarre circumstances of the last month. He wished he could slow down the whirlwind events galloping through his mind so he could glean some wisdom from them. Their significance seemed muddled, without purpose, chaotic. Had his team made a dent in the evil floating like an ethereal spectral among the ordinary citizens of the city? Was the world a safer, kinder place due to their efforts? He grunted, feeling a combination of mixed emotions. He returned to his computer, banging out his reports.

Since the terrible abduction of his daughter Sara, his family had recovered and was happily settled back into their routines at their home on Chipmunk Coulee Road. Lillie had returned to her bright, inquisitive self, spewing questions at a rate that made Jim's and Carol's heads spin. Henri provided many moments of toddler comedy. He seemed to have escaped any permanent insecurity from the whole experience. Carol was beginning to accept the fact that being married to Jim would, from time to time, include unanticipated events that might threaten their family's happiness and security. She wasn't happy about it; they'd had many late-night discussions about the dangers of his job. She still struggled with the complexities of confronting evil. But with each incident, she'd gained in her understanding of the conundrums of Jim's profession. She was learning to deal with the insecurities of being a cop's wife.

Although things had not worked out as well with Sara, Jim felt a buoyant expectation that she was doing what she had to do to heal. He had not followed or tracked her down, but not hearing her voice or seeing her face was killing him. Instead, he'd given her what she asked for—freedom to pursue her self-appointed program of restorative healing at her own pace. Whatever that entailed, he wasn't sure, but he hoped it was working. Perhaps Father Knight was having a positive influence. He hoped so.

His phone buzzed. *Another irritating interruption*, he thought. He was tempted to ignore it, but at the last minute, he grabbed it and answered.

"Higgins," he said, not hiding his exasperation.

"Dad?"

"Sara?"

THE END

ABOUT THE AUTHOR

Sue Berg is the author of the Driftless Mystery Series. She is a former teacher, and enjoys many hobbies including writing, watercolor painting, quilting, cooking and gardening. She lives with her husband, Alan, near Viroqua, Wisconsin.

The Driftless Mystery Series set in the beautiful Driftless region of the Upper Midwest does not disappoint. With complex characters, intriguing plots, and surprising twists and turns, this series will delight you with its ability to entertain while upholding the values we all treasure; love, faith, loyalty, and family. It is destined to become a beloved and enduring legacy to the people and culture in this unique part of the country.

COMING IN
APRIL 2024

JIM HIGGINS'
ADVENTURES
CONTINUE...

Look to the next page for an excerpt
from *Driftless Insurrection*.

1

WEDNESDAY, MARCH 20

The blizzard blew in with a savage wallop out of Alberta, Canada. It scoured the countryside of western Wisconsin like a Brillo pad. Fierce arctic winds and blinding snow squalls growled and hissed and screamed until small trees on the bluffs and hillsides bent to the ground like subjects prostrating themselves before a cruel taskmaster. The drifts behind the Tip Your Hat tavern in Genoa, Wisconsin, seemed like something from a make-believe fairy tale, frozen hard as rocks, the tops hissing with windswept pellets that blew in frenzied swirls. Across from the tavern beyond U.S. Highway 35, the Mississippi River seemed to disappear when whiteouts reduced visibility to zero. As the wind blew, the dark shrouded bluffs on the Minnesota side of the river became invisible across the two-mile-wide expanse of water.

Jed Klumstein, the proprietor of the Tip Your Hat tavern, was huddled under a heap of quilts in the bedroom of the apartment above the bar. The howling of the cold wind outside his window woke him when it was still early. The blue light of a false dawn barely penetrated the frosted window next to his bed. He lifted his

SUE BERG

head wearily from his pillow and listened to the rapping of frozen snow pellets on the weathered siding. He ducked back underneath the quilt again like a turtle hiding in his shell. *Another storm,* he thought disgustedly. *The third one in March. When are we gonna get a break?* He drifted back to sleep, nestled in the warmth of his bed and the quiet inside the apartment.

By seven o'clock in the morning, the roads throughout the Mississippi River Valley were drifted over with more than sixteen inches of fresh snow, making travel virtually impossible. Schools and businesses were closed throughout western Wisconsin. Davy Jones, the La Crosse County sheriff, asked citizens to remain at home and refrain from travel until the plow crews could get a handle on the record snowfall. Most La Crosse businesses closed until noon while the streets were cleared and the snow was hauled away. U.S. Highway 35, the Great River Road, was the only highway that had been kept open throughout the night in an attempt to make it accessible for any emergencies that might occur, but road crews found the task difficult in the blinding snowfall. Their work seemed pointless; the snow continued to blow, hampering any kind of travel.

At seven-thirty, an urgent pounding on Jed's upstairs apartment door rousted him from his warm cocoon. Sitting on the side of his bed, he slapped his feet on the icy floor, then instinctively snapped them toward his chest. Squinting, he scanned the bedroom in the dim morning light and grabbed a pair of wool socks from a pile of clothing he'd haphazardly dropped near his bed the night before. Stuffing his feet into the socks, he stood and stumbled toward the door. The pounding continued unabated.

"Yeah, yeah. I'm comin'," he muttered as he walked through the dark living room. Scantily dressed in a T-shirt, boxers, and the wool socks, he pushed off the security chain and whipped the door open.

"What?" he yelled at the figure standing in the hallway. "What's so damn important that you have to beat my door down in the middle of a friggin' snowstorm?"

"Sorry, Jed. I didn't mean to bother you," the young teenager said, his brown eyes apologetic. He scanned Jed's get-up from head to toe and smiled to himself.

"Bobby?" Jed asked, softening his tone, squinting in confusion. The cold wind whipped up the stairway, and he opened the apartment door wider. "Don't you have school today?"

The young man was sensibly dressed to meet the elements—a stocking hat, ski jacket, snow pants, and boots. "No, we don't have school today. Haven't you looked outside? It's a real live blizzard!" he said with an enthusiasm about inclement weather that only the young possess.

"Come on in. It's freezin' out there," he said begrudgingly. "I'll make you some hot chocolate." Bobby pushed past Jed and walked into the chilly apartment.

"That'd be great," the teen chattered.

"If you're lookin' for your dad, I don't know where he is," Jed said, shutting the door. "He hasn't shown up the last few nights."

"I guess you didn't hear. My dad's at the Tomah VA. He's getting dried out in the detox wing. He left the beginning of this week."

Jed's eyes softened with pity. "Sorry, Bobby. I didn't mean to bark at you. I didn't know about your dad."

"That's okay," Bobby said sadly. His eyes reflected a worry that seemed to age him beyond his years. "I hope it'll stick this time. Did you know it takes an average of seven interventions before an alcoholic can finally come clean?" He watched Jed stumble around the kitchen in his comical get-up.

"That's a fact a kid your age shouldn't have to know," Jed said as he ran his hand through his thick brown hair. He fussed around in the small kitchenette getting a pan out of the cupboard to heat milk. Setting it on the stove, he flicked on the burner. He turned to face Bobby, who'd found a chair by the small kitchen table.

"So, who's watching out for you while your dad's in the hospital?" he asked. He poured some milk in the pan and reached in the cupboard for a can of Nestlé chocolate mix and a bag of marshmallows.

"Nobody," Bobby said, dropping his eyes to the floor. "But I'm pretty good at taking care of myself."

"I can believe that," Jed said with resignation. "You've had enough practice." He stumbled into the bedroom to retrieve some clothes. When he came back into the kitchen, Bobby continued his litany.

"I'll be fourteen in May. I know how to clean, and I can cook some basic stuff—eggs and pancakes and hamburgers. Laundry's a breeze. I don't need a babysitter, but I do need a job, and I was hoping you could give me one. I wanna start saving for a car."

"A job? What makes you think you can work at a bar? You're not old enough. Besides, you're too smart to engage in the kind of activities that go on in my establishment."

"I know that, but I thought I could shovel snow out front and out back by the dumpsters. And I could clean the bathrooms in the morning before I go to school," he suggested.

Jed made a wry face, turning over the proposition in his mind. "Well, I guess that would be helpful. It won't pay much. How's seven bucks an hour sound?"

"Eight, and we'll call it a deal," Bobby said confidently.

Setting the hot chocolate in front of the teen, Jed scowled. "What? You're negotiating your salary already? Maybe you should be a lawyer."

"Nope. I'm gonna be a cop," Bobby said proudly.

"God in heaven! Drink your milk," Jed said, looking out at the swirling white of the snow beyond the window. It seemed to be letting up some.

Realizing Bobby had probably not eaten, Jed decided to make breakfast. While they ate, he did a quick inventory of the teen. Bright brown eyes looked out from a ruddy, scrubbed face that was just beginning to be shadowed with facial hair. His dark mop of hair lay thick and straight and hung almost to his chin. He had grown over the last year, and now his body had taken on a distinctive masculinity that would eventually produce a strong, tall, athletic, strapping man.

Jed knew the last few years had been rough for Bobby Rude—an alcoholic father, who was emotionally absent, a mother who'd abandoned her family a couple of years ago, and hours spent by himself worrying and fretting over his drunk dad. *The kid's a survivor. That's for sure,* he thought. But he knew Bobby's haunted look came from too many years of responsibility that his father refused to shoulder—a father who had flushed his life down the toilet.

After they wolfed down eggs, bacon, hash browns, and toast, Jed stacked the dishes in the kitchen sink.

"So, you want to start work today?" he asked, feeling more human with some food in his gut.

"Sure. You just tell me what to do," Bobby said enthusiastically.

"Come on, then," Jed said as he grabbed his outdoor gear by the door and began descending the stairs. "We'll start with the snow shoveling. That'll take you a while. You can wear off some of that breakfast."

The bar was dark and smelled of smoke and whiskey and spilled beer. Jed walked behind the long counter and flicked on the overhead lights. The bar was an oak monstrosity that featured carved gnomes in various poses intertwined with leaves and acorns. Jed had picked it up on an online auction. It had cost him more to haul it than what he'd paid for it. Opposite the bar, several booths lined the wall, and toward the back of the building, he'd installed a number of round tables with chairs for the snack food and pizza he served during happy hour and the Packers games. A large pool table also filled the center of the back room.

Jed turned and went toward the back entrance, where a small vestibule held a collection of tools neatly stacked on shelves, a broom and dustpan that hung on a hook, and a snow shovel that stood in the corner waiting to be used. Grabbing the shovel, he handed it to Bobby.

"Here. You use this, and I'll fire up the snowblower. We'll clean out the dumpsters first," he said.

Bobby grabbed the shovel, adjusted his gloves, and followed Jed outside. The wind had switched to the west; the cold took their breath away. The world had become a white wonderland of sculpted snow drifts. The sharp features of the rock outcroppings along the limestone bluffs had softened with the snowfall, and the edges of trees and houses and roads blurred in the intermittent bursts of arctic wind. Between gusts, everything was hushed as if someone had laid a huge white blanket over the scenery. When Jed slammed the back door, snow came loose from the roof and plummeted off the edge, just missing them. Bobby grinned happily.

"Ain't this somethin'!" he said with a lopsided smile. "It's beautiful!"

Jed shook his head. The innocence of youth. "Beautiful to a poet, maybe. But you probably won't be saying that in another hour," he said sourly.

Jed walked to the utility shed and removed the snowblower. After numerous attempts at pulling the starter cord, the machine finally coughed to life. Bobby was already scooping out the snow by the back entrance. They worked a while and were making good progress when Jed noticed a darkened area beneath a snow drift next to one of the dumpsters. Frowning, he stopped the snowblower, letting it idle as he walked up to the mysterious hump. He kicked at it, thinking it might be a dead animal. Possibly a deer, coyote, or dog had been hit on the road and crawled here to die, or a sack of garbage had missed the dumpster and had been covered by the snowfall. When he kicked the lump, the sole of a hiking boot revealed itself.

Jed stepped back in horror. After a moment, he leaned forward and swept away some of the snow covering the body with his hand. A red ski jacket and blue jeans lay lumpy and frozen beneath the drift.

"Oh, my God!" Jed whispered. He began digging energetically, brushing and scooping snow frantically into a heap next to the body. By this time, Bobby had joined him and was standing by his side.

"What're you doing?" Bobby asked, peering over Jed's shoulder.

"You find something?"

"Yeah. Somebody's buried under here. Help me. Maybe he's still alive," Jed said, panic-stricken.

"Are you kidding me?" Bobby asked. His eyes widened with shock.

Jed looked back at him over his shoulder. "Do I look like I'm kidding? Come on. Help me!" he said, his voice edged with desperation.

They continued to uncover the body. Jed's stomach turned over at the thought of someone dying in a drift in subzero temperatures only a few feet from the door of his tavern. When they tried to turn the victim over, he was already stiff with cold. Jed realized the man was dead. He flipped his cell phone out of his pocket and dialed 911.

"What is your emergency, sir?" a detached voice asked.

Jed identified himself. "I found a dead person buried in a drift behind my bar down on Highway 35 in Genoa," he said. He'd forgotten about Bobby, who stood next to him and was listening intently to the conversation.

"Holy moly," Bobby whispered. "First a blizzard and now a murder."

Jed covered the phone with his hand. "We don't know that yet," he said impatiently. "Don't be jumping to conclusions."

Bobby Rude's brown eyes hardened, and he met Jed's angry gaze with one of his own. "How many people have you found in a snowbank with their skull caved in?" he asked. "If that isn't murder, then tell me what is."

SUE BERG